Sword of Justice

CHRISTIAN CAMERON

First published in Great Britain in 2018 by Orion Books.
This paperback edition first published in 2019
by Orion Books,
an imprint of The Orion Publishing Group Ltd
Carmelite House, 50 Victoria Embankment
London EC4Y 0DZ

An Hachette UK Company

1 3 5 7 9 10 8 6 4 2

A CIP catalogue record for this book
is available from the British Library.

ISBN (Mass Market Paperback) 978 1 4091 7282 6
ISBN (eBook) 978 1 4091 6526 2

Sword of Justice

Christian Cameron is a writer and military historian. He participates in re-enacting and experimental archaeology, teaches armoured fighting and historical swordsmanship, and takes his vacations with his family visiting battlefields, castles and cathedrals. He lives in Toronto and is busy writing his next novel.

Also by Christian Cameron

The Commander Series
The New Achilles

The Chivalry Series
The Ill-Made Knight
The Long Sword
The Green Count

The Tyrant Series
Tyrant
Tyrant: Storm of Arrows
Tyrant: Funeral Games
Tyrant: King of the Bosporus
Tyrant: Destroyer of Cities
Tyrant: Force of Kings

The Long War Series
Killer of Men
Marathon
Poseidon's Spear
The Great King
Salamis
Rage of Ares

Tom Swan and the Head of St George Parts One–Six

Tom Swan and the Siege of Belgrade Parts One–Seven

Tom Swan and the Last Spartans Parts One–Five

Other Novels
Washington and Caesar
Alexander: God of War

Writing as Miles Cameron

The Traitor Son Cycle
The Red Knight
The Fell Sword
The Dread Wyrm
A Plague of Swords
The Fall of Dragons

Masters and Mages
Cold Iron
Dark Forge
Bright Steel

For my father-in-law, Gavin Watt;
re-enactor, leader and historian without peer

GLOSSARY

Arming sword – A single-handed sword, thirty inches or so long, with a simple cross guard and a heavy pommel, usually double-edged and pointed.

Arming coat – A doublet either stuffed, padded, or cut from multiple layers of linen or canvas to be worn under armour.

Alderman – One of the officers or magistrates of a town or *commune.*

Aventail – The cape of *maille*, or in some cases textile, that was suspended from a basinet or great helm to protect against rising blows to the neck. Attached by means of vervelles and laced on.

Bailli – A French royal officer much like an English sheriff; or the commander of a '*langue*' in the Knights of Saint John.

Baselard – A dagger with a hilt like a capital I, with a broad cross both under and over the hand. Possibly the predecessor of the rondel dagger, it was a sort of symbol of chivalric status in the late fourteenth century. Some of them look so much like Etruscan weapons of the bronze and early iron age that I wonder about influences . . .

Basinet – A form of helmet that evolved during the late middle ages, the basinet was a helmet that came down to the nape of the neck everywhere but over the face, which was left unprotected. It was almost always worn with an *aventail* made of *maille*, which fell from the helmet like a short cloak over the shoulders. By 1350, the basinet had begun to develop a moveable visor, although it was some time before the technology was perfected and made able to lock.

Brigands – A period term for foot soldiers that has made it into our lexicon as a form of bandit.

Burgher – A member of the town council, or sometimes, just a prosperous townsman.

Commune – In the period, powerful towns and cities were called communes and had the power of a great feudal lord over their own people, and over trade.

Coat of plates – In the period, the plate armour breast and back plate were just beginning to appear on European battlefields by the time of Poitiers – mostly due to advances in metallurgy which allowed larger chunks of steel to be produced in furnaces. Because large pieces of steel were comparatively rare at the beginning of William Gold's career, most soldiers wore a coat of small plates – varying from a breastplate made of six or seven carefully formed plates, to a jacket made up of hundreds of very small plates riveted to a leather or linen canvas backing. The protection offered was superb, but the garment is heavy and the junctions of the plates were not resistant to a strong thrust, which had a major impact on the sword styles of the day.

Corazina – A *coat of plates*, often covered in cloth, especially velvet. The difference between a common soldier's *coat of plates* and a corazina is that the plates in the corazina are more carefully formed in three dimensions to provide a much better fit and better protection. The corazina is better in many ways to solid plate: it moves with the wearer. However, it is only as durable as its weakest part, the cloth covering, which wears quickly.

Cote – In the novel, I use the period term *cote* to describe what might then have been called a gown – a man's overgarment worn atop shirt and *doublet* or *pourpoint* or *jupon*, sometimes furred, fitting tightly across the shoulders and then dropping away like a large bell. They could go all the way to the floor with buttons all the way, or only to the middle of the thigh. They were sometimes worn with fur, and were warm and practical.

Demesne – The central holdings of a lord – his actual lands, as opposed to lands to which he may have political rights but not taxation rights or where he does not control the peasantry.

Donjon – The word from which we get dungeon.

Doublet – A small garment worn over the shirt, very much like a modern vest, that held up the hose and to which armour was sometimes attached. Almost every man would have one. Name comes from the requirement of the Paris Tailor's Guild that the doublet be made – at the very least – of a piece of linen doubled – thus, heavy enough to hold the grommets and thus to hold the strain of the laced-on hose.

Gauntlets – Covering for the hands was essential for combat. Men wore *maille* or scale gauntlets or even very heavy leather gloves, but by William Gold's time, the richest men wore articulated steel gauntlets with fingers.

Gown – An overgarment worn in Northern Europe (at least) over the *kirtle*, it might have dagged or magnificently pointed sleeves and a very high collar and could be worn belted, or open to daringly reveal the *kirtle*, or simply, to be warm. Sometimes lined in fur, often made of wool.

Haubergeon – Derived from *hauberk*, the *haubergeon* is a small, comparatively light *maille* shirt. It does not go down past the thighs, nor does it usually have long sleeves, and may sometimes have had leather reinforcement at the hems.

Helm or haum – The great helm had become smaller and slimmer since the thirteenth century, but continued to be very popular, especially in Italy, where a full helm that covered the face and head was part of most harnesses until the armet took over in the early fifteenth century. Edward III and the Black Prince both seem to have worn helms. Late in the period, helms began to have moveable visors like *basinets*.

Hobilar – A non-knightly man-at-arms in England.

Horses – Horses were a mainstay of medieval society, and they were expensive, even the worst of them. A good horse cost many days' wages for a poor man; a warhorse cost almost a year's income for a knight, and the loss of a warhorse was so serious that most mercenary companies specified in their contracts (or *condottas*) that the employer would replace the horse. A second level of horse was the lady's palfrey – often smaller and finer, but the medieval warhorse was *not* a giant farm horse, but a solid beast like a modern Hanoverian. Also, *ronceys* which are generally inferior smaller horses ridden by archers.

Hours – The medieval day was divided – at least in most parts of Europe – by the canonical periods observed in churches and religious houses. Within these divisions, time was relative to sunrise and sunset, so exact times varied with the seasons. The day started with *Prime* very early, around 6 a.m., ran through *Terce* at mid-morning to *Sext* in the middle of the day, and came around *Nones* at mid-afternoon to *Vespers* towards evening. This is a vast simplification, but I have tried to keep to the flavour of medieval time by avoiding minutes and seconds. They basically weren't even thought of until the late sixteenth century.

Jupon – A close-fitting garment, in this period often laced, and sometimes used to support other garments. As far as I can tell, the term is almost interchangeable with *doublet* and with *pourpoint*. As fashion moved from loose garments based on simply cut squares and rectangles to the skintight, fitted clothes of the mid-to-late fourteenth century, it became necessary for men to lace their hose (stockings) to their upper garment – to hold them up! The simplest *doublet* (the term comes from the guild requirement that they be made of two thicknesses of linen or more, thus 'doubled') was a skintight vest worn over a shirt, with lacing holes for 'points' that tied up the hose. The *pourpoint* (literally, For Points) started as the same garment. The *pourpoint* became quite elaborate, as you can see by looking at the original that belonged to Charles of Blois online. A jupon could also be worn as a padded garment to support armour (still with lacing holes, to which armour attaches) or even over armour, as a tight-fitting garment over the breastplate or *coat of plates*, sometimes bearing the owner's arms.

Kirtle – A women's equivalent of the *doublet* or *pourpoint*. In Italy, young women might wear one daringly as an outer garment. It is skin tight from neck to hips, and then falls into a skirt. Fancy ones were buttoned or laced from the navel. Moralists decried them.

Langue – One of the sub-organisations of the Order of the Knights of Saint John, commonly called the Hospitallers. The *langues* did not always make sense, as they crossed the growing national bounds of Europe, so that, for example, Scots knights were in the English Langue, Catalans in the Spanish Langue. But it allowed men to eat and drink with others who spoke the same tongue, or nearer to it. To the best of my understanding, however, every man, however lowly, and every serving man and woman, had to know Latin, which seems to have been the Order's lingua franca. That's more a guess than something I *know*.

Leman – A lover.

Longsword – One of the period's most important military innovations, a double-edged sword almost forty-five inches long, with a sharp, armour-piercing point and a simple cross guard and heavy pommel. The cross guard and pommel could be swung like an axe, holding the blade – some men only sharpened the last foot or so for cutting. But the main use was the point of the weapon, which, with skill, could puncture *maille* or even *coats-of-plates*.

Maille – I use the somewhat period term maille to avoid confusion. I mean what most people call chain mail or ring mail. The manufacturing process was very labour-intensive, as real mail has to have each link either welded closed or riveted. A fully armoured man-at-arms would have a *haubergeon* and *aventail* of maille. Riveted maille was almost proof against the cutting power of most weapons – although concussive damage could still occur! And even the most strongly made maille is ineffective against powerful archery, spears, or well-thrust swords in the period.

Malle – Easy to confuse with *maille*, malle is a word found in Chaucer and other sources for a leather bag worn across the back of a horse's saddle – possibly like a round-ended portmanteau, as we see these for hundreds of years in English art. Any person travelling, be he or she pilgrim or soldier or monk, needed a way to carry clothing and other necessities. Like a piece of luggage, for horse travel.

Partisan – A spear or light glaive, for thrusting but with the ability to cut. My favourite, and Fiore's, was one with heavy side-lugs like spikes, called in Italian a *ghiavarina*. There's quite a pretty video on YouTube of me demonstrating this weapon . . .

Paternoster (sometimes **Pater Noster**) – A set of beads, often with a tassel at one end and a cross at the other – much like a modern rosary, but usually straight rather than in a circle. The use of prayer beads was introduced to Christianity in the twelfth or thirteenth centuries, from Islam and further east.

Pauldron or Spaulder – Shoulder armour.

Pourpoint – a somewhat generic word in the time of William Gold. In the fourteenth century, the garment's name refers to the piercing of the fabric during the quilting process. Raw cotton was most frequently used as the 'filler.' Pourpoint does not, in fact, refer to the act of pointing one's chausses or leg armour to the garment. According to *Le Pelerinage de la Humaine* (1331), 'Because the gambeson is made with many prickings (stitches), that is why it is also called a *pourpoint*. It is understood that a gambeson with many prickings is worth a lot, and one without these prickings is worth nothing.' (With thanks to Tasha Dandelion Kelly at cottesimple.com)

Prickers – Outriders and scouts.

Rondel Dagger – A dagger designed with flat round plates of iron or brass (rondels) as the guard and the pommel, so that, when used by a man wearing a gauntlet, the rondels close the space around the fingers and make the hand invulnerable. By the late fourteenth century, it was not just a murderous weapon for prying a knight out of plate armour, it was a status symbol – perhaps because it is such a very useless knife for anything like cutting string or eating . . .

Sabatons – The 'steel shoes' worn by a man-at-arms in full harness, or full armour. They were articulated, something like a lobster tail, and allow a full range of foot movement. They are also very light, as no fighter would expect a heavy, aimed blow at his feet. They also helped a knight avoid foot injury in a close press of mounted mêlée – merely from other horses and other mounted men crushing against him.

Sele – Happiness or fortune. The sele of the day is the saint's blessing.

Stradiote – A Greek or Albanian cavalryman. By the late fourteenth century, Greek cavalry probably resembled Turkish cavalry; certainly by the mid-fifteenth century they were expert scouts and were practicing horse-archery. In *maille* or scale armour, if contemporary saint's icons can be used as evidence.

Shift – A woman's innermost layer, like a tight-fitting linen shirt at least down to the knees, worn under the *kirtle*. Women had support garments, like bras, as well.

Tow – The second stage of turning flax into linen, *tow* is a fibrous, dry mass that can be used in most of the ways we now use paper towels, rags – and toilet paper. Biodegradable, as well.

Villein – A serf or unfree agricultural worker.

Vedette – A cavalry scout or guard on watch.

Yeoman – A prosperous countryman. Yeoman families had the wealth to make their sons knights or squires in some cases, but most yeoman's sons served as archers, and their prosperity and leisure time to practise gave rise to the dreaded English archery. Only a modestly well-to-do family could afford a six-foot yew bow, forty or so cloth yard shafts with steel heads, as well as a *haubergeon*, a sword, and helmet and perhaps even a couple of horses – all required for military service.

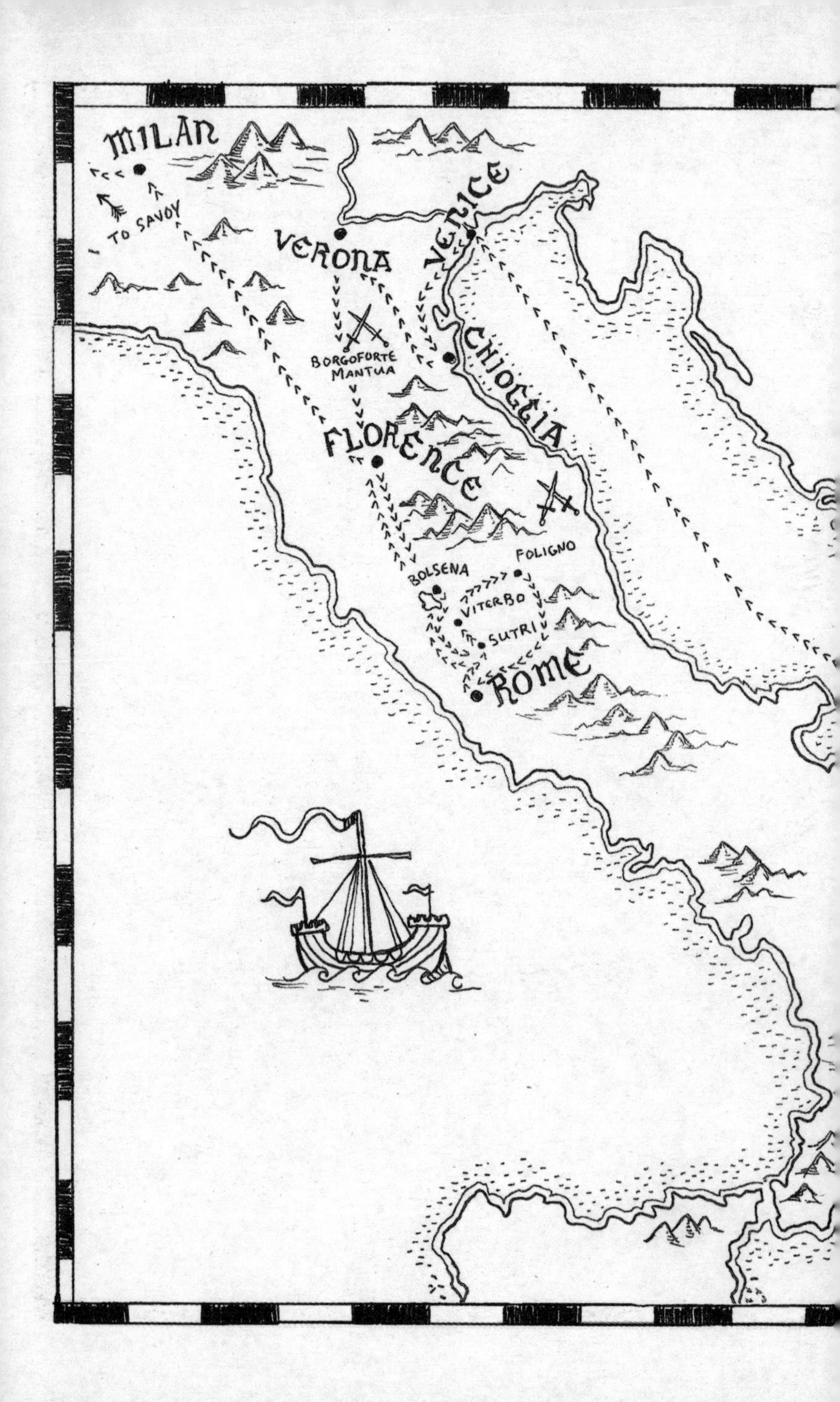

MILAN
TO SAVOY
VERONA
VENICE
BORGOFORTE
MANTUA
CHIOGGIA
FLORENCE
FOLIGNO
BOLSENA
VITERBO
SUTRI
ROME

Sir William's Travels
TO CONSTANTINOPLE
THESSALONIKI
ATHENS
CORINTH

PROLOGUE

Calais, June 1381

William Gold, knight and Captain of Venice, came down the stairs early in a plain brown cote-hardie that looked to be twenty years out of date. He paused at the common room barre and took an apple from the pewter dish that sat there, and rubbed it on his cote-hardie like an apprentice. The pot-boy, busy polishing the counter with walnut oil, nonetheless managed a full bow, as if Sir William was the King of England.

'What's your name, lad?' Gold asked after two bites of his apple.

'Which it is, William, my lord.' The boy flushed a very unbecoming bright red that showed all the pimples on his acne-scarred young face as almost white.

Gold smiled. 'I'm not much of a lord, young William.' He ate the rest of the apple in six bites, and then he ate the core as well. 'How d'ye come to be a pot-boy, then? You look hale.'

'He is a distant cousin's second son,' the keeper said, emerging from behind his writing table, rubbing his eyes and wondering if Sir William had been sent to encourage early rising. 'It is a long story.'

Gold smiled at William. 'Can you pull a bow?' he asked.

The innkeeper frowned. 'Now, see here, good sir knight. My cousin will think I have done him no favour—'

'I'm naw the best,' the boy said, cutting across the publican, 'but I can pull me da's bow to the mouth.'

'How many times in a minute?' Gold asked.

'My lord, I can show you,' the boy said. He had a broad back and long arms. He turned and dashed for the family stairs in the yard.

'Sir William,' the innkeeper pressed, as soon as the lad was gone.

The red-haired knight turned and met the innkeeper's gaze. His face wore what the innkeeper's wife would have called a 'man-of-business' look. 'What do ye pay him?' Gold asked.

'Sir knight, there is no question of payment. I have taken him to raise him to—'

'No wage? Just keep?' Gold said. His voice was light. 'Listen, messire. If I take him, he'll either make his fortune or be dead. It's his choice. Saint Augustine and Aquinas are in agreement about free will, eh?'

'I take it unkindly—' The innkeeper tried to protest.

'That's too bad,' Gold interrupted. 'I never seek to anger any man. But that boy is wasted here, and I challenge ye: you know it yourself.'

Young William reappeared with a bow. It was long – almost as long as Sir William. It showed evidence of both green and white paint, and its belly was as thick as a lady's wrist.

'You are from Cheshire, then?' Gold asked.

The boy flushed. 'Which me da' was,' he said.

'Your da' served the king. Crécy?' Gold asked, with an eye to the paint.

'Aye, my lord.' The boy strung the war bow with difficulty.

Gold took it from him. 'This bow was once a mighty warrior,' he said. 'But, like me, it has some marks of age, and I misdoubt it has anything like the pull of youth.' He pointed it at the floor and then raised it, swiftly, like a hawk rising to a lure, and Aemilie, the keeper's daughter, just emerging from the family stairs, stood transfixed as the bow centred on her …

Sir William let the tension off the bow gradually. 'Not so bad, after all. A master made this, sure enough, but it cannot go to war again. Still, show me your draw. And, demoiselle, pardon me for affrighting you.'

'Sir knight, it would take more than an empty bow to affright me,' she said.

The innkeeper winced to hear her tone. In the eyes of a father, there was no man in God's creation more unsuitable for his daughter's adolescent affection than the red-haired knight.

But she smiled warmly at young William. 'Let's see you pull it,' she said. 'Go and show Sir William, now, Bill. I know ye can.'

Out in the yard, the boy carefully positioned his feet. Sir William had a second apple, but after a bite, he grinned. 'There's nothing to put strength in a man like the smile of a beautiful woman,' he said.

Young William caught his smile and managed to relax a little. Gold saw him clear his head of rubbish, saw him give a little shake with his shoulders, and then the great bow went down like a diving swallow and then up, high in the air. The boy's shoulders quivered, but the string came all the way back.

'One,' Gold said.

The boy let the tension off and took two deep breaths, and then, almost as swift as the swallow he imitated, the bow went down again. The muscles across his shoulder blades stiffened, and the bow came up.

'Two,' Gold said.

One of Gold's archers came out – a swarthy man with an odd face, narrow eyes and skin like crackled parchment. He stood close by Gold.

The boy thought the archer looked like a demon from Hell. He tried to quell his pulse; he'd never managed more than three pulls in succession.

He breathed out, and began . . .

'Three,' Gold said.

'Not fucking bad, by Jesus,' said the demon, who ducked his head as he said the name Jesus.

'John, when you bow your head at the name of Jesus, which, may I add, you are using blasphemously,' Gold said, 'it makes no sense.'

'Every fucking sense,' John the Turk said. 'Eh, boy. Don't stop for me.' The swarthy man looked back at the knight. 'Jesus,' he bowed his head, 'is God. Yes?'

'Yes, John.' Gold sounded weary. The boy's bow went down, trembled a little at the fetch, and then rose again, an avenging angel.

'Four,' Gold said. 'Give me one more, lad.'

'Well trained, boy,' John grunted. 'So I swear by God, and I bow my— *Jesu! Damnatione!*' John spat.

The bow had exploded with a sharp crack.

The boy, despite his august audience, fell on his knees, the pieces of his father's bow across his lap, ignoring the blood that the whiplash of the bowstring had drawn from his bow hand.

Gold looked back. Aemilie and her father were both standing in the great mullioned window that was the hallmark of the inn, the best in Calais. Master Chaucer was leaning in the doorway.

Shaking his head at the Tartar's blasphemy, Gold approached the boy.

'I'm sorry it broke,' Gold said, putting his hand on the boy's shoulder. 'But you have the makings of an archer, eh, John?'

John nodded. 'Take him.' He turned without bowing and went back towards the barn.

'Why not leave him and let him live?' Chaucer called from the doorway, a little too loudly.

'Oh, master, I want to go!' Young William was fighting tears. His father's bow had been his most prized possession.

'You are too young to know anything,' Chaucer muttered, approaching the pair. The small, wiry man stood very close to Sir William, who was a head taller. 'Let him go, William. Your tales go to his head. He'll just die, face down in the mud somewhere. Or the plague will take him, or dysentery, torture, raped by captors, gutted like a fish, puking blood ...'

Gold shrugged. 'You would know,' he said mildly. 'And yet he might ride back here in ten years in a coat of plates, riding a tall horse with a squire and a full purse.'

'A killer,' Chaucer said bitterly.

'There's more to the life of arms than killing, Master Chaucer,' Gold said.

'Aye, I can hear the same poem from a Southwark strumpet, who'll tell me she brings comfort and love to loveless men, when all she does is fuck them,' Chaucer spat.

Gold's face turned a bright crimson, and then returned to its normal shade. 'You are hard on your fellow men, Geoffrey,' he said. 'But then, you are hard on yourself. Let the boy decide for himself.'

'He can no more decide for himself than he could choose chastity if ...' Chaucer caught himself, but his glance at Aemilie revealed the pattern of his thought; the girl flushed, and her father put a hand to his dagger.

Gold shocked them all by passing his arm around Chaucer and locking him in an embrace. 'I hear ye,' he said. 'We'll leave this for the morn. I'm off to prayers.'

'I'll come,' Chaucer said.

The two men walked off in what appeared perfect amity, leaving a boy and a broken bow in the yard.

John the Turk appeared with a new, white yew bow, almost as tall as Sir William himself, and its belly thicker than Aemilie's wrists.

'Spanish,' the Kipchak said, running a hand down the smooth wood. 'The best. For you.'

'Sweet Virgin, I cannot afford such,' young William said.

John the Turk knew a great deal about bows, but more about young men. He nodded gravely. 'You broke good bow in service of company,' he said. 'We replace it, eh? We have a bundle of sixty.'

'Sixty?' the boy asked, stupefied at such riches.

The Kipchak shrugged. 'And another sixty in Italy. War is bad for bows.'

He grinned his odd grin and went back towards the barn.

Aemilie glanced at her father. 'I don't understand them,' she said.

'The one who looks like the Devil?' the keeper asked.

'Nay, Pater. The knight and Master Chaucer.' She looked after the two men.

Her father was watching the strange man with the slanted eyes walking away from them. 'I don't really, either,' he said. 'But I'm going to wager that when men spend enough time together, and experience enough ... even if they mislike each other, in time ... they are like brothers. My brother and I used to fight like that.'

'I like him, Pater,' she said. 'But I'm not going to play the fool.'

He ruffled her hair. 'He's a fine man,' the innkeeper admitted. 'But also the Devil incarnate.'

'Oh,' she said. 'By the Virgin, Pater, do ye think I don't know?' She shook her head and went to find her mother.

The rain started before Matins were over, and came down like Noah's flood, and even Sir William, usually so debonair, looked like a drowned cat and smelled like wet wool when he returned from church. Master Froissart, late from his bed, was drinking small beer in the common room. When the damp men had changed into dry garments and the fire had been touched up, Sir William took a chair by the chimney and drank off a huge jack of hot porter.

'Ah,' he sighed. 'England. Italy has nothing like that.' He wiped his beard.

'Passports?' Froissart asked.

Gold looked over the common room. A dozen of his men-at-arms and most of the archers were packed in the low room, as well as several off-duty servants and some local Englishmen – a shoemaker and a cutler. Gold shrugged.

'I suppose now is as good a time to say it as any,' he said. 'There's trouble in England, gentles. They say the commons have risen against the lords, and that there's been a lot of killing.' Gold looked over the room, and then at Chaucer. 'They say Sir Robert Hales is dead, murdered by the crowd.'

'Christ,' Chaucer said.

'Aye, and I will pray for his soul. He was a good knight, whatever his sins.' Gold looked into the fire. 'He was with us at Alexandria …' He shook his head. 'Any road, gentles, the way of it is this: the castle is holding our passports until such time as they have a ship out of the Thames or the south ports that gives them cause to hope.'

'That could be weeks,' Froissart said.

'Aye,' Gold said. 'And all my profits wasted on good living in a fine inn.' He raised an eyebrow at the keeper. 'If it hasn't resolved itself in a week or two, I'll be headed back to Venice.'

'More stories!' called a voice.

Chaucer laughed. 'I think you have a willing audience,' he said, and then more soberly: 'The Italian wedding?'

Gold looked at Froissart. 'It's not just my story, although I know an ending that mayhap you do not. But you were both there; you'll interrupt me constantly and insist that I tell the truth.'

Chaucer laughed. 'You really should have been a scribbler, like me,' he snorted.

Froissart leaned back. 'I would like to understand what I saw in Milan,' he said. 'I still … It was beautiful, yes? And terrible?'

'Aye,' Gold said. 'So it was. The worst year of my life, in many ways. But the year before it was wonderful.'

'Made your reputation,' Chaucer said.

'Perhaps,' Gold said.

At the far end of the room, young William the pot-boy had just slipped into a corner, eyes bright with expectation. Sir William reached behind him, hiding a smile of satisfaction, and his squire handed him a well-thumbed book of hours. The knight laid it on the table. Chaucer leaned over, flipped a page, and exclaimed, 'You are a scribbler!'

Sir William smiled. 'It started one afternoon in Venice; I was copying itineraries, the year I served the Green Count. Look, it's not much; just the weather, usually.'

'And the saints' days,' Froissart said. 'And these little crosses. What are they?'

'Men I killed,' Gold said. 'I pray for them. I like to remember who they were.'

PART ONE

OUTREMER

April 1367 – August 1367

There I was with an arming sword in my hand, and I was desperately outmatched. A trickle of blood running down my right bicep, my old arming coat cut through all eight layers of linen, and sweat blinding my eyes.

I made a bad, hasty parry, but at least I wasn't deceived by my opponent's devilish deception. From the cross, I pushed, eager to use my size and strength against the little bastard, but he was away like a greased pig. He evaded my winding cut at the face with a wriggle and we were both past, turning, swords back into *gardes*; he in *the boar's tooth* and me with my sword high …

He raised his sword, a clear provocation, given he was so damnably fast.

I shook my head to clear the sweat. Backed a step in unfeigned fear.

He glided forward, perfectly controlled. I dropped my sword hesitantly into a point forward *garde*; I couldn't allow his point so close to my heart …

And then, out of my hesitation, I attacked. My wrist moved; my blade struck his a sharp blow. And I snapped the blade up into a high thrust, right at his face.

He had to parry. And he had to parry high.

I rolled my right wrist off that parry, rotating my heavy arming sword through almost a full circle, from the high cross all the way around, my thumb flat against the blade for control, and my blade just barely outraced his desperate parry to tag him under the arm, where no one has a good defence.

He burst into peals of laughter, spun away with my sword tucked under his arm, and sprawled to the ground in a pantomime of death. My son Edouard flung himself on the prostrate Fiore and pretended to shower him with dagger blows.

Fiore was laughing. 'I just taught you that!' he roared.
And he had. Just the day before.

It was a glorious spring of training, and we were all on the island of Lesvos, in Outremer. In the year of Our Lord 1367, I had reached the end of my desire to go on crusade. I'd be too strong to say I was sick of the whole thing; that came later. But I doubted the very basis of the idea. It was clear to me that the Infidel were neither so very bad nor so easy to convert. I had, I fear, spent too much time with Sabraham; I began to see the wisdom in the Venetians and the Genoese, who traded with them every day and seemed to know a great deal more about the Infidel than anyone in Avignon or Rome or Paris.

Spring in Outremer is as magnificent as spring in England. Lesvos is the most beautiful of the Greek islands, with magnificent contrasts: steep, waterless valleys like the Holy Land, which is close enough, for all love; and then lush greenery and magnificent fields of flowers; hillsides like a Venetian miniature; roses. Gracious God, it was beautiful. And as Emile recovered from pregnancy, having given us Cressida, we wandered the fields of my new lordship, and we were like sweethearts. The only cloud in the sky was that Sir Miles Stapleton, one of my closest companions, was recalled to England to marry and take up his uncle's lands. His uncle of the same name had been killed at Auray, in '64. We threw him an excellent revel; before he left, we all wrote letters and I sent Hawkwood a long one, as well as another for Messire Petrarca in Venice and Marc-Antonio added a long one for his family. Finally, I wrote a long letter of eight or ten pages to my sister – some of it in the Latin I had laboured too hard to master with Sister Marie. I sent her some saffron and some ambergris and a few other drugs and spices in a packet, and I sent her a bolt of silk.

Losing Miles was hard. The four of us – Miles and Nerio, Fiore and I – had been together a long time. And we had seen a great deal; we'd lost Juan; we'd been to Jerusalem. I knew when Miles left that soon I'd lose Nerio, and eventually, Fiore. On the other hand . . .

I had Emile. My life with Emile remained as fine as a dream.

I had a new horse, a magnificent horse, a gift from the Prince of Lesvos. At first, I thought that no horse would ever replace Gawain, but Gabriel, as I called my new charger, was big and glossy and intelligent, and the more we trained together, the better I liked him.

After Miles left for Venice in February, Gabriel and I were training hard for the Prince of Lesvos's tournament at Mytilene, which was to be given on Ascension Day. Actually, our entire little company was training; Nerio, my good friend and one of the richest men in the Inner Sea, was hiring us to defend his holdings in Achaea. That is to say, to defend them by conquering them. He did a little training – if by training you mean being fitted for new armour he was having made in far-off Bohemia – while parading around with his magnificently beautiful Greek mistress. Occasionally he deigned to cross swords or lances with my friend Fiore, who was in many ways his foil: poor, when Nerio was rich, devoted to training, where Nerio was lazy to the point of indolence, chaste, where Nerio's pursuit of women had something unhealthy about it. They quarrelled constantly, yet they were the quarrels of an old married couple, and each knew full well how to land a blow on the other, in conversation or in combat. Indeed, it had become impossible for me to touch Fiore on foot, and hard for me to shake his seat on horseback, but Nerio, who, to be fair, I could strike almost at will with sword or spear afoot, seemed to trouble Fiore a good deal.

At any rate, training for a great tournament is a fine way to pass a spring, in between dalliances with one's lady and playing with children in a pleasant, airy house full of good food and laughter and one's best friends.

It doesn't make much of a tale, though. I remember a perfect, golden sun, not too hot, not too cold. I remember making love with my wife under our lemon tree, giggling lest we be caught by our servants. I remember swaggering swords with Fiore in our courtyard, and jousting with Nerio, day after day.

One of my favourite memories is that of watching Fiore with a wooden waster in his hand, haranguing all of our knights and men-at-arms and a few others – two local Frankish-Greek boys and half a dozen of the prince's men-at-arms – who had all come to our School of Mars. Or Ares, as the Greeks would say.

He had just effortlessly dispatched three good knights, allowing each just one blow. They made a little line and came at him; one swung a great blow, one thrust, and the third, rather remarkably, threw his sword.

Fiore just laughed. To each blow he responded by a rising cut from a low, left-hand *garde*, the *garde* he called *the boar's tooth* or *Dente di Cinghiaro.* The cut came out of the low *garde*, false edge up, crossed the incoming weapon with precision, striking it away, up and left, and then descending like an avenging angel in the same line to strike the knight on the head, arms, or neck. The thrown sword he sent out of the lists like a boy hitting a stick tossed by another boy – same *garde*, same cut.

Oh, no, gentles. There's nothing false about the false edge. Look here: I talk about swords all the time. Let's look at mine. Here she is: four feet of steel, a long handspan of hilt and the cross guard as wide as the hilt is long. Not one of those new long hilts you see in High Germany; those are for men who never have to fight a-horse, and never have to fight close, either. A good wide blade, too; narrow blades break, and they don't cut.

A true sword has two edges. Saracen swords have but one edge, because they are simpler men than we, perhaps, or less deceptive, or really, just because their smiths use a different temper process and they can only get one edge hard as good steel ought to be. But in Milan they can make a blade that's straight as truth and has two sharp edges that run to a point fine enough to punch through maille. That's the whole point of the weapon, really, the point. It is mightier than the edge. But for all that, we play a lot with edges; and of the two, the true one is the one under your hand when you grip her – put a finger round the guard if it helps you, and there you are. The true edge is the one that it is natural to cut with: raise your arm and drop it, and you are cutting with the true edge. The false edge is the one on the back, and there's no false thing about it but the name. The true is the downstroke and the false is the reverse, and a better philosopher than me would point out that when you change grip, true and false are reversed, and that on a new sword it's impossible to tell the two edges apart.

I have found Truth and Falsity to look very similar in my time.

Regardless, there was Fiore, with a wooden sword. His *falso*, his false edge cut, had opened up his adversary, and then his own cut came down the line that his *falso* had traced with a precision and fluidity that was beautiful to watch.

'That's all I have to teach you,' Fiore insisted. 'The whole of this art is in emerging like a wild animal from the cover of the outside lines to strike the opponent's weapon and win the centre – and then to strike like the leopard.'

Now, this is the part that I always love when Sir Fiore teaches. Everyone nodded; after all, they were all professional men-at-arms, who at least notionally fought and killed for their livings. But, *certes*, not everyone fights the same way, and many good knights are merely brave enough to set their spear and push in the stour or the mêlée. They have no more idea of the art of *armizare* than they have of *tactica* or *logistica*. They put their heads down and they fight manfully and they survive.

A handful practise the art – really practise it. Fewer yet understand it; even fewer have the kind of cold rage that allows them to kill without mercy or passion. They are the most dangerous, but they are bad knights, because a killer without mercy is nothing but a killer – a rabid dog who needs to be put down. I have known a few such, as you will hear.

Bah, I lose my way. My point is that in this huddle of good men-at-arms, every head nodded understanding, and yet I could tell from the confusion of their bodies that not one in ten understood a word he said. Good men-at-arms smiled fearfully and hoped he would not call on them to demonstrate anything else.

I still laugh to remember it. Why is it that none of us is really brave enough to step forward and say, 'Aye, master, I have no idea what you just said?' Eh? To swordsmen or priests or even wives, I trow.

And yet we did learn that spring. If Jerusalem hardened us into something a little special, if the Holy Sepulchre made us something other than brutes, it was Fiore who gave us the art, and there were not fifty men-at-arms and archers in God's creation with a better understanding of the principles of fighting with spear or lance, sword or axe. Marc-Antonio, my squire, showed every sign of being a fine man-at-arms; Achille, Nerio's squire, who seemed too soft for a life of war, proved to be an incredibly dexterous swordsman. One day he disarmed me and I had to embrace him. And, of course, Sir Bernard and Sir Jason and Sir Jean-François were the best of knights and yet seemed to learn willingly enough, something I have often noted in the truly excellent. Prince Francesco's son joined us often, sometimes with three or four friends. Only one of his former companions had stuck with him through the changes he was experiencing; he had served as a man-at-arms and his friend Alessio had followed him to war. That spring, both of them worked hard with Fiore, to master the art of arms.

And what Fiore did for the art of arms, Rob Stone and John the Kipchak tried to do for the archers, honing them at every skill: fletching their own arrows, or long bowls at extreme ranges, or rapidly rolling arrows off their fingers, loosing and loosing again, while they *ran.* John made most of the English at least passable at shooting from horseback with Hungarian bows we bought from a Turk merchant. And Rob Stone, Gospel Mark and John all spent time making every man, even our Kipchaks and our Greeks, at least passable while dismounted on the flat.

It was all beautiful, if preparation for war can be accounted beautiful.

And I'll bore you for a moment and say that my children – and by then they were mine – were part of the delight. Young Edouard had begun to play with swords, rising eleven years. Fiore said twelve, but the boy wanted a sword, and he'd begun to use rough and tumble too often on his sister, so I made him a waster and sent him, across his mother's tears, to the prince in Mytilene and to Sir Richard Percy, to be a page and a squire.

It was as well I did, as you shall hear in time.

And playing with my daughters – a little one, too young even to hold up her head or focus her eyes, and an older mite for whom there was no doll as perfect as her sister, and she struggled like a saint with her own feelings of sisterly jealousy. The same Turk trader who had the bows had a load of silk, and I bought some and Emile made her a doll like a great lady, and she called it 'Lady Emma', and Lady Emma lived with her other ladies from Venice and Savoy. And I, the great knight, was betimes a horse, and betimes a huntsman to a princess, and a juggler, and a fool.

Great days.

Ascension Day was nearing, and we were in the very peak of training, and Fiore himself declared that he would do nothing for the last week, so that no man would miss his moment for a sprained wrist or a broken finger. Training hurts; men are covered in bruises and abrasions that shopkeepers never know.

Regardless, it was our first day free of training when the herald came on a small galliot flying a fine banner of the Virgin in a blue cloak, and under it the arms of Savoy. I walked down to the beach to meet him, thinking that perhaps it was the count himself; some said he would attend the tournament.

The herald bowed deeply, as if I was a great lord. Which, to be fair, I was, at least at a remove – I was lord of my lady wife, and she was a great lord. And I had three small lordships in my own right: one on Cyprus, that paid in gold; one on Lesvos, where I lived; and one in the Italian Alps, which I had never seen.

Well. I started my life of arms as a cook's boy. I am never less than delighted by the deference of my peers or my people, as it is new to me every day. I suppose I imagine I'll wake one day and find that I'm turning a spit and it was all a boy's dream, eh?

Ah, the herald. So he hands me a scroll. I still have it. It summoned me with my full knight service for a feudal levy for the Count of Savoy, at Constantinople, three weeks hence.

I was dumbfounded.

Now, in truth, the count was in his rights, but only just, and in an absurd way. No vassal could actually be summoned under Savoyard law to fight in the Holy Land; that part was absurd. He was stretching a point, because Emile was *in* the Holy Land. But the reality of the situation was immediately obvious when presented: he'd have to pay us all wages, and he couldn't really summon me with all my service – that is, all of Emile's service – yet, despite the absurdity, I had the men to satisfy him, because I had a small company. I actually *had* forty men-at-arms and forty archers – the whole service that Emile would owe if, for example, the Green Count summoned her at Turin.

The herald admitted over dinner that many of the count's men-at-arms were sick and more had gone home after Mesembria fell apart.

I looked at Nerio.

'I want to go to Didymoteichon, just as we planned at Christmastide,' Nerio said. 'I want to have friends on the Ottomanid side of this game.' He looked out of the window. 'But … he is your lord, and I imagine he'll esteem it a favour.'

'No, he will not,' Emile said. 'He will take it as his due. He makes outrageous demands and later pretends it was all a jest.' She shrugged; she was not one for pouting. 'He can be a good lord. But when he is not …'

The herald looked as if he might explode in defence of his lord.

I nodded. 'Forty days,' I said.

The herald looked at me.

'Marc-Antonio,' I summoned my squire. 'Take this fine young man and show him the delights of Methymna.'

When the herald was gone, I spoke to Emile and Nerio frankly.

'I know the law of arms,' I said. 'He gets forty days from when we respond, travel time included.' I shrugged. 'Two can play the game of loyal retainer. We have to go to Constantinople anyway, and by then, travel alone will have used eight days. Thirty-two days, and we'll end perhaps five days from Didymoteichon. Just in time to meet the Turks. We can send John and half a dozen Kipchaks across the lines to make sure that this Suleiman understands that we are accepting his invitation for, let us say, the first of July.'

Nerio nodded. 'And your feudal lord can pay the cost of transport!' he said.

'My other feudal lord has to accept the condition,' I said, and looked at Emile and drank wine. The Prince of Lesvos *also* had my knight service.

I sent the young herald back with our decision: the Green Count had to pay our transport and my other lord had to agree.

We arrived in the city of Mytilene a few days before the tournament. I wanted to talk to Prince Francesco, and to enjoy the good life of his court. He had jongleurs from Achaea and from Florence, and a singer from Provence. He kept a magnificent table, and, for an old pirate, he was the finest lord I've ever known – as good and bad a man as Hawkwood. And his son had grown on me – a difficult young man but increasingly a good companion.

Prince Francesco was originally a Genoese. He'd come out to Outremer in the fifties with a fleet of warships, and he'd ranged the coast of the Levant, taking prizes and burning and looting, a sort of sea-routier. About the time that the Black Prince was knighting Hawkwood at Poitiers, the Emperor of the Byzantines was marrying his daughter to Gatelussi and granting him a semi-independent principality on Lesvos, Chios, and Lemnos. These are the easternmost portions of Christendom since the fall of Acre; Methymna, on Lesvos, is only about three sea miles from Asia. Gatelussi got a bride and a fine little kingdom, and in return he provided the Emperor with a fine fleet and a very modern armed fist. The Gatelussi were excellent paymasters; they hired the very best mercenaries in Italy – Germans and English and Italians and Bretons and Gascons – and brought them out to the Aegean, where their superior training and armour gave them mastery of the seas around the islands.

I have always expected to retire on my estates there. It's a fine place, and with plenty of fighting. Francesco is an enlightened despot: his taxes are low, because he makes his income off terrorising the Turkish coast; his men-at-arms are too busy to brutalise the peasants. He is a patron of the arts.

He sat before me on a stool, while a servant fitted him with a sabaton that was slightly too small. He was trying a new harness; he planned to open the tournament himself.

'I have, hmmm, agreements.' Here the old pirate smiled like a fox. 'Hmmm, with most of the Turkish rulers this year,' Francesco said. 'I won't be fighting alongside your Green Count. And anyway, he has no army – most of his men-at-arms are sick.'

'I gather that new lords reached him from Savoy and Cyprus,' I said. 'Crusaders.'

Prince Francesco laughed. 'Fucking crusaders,' he said. 'The most useless ...' He looked at me. 'I don't mean the Order, or the professionals. But a bunch of Frankish lords with no idea what the conditions are here, no military training, no idea except to kill infidels.' He shook his head. 'Some of my closest allies are infidels. Old Uthman was far more reliable than the Pope.'

Once I might have been shocked. But now I was a veteran of Outremer. I knew, now, the dividing line between Christianity and Islam that had once seemed so stark was, like everything, a matter of shades of grey. I thought of the young men I'd met in one of the Turkish towns – curious, eager to dispute with us about the Trinity. I thought of the Dervishes. About the curious things men believed.

'I can see,' Prince Francesco said, 'that you are now one of us. So I say, another season of your Green Count harrying the Turks will only fragment good alliances. And anyway, he's attacking the wrong Turks.'

'Wrong Turks?' I asked.

'He's attacking the Ottomanids and not the Karamanids. He

probably can't tell them apart,' the prince said with contempt. Then he turned, with a sharp intake of breath. 'Careful there,' he said.

The armourer looked rueful.

'I need to open a rivet, lord,' he said.

'Just don't open my foot,' the prince said. 'Although, Sir William, now that I consider it, the Emperor might like us to ... bluster ... in the direction of the Ottomanids. They are dangerous allies.'

I changed tack. 'Will you go to do the deed of arms at Didymoteichon?' I asked.

'I probably won't break a lance,' the prince said, playing with his beard to hide a smile. 'But I'll be there, making a treaty with the Ottomanids for the Emperor. They have too much of our ground behind Constantinople already; your Green Count should have retaken Adrianopolis instead of Mesembria.' He shrugged. 'But ... with my fleet sitting off the coast to make sure everyone knows we mean business.' He nodded at a seat brought by a servant. 'Sit, William. You treat me like a great lord. I'm just an old pirate.'

A very successful pirate ...

'The Emperor is out of money; he paid thirty thousand ducats for Mesembria and Gallipoli. Now he needs to raise more funds. He needs to settle soldiers in the north, and stop the bloodsucking leech of a Church from taking all his money.' Francesco snapped his fingers and I was given wine. 'We need five years of peace,' Francesco said.

I toyed with my goblet, which was heavy and solid silver. I understood all his points, and he was my other feudal lord. 'So you forbid me from joining the Green Count?' I asked.

He shrugged.

'May I offer a suggestion?' I asked.

He sat back and flicked his beard. 'You're a smart lad, for an Englishman. Tell me.'

'The Green Count is going to make war on the Turks without the Emperor's permission,' I said.

'Against the Emperor's express request! It's as if he thinks war in Outremer is a fucking sport and he's going to hunt inside the garden,' Francesco spat.

I met his eye. 'What if, instead, the Emperor were to appear to be in control of the Green Count's expedition? Would the Turks not have all the more reason to negotiate?'

'Is this Nerio's idea?' the prince asked.

'No, my lord, all mine,' I said.

'He's rubbing off on you, and you may yet become Italian. So you go to serve the Green Count, and I hover off the coast with my fleet, and the Emperor and I pretend we're running the show.'

'Yes, my lord,' I said. 'And the Emperor can repeatedly and pointedly state that he "finds the young Crusaders difficult to control" and other such platitudes. The same platitudes that Venice and Genoa make to each other …' I smiled. 'And then, when we negotiate at Didymoteichon, the Ottomans will know that we have teeth. And you'll get your five-year truce with them.'

Francesco was pounding his armoured thigh with his hand, laughing. 'Jesus Christ, the same bullshit that Uthman used to say when he snapped up one of our towns!' he said. 'By God, Englishman, you have a head on your shoulders. I like it. And I have a terrible reputation for duplicity and brutality.' His eye twinkled. 'I'll make use of it.'

The tournament at Mytilene was magnificent as only the very rich can afford magnificence. We all had new pavilions of silk, at the prince's expense; need I say more? Everyone was in their best and, somewhere in Milan and Bohemia, armourers must have broken their guild rules and stayed up night after night to get so much polished steel into our hands. A galliot arrived two days before the first list was due to open and disgorged a small fortune in finished plate armour, straight from Genoa. There was a fountain by the fortress, rigged to give wine and not water, and the wine was delicious. At first, peasants and townspeople came in mobs to fill bottles and clay jars, but then the Gatelussi steward began opening casks just to give away, and the fountain ran on.

We ran our first courses in brilliant sunshine, and the good weather held all the way to the last day; it sprinkled rain from time to time, but it was not ever actually raining on the lists. The flowers remained in bloom, and the ladies of the town and the court, and my own lady wife, vied with *Natura* for the beauty of their apparel. Long dangling sleeves and high collars were the order of the day in France and Italy and Cyprus, and for the first day the ladies wore magnificent overgowns that might have been seen in Rheims or Ghent or Pavia. But by the second day, when the serious courses were being run a-horse, most of the women were in kirtles alone; the balance of beauty shifted slightly, from the richness of a brocade or a sweltering velvet to the curve of a hip or breast. As the heat of the second day built, so did the heat of the fights: hundreds of beautiful women with only a single layer of silk or linen covering them, stitched as tightly as craft and mothers would allow, has a certain effect on the fighting spirit, and a surprising number of men were stretched full length on the sand of the lists. The prince forbade Fiore and Richard Percy from having a third course after each pierced the other's visor with a lance of war; the prince's son Francesco unhorsed Nerio, and Nerio's rage was quick and hot. Fiore's comment that more practice might have brought him victory did not do anything to cool his anger.

Young Edouard waited on Sir Richard Percy as a page, and bore himself well, even when he had to control an angry horse that lifted him like a doll. I was watching him, even as Francesco dropped Nerio – shoulders set, head high, determined to hold the horse he'd been given.

Marc-Antonio rode in arms, the first time I had allowed him. He was not Galahad, nor yet Lancelot, but he held himself well and was never unhorsed, although he came close to going down against Percy. Achille, Nerio's squire, was excellent as well, holding his own against wily older knights like me and managing to score a point against Fiore, breaking his lance despite Fiore's attempt to use his lance at the cross, as he taught. Alessio, the young prince's friend, was unhorsed by Percy but kept his seat against Fiore.

I was adequate, but Jean-François stretched me across my saddle as he had on Cyprus. I didn't come off. Otherwise I broke most of my lances easily; Sir Bernard and I broke three and received a great many flowers and a long burst of applause.

But it was Fiore's week. Aside from his very dangerous encounter with Percy, he rode perfectly, dropping men left and right, and his score was unassailable by the time I reached him. I was surprised by his fire; he was clearly playing to win. I didn't want to be unhorsed, and I was on the stage of chivalry: Emile was watching. So I went and kissed her, to make the crowd roar, and it was then that I saw a young woman throw her arms around Fiore – not an everyday sight, I promise you.

Aha, thinks I. *That's how the sail is setting.*

Fiore fell in love in odd ways and quirky moments; his last lady love, so to speak, had been Janet. Not that she ever returned his fervour, but he learned a great deal from it; despite his lack of intuition, he understood the art of courtly love surprisingly well. Perhaps because he read books and memorised things.

All this went through my head in a moment. The young woman was unknown to me, and I pointed her out to Emile.

'Goodness!' Emile said. She was delighted. 'Beautiful. I will find out directly.'

Emile had the confidence of the beautiful aristocrat; she had no hesitancy in pronouncing the girl 'beautiful'. And she was. She had brown hair that hung far down her back, a crown of flowers and a kirtle of golden silk. She was 'somebody'; even her red leather shoes spoke of her station, and her very slim waist was girded with a chain of gold, which she took off and wrapped around Fiore's arm.

Oh, my.

'I think I'm about to be made an object lesson,' I said.

Emile kissed me, and very softly bit my lower lip, something that has always inflamed me. 'I want my knight to be the best knight,' she said.

It was like a shock – the look in her eye, lecherous and demanding. Courtly love need not end with marriage – far from it. My lady made her demand as she had every right to do.

I bowed, and vaulted onto my courser. My lady love had borne three children, and she still stood straight as an arrow, and she wore her kirtle over her naked body on a hot day, and nothing, for me, had changed since the first day on the bridge when I fought the *Jacques* for her and under her eye.

Prove your worth.

Fiore was, with Nerio, and Richard Musard, my first and best friend. But by the law of arms, we put that aside when we went into the lists. He was going to attempt to unhorse me for the slim lady in the golden kirtle.

I was going to return the favour, for the slim lady in the blue silk kirtle.

I had a new helmet, of which more later, but I did not feel that it was up to the rigours of jousting, and settled for my old and somewhat dented great helm, newly painted red and with one of my lady's sleeves floating from the crest. I took a moment to pray; I find that a prayer can put me in the right space for fighting, and after I prayed, I imagined the cross of the lances …

My horse was in a fine state – fully worked up. I'd practised all spring. I sometimes beat Fiore, even then. Nothing was impossible.

I kept my lance erect as long as I could, so that Fiore would not slam his lance atop mine and void my blow. And I did not aim at his shield; I went for the crest on his helmet, where a fine piece of golden gauze floated.

Fiore's lance slammed into my shield and split it, but the shaft shattered like glass.

My lance had torn the golden veil off his head and I rode down the list with that dainty bit of silk dangling like a brag from my crenellated lance tip.

I was coming to Fiore's end of the lists, so I rode to the golden girl and placed the silk in her hands.

She flushed.

I turned my horse and trotted back, and popped my visor. There was Fiore, and I saluted him, and he gave me a glare of hate.

I suppose I rolled my eyes. The crowd was cheering me, and my wife's eyes were big enough to bathe in, all the way from where she sat by the princess.

'Sir Fiore requests that you take up a lance of war to engage in the next course,' a herald said to me, as Marc-Antonio got water into my mouth.

I spat the water, took a drink, and patted my horse's neck. 'Tell Sir Fiore that such is my love for him that I would never consider using a lance of war against him,' I said.

I picked up a lance with a crenellated tip. So did Fiore; he wasn't lost to reason.

But he was coming for me with blood in his eye.

I decided to go for his visor. He had a new helm, a great helm with a visor in the Italian style. The visor was broad and a little flat for my taste, and I thought I might be able to seat my coronal, the tip of the lance, against his eye slit.

Seventy paces away, Fiore decided that my old helm had enough dents in the front that he could seat his coronal against it.

We charged. Both horses seemed to know that this was the

important course; both were tired, but in excellent condition, and we exploded into the lists like bulls into chutes at a fair. I got my lance into the rest under my arm, and my tip came down …

My lance *exploded.* It was the strangest feeling, and my hand hurt for half a day. I had to let go of the butt of the lance; my hand was numb. I rode by Fiore and he was untouched – not even rocked – but his lance was gone too.

The crowd was roaring. Almost everyone was on their feet, and I had no idea why. I just rode down the list, empty-handed, because I'd dropped the broken butt of mine, and I waved at the crown and turned.

This time, when I saluted Fiore, he reached out his hand and we touched our fists together. The crowd roared again.

A herald met me as Marc-Antonio handed me water.

'The prince forbids a third meeting. You have done enough,' he said.

I bowed. There's nothing to be said on these occasions. You can argue later, or whine about it, but when the Lord of the Tourney says you are done, you are done.

I trotted my courser down the list to where the prince and princess and my lady were seated and saluted, and the princess threw me a white rose, which I still have somewhere. And Emile looked as if she was going to eat me right there.

Bless her.

I trotted back to my end of the lists, and Marc-Antonio held my stirrup while I dismounted. 'What the hell happened?' I asked, a trifle pettishly.

Marc-Antonio made a face and handed me a jug of water. Achille, who was getting Nerio ready, glanced at me, full of obvious admiration.

'You don't know?' Nerio asked. He was already on his charger. 'By the Virgin, it was pretty, Guglielmo. Lance head to lance head – a perfect strike to the tip, and both lances shattered.' He shrugged. 'I have never done it. Never even seen it.'

'Five points,' Marc-Antonio said. In Mytilene, in accordance with the French fashion, a broken lance was worth one and driving the opponent to the ground was worth three; there were a few other scores. But tip to tip counted five.

I laughed. 'I thought I'd hit his horse or something,' I said. Marc-Antonio got my breast and back open and off me; suddenly the hot air of Lesvos seemed cool. I finished the water, took another, drank some, and poured the rest over my head.

Fiore appeared, and gave me a nice steel embrace. 'You bastard,' he said. 'Just once, I want to impress a woman, and you try to steal my glory.'

As Fiore had no sense of irony, I knew he was speaking the truth. So I embraced him again. 'I'm sorry,' I said. 'But you cannot expect me to lie down. Not in front of *my* lady.'

'No,' Fiore said. He sighed. 'Well, tip to tip was excellent.'

'And anyway, tell her you trained me,' I said.

Fiore brightened. 'I already did,' he said.

You and Hawkwood and Boucicault and the Order, I thought.

It was Nerio who found out who the girl was.

'Genoese,' he said. 'Bianca by name. But not really so very Genoese, either; the family lives in Padua and Genoa and Monaco, and they're in banking. Part of the endless Doria family. What is a woman that handsome doing with Fiore? He won't even know what to do.'

Emile slapped Nerio, not so lightly, on the shoulder. 'Fie on you, sir. First, because I believe that Sir Fiore knows right well what to do, and second, because you are so uncourtly as to imagine that the lady might not be able to … explain.'

Nerio laughed so hard he staggered.

'I find myself justly reprimanded,' he admitted, wheezing. 'But, my dear lady, the very picture of Fiore demanding explanations …'

I tried very hard to stare out of the window. Whenever Fiore was presented with something he didn't understand, he expected careful, minute explanations, and he would demand repetition until he felt he fully understood.

'I need to try this,' Nerio said, seizing a breath. 'Oh, fair lady, I am but a poor innocent and need to be instructed in …'

Emile glared.

The next day was axes afoot. This was very much a northern form of sport; most of the local gentlemen didn't even own an axe. We gave some good blows that day, and I received one from Richard Percy that almost ended my tournament. I managed to keep my feet mostly by clinging to his staff like a babe to his mother.

But Sir Jason won. He practised a little differently from Sir Fiore; his method was simpler, and to be frank, he was bigger. He didn't take Sir Fiore down, but he staggered him and *almost* hooked his ankle. Watching the two of them fight was a treat. They were excellent, and we roared for them, and I explained to half a hundred Greeks near me why the axe was a fine weapon, and I was told several times that we were mad heretics. But in the nicest way.

Told this way, the life of arms sounds delightful. But of course, you are exhausted when you finish even one bout; three times in the list on foot and you begin to prove your worth. And the blows hurt, despite the armour – muscles tear, bones crack. Not always, but sometimes. It can be hard to rise the third day, much less the fourth, and do it again. It is practice for war; in some ways, it is worse than war. There is no rage of battle to buoy you up, and everyone watches everything that you do; you are on stage, and the audience is other knights. Any error is discussed – bad temper, dishonesty, a foul blow …

All the things that seem to come so naturally when you are hot and tired.

It is meant to be difficult. A tournament is not to test your skill in arms. You are assumed to have skill. It is meant to test your *chivalry.* If you don't think that the social skill of chivalry has practical military application, you are not listening well. Of course skill at arms matters. On a dark night, when you propose to climb a pile of rubble and storm a breach full of Turks, men will follow you if they think that you are an expert killer who will bring them home alive. But they also follow you because they think the loot will be fairly divided – because they think that you will see and speak of noble actions, not steal the credit from some lesser man who does something remarkable, not leave a wounded comrade to die alone when it all goes to shit.

I can tell what kind of leader a man is by the way he treats his squire in the moments before he goes into the list. A little fear, a lot of anticipation – a man can be full of himself just then.

An excellent time for abruptness, or temper.

But *gentilesse* in these conditions is a sure sign of military grace.

Sir Jason won with the axe. He was splendid, and almost too humble, and when he knelt to be kissed by the princess, he later told me that he felt like a fake. This from a man whose *backhand* axe blow can knock me from my feet.

The fifth day was the sword on foot. So many men were injured that they had eliminated the spear; swords were relatively safe. It is too bad – the spear is one of my favourite weapons.

In the very first fight, Nerio and Fiore took themselves out of the deed. I have no idea what was said, but both men grew heated and, exactly like the first day, they both struck, very hard, and the point of each longsword went through the other's visor. Each punctured the other's cheek; both bear the scars to this day, and neither man could eat whole food for a week.

Let me make this simple. They were the two best swords. Percy was good, and Bernard was almost as good as me. But it was mine to lose.

I lost. I lost to Bernard; he surprised me, a sudden, brilliant direction change that he must have practised very hard, and down I went. In his last bout – with, of all people, Marc-Antonio – he was careful. Marc-Antonio landed some stout blows, and for a moment I thought my once pudgy squire was about to win a deed of arms, but Bernard knew his own limits and his fatigue. He finished with the same brilliant throw that had put me down, and was crowned with laurel and allowed to kiss the princess.

I have fought many times in many deeds, from Poland to Spain, England to Morocco. I fought once for the Khan of Tartary. But that was one of the hardest lists and best fights I've known. So much skill, so many gentlemen who'd practised so hard, with such good masters. Before a year was out, I'd be facing men in front of a crowd of twenty thousand in Milan, but the lists at Mytilene had the better men.

I had some magnificent bruises. And a fairly ugly gore: someone's spike or sword point had slipped between the plates of my brigandine and gone a finger's width into my side.

My wife had always liked a little blood. Which is good, as I always seemed to have a little to share.

I like to think that's the night we made our son.

Prince Francesco loaded his galleys immediately after the tournament. In fact, while the tournament was still ongoing, I saw four dismantled trebuchets being laid under the benches of a galley, which startled me, as I had thought the prince had said we would not be supporting the Green Count against the Turks. However, while I had been sitting with the prince watching Bernard beat Marc-Antonio, he'd turned, as if we'd been in conversation all along, and nodded. 'Tell your other master you may serve with him,' he said. I sent Marc-Antonio to the Green Count as soon as his hangover wore off.

Emile was making her own plans to travel to Venice. Our spring of pleasure was at an end; her steward was begging her to return to her estates – my estates – in Savoy, and she could not live forever on Lesvos, pleasant as it was. She and Sister Marie and Sister Catherine, who looked after our children, were planning to take her household knights, covered in honour from the lists, and go home. It was Emile's contention that she could return to Venice in time to meet me in the autumn; I doubted it.

So, four days after the tournament, as my borrowed Lesbian galley was packed with food, and a horse transport with horses, on the beach under our castle, she was also packing, for a different trip. We chatted; we had decided, as if by mutual consent, to maintain the pleasure of our amorousness in Mytilene and not to be so serious. We did well, right through the evening. It rained, and we made love in our bed.

And afterwards, my wife burst into tears.

'We will never come back here,' she wept. 'I am a fool. I should give away my lands and live here forever. What do I want with estates in Savoy? I can have you and my children every day and an orange tree that also bears lemons.'

Once, I might have murmured some platitude about feudal duty.

But I felt it too. We were at the end of something beautiful.

The next day, on the beach, she bit my lip like a wanton, and rolled her shoulders and smiled as if I might throw her down on the beach. I kissed Maggie and my own daughter, although they were both mine by then. Edouard was staying with Prince Francesco as a page. Emile was sailing on a Genoese ship, with Fiore's leman, to whom he was unofficially affianced, and her father, who owned the ship and disapproved heavily, but who was also somewhat star-struck by Emile and her obvious riches and nobility.

My wife patted Fiore's hand and promised to make it all right before the ship touched at Ancona.

Then she kissed me again, and went up the plank from the beach to the galley's stern, and walked serenely to the rail, whence she waved twice before the ship turned out into the straits and bore up for Lemnos.

She never returned. The orange-lemon tree is still there; I've been to it a few times, and I always cry. I have known other women, and loved them well, but my heart is in that tree, and it is the garden of my love until I die.

I was sombre when I reached Constantinople, although the city moved me all over again. However decayed she might be, she is the most magnificent city in the world, and when you have visited Hagia Sophia, you have seen a glimpse of Heaven.

I rode a borrowed horse to Blachernae to have an audience with the Emperor. That is, Prince Francesco had an audience, and I stood, bowed, scraped, and was perfectly silent, although there was something particularly gratifying about hearing my titles rolled off in Greek. And when they were done discussing the Ottomanids and the Karamanids and the Genoese and the Venetians and the Order and the Pope as if they were all equally dangerous rival tribes, the Emperor indicated me with the smallest motion of his hand and I approached the throne.

The Emperor, descendant of the Emperors of the Roman Empire, lord of the mightiest city in the circle of the world, had on no jewellery whatsoever. I knew why; he had pawned every jewel he owned to pay the Green Count so that the count could pay Nerio.

'Syr Guglielmo,' he said, making my knighthood sound like part of my name, 'I have no treasure to heap on you, but I have a title to give, because titles are cheap. This one is not cheap; it is, I think, exactly as you deserve, you and your three friends.'

That's when I was made '*Spatharios*'. Many Englishmen have been *Spatharios*. Indeed, once we formed the whole of the Emperor's guard. But it meant 'sword bearer' and entitled the owner to go armed, even in the presence of the Emperor.

'The title is as old as Rome,' the Emperor said in his soft voice. 'Wear it well.'

Then the Emperor looked at the prince. 'And now, we must speak of the Church,' he said.

I bowed deeply, kissed the toe of his shoe, and withdrew.

Gatelussi shrugged. Bad form, with an emperor. 'If we must,' he said. 'Majesty,' he added.

I can see that Froissart and Chaucer know what I'm talking about, but the rest of you do not. So, sometime in the eleventh century, about the time that William the Bastard was taking an army to conquer England, the Patriarch of Constantinople and the Patriarch of Rome, whom we call the Pope, had a quarrel. Rather, the quarrel was already quite old, and it became something not unlike open theological war. Until then, Christians in Greece and Christians in England had the same faith, and they took communion together and exchanged books in monasteries all across Europe, from Antioch to Dublin ...

When the schism happened, it was almost unnoticed in the west. The west had long accepted the Patriarch of Rome's commands; the east never had. Or so I'll guess. But suffice it to say that three centuries of crusade and war and betrayal and savagery had deepened the divide between the Greek Orthodox rite and the Western rite to the point that each considered the other heretics, and indeed, I knew churchmen who believed that schismatic Greeks were worse, morally, than infidel Saracens.

Let me add as a further aside that mere fighting men like me tended to take a more pragmatic view. I have heard Mass in many a Greek church, and if I go to Hell for that, I'll probably laugh, after all the other sins I've committed. Or perhaps not; it will, after all, be Hell.

Regardless, by the middle of our century there was rapprochement. It had become clear to the west that the fall of Constantinople would be terrible for all of Christendom. It had become clear to the leaders of the renewed Byzantine Empire – that's another story, how the Greeks took back their own from the Latins, but let's leave that for now, shall we? So, as I say, it had become clear to the Emperors that without some sort of alliance in the west, they were doomed. Alliance with the very Latins who had just attempted to conquer them, or alliance with Islam. And, to be fair, they tried both.

In the end, Latin Christians appeared the more reliable allies, although I suspect it was a close contest. And when the Green Count rescued the Emperor – that is, when Fiore and Miles and Nerio and I rescued him – we cemented that alliance, all unknowingly. The Emperor vowed to renounce the Greek rite and adopt the Latin rite, in return for subsidies of money and direct military aid such as that offered by the count.

I'm boring you. But you *must* understand this to understand the war that was brewing – the war we have today.

Prince Francesco shook his head, as I say. He was literally biting his lower lip, trying *not* to speak his mind.

The Emperor sat back on his throne and put his elegant head in his ascetic saint's hand. 'Listen to me, Francesco,' he said, as if they were the butcher and the baker arguing politics. 'I *must* declare for the Latin rite. I need the money. I need the armed might of your Latin knights. I need the friendship of the Pope.' His eyes narrowed. 'And I need to curb my patriarch and his fanatics, or I will be carried away like a boy on a runaway stallion. Except this stallion is running east, not west.'

Gatelussi tugged at his beard, bowed, and said nothing.

'Ah, come, my old friend. Most reliable counsellor. Vicious pirate. Speak to me.'

'I will speak, with the Emperor's permission,' Gatelussi said carefully.

The Emperor nodded.

Prince Francesco glanced at me and shrugged, as if throwing caution to the winds.

'The Patriarch and the Church will never accept the Pope,' Gatelussi said. 'Your own Church … That runaway stallion …'

'My own Church, that refuses to accept any form of tax, that is the largest landowner, that pays for not a single soldier,' the Emperor said bitterly.

'Exactly,' Francesco said. 'If you do this, they will depose or murder you – and besides, no one in the city will accept your decision. No one. The horse is already running. I am not certain that your Church even recognises that you are essential.'

'You overstep your bounds, cousin,' the Emperor said.

Francesco Gatelussi shrugged. 'As long as you dangle the possibility of conversion, the Pope will help us,' he said. 'As soon as you actually convert, they'll see how little they've accomplished …'

'Enough,' the Emperor said. 'I do not serve my people to plot duplicity.'

'I do,' Gatelussi said cheerfully.

I was in shock. That is, I had heard a rumour that the Greek Emperor might return to the Latin faith; such a reunification would have incredible consequences, for everything from the profitability of Venetian trade to the possibility of the reconquest of Jerusalem. I could imagine who, in Europe, would be for or against the reunification. For example, I could see that Genoa would be against it, as they would lose trade and power. What I didn't understand was the authority of the Greek Church. I had three – or even four – feudal masters. I didn't find it odd to serve Gatelussi and the King of Cyprus and the King of England and the Count of Savoy, and mayhap another for pay. Why did the Greek Church buck like a young colt at the rule of the faraway Pope?

They went on for some time, about the patriarch, and his politics, and the customs to deprive the Genoese of some of their income. Genoa, of course, would be against reunification; their profits would dwindle away.

I lost interest, staring at the shabby-genteel wall hangings and the magnificent mosaics undimmed by time. I stood there and wondered if the reunification might really happen. I still wonder. It was the brainchild of Father Pierre – his dream, and the dream of my Hospitaller brethren. I certainly already had a side.

When we left, the chamberlain bowed deeply to me and proclaimed me *Spatharios*. I gave him a gold florin, which he accepted cheerfully. As I have said, I have some other titles from the Greeks; they are meaningless. But all four of us – Miles, Nerio, Fiore and I – were named *Spatharios*, and I use the title to this day. I like to imagine that I stand at the head of a long line of men who have guarded the throne, back to the days of the Caesars.

We mounted our horses and rode through the city, much of which was empty – a city built for perhaps a million people, with perhaps the population of London living in it. There were no slums; everyone had a good house. It had been sacked in 1204 and taken again in 1260 or thereabouts, and the plague was terrible there. And yet it was having an almost miraculous recovery. Almost everywhere you looked there were heavy wooden cranes and scaffolding – repairs, even new construction on old foundations.

Prince Francesco glanced at me. 'The Empire is not done yet,' he said.

'I didn't think that it was,' I said.

We walked our horses, avoiding a huge pile of building materials piled in the street. I suppose I asked him some questions about the schism, because he raised an eyebrow. 'You can read?' he asked.

'Yes, my lord.'

'Latin?' he asked.

Well, I had indeed spent almost a year working on my Latin with Sister Marie. She was gone with my wife, but I could, with care and time and a little help from Nerio or Fiore, make my way through Latin. I was, that spring, reading Saint Augustine.

'You might consider … becoming acquainted with the whole of the Filioque controversy,' he said. 'I am not making a jest. In the end, we will need to understand this foolish schism to overcome it.'

I just frowned. 'I am a man of arms,' I said.

'I used to tell myself that,' Gatelussi said. 'Now I find that I need to understand each issue myself. Even if I need to be lessoned by experts, I cannot be ignorant.' He raised an eyebrow at me. 'Life was easier when I killed everyone I didn't like.'

I laughed.

He smiled. 'At least the Emperor approved our little expedition,' he said.

'He did?' I asked.

'Not in so many words,' Prince Francesco said with a gentle smile. 'But he did. The Green Count is off Regium. He's trying to lay siege to a Turkish fortress with no engines. At least it's a Karamanid town; we will help him take it.'

The count had never been so glad to see me. I might have been touched, if I had liked him better. He and Richard Musard came down to the pebble beach together, and when I knelt, the count raised me.

He appeared even more moved when Prince Francesco landed.

'I brought a siege train,' Prince Francesco said. 'And between our shared liegeman, Sir William, and my own people, I bring you two hundred good men.'

Count Amadeus nodded. 'I'm pretending to lay siege to this place with six hundred men,' he said. 'The blessing of Saint Maurice on you for coming.'

Indeed, it was all very debonair, despite the small numbers.

The Turkish garrison sent out a champion every day, and one of the Savoyard knights would fight him. It appeared to me that the Savoyards enjoyed these single combats so much that they didn't mean to prosecute the siege at all. It was a little like a tournament, with the added element of danger, but only two men had been killed in fifteen days of siege – one Savoyard, one Turk.

The Savoyards didn't love us, though, and when Fiore offered to take a turn with one of the Turks, he was brusquely told that the sport was for gentlemen, not routiers, by a tall, handsome Savoyard knight, Georges Mayot.

I had thought that I'd become quite a mature man, that spring: husband, father, pious Christian.

Apparently not. I stepped between the sneering Savoyard and Fiore. 'I tell you what,' I said. 'I'll fight you right here, and save you the trip to the castle walls.'

The Savoyard frowned. 'It's time someone cut your comb, cock,' he said, and drew.

'Why do you get to fight instead of me?' Fiore said. 'He insulted me, not you.'

'Draw or I'll gut you,' spat the Savoyard.

'I challenged him,' I said to Fiore, trying to push past.

The Savoyard cut at Fiore, a man whose sword was in his sheath. I make no excuses for him.

Fiore had been wounded almost to death five months before, and he had just fought in a tournament.

His sword rose from the scabbard like a stone from a siege engine. He crossed his adversary's blade early in his cut, and his left hand slammed out, striking the man's elbow so hard there was a crack as his joint was overstressed, and he was turned and Fiore's sword was at his throat.

'Beg my pardon, you idiot,' Fiore said. 'And if that's the measure of your skill at arms, don't humiliate us in front of the Turks.'

The Savoyard eventually begged his pardon. Fiore handed him back his sword.

'It's amazing how quickly Fiore makes friends,' Nerio said.

Fiore glared at Nerio. 'What was I to do?' he asked.

'If you'd killed him instead of casually humiliating him, things would be better,' Nerio said. 'That's all right, my dear. It was beautiful to watch.'

Fiore glanced at me. I admit, I was laughing. 'I miss Stapleton,' Fiore said. 'When he was here, you didn't gang up on me.'

Nerio paused. 'I hate to be unfair,' he said. 'Shall we gang up on William instead?' He looked out to sea. 'I hate all this waste. No one cares whether we take this town or not. We are not reconquering the Holy Land. We're kicking an anthill.'

Well. As I said at the start, we were all losing our taste for crusade.

After five days, Prince Francesco lost his patience and set up the trebuchets. He didn't ask the count's permission; he was, after all, the Emperor's Admiral, among other offices.

The first stone struck one of the ageing, Roman-style square towers. The whole corner collapsed – tower, underpinnings, curtain wall and all.

The Turks surrendered. Immediately.

I *swear* the Savoyard knights muttered that we'd ruined everything.

The scenes that followed had the quality of a dark jest, the sort of jest that can lead to blood. We entered the town after taking the garrison. That is, my people took the garrison under guard and led them to the prince's fleet, where they were all fed. The Karamanid captain was called Mehmet Bey, and I sat with him, ate the food so that he knew it was not poisoned, and smiled often. I even trotted out my fifty words of Turkish.

John the Kipchak came and sat with us.

'He says, am I slave?' John rendered.

'I don't think so,' I said. 'I think you'll all be ransomed.'

The man ate better after that. I went and asked the prince. He was in the town, which proved, when I was inside it, to be very small and smelled terrible. Even fifteen days of siege is enough to pile up quite a lot of carrion and garbage.

I found him shouting at Count Amadeus, who was shouting back.

'Are you a fucking idiot?' Prince Francesco asked. 'How will the garrison be fed?'

'Your ships can feed them,' Amadeus roared, 'if you are not too much of a coward to—'

'Coward? Listen, you French turd, I was killing Saracens when your mother was a virgin!' Francesco was clearly very angry.

Swords were drawn. I pushed in until I was between the two men, and there I was, eye to eye with Richard Musard.

In my Anglo-Norman French, I said, 'My lord, he is merely angry,' to the count, who had his hand on his hilt. There was Georges Mayot again with his sword in his hand. I wondered if his elbow hurt. Two more Savoyard knights also drew.

Musard began speaking, low and fast, in his excellent French.

I went to work on the prince. 'Your Grace,' I said, 'you are both angry and tired.'

'This … this popinjay … thinks he can leave a garrison in fucking Asia.' He hissed the words in Italian.

'My lord, the Turkish captain wishes to know if he is to be ransomed.' I asked this in a level voice.

Gatelussi shook his head. 'No, by Christ. Let him and his people go, with their horses and arms. I want no quarrel with Ustman Bey. And this is his second son, eh?'

'I have no idea,' I admitted.

Gatelussi shook his head. 'These fools want to kill the garrison and loot the town,' he said. 'Fucking foreigners.'

I had never seen him like this. He was always the cold, calculating professional. I bowed, and caught his son's eye. His son slipped up and put an arm around his father. Musard had the count's helmet under his arm. He gave me a wink.

'How will we divide the town, then?' the count asked.

The prince's son shrugged. 'We took it. You did nothing but play military games. We had our tournament in Mytilene; it is nothing to us if you choose to have yours here, but *we* took the town.'

The count looked genuinely surprised. 'No, I took the town,' he said. 'I am in command. And all of you are serving me.'

The prince looked as if he might immolate like a phoenix, but his son was calm. 'I am sorry, my lord. A simple misunderstanding. My father is the Emperor's admiral. You are a visiting noble. You only make war here with the Emperor's permission. You have no *command*.'

'I have no command?' Amadeus asked. 'My soldiers have done all the fighting …'

I stepped in again. 'My lords, as I serve you both, may I speak? My prince, the count deserves better justice than this. His soldiers have taken Gallipoli and Mesembria; they have served the Emperor many times. And, my lord count, the prince is the Emperor's commander in these waters and, in addition, he has been with you in almost every campaign, and his siege engines were, in fact, the tool that took the town.'

Amadeus looked at me, considering. 'So?'

I glanced at Prince Francesco, afraid of his rage. 'The town is worthless,' I said. 'The walls are crumbling. Look for yourselves what a single blow from a modern weapon did. We have neither the stonemasons nor the time to restore the walls and tower, which means that the next Turkish brigand to stroll by will take it from us and butcher the garrison.'

The count looked out from the walls for a moment. And shrugged. 'Ah, *bien.* Very well, then,' he said. 'I concede your point. My blood was hot. Your Grace, will you accept the apology of a hot, tired man?'

Now, let me just say, here, that I was not really fond of the count. But suddenly, in one gracious apology, he made himself a better man in my eyes. A popinjay – sometimes a hypocrite, and a very difficult, very rich hypocrite. But an apology is a fine thing, and many of us might learn from this.

At any rate, Prince Francesco stood rigid a moment, afraid, perhaps, that he was being made game of. But then he unbent, literally; he smiled warmly and clasped the count's hand.

'My lord, you speak like a true knight. Listen: the only thing of value in this town is the lives of the garrison. They are probably worth a thousand ducats. Let us split their value.'

The Green Count nodded. 'Done. But, Your Grace, if this little town is worthless, why am I attacking it?'

Prince Francesco drank off a cup of watered wine his son put in his hand. I poured another from the same pitcher and put it in Richard's hand, and the count drank it off. Both men were red in the face, hot and tired, standing hatless in the full beat of the sun.

Musard was actually pleading with me, wordlessly. Prince Francesco was on the edge of another explosion, I could tell.

I stepped forward again. 'My lord, every one of these towns in Turkish hands is a nest of petty pirates – local fishermen prey on every passing ship, Genoese, Venetian, or Greek.' So Richard Percy had told me. Of course, he went on to say that the deadly galleys of the Gatelussi swept the coast clean every two or three seasons and made a profit at it. 'And, my lord, you *wished* for a further *empris*, to engage with the infidel enemy.'

Prince Francesco glanced at me, the way your wife does when you say something painfully obvious at the dinner table. His son Francesco winked, and I knew that I was on the right track.

Amadeus shrugged against the weight of his armour. 'I agree,' he said. 'I still do. I swore oaths at home to fight the Infidel – yet I am here and nothing is as I expected.'

We were standing in the sun in a tiny fortified town on the coast of Asia and the Count of Savoy had just begun to see the complexity of the world of Outremer. I tried not to look at the prince. Instead I said, 'My lord count, last year when the Bulgarians took the Emperor, some of us thought ... that the Turks, at least the Karamanids, must be in league with them.'

'Ah!' the count said. The idea pleased him. Of course it did; it put the seal of crusade on *all* his actions. 'Yes, Richard has mentioned this.'

Prince Francesco raised his hand, silencing me even as I began to speak. 'So, if nothing else, we show that we can still chastise them for interference.'

Amadeus smiled cynically. 'This I understand. This is exactly like the politics of home. Savoy and Montferrat and Milan.'

Prince Francesco nodded. 'My lord, I grew up on the politics of that coast – Genoa and Montferrat and Monaco. It is the same. *It is the same.* Religion is not the dividing line here any more than it is at home. The King of Bulgaria will make common cause with the Turks if it wins him a kingdom. Suleiman Bey will attack Uthman Bey with the help of the Emperor if it will get him a city in Europe.'

I met Richard's eye. I had a notion, then, of how much time he must have spent managing his master's chivalric urges and his politics.

But the Green Count nodded slowly, and a smile crossed his face. 'Well,' he said. 'Where to next?'

Two hours later, I released all of the Turk garrison, and I gave them their warhorses, although we kept their fine herd of remounts. I clasped hands with young Bayzid Mohamet after I had led him and all his men through the trebuchet battery, where six hundred Greco-Genoese oarsmen were sweating off their sins and dismantling a league of sandbagged entrenchments. Richard Musard and I had arranged it all, so that every man we had was out at once – all the knights, every man-at-arms and archer, all the oarsmen and marines …

'He says, if he'd known how big our army was, he'd have surrendered the first day,' John translated.

I just smiled.

'He says, his father thought there was a treaty … and that you Christians were … far away.' John was trying not to laugh.

'Tell him that the Emperor is thinking of new arrangements. And these towns were never part of the treaty between old Uthman and the old Emperor. And tell him that you think we're just the vanguard of a mighty army; the King of Cyprus and the Knights of Saint John are coming, too.' I nodded to the Turkish captain.

Remember, we had just sacked Alexandria.

Bayzid galloped off in a haze of dust, desperate to warn his father that the Christians were on the march.

A small Turkish pirate boat sailed close to the wind, lateen sail tight as an altar cloth at Easter, with two Gatelussi galleys giving chase right to the low stone harbour wall of Tepecik, when a hail of Turkish arrows from the harbour tower drove them back.

Just then, a storming party emerged out of the dust near the town with two scaling ladders and went for a tower, and the whole garrison turned out, dashing for the new threat.

The Turkish pirate galley kissed alongside the pier, her oars in, coasting. It stopped as two men leaped onto the pier and cast lines around the bollards, which groaned as they took the weight of the little ship.

And then we burst up from under the sweltering tarps amidships on the Turkish galley. Fiore was there, and Nerio, Prince Francesco's son, Francesco, Richard Percy and Richard Musard and a score or more others. We'd lain under that evil, hemp-oil-stinking tarp for an hour, wavering between boredom, terror and sea-sickness, and every man of us was delighted to be ashore.

None of us had ever been in the town before. We got on the pier, fetching swords dropped in the bilges and all the other accidents of war, while the oarsmen, mostly Genoese, picked up their crossbows and their javelins and came ashore behind us.

Perhaps two dozen Turks formed at the base of the pier to stop us. Arrows flew; Marc-Antonio got pinked.

One volley from the oarsmen shot them flat. The survivors ran before we got to them, and we followed, more like a wave than a compact mass; these things have to be done all at once or not at all. We went up through the town, climbing steep streets only wide enough for three men. Twice we had sharp fights, but we had numbers and armour, and as soon as any group of Turks made a stand, the oarsmen would sweep through alleys and side streets and take them in the flank or rear. We got to the land gate, a small gatehouse of stone, and the Turkish captain threw down his spear and surrendered. It was, in its own way, a perfect attack, and as we'd lost no men and our blood was relatively cool, the taking of the town was not followed by one of those scenes from Hell so common in Europe – nor like Alexandria. We didn't outrage the women, who were, after all, Christian Greeks.

The banner of Savoy went up over the gate, and it proved that some of the Green Count's routiers had successfully taken a tower. It turned out that the count had led them in person. We'd refused to allow him on such a daring and risky *empris* as the attack on the harbour, and so he'd run off and stormed a tower with one rickety ladder.

I was the first man from the storming party to reach them.

'Messire Guillaume,' the count said. He embraced me as if we were old friends. 'I saw the galley come in. Brilliantly done, sir.'

Well, well. I found his praise sweet. It is hard to dislike a man who treats you as an authority. That night I was much in demand, and I served the count and the prince at table, along with Richard Musard.

'You see?' Musard said. 'He really is a great man.'

'He is growing on me,' I confessed. The way in which he had conceded my point – that is, the prince's point – about command showed a degree of restraint and graciousness that I hadn't seen from him in Bulgaria.

Just after the taking of Tepecik, a fly landed in the ointment of my pleasure in the campaign, but the blessing, or the fly, was not unmixed.

The fly took the shape of Florimont de Lesparre. He arrived with a dozen Gascon men-at-arms on a small galliot flying Cypriote colours, and he presented himself as a captain in the service of the King of Cyprus.

We were lying in the harbour of Tepecik, about twenty miles from Constantinople. The little town had a fine harbour and made a good place to refit. So we lay there, protected from weather and Turks, arranging to ransom our captives and loading water. I happened, by good or bad fortune, to be aboard the count's great galley when de Lesparre came in, and I knew the bastard as soon as he stepped aboard. He was politely received by the count's people, but the count, who was sitting aft under an awning, drinking wine from his silver cup, sensed my feelings and put a hand on my shoulder.

'Messire Guillaume?' he said courteously.

'That man is no friend of mine, my lord,' I said. I was hesitant even to say it. The Green Count had not always proven himself my friend, and he'd certainly listened to Turenne's slanders, which de Lesparre had also repeated, if you remember.

Amadeus met my eye. Truly, until that moment I had seldom been so close to him. He had my sleeve, and he was endeavouring to be private with me, even at the rail of a ship. 'You are my man,' he said.

At the time, I suppose I thought little enough of it.

As soon as de Lesparre saw me, he pushed Richard Musard – never a good way to seek favour, I find – and came to the foot of the count's command deck. 'My lord count,' he called out, 'it does you no honour to be seen with a man as ill-reputed as that fellow Gold.'

The count ignored him, raised an eyebrow to me, and then walked across the deck to his seat, almost a throne, under the awning. By doing so, he disappeared from de Lesparre's view, as the command deck was a span higher than the rowing frames.

'Come and stand by me, messire,' the count called to me.

I stood very straight and prepared to face whatever the count might say. I walked across the deck, just as de Lesparre came up the three steps to the command deck.

One of the Savoyard men-at-arms – Georges Mayot, whom I have mentioned – met him at the head of the steps and barred his path. What I remember best was my sense of wonder as I realised that the count was planning to humiliate de Lesparre. For me.

'You have been a good soldier for me,' he said. He reached out his hand, and a servant put a gold chain in his hand. 'I summoned you on whim – as much to annoy my cousin as for any other reason. Yet you came with a full complement of good men. I can't pay you right now, but, by God, messire, I repay; service with service and honour with honour.' He held out a gold chain, and on it was a badge emblazoned with his own arms in red enamel. 'This is not some trinket – it is my own. I ask you to wear it in my name; as my vassal who has served with good loyalty, in Outremer, when men I thought better of went home or never attended their lord.'

De Lesparre was watching.

I took the chain, and the count helped me slip it over my shoulder, like the baldric of a hunting horn. I have pawned it a dozen times, but I still own it; indeed, if you allow me, I will produce it later.

De Lesparre made a sound, almost like the growl of a cat.

'Please allow the Sieur de Lesparre forward now,' the count said.

De Lesparre came forward and knelt. Musard followed him up the steps, looked at the chain, and grinned. Then he brushed past me.

So I stood while de Lesparre knelt. Richard oversaw the service of a plate of sweetmeats; after the count had taken some, I was offered the same dish. Listen: this may sound like no great thing to you, especially those of you who have never served the great, but this was, in public, the most intimate way of showing approval. I ate everything I was offered and drank off a cup of wine.

A bowl of rose water was brought. We dipped our hands; a page stood while we wiped our hands on a beautiful Italian towel. All this took perhaps five minutes.

'Ah, Messire de Lesparre,' the count said. 'You may rise.'

'You offend my master, the King of Cyprus, by behaving so,' spat de Lesparre.

The count shrugged. 'Perhaps,' he said. 'But as you came into my presence without my permission—'

'By God, as the ambassador—'

'And like many Gascons, you seem not to know your place—'

'By God, my lord—'

The count leaned forward. 'I have not given you permission to speak. Go away. Come back with manners. You are dismissed.' The count beckoned to a servant for another plate of sweetmeats.

'You are under the spell of this miscreant, and that Moor!' spat de Lesparre.

Mayot stepped between them. 'Out,' he said.

De Lesparre was a very tall man, and he drew himself up. At the steps, he whirled on Mayot. 'I make a bad enemy,' he hissed, loud enough for us all to hear.

Mayot, who was one of the Savoyards I didn't particularly like, shrugged with unfeigned indifference. 'Save it for someone weak,' he said. An excellent answer, and one that raised him in my estimation.

We took one more Karamanid pirates' nest on the coast of Marmara, and Amadeus proposed that we go farther south and clear the European shore of the Dardanelles, the peninsula south and east of Gallipoli. As this would restore the Emperor absolute sovereignty from Bulgaria to the sea, the prince agreed immediately, and we spent the next two weeks making war with speed and efficiency. We had twenty galleys – a level of maritime superiority that no Turkish bey could match – and the Ottomanid army watched helplessly from across the straits as we swept along the coast, taking each town, freeing the Greek population, taking or slaying the Turkish garrisons and burning the Turkish shipping we found, unless Prince Francesco wanted to keep it for himself.

It might have been a wonderful time, except for de Lesparre and his mates; their hatred of me was palpable, and they lost no opportunity to pick on my people, to insult us, to dog us. Achille, Nerio's squire, killed one of them in a dagger fight, and it was all I could do to keep him from being tried for murder before the count.

Yet the count had turned from an enemy, or at least a very cautious ally, to a true lord. Was it rivalry with Prince Francesco? Or was it Richard, whispering in his ear? Whichever way, he was constant; he protected me from the worst of de Lesparre's slanders and made the Gascon feel so unwelcome that he sailed for Rhodes a week before the rest of us. He left us swearing that we were all cowards and miscreants and that he would go support his true lord, Peter of Cyprus, which led the count to ask why he'd come with us in the first place. Some high words were spoken.

We took the last town, Enea Cossea, which the count's doctor, Guy Albin, who could read Greek, assured me had been the ancient Thracian town of Maitos. I thought de Lesparre gone forever; if I had known better …

Bah. After we took Maitos, we sent word to the Emperor, and even Prince Francesco rejoiced in private, because the little campaign had done much to secure the heartland of the old Byzantine Empire.

The count was going home; he had a fever among his knights and archers – not as deadly as plague, but bad enough for all love. By the grace of God, we did not have it. Indeed, the last night, when the count commanded me to attend him, Prince Francesco and his son were against my going, but I insisted. I went across to his ship and was warmly received. Guy Albin, as I have mentioned, the count's English physician, was attending him, and explaining that he thought that the fever was from bad drinking water.

Richard was just serving the count his meat, so I went to the ship's rail with Master Albin, and we shared the blessing of the day in English, and told each other a tale or two. It was a pleasure to talk to a man who had been born in Kent and knew the same London I knew as a boy. Sir Richard Percy was English, like enough, but the north country from which the Percys hail is as different from London as France is; northerners are a different race, near enough. And his English could be very hard for me to untangle, whereas Albin's was good, simple London English. He liked a good story and he listened well; he also liked a dirty story, and I must tell you his tale of the miller and his pretty wife. But he was not a coarse man, and he liked to talk about God, and we often discussed the Gospels.

'Are you still shopping for a physician for your company?' he asked, after we'd discussed the healing of the man born blind.

'I am,' I admitted. 'I wish I could hire you away from the count.'

Albin shook his head. 'But my assistant is my nephew, Peter.'

'You were going to send him for my wife,' I said, perhaps a little sharply.

Guy shrugged. 'Sir William, crossing the sea in winter …'

I clapped his back. 'Never mind me,' I said. 'She was well attended, and by women, which she preferred.' I glanced at the count. 'Your nephew is available?'

'He wants to stay in Outremer,' Guy said. 'I admit that there is much to be learned here. There are texts available in every Greek monastery that are either forgotten at home or never known – Aristotle, Galen, Plato, Hippocrates …' He shrugged. 'But he's a decent leech, for man or horse. He has studied at Oxford, although he does not have a master's rank.'

'A master's rank?' I asked, because physicians aren't educated at Oxford. Padua has such things, and Bologna. Oxford is for priests.

'He started to be a theologian,' Albin said.

I had a hard time picturing a theologian in a company of lances.

On the other hand, a trained doctor was a precious thing. 'Of course I'll take him,' I said.

'I'll have him pack,' Albin said with a bow.

Shortly after, I was attending the count.

'You won't sail with us, Messire Guillaume?' he asked.

'My lord, I have agreed to help my friend Nerio reclaim his patrimony in Achaea,' I said.

'But you will come to Venice in the autumn?' he asked. 'And your lady wife is already there?'

'Yes, my lord,' I said.

The count nodded. 'This ended better than I had imagined,' he said. 'Do you think, Sieur Guillaume, that we have achieved something to build the confidence of the Greeks in us?' He rubbed his beard. 'I have leaned hard on my cousin, the Emperor, to convert. Now I wonder.' He shook his head. 'None of this is as I imagined.'

I took an offered stool and sipped a cup of wine. 'My lord, the Greeks I know best served Pierre Thomas and now the west well,' I admitted. 'But they say your expedition has put heart into the city and the Emperor.'

Amadeus smiled, then. 'We began badly, Guillaume. Come to me in Venice, or wherever I am in Italy. There is always a place for you at my table.'

I rose and bowed. I didn't tell him that I had a prior pledge with the notorious routier and enemy of the Savoyards, John Hawkwood. But I was coming to like him better.

And it was a wrench to say farewell to Richard.

We sailed from Maitos in June. I think that I have mentioned how fast war uses up material, but when we sailed from Maitos, the Gatelussi galleys were scarcely seaworthy, with leaky hulls, sails worn thin, and enough broken oars that only about two thirds of the rowers could pull at a time. We'd lost one of the big ship's boats in the surf near Gallipoli, stove in on a rock, and all of us were tired. Our horses were in poor condition, and armour needed work; most of the archers and crossbowmen were out of shafts, or near enough. Five sieges in a month and we were out of everything except victory.

The prince took us to one of his holdings, the island of Lemnos, one of the richest of all the Aegean islands. He had a palace there, with an armoury and a shipyard, and in two days of near feverish work, our galleys were refitted and our horses fattened and our armour polished.

When all the work was well along, Prince Francesco brought me aboard his own galley, with his son and Nerio and Fiore and a handful of others, including Albin's young nephew, and Giannis Calophernes, and we ran out for what I thought was a pleasure cruise. It was a beautiful day, and I knew from Marc-Antonio that they had loaded food; no one had much armour, and the only weapons we had were our swords. We sailed for two hours, as the coast of Asia grew before us, and we landed in Asia just south of the opening of the Dardanelles.

Soon after we landed, a cluster of Greeks came down to the beach. One of the prince's men hailed them, and they brought us a dozen sturdy ponies, which we rode up the beach and over towards the headland.

After a ride of no more than a few minutes, we came to a low precinct wall, the sort you see all over Greece; this one was distinct, and built with some red-grey local stone. Prince Francesco strode into the precinct and stopped by the remnants of an altar. I'm no scholar, but by then I had seen enough sway-backed Greek altars to know one when I saw one.

'Do you know where you are?' Prince Francesco asked.

'Asia?' I asked.

I glanced at Nerio, who had the best education among my friends. He wrinkled his nose. 'Somewhere with cats,' he said.

Fiore shook his head.

Peter Albin looked around as if he was in Heaven. 'It is an ancient temple,' he said.

'Yes,' the prince replied, 'but whose temple?'

His son stood there, insufferably smug as all young men can be.

Nerio guessed, 'Apollo.'

Fiore crossed his arms. 'Zeus?' he muttered. 'Jupiter?'

Prince Francesco shook his head.

'Mars?' Peter Albin asked. 'Ares?'

Young Francesco laughed. 'Even the Greeks seldom built temples to the god of war,' he said. 'Who worships war?

Prince Francesco looked at us all triumphantly. 'This was the tomb and hero-place of Achilles,' he said. 'Achilles and his lover-mentor, Patrokles.'

'Jesu!' Peter Albin said. 'We're at Troy, then!'

We all smiled at his enthusiasm, which was infectious. Prince Francesco nodded. 'You landed on the beach where the Greeks beached their ships, and the local Greek bishop told me that this was the tomb of Achilles, and that mound there, just at the edge of sight, is the remains of Priam's Troy.'

The dozen of us spent the day climbing over the ruins. I still have a gold bead that I plucked from the ground. Marc-Antonio found a bronze arrow point, and then everyone wanted one and the hunt was on. I thought Peter Albin might knock Marc-Antonio down for his find, but he found a small bronze lion instead, something that we all agreed might have been a shield decoration.

We ate our food on the wind-blown beach, and handed our ponies back to the locals, who ate with us, and proved to be the local bishop and some of his people. He spoke, in Greek, about the siege of Troy. He recited a piece of poetry, and Sir Giannis translated.

'This is Homer,' Giannis said at one point.

I had heard of Homer – indeed, Dante mentions him, and Abelard – but I had never read any. It was odd and beautiful to sit on a beach with my friends as the sun set over Europe, hearing the words of a bard from over a thousand years before our Saviour walked in the Holy Land – an event that seems ancient enough to most of us – and yet the story that Giannis translated was as modern, as good, as the very best chivalric chansons of my youth.

When the bishop left us, we made a fire and camped on the open beach, drinking wine.

'What did you think of my bishop?' the prince asked.

'I liked him very much,' Giannis said. 'He was an honourable man. And very educated.'

Peter Albin's eyes were wide and shining like a boy's, for all that he was my age or a year older. 'I want to find a copy of Homer,' he said.

Sir Giannis nodded as the fire crackled. 'I could perhaps find you a copy. Or you could pay to have one made in Constantinople.'

'What did you think of the story?' Prince Francesco asked me.

I think that I shrugged. 'The arrogant, greedy commander? The great warrior who does not feel he is receiving his due from his lord?'

'I think that you just claimed to be Achilles,' Nerio said.

'Nay. If I said the story was the same ... then Agamemnon would suddenly turn warm and give Achilles everything he wants.' I was laughing, but Prince Francesco was not.

Albin leaned forward. 'Your Grace,' he asked, 'do you think that it *really happened*?'

The prince stared into the fire awhile. 'Something happened,' he said carefully. 'And it happened here. Isn't that … odd? Here we sit; we've just fought a campaign of our own in these waters, and Troy looks on us as we sail by, and Achilles, perhaps, judges us. Is it all a fable?' He shrugged. 'I grew up on tales of Troy, but in many of them, Hector and Achilles are cowards and other men like Diomedes are the great ones. But Homer …' He shrugged again.

Sir Giannis smiled with a little tinge of bitterness. 'To us, Homer is like a fifth gospel,' he said.

Perhaps it was because we had been to Jerusalem, where the past seems to walk with the present, but the bishop and his tale made it all real to me, and I slept fitfully. Mayhap it was just cold sand and the wrong cloak, but I woke often, and I felt as if a host of shades marched past me in the night, and charged with a shout. It was an unseelie night, as if the Trojans still walked their ruined walls, and the Greeks licked their wounds on the windswept beach. I would not willingly return to Troy. But from that night on, we all spoke more of the distant past; we were in Outremer, where Jesus and Alexander and Achilles and the Apostles and the legions all walked or marched, and the past was palpable there.

The next morning we rose early, ate lobster for breakfast grilled on a fire right there on that beach, and sailed back to Lemnos.

'I wanted you to see Troy,' Prince Francesco said, with his arm around my shoulder. 'I know that you and Nerio will leave me soon. I will miss you. And I am not Agamemnon.'

It is good to be loved.

Two days later, our little fleet of eight galleys beached at the port of Trajanopolis, or so Peter Albin called it. The Greeks called the port Ainos, but many of them called the whole area Trajanopolis, or Traianopolis. Albin told us all about the Emperor Trajan, who sounded like a good knight and a good king – a veritable paladin, in fact. There are baths there as ancient as any I have ever seen, and we all worked the stiffness out of our wounds there while the prince collected taxes.

The next day, I rode with Marc-Antonio and young Albin all the way to the fortress of Avantas, which towers over the plain, and Peristera, 'the pigeon'. A few years before, a handful of archers had held the place against a Turkish army, and when I heard the tale, I thought it exaggerated. But when I met one of the archers, a tall, thin man with the pointed beard and thin face of a Greek icon, and when I climbed the track to the castle and saw the plain at my feet, I believed. The archer, with a mad grin, pulled a Turkish horn bow to his ear and loosed a shaft into the fields four hundred feet below us. The shaft seemed to travel forever, and I had a notion, then, of how a handful of men might dominate an army.

Sir Giannis told me that the man was now almost a beggar, having lost his farm to the Turks.

'Sign him up,' I said to John the Kipchak.

John watched the man shoot, and gave him a gold florin. His name was Christos Lascaris, and you'll hear more of him.

It was a beautiful area, very different from the Greek islands like Lesvos and Chios, which resembled the Holy Land. Thrace was more like the north of England; even in high summer, the leaves were green and the valleys rich and well-watered. It was fine, fertile land, with good farms, and it was here that the Kantakouzenoi had made their main effort to rebuild the Byzantine heartland; there were new fortresses and towers and churches all through the hills. And if the politics of Outremer bores you, you've come to the wrong table; the Kantakouzenoi were the scions of a powerful family like the Percys or the Mortimers in England. John Kantakouzenos had declared himself Emperor and had, despite everything, been a good one. His sons were very powerful within the empire, and ruled most of the Morea that was not ruled by Frankish princes like the Florentine Acciaioli and the Venetians at Negroponte and the old French families in the north. But despite their efforts, or because of their recent civil war, the Turks were everywhere past Avantas; we couldn't even find a bishop.

All of this made for some interesting diplomacy as we rode abroad with an Imperial banner. Thrace was virtually a Turkish despotate, and with the Turks holding Adrianopolis (which they called Edirne) and having recently taken Didymoteichon, you might have expected the Byzantines to unite in the face of the threat to Constantinople, which was less than a hundred miles away on the Via Egnatia.

Or maybe not. If you know the Scottish Borders, you know that not everyone unites in the face of an external threat, eh? Both sides tended to call on the Turks to win disputes. Prince Francesco and his son explained all of this to me as we rode through the brilliant sunshine from the new fortress at Avantas, away from the sea and up into the hills. We had perhaps two hundred men-at-arms and forty archers. The priest at Avantas declined to provide guides, because Prince Francesco was representing the Emperor and they claimed on some legal quibble that he had no legal right to go armed in Thrace.

Sir Giannis was sombre. 'This is bad,' he admitted. 'Very bad. It should not be like this.'

The garrison at Avantas was mostly imperial troops from Constantinople, and as such had been delighted to see us, but as we went north, we were met with grim hostility from Greek peasants.

A day later and we'd intercepted a Kantakouzenoi raiding party. We were in no-man's-land, between the Turks and the Greeks, and our Kipchaks had caught the Kantakouzenoi on the move and followed them to their camp on the heights.

Prince Francesco chose his son as an ambassador and sent me to watch over him – and Nerio to watch me, I suppose. We rode over stony fields to the base of a long ridge, and then we were blindfolded and taken to their camp. There were two Kantakouzenoi, both older men: Matthew Asen, who I later learned had been Emperor briefly, and Thomas. They were plainly dressed in good wool, and they had recently worn maille over it; their hair was matted from helmets. Their horses were as good as mine and both had bow cases on their belts like our Kipchaks carried: open at the top, flat, wider at the bottom, for holding arrows flight-side *down* like the Mongols. They wore curving swords like Kipchaks and their saddles were like Kipchak saddles. Thomas was as blond as my sister and Matthew was dark and heavy. Matthew wore a high hat, like but unlike a Mongol hat.

Young Francesco dismounted immediately when we were close. Marc-Antonio took all our horses, and we walked forward. The Kantakouzenoi remained on horseback. There were at least a dozen soldiers present: the stradiote or *pronoi* cavalry that is too light to stand a charge of knights, but otherwise almost the equal of Mongols. I looked them over carefully; they looked hard, and completely capable. Above us on the slopes stood the stones of an ancient wall, and it was lined with men, and the sounds of horses – maybe four hundred. Enough to give us trouble.

Young Francesco addressed Matthew, the Despote, from one knee. He was respectful and cautious, and it was an excellent performance. The young man had, in the last year, shown himself a capable soldier, and now he showed himself capable of thought and lordship. I applauded inwardly.

'... And Sir Guglielmo D'Oro, *Spatharios*, and Sir Renerio Acciaioli, also *Spatharios* of the Emperor John V ...' I heard go by in the Italo-Greek of the conversation.

'Lord of Morain,' I muttered. 'Baron of Methymna.'

'Duke of Nothing,' muttered Nerio. 'Count of Empty.'

The Despote of Thrace raised a hand and blessed us. 'I am always pleased to meet messengers from our cousin the Emperor,' he said. He didn't smile, but neither did he frown. 'Your father is with you, I think?' he asked.

'Your Grace, my father sent me merely to ascertain who might have come down the pass, and would be delighted to receive you,' Young Francesco said.

The despote nodded, looking down the pass at the olive groves below, among which the rest of our men were waiting. 'I do not believe that my guards would be happy with me if I rode into your little army,' he said. 'Let us have our discussion right here.' He glanced at me. 'I have heard of you. You did my people a favour. In Athens.'

I smiled. 'Perhaps, my lord,' I said. 'We co-operated long enough to defeat the Turks.'

The Despote Matthew managed a very Greek smile: thin lips, half his face. 'When the Emperor's galleys and mine combine with the Knights of St. John and the Venetians,' he said, 'Hell might not actually have been said to have frozen over, but I imagine it was quite cold for a bit.'

Giannis, who was translating, let loose a bark of laughter before he revived enough to pass on the despote's comment.

We all laughed, and the atmosphere lightened. The sun was dropping and it was becoming cooler. We had brought wine with us, and Marc-Antonio and Achille bustled about, sharing it. I watched a pair of the *stradiotes*; their hands came away from their sword hilts, and when one bent to take wine, his eyes met mine and he twitched an eyebrow, as if to say, 'Eh, we're just posturing, leave me alone.'

Francesco's Greek was very good, and he bore the brunt of the conversation. The first part was very stilted, or so it seemed from the translation. After one joke, the despote retreated behind an ancient court ceremonial practice, and the prince's son was forced to roll the despote's titles off his tongue fluently at each address, so that the simplest sentence had to be preceded with a full list of honorifics. After a quarter of an hour, the despote raised his hand and encouraged Francesco to address him as 'your grace', which shortened the proceedings enormously.

In short, the despote denied that anyone had authorised our coming, despite an ornate purple vellum document bearing the Imperial seal, and said that we would make trouble with the Ottomanids at Didymoteichon.

In vain, the young prince explained our invitation and the reasons for our numbers.

We were at a deadlock. No one had spoken of using force; the tone of discussion was urbane, even courtly, and we might have been at Blachernae. Down in the valley below us, pavilions had sprouted like mushrooms on a damp night in the woods, and firelight winked among the olive trees.

'I repeat, you have too many men,' the despote said. 'Send them back.'

Nerio glanced at me. I nodded, and the two of us walked forward cautiously, so as not to startle any of the armed men. Let me note here that we were in full harness and had our war swords on; we were not without resource. But the formality of the proceedings was a thin veneer. We were in the desert, and in the desert there are lions, and there are hyenas.

I bowed. 'I am Sir Guglielmo,' I said. I waited while Giannis translated. 'This is my company of lances – almost half of the men you see. We have our own invitation to visit Didymoteichon, and we travel with Prince Francesco from friendship. My men have served the Emperor all year, in Bulgaria and elsewhere.'

Nerio bowed: a full *reverentia*. 'Your Grace,' he said. 'I am now one of the Frankish lords of Achaea. When we have visited the Turk,

I plan to take Sir Guglielmo's company across Thrace, by the Hot Gates, and into Boeotia to retake what is rightfully mine. We will not, strictly speaking, be neighbours, but I promise you that I can be a good friend.'

The despote, five feet above us on his horse, looked annoyed. He spoke briefly in Greek, to Francesco.

'He asks the young prince why his father claimed that they were all his men? And he wonders aloud if his hand is so light that a Frankish lord plans to cross his whole realm in arms without asking his leave?'

Nerio raised an eyebrow. 'Tell him that I *am* asking his leave. Now. I have been busy heretofore, fighting the Infidel, as is the duty of all Christian knights.'

Giannis, who knew Nerio all too well, raised a dark eyebrow. But he translated fluently, and the despote's face cleared.

'Indeed,' the despote said, 'if all Frankish knights did as much, instead of murdering Greeks and harming our Church, we might be better friends.' He spoke on, and grew heated.

Giannis flushed. 'He says, as to your being a Prince of Achaea, no man of his blood would ever admit that a single finger's breadth of Boeotia belongs to any Frank. It is a typical piece of Frankish arrogance to tell a prince of the Imperial House of your aspirations to steal his land and call this theft "friendship". Nonetheless, he recognises your famous name and he says that your father was an honourable enemy. And that you should be very cautious, as you are perhaps the most valuable ransom in all Outremer, Sir Renerio. Bandits and thieves might form armies to take you.'

Nerio grinned as if this was a compliment. 'I always take care, Your Grace,' he said. 'As to thieving, I beg leave to remind Your Grace that if the Franks took Achaea from the Greeks, so they, in turn, took Thrace from the Thracians and Dalmatia from the Slavs. It is the way of the world, despote, and I can make no apologies.'

The despote frowned as Nerio's sally was translated. 'There is a difference between the will of God and the will of Satan,' he spat.

Nerio opened his mouth, his nasty, sneering smile ready for combat. I loved him like a brother, but I knew where this was going.

'No, Nerio,' I said. 'Or I will call you Fiore.'

Nerio looked at me.

'Your Grace, I am a simple soldier, and I wish to fight in a deed of arms at Didymoteichon. I have a contract to support my lord Renerio.' I smiled and tried to look like a bluff, simple soldier, if such exists. 'It would be financially ruinous for us to turn back to the ships that brought us, which may already have sailed. May we pay a tax – perhaps to support the cost of watching us? I well know the dangers of soldiers loose in rich lands.'

Princes love money, because they never have any. It must have cost Despote Matthew a pretty penny to keep a little army in the field, and for me, it seemed that he couldn't want a fight any more than Prince Francesco. Especially as there were Turks everywhere.

But he shook his head. 'Out of the question,' he said. 'I will not appear weak. I will allow ten men to go to Didymoteichon, and then only under guard and without arms.'

Again I spoke, because Francesco was angry and Nerio was indignant. I glanced at both, and in one look knew they would follow my lead.

'Well, we'll see if you feel differently in the morning,' I said.

The despote raised an eyebrow. 'I have not dismissed you,' he said gently. His men put their hands on their swords.

I bowed yet again. 'Your Grace, I am from England, where we prize plain speaking – even from kings.'

'Yes,' the despote said. 'I know of Englishmen.'

I nodded. 'So, my lord, I don't really need your permission to ride to Didymoteichon.' I smiled. I tried to sound like Hawkwood. 'You do not own this ground. You ride armed for fear of the Turks. I can do as I please. And you'd have to come down off your mountain to stop me.'

The despote turned first white, and then red. His skin was tanned brown, and yet the colour change was plain as plain.

'Oh, I see,' muttered Nerio. '*This* is diplomacy.'

I shrugged. 'I am perfectly willing to be reasonable,' I said. 'This is strictly business, Your Grace. If you delay me, you cost me money, and I will take action.'

'I can put three thousand men in the field to stop you,' the despote said.

'Perhaps you could,' I agreed. Giannis was a little white around the nostrils as he translated. 'But wouldn't it be easier to accept a small tribute from us and let us pass?'

Francesco bowed. 'Your Grace, it is nearly night, and we are all hungry and tired. Sir Guglielmo speaks, perhaps, too strongly, but surely none of us want such a solution …'

'Go,' said the despote.

We rode back down the pass, and Nerio turned to me in the ruddy light of the Greek sunset and his smile was not a happy one. 'Remind me not to use you as a negotiator,' he said.

'This from you?' I asked. 'You were about to come it the high and mighty Florentine—'

'You told him you'd burn his farmers out!' Nerio said. 'I would merely have *hinted* that I *could* burn out his farmers. Your way is crass.'

'All Englishmen are barbarians,' I agreed.

'He really has no choice but to let us pass,' the prince said. 'I have his father's seal.' He shrugged. 'William, if there are four hundred of them, they can't have all their horses up on that mountain top. I would esteem it a favour if you would ask John to find their horses. It is not an order; you and Nerio have to live with the consequence of what we do here.'

I called for John, and he came, and when I laid out my request, he shook his head.

'Let me do this my way,' he said. He explained, and Nerio laughed.

'Mongol diplomacy,' he said. Prince Francesco laughed too.

In the morning, we met with the despote in the same place. This time, the prince accompanied us, and six of the prince's men-at-arms, and John. We also brought water and a small shelter and some stools. The despote dismounted too and joined us in the shade.

The conversation repeated the pattern of the evening before: etiquette followed by conversation. But the despote didn't show any sign of changing his mind.

'If I let you through this pass,' he said finally, 'you are in the heartland of Thrace, and if the good Sir Guglielmo threatens this valley and its farms, imagine what damage he can do to my heartland?'

He smiled at me. He was a very intelligent man, and he had considered what I had said. Interesting.

'My lord,' the prince said, 'we will not do you any harm.'

'How can I trust you?' he cried, throwing his hands in the air.

The prince glanced at John.

John stepped forward and tossed a twist of indigo blue yarn on the table, and then bowed.

The despote looked at the yarn.

One of his guards looked at me. He muttered something in Greek, gave me a hard stare, and many hands flew for hilts. Prince Francesco leaned back and ran his fingers thoughtfully through his beard. 'We didn't steal your horse herd last night,' he said.

'What makes you think you could have done such a thing?' the despote asked.

John the Kipchak laughed his deep laugh. 'Lord, every one of your horses has this yarn tied to its tail.'

'*Christe Pantokrator*,' the despote's brother swore. He shot to his feet and went out into the beating sun.

He came back in, shaking his head. He threw a bit of yarn on our little folding table in front of the despote.

'It is true,' he swore, in Greek.

The Prince of Lesvos smiled very much the way Hawkwood might have.

And, as it proved, we paid two hundred gold florins as a 'tax' to pass, and the despote 'allowed' us to ride on. A dozen of his *stradiotes* shadowed us for the next two days.

Prince Francesco gave John a belt covered in gold and silver fittings which he still wears.

And we came, at last, to Didymoteichon.

Didymoteichon means 'the city with two walls', and it sits on a steep hill at the juncture of two good rivers. The Kantakouzenoi built, or rebuilt, the fortified town to be their capital, and then they refortified it, making it even stronger, about the time of Crécy. But in the year of Poitiers, the Ottomanids took it without too much trouble, despite all the walls and the garrison. The Turks took Adrianopolis, too – the third city of the empire – the only city in Thrace that had resisted the Slavs, the Bulgars, the Huns, and all the other waves of barbarians that had washed through Greece except Thessaloniki, of which more soon. The Turks called Adrianopolis 'Edirne' and made it their capital city in Europe; it still is, to this day. But Didymoteichon was their second city, and it has something wondrous about it. Perhaps it is the height of the acropolis, or citadel, perhaps the strength of the walls, the profusion of Christian churches even now, the beauty of the red-tiled roofs, or the richness of the farms in the well-watered valley. I took one look at it and wondered why we'd wasted our siege engines on Mesembria and Gallipoli when we could have restored this gem to Christendom. It was the second place that I ever saw that I wanted for my own – as good, in its way, as Methymna on Lesvos.

I never got the chance to see inside the walls, though, for the Turks – although they met us at the border and escorted us with a degree of friendliness that contrasted sharply with Matthew Asen and his little army – did not trust us in the town. They did let us know, in gifts and body language, that they wanted Prince Francesco's peace treaty: the message of our raids had been heard, loud and clear. Or so it seemed.

I had most of two days riding alongside Holgai, the Turkish captain of our escort, and during that time I understood why John had found our operations in Bulgaria so funny. Here were the Turks – perhaps a hundred leagues from Mesembria, or a little more. They were gradually conquering the Greeks; *they* were the infidel enemy. Yet we'd spent our treasure and blood fighting the Bulgarians.

Even the Turks were puzzled.

On the other hand, the Turks were all too well aware that their army was locked in Asia, and that we'd just reconquered the whole of the Gallipoli peninsula. It was a little unnerving just how much Holgai knew: he knew where I had fought, who I had taken captive; he knew all about our quarrel with the despote.

The local pasha, yet another Suleiman, suddenly changed his course and made a great pretence of rage, demanding that we return all of the towns we'd taken on the peninsula before he would meet with Prince Francesco. And the prince told us that, for once, he was negotiating from a position of strength, with a fleet offshore and the potential for an endless torrent of green-clad crusaders crawling around the shores of Europe and Asia.

We left our escort at the gates of Didymoteichon, and they assumed we'd camp in the ditch, where they'd prepared a market for us to buy food.

Instead, we moved almost a mile to a hill that Sir Giannis knew and made camp, and Fiore and Nerio decided between them that we would fortify it. The hill had some water from a spring and its own ring of old walls. We raised our tents and pavilions, and on the first night, we set to work digging. Even the boys wove baskets to be filled with dirt, and every shovelful was studded with bits of the past: old pottery, and bits of iron, and one of the archers found a gold ring with a seal, a woman's head with snakes.

We lost a night's sleep, but, by morning, we were virtually impregnable, with trees and plashed greenery and new earthworks all along the lower slopes.

That afternoon, a hundred Turks in silk kaftans and glittering maille swept by the base of the hill with many a shout, and after they left, a haughty Turkish officer arrived and ordered the works dismantled and all our weapons handed over to him.

Marc-Antonio, who had some Turkish and a good deal of Greek by then, and Sir Giannis, whose Greek and Turkish were our best, came to me because Prince Francesco was asleep. I was awake, and fully armed, and I mounted Gabriel, my new warhorse, and rode down the ridge to our 'gate', where Rob Stone and Ewan the Scot had taken position in tall oak trees behind screens of woven leaves. Both men were quite expert at this, and had cunningly pruned the branches to give them clear shots out into the plain before our gate. Hector Lachlan had the watch; Pierre Lapot was leaning against the base of a tree, sharpening an axe.

I felt as safe as a man could, riding out to parley with the Infidel. I took Marc-Antonio and Sir Giannis, caught Ewan's eye to make sure he was covering me, and rode slowly down the last of the hill to where the Turkish captain sat on a beautiful golden horse with dark legs and mane.

'He asks if you have come to surrender,' Sir Giannis said. 'I can't tell whether he is mocking us or merely trying to be funny.'

'Tell him I will be happy to accept his surrender,' I said. I was armed cap-à-pie, and my new helmet had a catch to hold the visor open, an innovation I valued extremely highly. I had my best plumes in my helmet and my brigandine's velvet was clean and brushed. Gabriel glowed with magnificent vitality.

I smiled.

The Turk grinned. He said something to his lieutenant, who was every bit as red-headed as I am myself. They both laughed; it didn't appear bad-tempered.

The Turk leaned forward, crossing his hands on his saddle-bow, relaxed, both hands showing, no weapon. He spoke at length, periodically meeting my eye.

'He says no, he doesn't feel like surrendering. He tells me his name. He is Everenos Bey, commander of one hundred knights and a horsetail lord. He tells me of his father and the piety of his mother.'

'Ask him, where is Sir Holgai, who led our escort?' I asked.

The Turkish captain nodded, as if well pleased that I had asked. 'Holgai has gone to Edirne with a message,' he responded through Sir Giannis, although I understood him well enough.

'In that case, tell him I am William Gold, also a horsetail lord and commander of one hundred; tell him that I am a volunteer with the Order and my sister is a famous religious woman.' I smiled. I'd never had cause to mention my sister to a Turk before. But I mimicked his ease; I handed my gauntlets to Marc-Antonio and then my helmet, and when I pulled off my helmet, unhinging the cheekpieces of the newfangled thing, both Turkish officers smiled.

I pointed at my red hair and at Everenos's lieutenant's head.

'He says, you two could be brothers.' Sir Giannis was laughing.

And indeed, we might have had the same mother and father; he was a big man, like me, and his beard was as red as mine. He was younger, perhaps twenty or twenty-one.

'Tell him that I do not know my brother's name,' I said.

Sir Giannis must have said more than that. But the Turk nodded and barked something which I caught.

'He is called Timurtash, an Eastern name. He must mean Eastern Turk.'

I bowed.

Timurtash inclined his head.

Everenos spoke at length.

Sir Giannis shrugged. 'He says, now that he meets you and you are so cheerful, he is sorry to bear bad news, but his lord the Sultan and the governor of the city require all the Christians to disarm and cease to fortify their camp.'

I had on my hip de Charny's dagger. I thought about it for a moment, but spontaneity is everything in chivalry. I untied the lace which held it to my belt, and held it out to the Turk.

'Tell him to think of this as a symbol of all our weapons, which we offer in bond. Tell him this weapon belonged to a great warrior, a saint among warriors, and I would never dishonour it. Tell him that I will demand it back, but offer it in surety for our good behaviour.' I held the dagger out, glinting in the sun.

De Charny had fought the Turks at Smyrna.

Giannis's voice went on. I could understand a few words, but not many. I could see the surprise, and some indecisiveness, on the Turk's face. He looked at the dagger; then, as spontaneous, perhaps, as my gesture, he took it. He drew it, looked at it, and sheathed it.

'He says, this is not what his master ordered, but he will see if it will do.'

He saluted with a wink, and he and his Judas-headed lieutenant rode off in a swirl of dust.

I turned Gabriel and walked back up the path to our 'gate', where Nerio lounged in full armour against a tree, his charger, saddled, in his hand. Fiore was against another tree, cleaning his nails with a rondel dagger, a terrible habit he'd picked up from Nerio.

'You may yet make a diplomat,' Nerio said. 'What did you tell them?'

I explained, and Fiore frowned. 'But ...' he said. 'De Charny's dagger?'

I admit that in the aftermath I felt foolish, like a man who spends too much money on a horse in the market, or who tells a girl he loves her ... and isn't sure he means it.

But, on balance, they seemed people of honour, these Turks, and I wanted to ... challenge them, I suppose. Challenge them to behave honourably. And I'll comment, from years with the Turks and some of the other easterners – Kurds, and Syrians, and of course Mongols – that they all share this trait. They are, most of them, deeply honourable men, but you must summon them to it – like a challenge, or calling out. Perhaps this is because they do not see Franks as men of honour; I have seen Franks behave very badly in Outremer. But, for whatever reason, my experience is that when you offer honour, you receive it, in England and in Outremer.

Be that as it may, we spent a day resting. The farmers, who were for the most part Greeks, were afraid of us, but we convinced a few to open a little market at the foot of our hill and Prince Francesco insisted that we pay in hard silver, and our little market grew rapidly.

The next day was Sunday, and Father Angelo said Mass for the Latins, and then he read the Bible during the afternoon, and I remember sitting in a pleasant near-doze, listening to the story of Mary and Martha. Father Angelo read the story in Latin, which I understood well enough, but then he repeated the tale in French, and then Italian. The archers who spoke French, like Ewan, then passed the tale on to those with no French, like Tom Hicks, a big lout from Southwark who was the worst archer of the lot, but a hard worker. Likewise, John the Kipchak, who knew some Italian and some French, passed the story to his mates in his own tongue; Sir Giannis retold the story to our Greek camp boys, so that we were the Company of Babel, which is what the prince christened us.

Sir Richard Percy shook his head when the story was over. 'If I died, and Sir Jesus came too late to save me, my sister would ha' gi' him a piece of her mind, I ha' no doubt.'

That got a laugh.

'But it was all for the greater glory of God,' Father Angelo said.

Sir Richard shrugged. 'Sir Lazarus still died, Pater, and that can't ha' been any kind o' pleasance, eh? And then, he was dead full three days.'

'Four,' said Rob Stone, shaking his head. 'He stank!'

'An' all I can wonder is, what did Lazarus think? Were he in Hell, Pater? Waiting to be raised? The fear … he must ha' suffered. Like a man dying on a battlefield, knowing no man is coming to help him and the ravens is on the way.'

'But Jesus came for him …' Father Angelo said.

'Why does God need all that glory from us?' Rob Stone asked. 'I mean, he's God.'

Instead of flaring up like many priests I've known, Father Angelo laughed. 'I thought this was a company of lances? And it turns out I've fallen into a nest of theologians.'

Master Stone stood his ground. 'You priests tell us these things. Well, I think on 'em.'

'As do I,' Sir Richard said.

I nodded. 'As do I,' I confessed.

Father Angelo fingered his beard. 'I have only been with you a winter, but I see this is not as I imagined. Is it, perhaps, that men in imminent fear of death spend more time thinking of religious things?'

'No,' Fiore said. I hadn't even realised he was present. 'No, Pater. It is this company.'

'It's the Holy Sepulchre,' said l'Angars.

I met his eye. 'Yes,' I said.

'Ahh,' Father Angelo said.

Pierre Lapot scratched his scraggly beard, which he was now growing in double points, like an image of Satan. 'We're going to be the most holy company of mercenaries in Italy,' he said.

The next day, my new friend Everenos Bey rode to our barrier and announced that we would be received by the representatives of the Sultan, who was in Edirne, and that there would be games 'in the Frankish manner' on the following three days. A train arrived from Edirne that afternoon; it passed unmolested under our little mountain, and I think it was offered to us as a provocation, in case we meant harm. Or perhaps not, as it turned out. The Sultan's officer, Angrium Pasha, came with that train, as well as a treasury to pay the troops at Didymoteichon, and a long line of merchants.

That evening, two men in long gowns appeared at the barrier of our camp with servants. They asked for me by name, and I rode down the hill to meet with them.

They proved to be Jews of Edirne: a teacher, which they call a rabbi, and a merchant, his brother.

The merchant was obsequious, in a way that always irritates me; when a man is servile in a way that suggests that he doesn't actually believe you are superior in any way. It was a little like being mocked.

'Oh, great lord,' he said. Both men dismounted, with their hats in their hands. The merchant, Isaac, bowed deeply. The teacher, Benjamin, bowed a good deal less.

'How may I help you?' I asked. I'd been taken away from my food, and I was not in the best of moods.

'Oh, great and gracious lord,' Isaac said. 'My brother and I, worthless Jews as we are, beg you to allow us to travel with you to Corinth.' Isaac's eyes burned with intelligence, and a certain relish, that I, a gentile, would be amazed that he knew we were going to Corinth.

My desire to punish him for his arrogant servility warred with the Order's unstated support for the Hebrews. The Order protected Jews whenever it could; I had met a few knights with rabid hatred of the race, but never a knight in any position of authority, and officers like Sabraham were far more common. Sabraham had rubbed off on me.

Also, I had learned a little from Father Pierre Thomas, despite my sins.

'I'm sure that we can find you a place,' I said politely. 'How many in your party?'

'Fourteen,' Isaac said. 'I know it is many, but we will have our own food. It is very important to us, and we will pay you.'

I suppose the Devil was in me; a devil of humility, because Nerio and I needed money that summer. He had a piece of paper worth thirty thousand ducats in Venice or Genoa, but in the wilds of Thrace, it was worthless, and my lances were living out of my purse.

But I smiled in a manner I hope was gracious and said, 'Such is my love for the mother of Jesus, who was a Jew, that I will charge you nothing, and only ask your blessing when we part.'

Isaac went as red as a beet.

Benjamin laughed silently, rocking slightly back and forth.

'He thinks he's so smart,' Benjamin said – his first words. In clear Norman French, as you might hear in London.

'You're English!' I said.

Isaac shook his head. 'We're Jews,' he all but spat. He spoke at length to his brother, in a language I didn't know – Hebrew, or some other cant.

Benjamin finally shrugged. 'You are an English knight of the Order?' he asked.

I shook my head. 'No, sir. I am a volunteer with the Order from time to time. Not, in fact, at the moment.' I showed my devotional ring. 'But I consider myself a member of the Order at all times.'

'Do you know Fra Peter Mortimer?' the rabbi asked.

'Yes,' I said. 'My master in the faith and in knighthood.'

The rabbi threw his hands in the air with a certain theatricality. He spoke at his brother – at him, in that he was clearly attacking him in some way.

'Isaac would trust you better if you took our money,' the rabbi said. 'I will choose to trust you for Fra Peter's sake, and because I have heard of you and of your sister.' Both men remounted.

I bowed, eager to get back to my food and not really giving them much thought. I had, at that point, known few Jews, and they were in many ways more alien to me than Turks or Syrians or Greeks. But Isaac, who seemed mercurial, paused and looked back at me. 'The Sultan's pasha, Angrium, is deeply troubled by your presence here.'

Well, I knew they'd come out from Didymoteichon. It wasn't much of a guess that they'd come all the way from Edirne. 'You know the pasha?' I asked.

He turned his mule – a big and very practical animal that told me much about the man. 'I do,' he said guardedly.

The rabbi fingered his beard. I suspected that this was the actual purpose of their visit. We were in unofficial negotiations.

'Why is he troubled?' I asked. I play a bluff innocent very well. I didn't need anyone to tell me why the Turkish warlord of a newly conquered province, who'd just been cut off from his bases in Asia by our fleet, would be terrified to find a small but elite army on his doorstep, coming to 'negotiate'.

He met my eye. I suppose I smiled, and my smile gave away my lack of innocence.

His eyebrows moved a tiny fraction.

'The pasha feels, perhaps, that the Prince of Lesvos is threatening him.' Isaac leaned forward in his saddle, very much at ease.

I considered for a moment riding off and leaving them. I didn't have any brief to negotiate anything for the prince or the Emperor. On the other hand, I had a good idea what was at stake.

'Nothing could be further from the case,' I said. 'We were invited to participate in a tournament.'

Isaac smiled. 'Yes,' he said. 'There is some consternation inside the city about this tournament. Do you have among you some *converso* or renegade Turk or perhaps a Vardariot, a Christian Turk? The pasha's captain thought that it was … men of his own kind. A contest of archery and horsemanship. I am …' Isaac looked at me. 'I am trying to prevent a difficult incident, my lord. I know jousting. These men have no jousting in the manner of the French or Italians, and if men are killed, if they are humiliated, nothing will be served.'

He looked back at his brother, who had clearly prompted this approach in confidence, and I didn't need to speak Hebrew to read that Isaac was telling his brother, 'There, now, I've done it, and it's all your fault.'

I nodded. 'I have a dozen men-at-arms,' I said, 'who would like nothing better than to compete in the Turkish manner.'

Isaac brightened. 'They are Christian Turks?' he asked.

'No,' I said.

'Ah.' Isaac was trying to be diplomatic. And he still didn't think much of my intelligence. 'The Turks are very, very good at horsemanship and archery, Sir William. They will easily defeat any—'

'Perhaps we can have some archery on the flat as well as on horseback,' I said. 'And perhaps some fighting with a rebated spear on foot instead of jousting.' I laughed. 'We are negotiating the lists, yes? Why not just have the prince send a herald to the pasha?'

Isaac nodded. 'I think that now …' He managed a smile. 'I think that based on this conversation, perhaps that could be arranged.'

As it proved, after dinner, and after a long conversation with the prince and his son, we sent Marc-Antonio and Sir Giannis to the town in the morning. They returned unharmed and full of mutton and rice, and in the evening, Everenos Bey and Timurtash returned, and this time we had them into our little camp, and they sat cross-legged with us at a campfire as we hammered out the terms of the 'deed of arms' between two very different races.

Timurtash, in an aside to me, said in bad Italian that he knew we had some Turks among us, because he'd seen them. I called for Marc-Antonio and Father Angelo, and they translated so we could be sure what Timurtash was saying.

He was warning us that Christianised Turks might be badly treated.

I clasped his hand and told him we would not field any.

In the end, the prince agreed to the following events: mounted archery, twelve targets; archery on foot, two targets at set distances of fifty and one hundred paces; and a mêlée in armour with cane lances or javelins. In addition, we agreed that a Turk would run a course with sabre against another Turk, and a few of our knights would run jousting courses against each other, so that each race could demonstrate its own favourite sport.

The plain at our feet sprouted silk pavilions like the first bloom of flowers in spring, and courses and lists appeared as if by magic; our little market became the market of the whole tourney, and suddenly there were carpets for sale, beautiful ring maille, damascene daggers and other wonders from the east and west too.

We paraded our teams for each other. We were allowed six 'knights' for the encounter with cane javelins, and so, after much discussion and some politics, we had Sir Richard and Fiore, Nerio and me, young Francesco and l'Angars. For the mounted archery, of course, our entire team was Kipchaks. Both Sir Georgios Dimitri Angelus and Sir Giannis declined, despite being excellent, accurate archers, and none of their *stradiotes* felt up to the skill of the Kipchaks. And for archery on foot, we had three Englishmen, a Scot, a Turk and a Greek – the man from Peristera, Lascaris.

We rode out to the tourney grounds together, with the prince and his retinue in their best, us in our armour, and the archers as fancy as they could manage, with turbans in their helmets and all the dust beaten out of their jacks and brigandines. We made a brave show, but we were nothing like as magnificent as our adversaries, who seemed to be made of gold and silk, and whose horses were just as good as ours.

It was a fine day, without a hint of rain, and a huge pavilion was set up with half the walls rolled up so that the prince and the pasha could sit with their officers, emirs and beys all about them, drink iced sherbet and watch the games. The only thing missing was a crowd. In England or Italy, a thousand men and women would have watched the games, but here in Turkish Outremer the peasants were all Greeks, and despite our retinues having a dozen Greeks, the peasants seemed as uninterested in us as they were in the Turks. So the lists seemed curiously empty; there were no stands, and no women at all.

I knew that the prince and the pasha were negotiating the whole time we were fighting and shooting; I understood how the world worked, or so I thought. Five years' peace, without any further conquests: that's what Prince Francesco wanted. And after the Green Count's campaigns, and the sack of Alexandria, and the sudden appearance of galleys of the Order in these waters ... it didn't seem like too much to ask.

Our hosts clearly esteemed the archery on foot the least, for they put the event first – or possibly did so to humour us. Either way, our team dominated the butts from the first arrow to the last, and with a wave from the prince, Ewan and Rob, after the shooting was done, walked back to *two hundred* paces and dropped a dozen shafts into the target, to the delight of the Turks. Their pleasure was unfeigned; I think they planned for us to win this unimportant event and they were gracious about it.

They were less gracious when they discovered that our horse-archery team was all Kipchak. The Kipchaks are rivals of the Turks twice over – in the east, on the high steppe, and in the south, where Kipchak slaves become Mamluk ghulams.

There were ten targets, five on either side of the course, all small wicker shields covered in silk, brightly coloured. The course was about three hundred paces long.

One of the Turks played first. He had a green silk kaftan and long moustaches and a fine gilded-steel helmet under his turban. He touched his horse, so far from me that all I could see was the sun dazzle of the peak of his helm, and a roar announced that he had hit the first target. He shot, left and right, his body flexing, his horse changing lead; he always loosed with his horse on the same foot. He managed nine of the first ten; John told me later that he dropped an arrow at mid-course.

The eleventh and twelfth targets were different. Boys stood with two more little shields, and I was afraid that they were going to hold them and be shot. But the boys were safe; it was the rest of us who were in peril. They threw the shields like discs, rolling them along the ground. Both shields rolled almost side by side, very fast, one on the rider's right and one on his left. He leaned out and loosed into the one on his bridle side and hit it, and then turned, but by sheer bad luck his shield had hit a stone and skipped away, unhit.

Undaunted, the Turk followed it, his arrow point leading the shield, and he loosed, but by then the little shield had rolled in among the horses of our mêlée team, and his arrow skipped along the ground and pinked l'Angars' charger.

The Turks laughed.

L'Angars was off his horse in a moment, seeing to the beast, but the head had not penetrated his Arab's coat, and she merely had a long red slash on her withers. I could see l'Angars go red.

Timurtash was trotting up to me. He was laughing, and I didn't think he was laughing at us. I looked at the prince, and met his eye from fifty paces away and I swear he was willing me to good humour.

I turned to Nerio. 'Make light of this,' I said.

Nerio raised an eyebrow. But he concurred, and he turned his horse.

'Not the poor man's best archery,' he said, and Ewan the Scot laughed.

'Mayhap he's just used to shootin' Franks,' Rob Stone said.

Gospel Mark guffawed and Timurtash made a face.

I translated the comment about shooting at Franks and Timurtash laughed.

'Ten of twelve is not a good score,' he conceded.

I rode over to l'Angars. 'Don't show any temper,' I said quietly.

'But that was on purpose!' l'Angars said.

'We're on stage,' I said. 'The prince needs us to be calm and unruffled.'

L'Angars made an effort and cleared his face. 'I need another horse,' he said.

'Have mine,' Sir Giannis said. He had a beautiful small mare who could ride rings around most of our horses, even the good Turkish ponies we'd picked up in the Holy Land, and yet she carried l'Angars without much effort. The Gascon clasped the Greek's hand.

I went back to Fiore and Timurtash. They were speaking, through Marc-Antonio, about swords, and Fiore had the Turk's sabre in his hand.

The first of the Kipchaks came into the lists. I saw his horse give a little bob, as if bowing to the guests, and then the steppe pony was hurtling down the lists like an ugly equine thunderbolt.

The targets were alternated, some on the ground, some hung on spears, so that the archer had to go high and then low, high and then low, while also alternating sides.

'Is there a rule that a man must ride at a gallop?' I asked.

Timurtash laughed. 'No rule I know,' he said. 'Just ... men.'

The Kipchak, Kerchus, the shortest of all the steppe men, moved like a centaur, a dancing centaur, and his bow arm rose and sank in a rhythm, and he loosed regardless of what foot his pony was on, rolling arrows off his bow hand which clutched all twelve – no mean feat, let me tell you. Just try holding a dozen fully fletched arrows in your hand. As it proved, Kerchus was cheating; he was loosing flight arrows, almost like darts, because weight and penetration were not important, but as the boys started their shields rolling across the bumpy ground, he was ten for ten, and he chose the harder shield first, shooting down into the right-hand shield almost as soon as it left the boy's hand.

It was my impression that the boys, who were Turks, threw the little shields harder for the Kipchaks; certainly, the left-hand shield hit a hummock and leaped in the air the height of a man, sailing along like a thrown plate, at head height, and right in front of the Turkish military contingent in all their armour and finery.

Kerchus rolled his last arrow off his fingers and onto his string without a glance, his whole body seeming to follow the flight of the little buckler the way a dog watches a hare, and as he drew his bow he was leaning out, out ... Everenos Bey was less than three horse-lengths behind the flying shield ...

Kerchus loosed. John told me later that he barely drew, only pulling the horn bow to half its power; the lightweight arrow flew true, and transfixed the buckler in the air, and it fell to earth, and the steppe pony's pounding hooves were, for a moment, the only sound on the course, and then Timurtash gave a scream and all the Turks took it up, and Kerchus pumped his bow hand in the air.

I give the Turks high points on chivalry. Kerchus had run a magnificent course and they applauded him as one of their own, and Everenos Bey crossed the lists to toss the little buckler to the Kipchak with a grin.

The next Turk scored eleven out of twelve. He missed the same target that the first Turk had missed – the middlemost high shield, where the first man dropped an arrow. He hit both of the rolling shields to loud applause, which I was happy to see our own archers joined.

Ten or eleven was the rule; no one shot nine, and one Turk scored all twelve, to the wild approval of his mates. I lost count of the score, but Ewan the Scot and Gospel Mark did not; they were holding a book on betting and they had acquired both Frank and Turkish customers.

The last rider was John.

Gospel Mark looked up at me; he was on foot, and I on horseback, mostly because *all* the Turks were on horseback.

'Ten to draw, eleven to win,' Mark said.

John didn't do anything the way the other riders had done.

He entered the lists at a gallop, having started far off. I didn't see it, but he shot the sixth target, the high right-hand shield, *first*, as soon as his horse had a foot over the line. He had five arrows in his fist and six in his little belt quiver. He loosed the next five in order, very fast – so fast that he was, for the most part, loosing *ahead* and not to the right and left. At the sixth target, because he'd already hit it, he reached down and took all six arrows from his quiver and put them in his bow hand and drew, even as he passed the seventh target, which he hit over his shoulder. Then he made the next three shafts from the same position, shooting back over the rump of his horse, so fast that he was coming abreast of his tenth target as he drew, a simple low shield.

He passed it, and instead he shot the buckler that one of the boys was *holding*. The boy screamed and dropped the buckler, and the other boy threw his wildly and it sailed through the air, high as a bird, and John hit it for eleven.

But John was not done. He'd passed the tenth target, and now he turned with his last arrow and loosed it into the air, as if having a second shot at the flying buckler. His arrow flew, up and up, into the sky. I lost it in the blue and the sun, even as John skidded his pony to a stop in front of the grand pavilion, leaped from his mount and made a deep reverence to the pasha.

Behind him, his last shaft fell to earth. It struck the tenth buckler with a little *pop* as it penetrated the straw.

Timurtash gave a long throaty scream, and pounded his fist on his own shield.

'Now, Allah be praised, but that man is a magnificent archer. Is he yours?' he asked.

'Yes,' I said with forgivable smug pride.

'I will buy him from you,' Timurtash said through Marc-Antonio.

I smiled. 'No,' I said.

'Come, let us wager,' Timurtash said. 'I lead my team, you lead yours. The winner has him. I will put my horse – nay, all the horses of all the men on my team against him.'

Marc-Antonio paled.

Nerio laughed. 'Done,' he said.

Timurtash rode away, laughing.

I looked at my friend. 'Damn you,' I said.

'Don't be so pious,' Nerio snapped. 'We can beat them.'

'I wasn't planning on beating them,' I said. 'We're here to support diplomacy, remember?'

Nerio winced. I rarely saw him concede an error, but he glanced at Fiore, because he hated Fiore's criticisms. Luckily the Udine knight was still talking swords with Sir Everenos.

'A draw?' he asked.

'How do you manage a draw in a mêlée?' I snapped.

'All right, I'm an arse.' Nerio pursed his lips. 'I'll buy him back.' He smiled. 'Or he can just desert in a few days.'

John received the plaudits of the prince and the pasha, and I waved to him and he trotted over.

'That was brilliant,' I said, or something equally useless to the occasion.

He grinned. 'Even for me, that last shot was from God,' he said.

'Nerio just wagered you against all the horses of the other team,' I said.

John turned his head. He winked. 'Good bet,' he said. 'I get horse?'

Nerio gave me his annoying 'told you so' look.

'Yes,' I said.

'Good,' he said.

'You really think win?' John asked. 'Turks pretend happy, but mad as fuck.'

I need to note that John's Italian was almost as good as mine by then, until he was excited. For all his Mongol calm, he was very, very elated just then.

Nerio shrugged. 'They're Turks,' he said. 'They chose the game. It's not jousting or something we understand. I say we play to win.'

L'Angars agreed. 'They shot my horse!' he said.

Fiore raised both eyebrows. 'I do not understand,' he said. 'Why play any game, unless to win?'

Young Francesco pulled his new beard. 'You gentlemen are all so confident, but I promise you these Turks will be very difficult to unhorse with nothing but cane javelins.'

Fiore gave a little shrug. 'No,' he said.

Sir Richard looked at me. 'I'll follow your lead, but it sticks in my craw to just give the infidels the day, even for the prince. Let them win if they can.'

Well. There is chivalry in competition, and mayhap for a moment I was trying *too* hard to be a diplomat.

'Win it is,' I said.

*

The mêlée began with a lot of javelin throwing. It was almost formal; a Turk opened the dance by riding out, alone, from the neat line of his companions and racing along our rank. He tossed his javelin and hit Francesco's shield, and the crowd roared. Then Francesco rode out and tagged Sir Everenos, and so on. Francesco had played this game before, and so had Sir Richard, and they had talked us through it. I rode my 'course' and my little dart stuck in Timurtash's shield and he waved at me, and a moment later his came at me, and I had to raise my shield to catch it.

In the second encounter, the shafts were thrown with more intent. We'd been told that it was a major foul to strike a horse, just as it was among us, but it was not a foul to wound a man, and Everenos powered his second spear at me with a full overhand throw that sank the javelin's head four fingers deep in my jousting shield. I'm happy to say I raised my shield in a flash when he threw; Fiore was firm on the use of the shield, as with all else in *armizare.* I reached out and broke the shaft, as I'd seen Timurtash do, and Francesco too, while waving my approval, and when it was my turn, my Arab mare raced effortlessly along the sand, more excited than tired, and I threw at a Turk I didn't know. My hand started low, like a boy skipping stones, and then I rifled the javelin overarm from very close, and the man missed my throw and took the shaft in his thigh.

The Kipchaks screamed a war cry.

The Turks were silent.

There were no more cheers, and no more congratulations of fine shots, and Timurtash aimed for Nerio's unguarded face. His throw was like lightning, but Nerio had practised with Fiore; his shield caught enough to turn the blow. Francesco got his nose broken by a tumbling shaft meant for Fiore.

And then the second round was over, and we lined up at opposite ends of the course. The man I'd wounded was still in the saddle.

Francesco was struggling to breathe, so Percy turned to us.

'Last team to have a man in the saddle wins,' he said. 'Just like home,' he added.

No weapons at all, except fists and horses. And every man was wearing both sword and dagger. I had to wonder who would be the first to draw.

The Turks formed very close, exactly like the Germans in Poland had done, and they charged us. I spent a moment in admiration of their tactic.

Fiore glanced at me. 'Scatter,' he said, and we did.

There followed a fine show of trick riding. The Turks went up and down the lists, wheeling their six-man team as if they were one man – far better horsemanship than the Emperor's team had shown.

We just rode around them. It had a comic element; as Timurtash himself said later, it was as if they were the Franks and we were the Turks.

'I'm the bait,' Fiore said after two passes. 'Collapse their flanks.'

Now, you might have expected that I would be in command of this little team, but you would be wrong. Fiore had had two days to learn the rules and consider tactics. He was the leader.

He turned his horse. The Turks were neatening their line, a hundred paces away.

Fiore began to trot forward, alone, in the middle.

'Give him ten paces,' I said to Sir Richard, who didn't want to abandon Fiore to the Turks.

'They'll kill him,' Percy breathed.

'I doubt it,' Nerio said, and broke left as I broke right and the Turks charged.

They were six abreast, but the most remarkable thing happened. One of their centre two men saw a javelin lying in the sand; javelins are allowed in every phase, and he rolled down in the saddle, almost between the horses, and plucked the javelin out of the dust, an incredible feat of horsemanship. As he rose, he crossed the javelin across his chest and the next Turk, Timurtash, grasped it by the head so that they held it between them, and they went either side of Fiore.

Fiore rolled down, almost upside down, feet still in his stirrups, and he went under it like a dancing girl, scooped Timurtash's left foot in his own left hand and threw him from the saddle at speed. Timurtash hit hard, and lay still, and Fiore turned his horse hard to the right – that is, towards me – even as Percy and I descended on their end man, knee to knee and far more heavily armoured than our opponent.

He couldn't turn in; his mates were there. He hauled on his reins and his horse reared; he turned her on her hind feet, a beautiful move, and Sir Richard's reaching hand closed on air. But he was at a stop in the midst of the lists, and as he turned his horse, Fiore came behind him, slipped an arm around his shoulders and threw him to the ground.

Perhaps our archers cheered, but the Turks were silent.

I went along the back of their line, and they turned on me, four on one. In the end, a few heartbeats later, I was in the sand, although I had my arms around Sir Everenos and I carried him to the ground with me.

Francesco went down next, as he had lingered too long, and three of them converged on him. But then, in a swirl of dust, it was over, as Fiore and Percy both downed a man. That left the last Turk, a small man, to ride around the lists, trying to avoid Fiore, until Nerio dropped him with one of the few mounted punches I have ever seen thrown.

I had by then gone across the lists to Timurtash, who was conscious, and poured some water down his throat, and Marc-Antonio and two Turks and I pulled the other fallen men out of the lists.

Everenos looked at me and shook his head. 'I love my horse,' he said bitterly. 'Timurtash is a great fool.'

'I will sell you your charger back for a bowl of iced sherbet,' I said.

And so we held the lists at Didymoteichon, although none of the contests would have been recognised by the great knights of the past. I confess that I felt, and still feel, that somehow Fiore and his tactics took some of the spirit out of the contest; certainly, the Turks long debated the utility of our swirling approach.

'You learned all that from us!' protested Everenos. 'And you are all riding Turk horses!'

He had a point. Certainly, my own riding was far, far better than it had been before I came out of the Holy Land, and heavy jousting saddles seemed like thrones. On the other hand, while I have often heard easterners complain about our saddles, I note that our horses seem to outlast theirs, and Fiore says our saddles are better.

The prince came and sat by me while Marc-Antonio was unarming me.

'Ever occur to you to lose a match?' he said, a little ruefully.

'It occurred to me,' I admitted.

Sir Richard laughed. 'Don't blame Sir William,' he said. 'We all wanted to win.'

The prince nodded. To me he said, 'It is not as bad as it might be. The pasha is no soldier, and he is not altogether sorry to see the spahis handed a defeat.'

'And the treaty?' Sir Richard asked.

'They want Gallipoli back immediately,' the prince said. He shrugged. 'I gather that we are not officially negotiating. That is, all negotiations are forbidden by the sultan until the Emperor returns Gallipoli. So the tournament allows us to talk, but tomorrow they will pack up and ride back to Edirne.' He looked at Nerio. 'I worry about you, my lord.'

Nerio nodded. 'I worry too.' He smiled ruefully. 'It is like meeting someone's beautiful wife.'

'It is?' the prince asked.

'The pleasure is immediate; but the husband may follow you for a long time,' Nerio said. 'I am glad we won the mêlée, but …' He shrugged. 'In retrospect, William may have had the longer head.'

I shook my head. 'Nay, I was wrong. One should never play to lose, unless with a child.'

'Never is a long time,' Prince Francesco said.

'And the treaty?' I asked.

He smiled. 'We will be all right,' he said. 'We're merely being tested. Winning was probably the best course. We must look confident. We cannot afford to be humiliated.' He shrugged. 'Not unlike piracy.'

Later there was a sumptuous feast laid on in the great pavilion, and two hundred men sat on beautiful carpets and ate mutton with saffroned rice with raisins, a fine meal but a sticky one. And if a tournament without women is dull, a dinner without them is tedious to extreme. I also missed my wife; I missed having someone with whom to exchange a few barbs, and someone to comment. Emile's comments were always witty, unless she was in a fury, and she would have loved the Turkish camp and everything about it, and I was a little sad to be without her. I missed my children. I missed Lesvos.

I admit it. I was not yet thirty years of age and I was thinking about a little comfort. I am unashamed.

At any rate, the conversation rolled on, stilted, translated, and difficult, and most of it was sustained by a remorselessly cheerful Prince Francesco and the pasha, whose idea of humour became more wicked and malicious as the evening wore on. Of course, all the slaves serving us were Christian men, most of them Greeks; Sir Giannis knew one of them, and the man burst into tears on being recognised.

'See how he misses his wine?' the pasha quipped.

This bastard is trying to humiliate us, I thought

The Turks seemed to have no idea how long most of us had been in the east, nor that many of us spoke some Turkish and some Arabic, so that many casual asides about how dirty we were and how we smelled of pig fat and so on were easy to understand, or perhaps they meant to insult us. Let me remark, though, that the longer I lived in Outremer, the less pork I ate, and the more obvious the smell of pork became to me; I merely remark on it. Englishmen will say the same of garlic eaters.

'Perhaps my guests miss the company of women,' the pasha said. 'I have some beauties for you to admire. They will dance.'

A dozen women came out and danced; their bodies were handsome enough, but their faces were like stone.

'Admire them all you like,' the pasha said. 'I promise every one of them is as Christian as you are yourself – my master had them all from a convent near Patras.' He laughed, and so did most of the Turks, although I noticed that Timurtash made a grimace, as if he thought the remark in bad taste. But all the Turks turned and looked at us, to see what we'd do.

Nerio leaned back and watched them. 'I've had a few nuns,' he quipped. 'Most of them didn't look like that. How much for the lot? I'll buy them.'

'They are my master's,' the pasha said. 'Although I'm sure he would release them if peace were to be made.'

One of the young women sobbed, and a man struck her, and she was pulled away and then they were all removed through the back of the tent.

'You haven't heard my offer,' Nerio said.

The pasha glanced at him. 'I am speaking to the prince,' he said.

Nerio shrugged. 'I am much richer than the prince,' he said.

I looked at my hands in my lap, and I touched my dagger. Nerio was playing a dangerous game.

The pasha shrugged. 'You serve the Emperor?' he asked.

Nerio laughed. 'The Emperor is much more likely to serve me.'

'Renerio!' spat the prince.

Nerio sneered. It was an ugly face, and he knew it. I thought he was acting; I certainly hoped so. The silence in the tent was terrible. The Turks were done being polite.

'I'm sorry,' the prince said. 'This man is Italian.'

'I am the Duke of Corinth,' Nerio said. I had never heard him use the title before.

The pasha looked at him with interest. 'You are Catalan?' he asked. 'There is a Catalan garrison in Corinth.'

'Ah,' Nerio said. 'Thanks for that. I suppose I'll buy them, too. My father was Niccolò Acciaioli.'

At the name of the famous Florentine banker, several of the Turks started.

'And Allah has delivered you into our hands,' the pasha said, in Turkish.

'Not really,' Nerio said, also in Turkish.

Many hands went to daggers and swords.

Nerio just leaned back, uncrossed his legs, and laughed. He looked at me. 'I was not born to be a diplomat,' he said in Italian.

'I could have told you that,' I said.

The prince was on his feet. 'We will withdraw,' he said, and I saw a look go between him and Nerio.

'Perhaps I will keep you as ... guests,' the pasha said.

'There will be a lot of blood, and very few guests,' I said in my bad Turkish.

'I think it is time to stop pretending,' Gatelussi said abruptly. 'We have a fleet and an army. You are pretending that it is ten years ago, when the Emperor had no teeth. Now our teeth are sharp. Look at today – you cannot defeat us at anything.' He shrugged. 'If you refuse to sign a treaty, we will take what we want.'

'You dare!' the pasha spat. 'You are all vassals of the Sultan.'

The prince looked around. 'Yesterday's news. Today, I hold all the ports, your fleet is worthless, and your army is in Asia.'

'I will have you flayed alive,' the pasha said.

The prince sighed. 'You are a very great fool, and all of your people have heard you utter this threat. So here it is, fool: kill us, and see what you have next year. Certainly, no Turk in this tent will live to see a new year.'

'You lie,' spat the pasha.

'Let us see who is a liar. The words come easily from you.' Prince Francesco was calm; his delivery was slow. The pasha was angry and also afraid; his words came forth with too much spittle. 'And a true son of a Turk would never threaten a guest.'

The pasha turned red and white, as if he was diseased, and his eyes glittered. I didn't know that the local pasha was part Albanian; I didn't really know what was going on.

But Everenos Bey stood and snapped a string of orders in steppe Turkish, too fast for me. And men obeyed, backing to the tent walls and going out, many by the simple expedient of rolling under the walls.

He came and stood by me. 'There will be no more threats,' he said. 'Let us see what we see in the morning.'

'Are you a traitor?' barked the pasha.

'I could arrange for you to spend the night with the Christians,' snapped the bey.

To me, in fairly fluent Italian, he said, 'I will send a rider to Edirne. Do not take this pompous fool for our voice.'

I nodded. All the Franks were on their feet, and at a motion from me we gathered around the prince.

'*Ignore the Pasha*,' I spat in French.

'I will hang you from your heels,' the pasha shouted in Turkish. 'I will put hooks through the bones of your legs …'

The prince started walking towards the door.

'How I hate you, you unclean dogs!' spat the pasha.

'See?' Nerio said cheerfully. 'By comparison, we're *master* diplomats.'

But the prince stopped and turned. 'Hate is for amateurs,' he said, in Italian. We walked out into the night, collected our horses in air so thick that a dagger could have cut it, and rode up the hill to our camp. I doubled the guard.

But young Francesco said it was all negotiation.

'The pasha does what the sultan tells him,' he said.

His friend Sir Alessio agreed. 'It is always like this,' he said. 'The extreme demands, the string of captives, the humiliation, the insults. Next day, flowery apologies and new arrangements.'

'It is a test?' I asked.

Nerio shook his head. 'Remember how Sabraham used to say "they are not us"?' he said. 'Truer words were never said. I would hate to do business with them. Everything is a war.'

But then the prince laughed. 'That is exactly what they say of us,' he said. 'And the pasha is, in fact, a fool. He may be a tool in the hand of the Sultan, but he's overplayed. He keeps telling me that the crusaders have all gone home, when we have all of you right here with us to prove him wrong to his people. I was not altogether sad to see you win today, Nerio, and—'

'And I'm your pasha!' Nerio laughed.

'I saw you make the play – the tough upstart ...'

The two men laughed together, and for all that I loved Nerio and saw the prince as a fine leader, I was chilled, because the nuns were nothing to either of them. They had that ruthlessness that Hawkwood had; I lacked it.

'I would like to save the nuns,' I said.

'What, a dozen heretics?' muttered Nerio. 'Let the Turks have them.'

He saw my face and stopped. 'Guglielmo,' he said, his hand reaching out for mine.

'Do you bastards remember Father Pierre Thomas?' I asked. Fiore looked away, and l'Angars took a sharp breath.

The prince glanced at me. Our eyes met; he didn't flinch. 'I am trying to save all the nuns in the empire,' he said. 'I can't save these few women. And I beg you not to try. That's the response he wanted.'

I held his gaze.

He shrugged. 'Sir Guglielmo, in truth, my fleet is too small to fight all the Turks, and the emperor cannot afford to pay his army, such as it is, and now he owes the Venetians thirty thousand hyperaspers. The empire needs time to rebuild. The Franks sacked it, and the Turks – if they don't have time, they will fall, and then ...'

'Can you imagine what has been done to those women?' I asked. I was in France, in my head. Looking at the nuns that Camus had turned to whores. And their blank faces.

'Don't be so pious,' Gatelussi said. 'That's what happens to women, in war.'

'I know,' I said. 'That's why I will not let it stand.'

*

In the end, they were all with me. All but the prince.

I summoned John. 'We will rescue those nuns,' I said. 'I need to know where they are kept.'

He nodded. 'If Turks catch us,' he said, 'it will be very bad.'

'Noted,' I said. 'My plan is this: you find the women; Fiore cuts loose their horse herd after I set fire to the pasha's tent.'

John laughed. 'I love you, William Gold,' he said. 'Good Mongol plan.'

'No killing,' I said.

'That not so Mongol,' he said.

I have done this sort of thing before, and so has Ewan the Scot, who'd taken his fair share of English cattle, and we crept through the night past the outer guard posts, which were all manned by Turks on horseback keeping a very poor watch. We worked our way along the lists; they were unguarded and empty, and stretched like a highway to the pasha's tent, which was unguarded too. I'd had a notion it might be.

There were Turks in the streets between the pavilions for a while, but they didn't stay out late; men were tired, and most of them went to bed after a trumpet was blown. And then the camp was empty, and we were unobserved. I will never forget the long crawl down the lists over which I'd ridden so casually all day: the pats of horse manure, the dust, the spiders . . .

In the chansons, there are never any insects. In real life, everything bites. We were both completely unarmed; I had ordered it. If we were taken, I wanted no accusation of camp-murder. But unarmed is a form of nudity, and I felt very naked, crawling like a worm on my belly in a smelly old linen gown and my oldest braes and hose – more like a servant than a knight.

When you start on an *empris*, you imagine how it will be if you succeed, and yet, I was startled, somehow, inside myself, when we were lying in the grass under the pasha's tent ropes. His tent billowed and snapped in the breeze. The walls were back in place; there was a light away at the back, on the side of the city, but the rest of the huge tent was dark.

Ewan touched my wrist. 'What if,' he whispered, 'the women are in the tent?'

Oh, the things you never think of.

I lay in the darkness and prayed to the Blessed Virgin and Mary Magdalene for the salvation of those women. And I knew perfectly well that I was trying to rescue all the women I'd wronged myself – Richard and I ran brothels in France. We knew …

God.

You never escape your own evil, you know. Unless you are made like Nerio, or Gatelussi. Sometimes I envy them. But I am as I am.

I struck sparks from flint and got a burning coal on my little square of char cloth, and then I used a little dry tow, blew it to light, and instantly raised the flame to the eaves of the pavilion.

Silk burns quickly. Silk that has been all day in the brilliant Greek sun, oiled with a little linseed oil? The pavilion was like a giant lamp wick.

A man shouted, off to the left.

The pavilion caught with a rush; in ten heartbeats, we had a wall of flame behind us.

'Lie still,' snapped the veteran cattle thief. I obeyed. I wanted to run into the darkness.

Instead, I lay with the raging heat of the flaming tent above me. Most of the heat passed over, but it was uncomfortable, and then worse as the tent's hangings and furnishing caught, and there were screams, and I prayed …

The earth vibrated with running feet, and Turks appeared out of the darkness, perfectly visible against the fire. No one had any water, and the fire was too fast, and then they were shouting for the pasha.

'Now we run,' Ewan said, and we rose and ran off, first towards the water stores, with twenty other men, some of whom were Christian slaves. Then we lay still awhile, and then we were slipping off to the south. By then their guards were shouting that there was an attack, the crusaders were attacking them, and others were shouting that the horse herd was under attack by Mongols. It would have been delightful, except that we were in the midst of it.

A woman screamed, and then another.

I pinched a kaftan off a line between two tents; it was sweat-soaked, but it covered my gown, and changed my profile. Ewan wrapped a stolen strip of cloth around his head and we ran again.

The earth shook. A thousand horses broke into a panicked gallop to the north of us, and every Turk in the camp cried out, and turned that way, as if they were under a compulsion. They ran for the horse herd.

We ran the other way. We ran almost to the Turkish sentry line, and then we lay down in the dust and crawled. We might have spared ourselves the effort; the sentries were chasing horses.

It was almost an hour before I made it back to our camp. John had all the nuns in a tent; Sir Giannis was trying to talk to them. They were terrified of the Kipchaks, who had blackened their faces.

I went to Prince Francesco.

'It is done,' I said. 'We lost no one.'

He was furious. 'You have risked the lives of fifty thousand people against these twelve women.'

He didn't like piety, so I spared him mine. In my heart, though, I was full of joy. I still am. I am a knight. This is what knighthood is for.

In the morning, the pasha was gone. Angry men make mistakes; he made the mistake of accusing Everenos of burning his tent.

Everyone has politics, even Turks.

We waited for two days to hear from the sultan. The nuns stayed in two tents, and had the Kipchaks around them at all times. The Turks never mentioned them; we pretended we knew nothing. It was a curious game, but one I understood.

'We can't admit we have the lasses,' Gospel Mark said. 'They can't admit they lost 'em. Stands to reason.'

On the third day it rained like fury – it was more like England than Outremer, and we all had to look to our horses. The farmers didn't come, and we were very short on food.

Prince Francesco frowned at me over some stale bread. 'Here we go,' he said. 'They are calling our bluff. Cut off our food, and we have to act.'

But the next day the sun rose, and the farmers came. We ate well enough. I wondered if every Greek for twenty miles was selling us his oldest mutton, but old mutton is infinitely better than no mutton.

About noon Everenos came with Timurtash at his side. I rode down with Nerio and Young Francesco, and we saluted them.

'The pasha has gone north for a while,' he said easily. 'My master the sultan says threats are for children, and neither he nor your master are so young.'

Young Francesco bowed. 'This is true – nor did we ever suspect that the sultan was young.'

'My master says, let us make an equitable peace. He says, come to Edirne with thirty men, and you will be received like a son.' The bey nodded and flashed his toothy smile. 'I myself will provide an escort. And I am to say,' he raised an eyebrow, 'that the son of Acciaioli is to have a pass and firman, but is not welcome to join the Emperor's friend. Yet.'

He handed Nerio a pair of scrolls. 'You are free to cross the sultan's possessions of Greece and Morea,' Everenos said.

'The sultan's possessions?' Nerio asked.

The two men smiled.

'Did you have a fire the other night?' Nerio asked innocently.

'We might have, and we search high and low for the culprit,' Everenos said. 'Arson is punishable by death among us.' He looked around at us. 'Some slaves escaped. We assume they set the fire. If they are caught, it will be terrible for them.' He nodded, rocking in his saddle. 'So it would be better for everyone, perhaps, if they were not caught.'

'I have no idea what you are saying,' Nerio said lazily.

'Whereas I understand you perfectly,' I said, through Marc-Antonio. Everenos turned and met my eye. His were blue.

'You and I have always understood each other,' he said, in Italian. 'We could make this peace in as long as it takes an arrow to fly.'

I reached out and took his hand. 'Mayhap we'll have a chance someday,' I said.

He handed me de Charny's dagger. 'I have no more need of this,' he said. 'We know you now as men of honour, like ourselves.'

I embraced him. I was no friend to the pasha, but I could have spent a year alongside Timurtash and Everenos.

Nerio was going to say more, but I turned my horse and his horse followed mine, thank God.

I liked Timurtash and I liked Everenos, but I have seldom been happier to get well away from anywhere as Didymoteichon, and we left the two walls behind and rode away on tracks that only our Greeks knew. Lascaris was a good guide; so was Sir Giorgios's squire. We all rode together for a day, to a town that they called Mandritto, which sounds like the Italian for a right-hand blow, and made us laugh, and if the laughter was a little unnatural, still we were elated to be away. I bid farewell to my lord at Mandritto; I bent my knee and he forgave me for risking everything by rescuing the nuns.

'You can earn back my trust by taking care of my son,' he said.

I was surprised. 'My lord?'

The old prince shrugged. 'The sultan may have me killed at Edirne,' he said. 'I want my son free to avenge me.' He nodded. 'If it doesn't offend your delicate sense of morality, perhaps you'd kill a few Turks as well.'

I embraced Sir Richard. I little thought that it would be the last time I saw the prince, or five years until I next saw Sir Richard.

I thought only of the ten nuns who were wearing Kipchak clothes – the worst riders ever to grace steppe ponies – but the Turks were either fooled or pretended to be, and we left Everenos Bey at Mandritto. I shook his hand and embraced Timurtash, my near double. I never expected to see them again. Well, God works in mysterious ways, eh?

In a day we were on the Via Egnatia, the ancient road the old Romans built, like the highway near Chester in England: two carts wide, paved in stone. It went west, a ribbon you could follow with your eye, with country houses, inns, ruins and bandits. It runs almost all the way from Constantinople to Venice – well, Ragusa, anyway.

It was only on the third day out of Mandritto, when we rounded the corner of a hill and the Aegean was laid out at our feet, blue as blue for as far as the eye could see on a perfect day, that one of the women cried aloud.

'Thalassa!'

And the other women took up the cry. Then the tallest woman managed to get her pony close to Sir Giannis and they had a brief exchange, and he caught my eye.

'They want to know where we are taking them,' Giannis said. 'They want to go to Thessaloniki.'

Thessaloniki, or Salonika, depending on who was speaking, lay on our route. It was a major city, the second city of the Empire, and like many of the Italian communes, it had vicious internal politics, or so Giannis told me as we descended from the mountains to the coast road. The city regarded itself as virtually autonomous, and had in fact been ruled by a council of workers, farmers and sailors in the past.

'How'd they do?' I asked.

Giannis made a face. 'Not very well,' he admitted.

It turned out that they'd been overthrown by a moderate group of merchants who'd returned the city to the allegiance of the Emperor, but one of the results of the years under communal rule was the presence of a Venetian bailli and the development of the town as the easternmost port open to Venice; Genoa did their best to keep Pera and Constantinople closed, or at least difficult for the Venetians.

'It is a fine city,' Sir Giannis insisted. 'And returning to normal. And there are more than forty monasteries and nunneries for these women.'

The women kept very much to themselves; Marc-Antonio and Achille and I did most of their cooking, because they flinched when other men came close to them. I can't claim I saw much in the way of smiles from any of them. Giannis was our translator, slow and patient, and I wished every day that I had Sister Marie, whose Greek was excellent.

'I know they have been through a great deal,' I said one day. 'But I can tell they are … still afraid. Is it us?'

'Two of them are afraid they are pregnant,' Giannis said bitterly. 'They will not be admitted to a nunnery.'

Nerio shrugged. 'In Italy it is practically a requirement.'

Sir Giannis turned red, and one of the nuns clearly understood Italian. Her face hardened, and she turned away, white with anger.

'Jesus,' I spat, blaspheming in my anger. 'Do you say every stupid thing that comes to your mind?'

'Yes, he does,' Fiore said.

Nerio glared at me like an unfed cat.

'Nerio, those women have been raped by infidels, and where they are going, it is quite possible they will be held responsible – punished, made whores for their "sin",' I growled. And my anger was fuelled by my own self-knowledge. Oh, yes. I knew how it all worked.

Nerio could not, for once, meet my eye.

'Tell the good sister that I apologise. It was ill-said,' Nerio muttered to Giannis.

I tell this story mostly because when we reached Thessaloniki, we took the sisters to an inn outside the gates, not to one of the nunneries high on the hill in the city. And Nerio took charge. He insisted.

I let him go. I spent the morning billeting my lances, making sure we had fodder, and loaning men money. We were desperately short of hard coin. On the other hand, I had a good supply of silk and some saffron to trade, and Nerio had more, and I saw him in the market, which was as big, and as good, as the market in Florence. He and young Francesco spent almost an hour with the Genoese factor. After we had all done some haggling, both selling and buying, I met up with the two of them.

Nerio nodded to me as if I had not castigated him mere hours before. 'I have some news for you,' he said. 'But first, the Venetian bailli.'

I went with him to the Venetian bailli, who quite happily cashed Nerio's bills of exchange and my own, as well as paying us a thousand compliments on our campaign against the Turks and our visit to Jerusalem, about which he was surprisingly well informed.

'The Count of Savoy sent a ship in for greens,' he said. 'And one of our captains needed a foremast. And you have no friend in Messire Florimont de Lesparre, I think?'

'He does not seem to like us,' Nerio said.

'The feeling is mutual,' I said.

The bailli nodded. 'Well, he spews poison like a woman scorned, so beware. To me, he is a Gascon adventurer, while both of you come highly recommended by friends. But in other places … among other things, he claims that Sir William betrayed the crusaders at Gallipoli and served alongside the Turks, for money.'

Nerio looked at a spot of dirt on his glove. 'I think it is time that Messire Florimont was reminded of the cost of speaking so,' he said softly.

The bailli made a face. 'In fact, I would not have been disposed to pay Messire Florimont much mind. He is full of gasconades. But he arrived on the heels of the news that he had accused the King of Cyprus of cowardice. He did so at Rhodes; my brother is a knight there. He was present.'

I bowed. 'Your brother is a knight of the Order?' I asked, showing my ring.

He nodded. 'This is how I know your reputation so well, Sir

Guglielmo. You have nothing to fear from my city, I promise you. But Messire Florimont has apparently challenged the King of Cyprus to a duel. And the king has accepted.'

'*Bon Dieu*,' I muttered, and Nerio shook his head.

'What an idiot,' he said. 'Still, this man needs to be silenced.'

The bailli agreed. We shared wine, he offered us some shipping advice, and we negotiated some bills and sold him some saffron.

As we emerged, rich in gold if not spirit, Nerio shook his head.

'I need to be in credit in the west. I need Florence and Venice to see me as a hero and a defender of the faith. That's how I will raise funds.' He frowned. 'This glove is ruined.'

'Funds for what?' I asked.

He smiled. 'I plan to conquer all the Morea and Achaea,' he said. 'I intend to be Prince of Achaea. It was my father's dream.'

I whistled. I'd heard some of this, but never heard it all. 'You'll need soldiers,' I said. 'And isn't someone else the Prince of Achaea?'

He smiled. 'I can only afford you for sixty days,' he said. 'I need to go a bite at a time. Will you come back and serve me when I am ready? With a hundred lances?'

'Of course,' I said, taking his hand. 'Cup of wine?' I asked.

'No, I have a little detail to attend to,' he said with his easy smile. He shrugged. 'Listen: you need to know some things, and I know them already from the Genoese factor, who has just come from his home. The Prince of Achaea is the Green Count's cousin, Filippo. I know very little about the man, except that he and the count are at odds. It is a typical story: his mother died, and his father remarried, and now the Prince of Achaea is in danger of losing his inheritance in the Alps to a young, attractive woman and her darling five-year-old son.'

I played with my beard. 'What's that to me?' I asked.

He looked smug. 'Nothing, perhaps. But Filippo is trying to make war against his father, and that's news. The Green Count is going to return to find companies of mercenaries camped close to his castles, and young Filippo preparing war.'

I shrugged.

'Filippo, Prince of Achaea, is allied with, among others, the Bishop of Geneva, in attempting to break the count's hold on the vassalage of Savoy.' Nerio had that look – the look we all hated – when he knew something and we'd have to swim upstream through his vast sense of superiority to learn it.

'Ah, I mention Robert of Geneva and you are interested,' Nerio joked. 'But Emile's lands lie right there – indeed, I believe you hold a little knight's fee of your own up there by Chambéry, eh?'

'So this Filippo is allied with Robert of Geneva, and they are hiring soldiers?' I asked, to show I was still following.

Nerio smiled; the cat was about to pounce. 'Archbishop Robert sent Filippo his best captain,' he said. 'The Bourc Camus.'

I stopped dead in the street.

'Now I have your attention, yes?' he asked. 'Emile is riding home into the middle of a war, and the Bourc Camus is commanding the other side's brigands.'

'Christ,' I blasphemed.

Nerio nodded. 'I need you at Corinth. We have to move fast anyway. And then I'll let you go. The count will need to know this too, I suspect.'

'Is there more?' I asked.

'A few details. My Genoese source knows a great deal about Filippo; I may get him to sell me the rest. But the Green Count is not yet at Venice. You cannot ride off and save Emile yet.'

I remember shrugging. 'Emile is not a maiden in need of rescuing,' I said. 'She has good knights and good advisors.'

'Good,' Nerio said. 'I was going to tell you that, because I need you here. Now I must go.'

'A brothel?' I asked.

He grinned. 'Very close, my brother.' He called for Giannis.

I later learned that he visited the city's metropolitan, a cleric only slightly less powerful than the Patriarch of Constantinople. He took Giannis. I assumed he was going to a brothel and I didn't go. I can't remember what I did; I think I was arranging for fodder for two hundred horses. But Giannis told me afterwards that Nerio gave the patriarch one thousand Venetian ducats in gold. And a note from the Venetian bailli, and another from the city's military governor.

The patriarch graciously ordered that the ten nuns be taken into the noblest convent in the city; the two women who were pregnant were sent to have their children in the houses of two families who volunteered, and were then 'allowed' to return to the nunnery.

The next morning, I found Nerio kneeling on the hard stone of the Venetian bailli's chapel. He was not much for church at the best of times; Christmas and Easter and some casual blasphemy was more his style.

He glanced at me like a guilty boy who has stolen some pears.

'You saved those women,' I accused him.

He shrugged. 'Sometimes I am an ass,' he said. 'I regret it, like most people.'

We knelt there a while.

'I blame the Holy Sepulchre,' he said.

We took Mass together with Fiore and l'Angars, and went down into the town. And I will say that in the next day or so, all of us were drunk, we ate a great deal, and l'Angars and Nerio hired courtesans. We were never made to be priests.

Thessaloniki is a fine town, as old as Rome or older, with a dozen magnificent churches and superb walls. It has been stormed and sacked only once, and it would indeed be a hard nut to crack. It is a handsome town: there are new churches, as if to prove that the Empire is not yet dead, and the frescoes in one were so beautiful that I stared at them for an hour. Yet beside the new work is some very old: a magnificent church from the time of Constantine, and a fine triumphal arch with the Emperor surrounded by his knights in fine archaic armour. Sir Giannis and Sir Giorgios explained a little of the history of the town while we strolled about, and then we sat in little tavernas and listened to bards and minstrels as good as anything in the west – better, possibly. I heard a man sing a song in Arabic that he said he'd had from a sailor, and Gospel Mark met an English sailor from an Aragonese ship that was running down to Crete and we filled him full of wine.

It was early July and we'd already had a month of war and another month of 'diplomacy' that had felt like war most of the time. I paid my men and let them loose, confident that they'd come back.

The town was as full of news from the west as it was full of Frankish sailors. There was news from Venice only a month or two old, and the most amazing news was that the Pope had returned to Italy from Avignon. He'd come in May, and his return seemed to be tangled in conflict with my friend and former employer, Sir John Hawkwood. The politics were as complex as anything we'd heard in Outremer: it appeared that the Pope, on his return to Italy, had refused to meet with any representatives from Milan or any of the Milanese allies; on the other hand, it also appeared, if the traveller's tales could be believed, that the Milanese, or at least, their allies, including Sir John, had made at least one attempt to kidnap the Pope.

The Green Count was, by all accounts, held in the Lazzaretto in Venice because his people had plague. I heard our friend the English sailor say that he'd heard that the Pope had invited the Green Count to visit, and would ask him to command his armies, which worried me. Remember, I expected to find employment with Sir John on return to Italy, but the last thing I needed to complicate my life was to make war for Sir John against my feudal sovereign, the Count of Savoy.

And if that wasn't enough, it was widely said that the King of England was breaking off relations with the Pope because of the Pope's unwavering pro-French policies. I have to note that the Pope, even when we served him directly, had been notoriously biased in favour of the King of France. There were rumours of a direct alliance between England and Milan.

I listened to all the news from Italy, and wondered where Emile was. I sent young Francesco to gather news from Genoese sailors, and I sent l'Angars to gather news from French sailors, but it was Father Angelo Cavalli who seemed to know everyone and put us in the way of getting information on Corinth.

Nerio bought an itinerary from a Greek monk introduced by Father Angelo. Suddenly he had contacts in the Greek church, thanks to our priest and his donation to the patriarch; everyone seemed anxious to help him. So one evening, while Fiore practised against a post supporting the roof of the stable, Nerio laid out his itinerary and we drew it as a map, something that Hawkwood liked to do. Not a real map – just a set of circles ...

Maps and charts are still rare; in those days, only sailors and soldiers and pilgrims were interested in them at all.

At any rate, Nerio put a stack of gold ducats on the table.

'Corinth,' he said.

'Are you really Duke of Corinth?' I asked.

Nerio smiled. 'My cousin Antonio, the legitimate son, has chosen to represent himself as the duke,' he said. 'But I have his authority to install myself in the city, which is currently held by bandits.'

I leaned back. 'Really bandits?' I asked.

Sir Giannis looked at the stack of ducats. 'That should be twice as high,' he said. 'Have you ever seen the Acrocorinth?'

'No,' Nerio admitted.

Giannis shook his head.

'I doubt that they are actually bandits,' Nerio said, looking at the arc of the Greek coastlines rendered in charcoal. 'My guess is that they are Catalan mercenaries. Hired by the Duke of Athens to take my fief. Pretending to be bandits.'

'This sounds like Italy,' I said.

'It *is* like Italy, except that there are no rules – no Holy Roman Emperor, no Pope, no communes,' Nerio said with relish. 'We can do whatever we can get away with.'

I looked at the charcoal drawing. 'Still four days away,' I said. 'Why Catalans?'

Giannis ran his fingers through his beard. 'Ah,' he said. 'Sixty years ago, the Emperor hired the Catalans to rid him of the Franks.'

I think that I laughed and slapped my knee. It really was as good as a joke.

'Let me guess,' I said. 'The Catalans drove out the Franks and took it all for themselves.'

Nerio smiled. 'Well, Catalans at first. Later the Kingdom of Naples.'

'And your father,' I said. Sir Niccolò had been Grand Seneschal of the Kingdom of Naples.

'The Catalans needed Florentine banks,' Nerio said. 'I have decided that the Florentines no longer need the Catalans.'

'Hence your uncle, the bishop …' I said. I could remember that on our way out to sack Alexandria, we had run across Nerio's uncle.

'Who ought to be holding Corinth for me, but is away in the Morea, chasing a new bishopric,' Nerio said.

Giannis leaned back. 'Let me see this,' he said. His soft brown eyes turned on Nerio. 'You intend to storm the Acrocorinth,' he asked.

'Yes,' Nerio said.

'You are insane,' Giannis said.

Nerio shrugged.

'No, really, I must insist,' Giannis said. 'Wait until you see it.'

Nerio shrugged. 'Listen, Giannis!' he said. 'I don't care if it is high as Heaven and guarded by the legion of Archangels and led by Saint

Michael. It is mine, and once I have it, I'll be in the saddle of the whole of Greece.'

Giannis sat back and shook his head.

I looked at him. Giannis was a quiet, careful man – in many ways, very like the former legate, Father Pierre Thomas, who he'd followed for six years, and he had the same ascetic face and thoughtful eyes.

Giannis took a long pull on his wine and didn't meet my eye.

'You say this is impossible?' I asked.

He shrugged. 'If the place was *empty* it would be a challenge to climb all the way to the top of the citadel in armour,' he said. 'I believe it is almost fifteen hundred stone steps from the first gate to the citadel.'

I looked at Nerio.

Nerio shrugged. 'I have never seen us beaten,' he said. 'To me, this is a straightforward assault. We will have absolute surprise. We ride straight up to the gate dressed as monks, go in and fight our way to the citadel.'

'They close the citadel gates and we are trapped outside, laying siege for a year,' Giannis said.

'We can take down one gate,' Nerio said. 'I have purchased a device.'

Giannis looked at me, eyes fatalistic, only the faintest flaring of his nostrils indicated his feelings. I knew that he was asking me to intervene.

I admit, it sounded insane. But by God, gentles, it sounded like a great *empris* – the sort of thing that would be talked of throughout Outremer and Europe.

'How big will the Catalan garrison be?' I asked.

Nerio nodded. 'The patriarch here says one hundred and forty men. The bailli says the same.'

I looked around. 'Have you offered the patriarch . . .?'

Nerio nodded. 'I expect a little help in the citadel,' he said.

Giannis leaned forward. 'You promised him what? The restoration of the Greek church in Corinth?'

'Something like that,' Nerio admitted.

'Directly against the wishes of the Pope and even Father Pierre Thomas?' Giannis asked.

Nerio shrugged. 'Outremer is doomed as it is,' he said. 'The Pope has no idea what it's like out here. You have heard the news – the Pope isn't preparing to back the crusade! He's arming for war with Milan instead. And anyway, the schism between the Orthodox and the Catholic churches is a fool's bargain.'

'And you will heal the rift?' Giannis asked.

'I will ignore it,' Nerio said.

The two of them looked at each other. I could tell it was important to Giannis – this small point. His lips curved down, not quite a frown.

'If you have a traitor inside the citadel, and some magical device that will open a gate,' I said, changing the subject, 'I think it's worth a try.' I knew I was trying to convince Giannis.

Giannis picked up his sword. He looked at the hilt for a bit, and then shrugged. He caught every eye, as if making sure we were listening.

'We will all die,' Giannis predicted.

We rested for five days in Thessaloniki, and it was with difficulty that I gathered and mustered my lances. The Kipchaks were easy to find, and they sobered up quickly; the archers were more difficult to find, and several men had sold their kit, and their brigandines and basinets had to be ransomed from pawnbrokers. On the other hand, Gospel Mark had recruited the English sailor and two of his Aragonese friends, who, as it proved, could draw heavy bows. We also picked up a Breton squire and another Irishman, Patric Loily, who was also a competent archer. He was a pilgrim; he'd been all the way to Jerusalem, and he joined us when he asked for alms and Nerio gave him a silver mark. Hector Lachlan, who was at last recovering from all his wounds and looked like himself, and Red Bill, who was if anything bigger than the year before, welcomed the Irishman, and the sound of Gaelic was to be heard throughout our camp. Gaelic, two kinds of Spanish, Portuguese, Italian, Greek, Kipchak, English, Hungarian, Norman French ... even Hebrew, since our two London Jews had followed us to Thessaloniki and now asked to accompany us to Corinth. We were, as Fiore kept telling us, now the 'Army of Babel'.

'We should have recruited some Turks,' Fiore said.

'The scum of ten societies,' muttered Sir Giorgios.

'I prefer to think of us as the best soldiers of ten societies,' I said. 'Carefully chosen and brilliantly trained.'

Fiore nodded. 'Good point,' he said with his characteristic modesty.

*

I don't want you to think that all of our brilliant plans came to fruition. There's a sort of lie to telling a story like this; I leave out anything that I didn't like. So let me add, in lieu to hundreds of other details I've no doubt passed over or forgotten, that Nerio had planned to move us by ship from Thessaloniki to Negroponte, or even to the coast south of Corinth for a direct strike.

At the time, Nerio said there just weren't ships suitable to move all our horses, and I believed him. But more recently, I heard him tell the story himself, in his own hall in Thebes, and he said that when he bought the nuns their place in a convent, he spent all his ready money, which had a sound of authenticity to it.

Regardless, instead of sailing around the Chersonese, we had to march. We had about twenty lances, each made up of a knight or fully armoured man-at-arms, an armed squire, an armed archer mounted, and an unarmoured page to hold the horses. I say 'about twenty' lances because really we had thirty with men like Sir Giannis and Sir Giorgios and Nerio himself. In addition, we had more archers than our lances needed – almost another twenty archers; we had fourteen Kipchaks, and a dozen Greeks who were not as well armoured as a squire but not as naked as a Kipchak, either. Thanks to the campaign in the Holy Land and our good fortune and God's providence, we had two horses per man and more – a lot of very good horseflesh, too much to transport by ship. All told, with camp servants and our priest and our 'doctor', we were feeding a hundred and ten mouths and almost three hundred horses.

I know this may bore you, but it was my everyday life and it is now, and while Monsieur Froissart never mentions the cost of knightly deeds, I seem to feel the pinch every day, so here it is.

A horse that eats grain eats about as much, in terms of money, as a man eats in bread and meat. This is a rough guide. It costs a man about four soldi, silver Italian coins, a month to subsist. Soldiers like to do better than just subsistence, and so do soldiers' horses, so let's assume double that plus for each man – fifteen soldi a month for each man and his two horses. Assume roughly twenty soldi to a Venetian ducat, depending on exchange rates; imagine wastage and mischarging, and you can guess that every man will cost a ducat a month to maintain. That's before you pay them. We pay between sixteen and thirty florins a month to each lance, depending on the market; again, let's just imagine that in ducats. Every lance makes roughly twenty ducats a month. They have to pay for their own armour and tack, but the *compagnia* is usually responsible for horseflesh.

Now you know why our word 'soldier' comes from the Italian word for a silver coin, eh?

They'd all served at their own expense out in the Holy Land. But from Thessaloniki on, all our people were to be paid under contract with Nerio. Regular pay would improve morale, and also allow men to replace broken swords, expended arrows – our arrow supply was shockingly bad, with some men having only three shafts. We needed new saddles and bridles, and we had men who were using old bronze eating knives. I found a German cutler in Thessaloniki and I bought his entire stock of swords and daggers and handed them out to my archers.

Anyway, we were not a beautiful company when we rode out of Thessaloniki. But the first morning on the road, in sunny Thessaly, as we rested in an olive grove, I reminded them all that it was their first day under pay, and they cheered.

Ah, the life of being a soldier.

Three days out of Thessaloniki, we came to Thermopylae.

There are hot springs at Thermopylae, and while that may be obvious to a Greek speaker, I hadn't expected the sulphur smell, or the restfulness of the ancient baths carved into the side of the steep cliffs that lower over the sea coast. Sir Giannis took us to see the low hill where the Spartan king made his stand, and we walked all over the place where the battle was fought, imagining King Leonidas and his three hundred Spartans facing a whole army of Turks.

Fiore found the place very exciting, and after he'd been up the hill twice, and looked at the sea, he proposed that we put our harnesses on and exchange some blows, to honour the Spartan king.

The Greeks, Giorgios and Giannis, who were usually uninterested in our ideas of martial honour, fell in with the suggestion immediately and hastened to put on their armour, and there we were, grilling in an early August sun on a flat salt pan where the king of Sparta tried to save Greece. Nerio and I shattered lances on each other; Sir Giorgios and I exchanged some hearty blows with the longsword, and Hector

Lachlan and I swiped at each other with axes, although I was cautious and he caught my ankle with his hook and dumped me on the salt pan. The archers shot at marks, and volunteered to be the Persians for us, if we'd like to stand in a huddle together.

Giannis laughed aloud. 'You are not enough to darken the sun,' he said. 'Nor would we be able to fight in the shade.' Our two Jews laughed, as did Sir Giorgios. They all knew the quote – Giannis had to explain Herodotus to me. I agree that it was a capital joke, even when explained, and the Spartan king grew in my estimation. And indeed, as Sir Giannis recited to me bits of Spartan humour, his eyes seemed to grow brighter at the remembered valour of his ancestors.

We declined to allow our archers to make us targets, and later we bought fish from a dozen boats that came in, having seen our fires. The fishermen were delighted to take our hard silver. We built fires on the sand, and ate like kings and drank some terrible local wine, and imagined ourselves as the saviours of Greece while Giannis and Giorgios took turns telling the story of the battle and the sea battle at Artemisium that accompanied it.

It was a fine day. I'll never forget it.

I was lying by the fire, with Nerio on one hand and Giannis on the other, and Giannis was telling us about the Spartans. And then he turned to me and raised his horn cup of wine. 'Perhaps we will take Corinth,' he said. 'I think we should try. But only if Nerio swears he will uphold the Union of Churches. I will fight for that.'

And Giorgios raised his wine cup. 'And I. Indeed, I have fought for it for ten years.'

Nerio sat up, a little more like a debauched satyr and less like a battle commander. And as he sat up, I caught his twisted smile. His contempt for the 'Union' and for all men who held deep convictions was clear enough.

But then he shook his head. 'I swear to you by my father's name and the cross on my hilt that if we take Corinth, I will uphold the Union and make my lands a model for the co-operation of our faiths.'

Giannis nodded. 'For this, I will fight.'

Giorgios nodded. But to me, he muttered, 'I do not see our Nerio as Leonidas.'

*

I have said before that my company of lances, the company that brought me real fame, was born in the darkness of the Holy Sepulchre. But it was not just the Holy Sepulchre, with its magical reminder of our morality and mortality, that changed us. It was war in Outremer. I have never met a race of men so nearly perfect in the art of war as the Turks, although the Mongols seem to equal it, and facing the Turks required a constant devotion to details, from upkeep of horse harness to minutiae of food and water, that war in France and Italy never demanded.

But besides military proficiency, there is also spirit, and spirit is bred in many ways: shared adventure, and shared experience. I have found that moments can define men (and women) and change the way they see themselves. That day at Thermopylae was one such. We came to Thermopylae as soldiers, but after games and a fish dinner, and the tales we told, we were a different kind of soldier. I think that we all felt connected, somehow, to King Leonidas and his knights. And games provide soldiers with incentive to excel. War can easily become a matter of barbaric survival. It takes extra effort to make it more than mere brutality. I was still learning all of that, then, with some difficult precepts of chivalry as guideposts and with the Turks and Greeks as exemplars. But I was determined – that is, I think, we were all determined, l'Angars and Fiore and Rob Stone and Hector Lachlan – to be something more than mere men of arms.

I offer this philosophical aside to explain what followed. It is a famous exploit; I'm sure it is the reason Froissart is so patient with me.

So, there we are, on the beach at Thermopylae, about three days' ride from Corinth. Nerio came over to me and asked me if he could address the company.

I smiled. 'We are your company, just now, *patron.*'

Nerio grinned. Then he gathered us all together; he stood on the stump of an old tree, and his back was to the fire, and he addressed the company.

'Corinth is one of the mightiest fortresses in the world,' he began. 'It towers into the clouds, or so I'm told, and it is huge – more than a mile of walls. It is viewed by Franks and Turks alike as impregnable.' He looked at all of us. 'Yet I am paying all of you gentlemen to take it for me, because it is mine, and it has been stolen by a pack of Spaniards.'

I've mentioned it often enough, but I'll say it again: we English and Gascons had more experience of taking towns by escalade than any group of soldiers anywhere. The one real area of warlike endeavour in which routiers excelled over all other soldiers was in the storming of towns. We had practised methods of breaking in; we practised the skills that could seize a gate or open a drawbridge and, frankly, we had better armour and better hand-to-hand fighting skills than most garrisons. These same men had taken both the outwalls and the citadel of Gallipoli in the face of a Turkish garrison; a bunch of Catalans didn't sound like much of a threat. So men yawned, and someone wondered if there was more wine.

'Men will have marked our leaving Thessaloniki,' Nerio said. 'I put out that we were going to Athens, or maybe Patras, but my greatest worry is that the men who have dispossessed me of my lands will guess that we are headed for Corinth, because the only weapon we have is surprise. Corinth is deemed impregnable by the Turks – you can imagine how tough a nut it must be. But we will crack it, and the way we will crack it is by being in position to take it two mornings from now, at daylight. We will move fast; we will eat cold food. It will not be pleasant. But we will outrun rumours of our arrival.'

That got everyone's attention.

'One hundred and twenty miles,' Nerio said. 'Six days' travel for most travellers, and two sets of mountains. We have guides and food. We are going to fly.'

Men nodded. No one said, 'Sweet Christ, that's impossible', or any such foolishness.

Nerio nodded to all of us. 'I knew you were the right men for this task,' he said. 'We will rise early and move at dawn. We will move as fast as the horses allow; everyone should be ready to change horses all day.'

'Loot?' called someone. I assume it was Gospel Mark.

'None,' Nerio said. 'But double pay for the month if you take the citadel, and a five ducat a man bonus above that.'

'That's fair,' another voice said. There was a rumble of assent.

That was it. We'd taken Gallipoli. We'd marched to Jerusalem. Corinth was just another day's work.

*

Sir Giorgios took us inland almost immediately from Thermopylae, up into the hills that separated Boeotia from Thessaly, and we had a brush with some Greeks who shot arrows at our Kipchaks, wounding one man in the hand. Giannis rode off with his *stradiotes* for half a day while we pushed on; he visited the Greek bishop and put out the word that we were harmless, for Franks. Nerio rode to a castle that towered over the road and was well enough received. There was diplomacy at the local level. Romania, or Morea, was not like England at all; every lord was his own sovereign, so that a count or baron had his own tiny army, and his own rights of justice. Men tell me that England was this way once – certainly Italy can be so, at least around Rome and along the east coast. But it is terrible for the people of the land, and the peasants of Boeotia looked as poor, for the most part, as the *Jacques* of France during our *chevauchées*.

We moved fast. The advantage of having reliable native guides was not lost on me; I'd already come to the conclusion that information was a better weapon than a sword, and a good captain always paid well for his guides. Hawkwood always paid for spies and guides, and paid well; even when he couldn't pay his lances, Sir John paid his spies.

Sir Giannis and Sir Giorgios were better than spies or guides, though; they were friends and comrades who knew the land, and when they didn't know the details of a route, they could ask. Even I, with my title of '*Spatharios*' of the Emperor, enjoyed a certain status, and certainly as we crossed the plains of central Boeotia, through village after village, Nerio arranged that we flew the double-headed eagle at the head of our column, and priests came out and blessed us.

We came to the plain of Boeotia as the shadows were growing long, and Sir Giannis, who was leading us, took us well away from the town of Thebes on its lonely ridge. Thebes was held by the same Catalans who held Corinth. The sun was just setting in the west, and the fields of Boeotia were a fecund chequerboard of wheat and millet and rye, ten times as rich as the fields near Thermopylae, neatly laid out and irrigated. We went south and west, out of sight of the town, and we slipped over the dry bed of the Asopus.

I was busy shepherding our rearguard. We were tired: the bone-weariness of riding fast over rough country for two days without much rest and not enough food or water. The rearguard had not proven necessary at any time and the men in it, mostly archers, were 'tired of playing soldier' and tended to close up to the main body. I feared an ambush, feared a party out of Thebes, alerted to our presence, trying to have a snap at the column. In fact, one of the reasons I'm a good soldier, as opposed to merely a good knight, is that I'm so very good at being afraid.

At any rate, I got the rearguard onto the correct road with the help of John the Kipchak, and I left l'Angars in command of them and rode up a long, shallow ridge, to where I could see Nerio and Fiore and Sir Giannis with Benjamin the rabbi and his brother Isaac, all silhouetted against the pink sky. It was a beautiful evening, but then, Boeotia is itself beautiful.

Sir Giannis smiled his Greek smile as I came up.

'I waited for you,' he said.

I smiled. If I have done Giannis an injustice, I'm sorry. He was ordinarily a quiet man, who expressed himself in cautious smiles and very slight frowns and never committed himself too strongly. On occasion, passion for a subject, usually the history of Greece, would bring out a different man – forceful, even loud.

At any rate, the statement that he had waited for me was said in a level tone, but I knew that he meant it as an affirmation of friendship; he had truly waited, holding his passion in check, so that I would be there.

I had to grin. I liked him, even with his reserve. One of the best men I have known.

He waved a hand over the great plain.

'This was called the Dance Floor of Ares,' he said. 'The plain of Boeotia was the site of many great battles in the ancient world; the greatest of all was the Battle of Plataea. Plataea is that village over there where the farmers are burning off their fields. See?'

I did see.

He waved. 'The Greeks were over there,' he said. 'We're sitting on the ridge where the Persians formed their army, or so I have always imagined it. A million Persians and a hundred thousand Greeks.'

Nerio shook his head. 'A million? That's not possible.'

Fiore shrugged. 'Imagine feeding a million men?' he asked.

I just shook my head. I was finding a hundred men a challenge. I couldn't imagine a million men; even their latrines would be impossible. I tried to imagine the size of camp that they'd require.

And yet, *it had happened.*

Nerio was calculating, like the banker he was.

'A million men ...' he said. 'They would drink rivers dry.'

I was looking down at the green-lined banks of the dry ditch that was called Asopus. The river existed, in that the banks were green and the irrigation ditches ran into it, but there wasn't enough water in it to water our horses, much less the horses of a vast army.

'Who won?' Fiore asked.

'The Greeks,' Sir Giannis said. 'It was the day the Greeks won their freedom and avenged Leonidas.'

As we watched, the lights flickered out in Plataea.

Nerio had a fly-whisk riding whip he'd bartered from a Turk, and he used it to point at the distant villages. 'It's terrible, when you think of it,' he said.

'What is terrible?' asked Fiore, clearly annoyed.

Nerio frowned. 'The Greeks were enslaved by the Persians. The Athenians freed themselves at Marathon, and then had to fight again and again to preserve their freedom. Yet no sooner did they gain it than they fought among themselves for supremacy, like victors squabbling over spoils. Alexander conquered the world, so men say, and yet his empire did not outlive him because his generals squabbled among themselves, and eventually the Romans conquered it all, and the Greeks were a conquered people. And yet ... in the end, the language of the Roman Empire was Greek, not Latin; the philosophy and architecture of the Roman Empire were Greek.'

'Indeed,' Sir Giannis said, 'we still call ourselves Romans.'

'You read Greek?' asked the rabbi.

'A little,' Nerio said, with uncharacteristic modesty.

'Herodotus was from Halicarnassus,' Benjamin said. 'His people fought the Greeks. Thucydides was Athenian. His people lost. Yet a generation later, Athens had an empire again and Sparta was nothing.'

'So what is victory?' Nerio asked.

The Jew smiled. 'To a Jew, victory is survival,' he said.

Sir Giannis smiled too. 'Thus might speak a Greek, as well,' he said.

We camped in the ruins of the once mighty city of Plataea, below the little village, a village that Giannis assured me was full of Vlachs and where no one but the priest spoke any Greek at all. Yet the next day, when we clattered through their little town at the very break of day, there were dozens of men in tall fur hats in the streets, and they waved, and two little girls threw flowers, and when Giannis mentioned the name of Thebes, the men turned and spat.

'Thebes was, of old, their enemy,' Sir Giorgios said. 'It is something that these northerners continue to hate Thebes, when they are from Albania and the Thebans are all Spaniards.'

L'Angars was a more thoughtful man than his brutish face proclaimed him, and he shook his head as we clattered along. 'If a man is a Gascon,' he said, as if chewing his words carefully, 'and he gives his word to serve the King of France, is he then a Frenchman? Or if he then, in turn, gives his word to serve the King of England, is he then an Englishman?'

'He'd have to speak English,' Gospel Mark said.

'Nah, that's daft,' Rob Stone said. 'You speak French well enough, Mark.'

'So if an Albanian comes to Plataea, what makes him Greek?' Mark asked.

L'Angars nodded, agreeing with the question. 'Sir Giannis says these men do not speak Greek,' he said.

'And they dress differently, and they herd sheep, where the men on the plain grow wheat.'

'The men on the plain are Greek?' Lachlan asked.

'Partly Greek and partly Catalan and …'

'And everything else in the world,' Lachlan said. 'Except Erse. I don't think the Erse have made it here.'

L'Angars shrugged. 'So who is Greek?'

Gospel Mark made a wry face. 'Who is English, my lord?' he asked. 'Normans and Gascons and Irish and Saxons … Lachlan barely speaks English …'

'I'm not English!' Lachlan spat. 'I'm a Scot.'

Sir Giorgios smiled. 'But to me, a Greek, you are English.'

Gospel Mark laughed. 'Ye're daft,' he said. 'Sir Hector is no Englishman!'

And Lachlan looked as if he'd been stung.

But I looked at Sir Giorgios and understood him – that in addition to the way a man might feel about who he was, there was also how other men identify you.

I never asked these questions when I was cooking for Prince Edward's archers in Gascony. It was all simple then. But now I am a baron of Cyprus; I hold a parcel of lands from the Prince of Lesvos, and through him, from the Greek Emperor. And I hold lands from the Count of Savoy, who is in turn a vassal of the King of France. I accept money from a Florentine banker to fight his enemies in Outremer, and from Venice to fight Genoa. I have no knight's fee in England, no English wife, nor so much as a house or a field there.

Am I English?

We rode all day, to the west, along the Asopus valley, with Mount Kitharon towering on our left, lowering over us like a dragon over the plain below. The slopes of Kitharon stretch out to the skies, and Giannis told us that, in ancient times, men worshipped the mountain as a god, which no doubt sounds pagan and foreign and a little foolish, but when you look up at Kitharon, it has a majesty few mountains possess. And while the plains of Boeotia are a fine patchwork of neat Frankish farms, the mountain is all old woods full of game, or so Sir Giannis assured me. We passed a beehive-shaped structure at the edge of the woods, and I thought it was a chimney or a smithy, but Sir Giorgios told me that it was a tomb, so ancient that it might even date to the Trojan War and Hector and Achilles, and I dismounted for a while. Something made me kneel and pray there; it was like a scene in *Giron le Courtois* or *Lancelot*, and I rather expected to find a fountain and a maiden, or perhaps an old hermit to guide me to fight a pagan knight and win a magic sword.

Instead, I prayed in the cool, leafy green, and thought of the Holy Sepulchre, and fighting, and men who fought. And then Nerio came and demanded that I keep moving, as if I was a common soldier.

Ah, the life of chivalric romance.

At any rate, we moved fast. It took me half an hour of hard riding to catch the end of our column, with Nerio nagging me like a fishwife, and then we climbed a steep ridge on a track so narrow that we had to pass one horse at a time. I dismounted and led Gabriel myself, and left Marc-Antonio with his own horse and our riding horses; our two Greek brothers, Stefanos and Demetrios, about whom more anon, led the packhorses. We took almost an hour to ride over that ridge; it looked as high as the heavens but, like most of Outremer's landscape, proved smaller in fact than it appeared at a distance. The sun was almost destructive: armour burned when it touched you; even a buckle might be as hot as a fry-pan on a fire, and brass buckles got soft and bent. I've known knights of the Order who will have none but steel buckles on harness or tack, and in Outremer I learned why.

And while Boeotia and the 'Dance Floor of Ares' were criss-crossed with watercourses, wells, and Frankish peasants, the hills were as dry as the desert by the Dead Sea in the Holy Land, and dusty, so we were all parched. The Kipchaks warned us that we were being watched, so we had to close up our long files and look anxiously at the heights above us.

And then we were riding down off the ridge and we could see the Gulf of Corinth.

Nerio reined in with Sir Giorgios, who pointed at an impossibly high mountain at the very edge of the horizon.

'Acrocorinth,' he said.

'Sweet crucified Christ,' Nerio blasphemed.

I was used to the landscape of Greece by then, but that mountain seemed impossible, and more impossible for standing straight up like a column of rock from the sea, at least, when viewed from a distance of twenty miles.

'How high is it?' I asked.

Sir Giorgios shrugged. 'We will never storm it,' he said.

Nerio looked at me.

He was, perhaps, my best friend. Who was I to say no?

'We'll do it,' I said.

'No, you won't,' Sir Giorgios said. He smiled, as if to disarm anger. 'It is like threatening God that you will storm Heaven. If they have twenty men-at-arms, they can hold that mountain top against an army.'

Fiore looked at it under his hand. 'Too far for any detail,' he said. 'So not worth speculating.'

We rode down the ridge and through the brilliant afternoon, right down to the Gulf of Corinth and a tiny fishing village where every door was closed against us and the dogs barked. The Kipchaks stopped them from ringing their alarm bell beyond one clanging peal, and did so without killing anyone.

Sir Giannis found the priest, and arranged for water, and none too soon – we had men and horses already in a bad way. Greece is a cruel place to armies; I wondered why the Persians had wanted it, or why the Turks fancied it as, mostly, it seemed to be steep rock and desert. Beautiful, but hardly profitable.

From our tiny village, we moved rapidly west on a terrible path along the beach, often riding right along the shingle, on sand or gravel. The sand was fine; the round gravel was treacherous for horses' hooves, and we had to dismount. Now, men in harness are not fond of walking, especially on piles of shifting gravel in a boiling sun. The day stretched on, canteens were emptied, and Nerio kept us at it, and the mountain in the distance grew, sometimes hidden by an intervening ridge, sometimes vanishing behind a promontory.

But as the sun began to set in a western blaze of salmon pink and brilliant scarlet, the mountain was closer, and it seemed even bigger. It seemed impossible – a sheer rise from the ocean. The red sun began to gild the distant walls of the Acrocorinth and her citadel. We were perhaps four miles distant, on the darkling plain, known as the Isthmus of Corinth. The direct sunlight could not reach us to sparkle off our white harness or our spear points, as Nerio had planned.

The notion of a surprise attack seemed ... ridiculous. The Acrocorinth *was* as high as God's own Heaven. It towered over us like a huge dark cloud, and at the very top we could see, etched against the rose-pink sky, the lines of the walls. If they were visible at four miles, they had to be twenty or thirty feet high, and they went on and on.

At the edge of darkness, we made camp in a small bay on the north side of the isthmus. The base of the incredible mountain was perhaps two miles away; the town of Corinth was visible just over the hill, but Sir Giorgios had planned this part of the approach well, and we were virtually invisible to town and citadel. We had a spot of luck, too: John and our Kipchaks brought in a shepherd boy, who reported that a large force of Turks was moving through the same countryside as we were, a day or two ahead of us, going to raid the Peloponnese. The boy had been left behind. His name was Gregorios; he was fourteen, and my pages took him as one of their own. We ate his sheep. Let me add, if you seek to blacken my name, that he was a Vlach slave, taken captive in war; his owners abandoned him and his flocks to be taken by the Turks.

If they didn't want him, I certainly did. So did Sir Giorgios, who was happy to have a local guide.

As the moon rose – a summer moon and none too bright – the light shone down on the walls. We craned our necks looking up at the incredible majesty of that fortress. It was as far above us as a cloud in the sky on an English summer day, and I could see that the citadel, the actual Acrocorinth, was as high above the main gate as the gate was above the plain.

We had fires on the beach, screened with cut olive branches to be invisible from the west. The mutton was delicious, and there was bread and two cups of wine per man, knight or page or archer.

I knew we had no food after this. No wine, no fodder.

'You are staking everything on this assault,' I said.

Nerio shrugged. 'Yes,' he said. 'I hired the best men I could find,' he said, in Fiore's direction.

Fiore lay down in the gorse, or whatever Greeks call it – the low scrub full of thorns that decorates the Greek countryside and discourages courting couples, I suppose. Fiore was in a brigandine and was immune from thorns. I still thought him mad, but then I realised that he was studying the lofty fortress from a comfortable pose.

'We can take it,' he said.

I sent Marc-Antonio for l'Angars and John and Rob Stone, and we tramped down the low thorn bushes and sat in the darkness. We could see lights across the Gulf, and Sir Giannis pointed out the Vale of Delphi, where the ancients worshipped their pagan gods, and Naupactus, a strong fortress still held by the Emperor's people, although nowadays it is Venetian.

With the help of Sir Giorgios and the new boy, Gregorios, we drew the fortress in the sand.

Nerio was more subdued than I have ever known him. The fortress had frightened him; I could scarcely blame him. It was odd, though – as he was our *patron*, he was in charge, and the burden was on him, not me. I looked up at the fortress with some complacence. I know that's an odd word, but I felt a calm. Because it was clearly impossible, I knew that all I had to do was acquit myself well. It is much easier to fight well than to be in command.

The shepherd boy – let me hasten to add, greasy with mutton and relatively happy with his new masters – was nonetheless not full of answers. He didn't know of any secret approaches or hidden gates.

He had pastured his flock on the lower slopes, though, and he knew paths up to the walls.

'I've pissed on the walls,' he said. He grinned. 'I hate fucking Franks.'

We all smiled while he thought of what he'd just said. He looked stricken; Fiore laughed.

As an aside, I remember this night so well because of Fiore. He … how can I put this? He laughed. He laughed at the discomfiture of the boy, in a way that, I swear, he would never have laughed in the year I met him at Avignon. That laugh demonstrated a subtle understanding of the boy and his plight.

Fiore had grown. He knew how to talk to men, aye, and perhaps women. One woman, at least. He wore her favour, and he mentioned her from time to time, as if, by talking of her, he was closer to her. Her silk favour fluttered from his shoulder, catching the moonlight. Ah, love. Even for swordsmen.

I digress, but Fiore's laughter was not such a common sound that Nerio and I didn't glance at each other in wonder.

Fiore, remember, was lying in the gorse. He had a small stick, or baton, that he often carried – one of his many affectations, like big hats. He pointed with the baton at the lowering fortress.

'It is just an escalade,' he said calmly. 'If the boy can get us to a section of wall, and if it is unmanned, we're in. No different from any town in France or Italy. We take a ladder. Once we're in …' He shrugged. 'Well, it's just fighting.'

'We clear the gate,' I said. 'And open it to Nerio, who has most of the knights, *mounted.* We make a dash for the citadel.'

'*Christe Pantokrator*, we are going to storm Heaven on horseback,' Sir Giorgios said.

John the Turk raised both eyebrows. 'If you go to storm Heaven, on horseback is the best way,' he said.

Nerio looked at me. I understood Fiore immediately; he meant, in his laconic way, that if we made a dash and were quick enough, we might just snap the place up, the way we took Pont-Saint-Esprit and Gallipoli.

I agreed. When someone has a good, simple plan, there's no need to elaborate or waste time or energy.

'What if the wall is held against us?' I said.

'Take some archers to clear it,' Fiore said.

'Just like France,' said Rob Stone.

A fire burst, like the dawning of a new star, high in the fortress. A signal fire.

Nerio's head shot around like an owl's.

'We are discovered,' he said.

I scratched my chin. 'I doubt it,' I said.

'They have had a beacon every night,' the boy said.

'How many men on the main gate?' I asked the boy.

'Many!' the boy said. 'All in armour like yours!'

Nerio sank down on his haunches, his face as haggard as I have ever seen.

'How many?' I asked. 'As many as we are?'

'More than ten,' the boy replied. He was speaking a very odd Greek, but both Nerio and Giannis understood him well.

'Twenty?' I asked the boy.

He counted on his fingers for a while. 'More than ten,' he said, with doubt in his voice. 'Many.'

'And on the wall?' I asked.

'Many,' he said.

'You have a spy inside the fortress,' I said to Nerio.

'I can't wait around to contact him,' Nerio said. 'And he isn't really mine. It might take me a week to get him a message. We will be discovered tomorrow. Or we are already discovered.'

I was still scratching my chin under my scraggly beard. I thought of how neat and elegant I had become on Lesvos, with Emile in my arms every day.

'Our armour and our training will be better, no matter what,' I said. 'Our horseflesh is better than anything they'll have.'

'Why?' Nerio said.

'Don't interrupt,' Fiore said. 'Besides, I agree.'

'So the risk to us is not that great,' I continued. 'If we fail ...' I shrugged. 'We mount up and ride away. If they pursue, we ambush them and slaughter them.'

'You are cocky,' Nerio said.

'This, from you?' Fiore said. 'There's no one in a thousand miles who can take us in a straight fight.'

'I feel as if our roles are reversed,' Nerio said. 'I am not sure I like being in command.'

'It grows on you,' I assured him. 'Listen, ask any of the veterans. L'Angars, I appeal to you: are we not safe enough, trying the escalade?'

L'Angars shrugged. 'I'll say confession first, if you don't mind,' he said. 'But *oui, monsieur.* If the escalade fails, most of us will simply ride away. Where are these Turks, though? Surely this beacon is to alert some covering force?'

We all looked at each other.

'Be bloody annoying to get attacked by Turks while we're storming the place,' Rob Stone muttered.

'John, take your people and perhaps, if Sir Giannis will allow it, his *stradiotes,* and sweep west; find the Turks and amuse them?'

'If we fail …' John said.

'We'll need to get water right away,' I said, 'How about the town?'

'It's my town,' Nerio said. 'I don't want it sacked. Those are my townsmen and my peasants.'

I looked at the ground again. The town was almost a mile from the mountain fortress; the town was placed right on the isthmus, so that ships could approach either beach, from the Gulf of Corinth to the north, the Aegean to the south.

'We will need the town,' I said, 'if we fail – for food and water.'

'No rape and no theft,' Nerio said.

I nodded. 'You do it,' I said. 'I know you are the *patron,* but we don't need you to storm the citadel. Pick a dozen men, seize the town gate …'

'Lachlan,' Fiore said. 'He's deadly, but he listens. We need Nerio for his spy.'

'Perfect,' I nodded. 'Send for Sir Hector, with my compliments.'

Nerio was nodding too. 'If he only takes the gatehouse …'

'We are covered,' I said. 'We wake up tomorrow with water and food. Mayhap we come up with another plan.'

'Mayhap we learn to fly,' Sir Giorgios said. 'I think you are all mad, but then, I saw you take Gallipoli, so perhaps …'

Fiore looked up at the stars. 'This is a great *empris,*' he said. 'I will wager a clean pair of gloves against a golden-hilted dagger that we take the citadel. This seems fair, as I have clean gloves, and you are much richer than I.'

Nerio managed a nervous smile. 'So if we fail, I'll have clean gloves,' he said. 'I agree, but that means I'm wagering against my own success.' His voice tailed into silence, and for a long time the only sounds were the crackle of gorse as one of us shifted slightly and the distant crashing of the waves. I had never seen him so quiet.

It took us most of the night just to climb the mountain.

I took just ten men-at-arms; including Marc-Antonio and Fiore; Nerio took all the rest, save the Irish and Scots. He was not even to leave camp until we lit a torch on the wall, which we thought would be visible for ten miles. When we signalled, Lachlan would go for the gate of the lower town and Nerio would ride for the gate of the fortress – about two miles – which was a ten-minute ride for an armoured man on horseback.

My party rode to the foot of the mountain without a challenge. I felt naked; there were no trees for a mile, the steep slopes were denuded even of soil, or so it seemed. In the dark, everything made a ridiculous amount of noise, and dogs barked constantly. Morea is full of dogs, scrappy mongrels who are half-wild.

I knew in my head that John and his Kipchaks were off to the west, already moving through the darkness, but that did nothing to cure my heart's feeling that I was sticking out my neck and some Catalan or Turk was waiting to cut it off with an axe.

We left our horses with pages when the slopes became too steep for them, but a man could still climb them. There was even a sort of goat-path, which the boy Gregorios pointed out. It started above a neat stone culvert to siphon run-off from spring rains away from the old Roman road.

If you have never climbed a mountain in armour, let me recommend that you do it by daylight. At night, you cannot see handholds; if you lose your balance even a little, down you go. L'Angars fell when we were barely ten minutes above the road; he crashed all the way to the road and lay there for a long time while I considered whether I had the strength to go back and look at him. It was like that. He only fell a hundred feet, and at that, it wasn't a cliff; he rolled over and over.

L'Angars was made of rawhide. After lying on the road for a bit, he got up, shook himself, and started to climb up behind us.

I was tired before we had even made it a third of the way up the mountain, and my upper thighs had that terrible feeling of tight rope before we were halfway. I ordered a rest, mostly for myself. The archers were still fresh, and I wondered about leg harness on a mountainside, but armour, as I have no doubt said before, is the best choice in the dark: you need something to save you from the sword you cannot see. I lay full length as long as I could, and then got to my feet. The moon had moved a long way across the sky. L'Angars caught up with us, and I seemed to be the only one flagging.

This time, I sent Gospel Mark first, with the boy Gregorios, and I followed the archers. This proved to be a foolish plan, as the archers easily outdistanced us and drew further and further ahead.

In minutes, they were too far ahead to stop unless I sounded a horn or shouted, which seemed like a daft idea. So up we went, sometimes on hands and knees. We made a lot of noise, however disciplined we were; men had canteens that rattled, and armour itself is never quiet. The mountain was as still as a grave; the doves, which coo all day in Morea, were silent at night. There were no owls, and the only cries were distant sea birds. And dogs.

Some of our noise gave us away.

We were three quarters of the way through our climb to the lower wall, which was itself perhaps five hundred paces of steep slope above the road. Let me add that the wall itself rose and fell, and we had to climb all sorts of ups and downs to reach it – probably fifteen hundred paces forward to climb five hundred paces up.

There was a horn, off to the north. The gate was that way, almost three quarters of a Roman mile from where we stood. I said the walls were huge; the circuit was perhaps a mile, and we were as far from the gate as our boy could manage. I had wagered that the garrison would be in the gatehouse and the citadel, and not out on the long walls all night. I mean, their paymasters probably *wanted* them out all night, but soldiers are lazy, or at least I hoped the bastards were lazy.

Not lazy enough. Maybe if I'd known more about the famous Catalan Company and Roger de Flor that night, instead of learning about him later, in Italy, I'd have been more cautious. Anyway, we heard the horn, and then, after climbing another minute, we saw a new signal fire.

I climbed faster, ignoring my burning tendons and tensioned muscles. Up and up, a switchback, a little sheepfold. I tripped over a low wall and fell, down and down, and hit hard, my basinet ringing on a rock. But I had fallen forward into a defile and not back off the mountain, and after a minute my head cleared and I picked myself up.

No one waited for me.

Men were shouting in Catalan, right above us, and suddenly the walls shut out the stars. There were men with torches almost above us. I say suddenly because I have no memory at all of those last hundred paces. One moment I was picking myself up from my fall – wincing where my left knee now hurt and noting that the flange that protected my left knee was bent – the next moment, somehow, I was at the base of the great wall.

An arrow from a light crossbow bolt rang off my basinet, skipped off my pauldron like a punch in the shoulder, and shattered against the stones at my feet.

In a well-planned escalade, you arrive at the foot of the wall unnoticed, on flat ground where you can assemble and put up your scaling ladders, which you do in perfect silence. You beat the garrison to the top of the wall, and the town is at your mercy.

None of that happened.

Instead, heavy rocks began to appear out of the darkness. Gospel Mark took a stone right in the helmet and went down.

'Slings!' shouted someone.

I heard the little stones slapping against the ground and ricocheting off into the night.

'Ladder!' I barked.

'Going as fast as we can,' spat Rob Stone.

Another archer fell.

I took another hit in the pauldron, my left shoulder this time, and the pain was immediate and intense. I swore.

It was terrible: the darkness, the hail of stones, and crossbow bolts flying through the air like javelins from Jove himself.

All the archers were assembling the ladder. It struck me, suddenly, that this was insane – the ground sloped so sharply away from the walls that there was nowhere to put a ladder. And there were thirty men above us. The whole fortress was alarmed.

'Forget the ladder,' I snapped at Rob. 'Can you hit them?'

Stone turned and picked up his war bow, which lay already strung at his feet. He raised it, fitting a heavy arrow, and both bow and arrow shaft shone silver in the moonlight. A stone struck by his feet, the moonlight danced off a man's helmet up on the wall, and in one movement he raised his heavy bow, spread his shoulders and loosed.

His arrow went home; the shriek told its own story. That one arrow changed the night.

Men who are not being shot at have all the time in the world to pelt you with rocks, to whirl big slings at odd angles, to take their time with the placement of a crossbow bolt.

Add any return fire and those same men will behave very differently. In ten heartbeats, the hail of stones became an occasional *snap*, *crack* of a stone hitting the rock at our feet. The slingers stopped altogether after one of the Gascon archers feathered a slinger who leaned way out over the wall, as he had to to whirl his sling, and he fell at our feet, his neck broken from the fall, still screaming in shock.

I stopped watching and got to work on the ladder. The moonlight was full of tricks, but we couldn't light a torch because Nerio would think we were signalling him to attack.

Rob Stone said later that the shot-stour was won and lost by moonlight: the men on the wall had the moon behind them, so the men at the foot of the wall could see them silhouetted against the light of the sky. That's not my impression; my feeling is that the Catalans had it all their own way for a few minutes and had no heart for losses – two of their men had been killed and they all hid behind the pylons and crenellations.

I was still trying to fit wooden rungs into the ladder-sides while l'Angars and Fiore tried to get the ladder's folding legs extended.

Someone on the wall lit a torch. He did it behind the crenellations, but the effect was to bathe the back of the wall in an orange glow. Gospel Mark, up and functioning again despite a deep dent in his helmet from the rock he caught earlier, loosed with a grunt, and a second later, so did Stone and then Ewan, and there were shouts.

Ewan grinned like a loon and lofted an arrow impossibly high.

He shrugged. 'They're behind the wall,' he said. 'I can drop arrows there.'

'No one can do that,' Gospel Mark said.

They began to loose arrows while arguing what kind of shaft would be best for plunging fire.

I got another rung into the ladder. A shower of stones hit us, and Ewan cried out and dropped, cursing, blood flowing through his fingers – someone had thrown a bucket of gravel over the wall. A small stone had cut off his earlobe and it was bleeding like fury, but Ewan was damaged only in his vanity. His face was mottled in the moonlight, the blood like a black spiderweb across his face.

I got another rung into the ladder. I laid the thing along the base of the wall, and Fiore and I began to hammer at the sides, trying to get it to stay together.

Right at the base of the wall was the most dangerous place, because that's where they dropped the biggest stones. One hit my ladder and bounced away. The ladder had been with us since Pont-Saint-Esprit. It was English oak, and, though it was far from home, it was still strong.

'Ready!' I roared in English, a language I assumed my adversaries would not know.

Men ran towards me in the dark. By God, I lie. Men staggered and climbed and tottered towards me. The ground, if it can be called that, was so uneven that when Gospel Mark drew his bow, one foot was three feet above the other and he looked like he was kneeling sideways.

But they came. They got on the ladder, and pushed – there was some yelling. Stones fell on us, and Fiore was hit. There was cursing in six languages, but the ladder went up, and as soon as it scraped on the stone, all the archers left it, ran, hobbled or jumped to their bows, and began to send shafts profligately at the head of the ladder. This was our style; the archers weren't aiming, they were simply showering the area around the head of the ladder with arrows, and woe betide any enemy that tried to push the ladder down.

There was one brave man, though. The ladder shuddered and tottered, as someone very strong pushed it away from the wall, but the steepness of the slope and the eight men holding the base steady saved it.

There was nothing for it. Someone had to go up. Don't think less of me. We all hesitated.

Everyone looked at me.

That's how it is. They look at you, and you have to go. I don't know whether that's courage or cowardice, but when your friends look at you, even in the moonlight, you know what they mean.

Show me the way. That's what they are saying. *Lead me up*.

'Follow me!' I bellowed, and started up the ladder.

It was terrifying. I had lots of time to be terrified: long enough to not be able to see the head of the ladder; to wonder if it was too short; to think about how fucking obvious I was to the enemy; and how many rocks it would take to brush me off like a fly from a farmhouse wall in summertime. My legs felt like they were made of lead and my head hurt. Probably my fingers and toes hurt too.

I wasn't hit a single time. The reason was the archers. Their rhythmic, almost obscene, grunts at the base of the ladder rose out of the darkness at my feet like a hymn of comfort, and their shafts passed within inches of my back. No man ventured a shot at me save one crossbowman bold enough to peek out further along the wall when I was almost at the top. I never saw him, but I heard his scream, and then . . .

And then, by God, I was up. My pain was forgotten, and I was in between two merlons. I tripped, just as I had way back in France, and fell forward onto a man with a spear. His spear missed me in the dark and then we were tangled on the catwalk. I mangled him with my knees, my elbows, my fists and the pommel of my sword and then I was up. There were two dead men by the ladder, another breathing blood, and the man I'd just pulped. I had time to look left and right.

A crossbowman shot me from so close I saw his fingers move on the stock of his bow in the moonlight.

His shaft slammed into my right cuisse, just a finger's width to the outside of the ridge by my groin. An inch the other side and I was a dead man, but all the bolt did was knock me down and leave me a bad bruise.

I got my legs under me, and went for him.

He threw the crossbow and ran.

The fire behind the wall was big by then and no doubt served as a signal to the garrison that this was the location of the assault, because by its light I could see a dozen men coming up, the firelight washing their armour and their maille and brigandines. Franks, like me. Catalans.

The ground inside the walls was as steep as the ground outside. It might have taken the spirit from me, if I had had a glimmering of what was in store, but I did not, so I whirled and ran along the wall towards the gate. The slingers there were virtually naked – none of them wanted to face me – and they dropped off the wall. There were a dozen of them, and none of them stayed. One twisted his ankle in the drop, and he screamed and begged men to come and help him, wedged between two slabs of volcanic rock, lit by the pyre.

I ran on, careful of the drop on my left, and reached the head of the steps to the interior of the vast fortress at the same moment that one of the Catalan sergeants was climbing up them. He had a heavy pole-hammer.

I had a sword.

He should have thrust, but he whirled the head back, and I cut down on his gauntleted hands, and he was done. I probably broke all his fingers, and then my point scraped his nose and my left hand pushed him back down the steps.

Sic transit gloria mundi.

'Leave some for me,' Fiore said.

And we were in.

'In' wasn't worth all that much. We were inside the damned wall, but we were three quarters of a mile from the gate to the town, and the ground inside the fortress was … more mountain: slabs of rock, gravel, tufts of grass, and never a yard of flat.

I sank to one knee. I thought I was exhausted, which shows how little, still, at that age I knew about my body.

'Hold,' I panted. I doubt I roared it. Fiore was going down the steps. He looked back.

'Make them climb to us,' I said.

The Catalans had no interest in climbing, though, and formed a little line about twenty yards away. That might have been a good idea, except that Ewan came up the ladder and started dropping shafts among them. L'Angars followed him, and then, very quickly, the rest of my men-at-arms.

The Catalans ran. We panted and scraped along behind them.

'Does the wall run all the way to the gate?' I asked.

Gregorios didn't know, in any language.

'Stands to reason,' Gospel Mark said. 'Garrison here ought to be all goats.'

'Bring the ladder,' I wheezed at Rob Stone.

We headed off along the walls. The catwalk behind the merlons was not straight, but it was smooth, better by far than crossing that infernal stony ground.

At some point, we realised all the Catalans had run off. It might have mattered later but, for the immediate objective, it didn't matter a damn, and we moved from tower to tower. None were occupied, and we turned a corner and saw the gatehouse and the steep road running like a ribbon down to a moonlit sea, like in some tale of romance.

The sight of the gatehouse put heart into us, even though it was like a separate fortress, strong and tall, built into the side of the hill, a thousand feet above the sea.

But then, at last, we had a little luck. The door, four layers of oak board clenched with iron bolts, was open, and the catwalk was bathed in the glow of oil lamps from within the tower.

Of course it was.

There were crossbowmen up in the tower above us, shooting down into a milling pack of mounted men-at-arms on the road below us.

Why, you ask?

Because signals are for fools, and when the garrison lit their beacon behind the wall just before Rob Stone started throwing shafts back, Nerio assumed that was us *on the wall* and he galloped along the coast road and up to the gate …

Far too early. His best warhorse was motionless on the ground and his squire, Achille, was lying in Father Angelo's arms with a bolt through his left pauldron. It was fucking chaos out there, and my friends and my company were trapped like fish in the proverbial barrel by expert crossbowmen.

No one was looking at us. And the door was open.

I remember it as one of the longest runs of my life. I thought that I was tired, but God, or fear for Nerio, gave me wings, and I ran like Hector, heedless of the condition of the wall or the catwalk. But Fiore, for all his snaps at Nerio, was faster – he ran like Achilles, and I had to be second. He threw himself through that door heedless of what might wait on the other side.

We were in a room full of women. Perhaps ten of them – big, strong women with cooking implements and knives, and they knew we were the enemy as soon as we went in.

They screamed and came for us.

We didn't kill them. I'm proud of it. Our blood was up, our friends were at risk, and in a storming action there are no rules. But Fiore wasn't going to kill a woman, and I wasn't either. I took an iron poker on my vambrace and put the first woman down with a sweep of my armoured forearm across her throat. I kneed the next, caught her leg and threw her, pommelled another, and they broke, screaming, and ran or fell down the central steps.

'Up!' I called to l'Angars. Fiore stopped at the head of the stairs to breathe and because we needed someone to hold the steps behind us. L'Angars and I went up, with Ewan at my shoulder. Lascaris came up with l'Angars.

A bolt missed me.

Ewan got the crossbowman, and I was going up, my legs still, somehow, functioning, the spirit of war driving me, and I climbed. Another crossbowman flinched and didn't loose his bolt, and Ewan dropped him, too, and then I was out on the roof of the tower. My left arm was not functioning well, there was something wrong inside my helmet, and my legs felt like they were made of wood.

Despite all that, I could hear young Francesco roaring like a lion down in the dark, demanding that the men-at-arms stand fast.

'Saint George!' I called.

I was on the roof, and there were a dozen crossbowmen, most of them in their nightshirts.

L'Angars came up behind me, and I flipped my visor open, regardless of the crossbowmen.

'Saint George!' I roared.

Down on the road, I heard young Francesco call 'Saint George!'

Ewan's shaft dropped a man, and I turned to clear the wall.

They had cressets lit so that they could see to span their bows, and by that fitful light I saw a young man on his knees. I didn't speak a word of Catalan; he bared his neck.

Behind him, his mate used him for cover while he aimed at me.

I killed them both. I'd like to have spared the young man, but he was in my way, and I had time to cut up, and then back with a kick into the man with the crossbow. That's how I see it. It still sticks with me, but storming actions and escalades are terrible; everything dies.

Let's make this brief.

We killed them all. Mayhap we might have given quarter to the last two, but we did not. Aye. War is glorious, is it not?

*

The Gascons had the gate open before we cleared the top of the tower. Our men-at-arms burst in like water bursting a dam in spring and, as Nerio was dismounted, young Francesco led the charge up the road without an order or a word from anyone.

There were no wounded. The women were well up the slope, barely visible in the darkness. Nerio came in through the gate, and behind him were Sir Giorgios, his *stradiotes*, at least those who weren't with John, and a big mule, grunting in the darkness.

Nerio threw his arms around Fiore, and then me.

'Christ, I thought you were all dead,' he said.

'Christ, I thought the same, for a bit,' Fiore said.

Nerio paused. 'You made a joke,' he said.

Fiore made a face in the moonlight. 'I make jokes all the time,' he said. 'You're just too slow to understand them.'

'Citadel,' I said. It took all the willpower I could muster to get my leg over Gabriel's back. The saddle was comfortable. The high back supported me, and I swear I could have gone to sleep. I probably grunted. My shoulder was aching, waves of ache that meant it was probably broken.

'Citadel,' Nerio said. 'You stay. I can do this.'

'I wouldn't miss this for anything,' Fiore said. 'We are about to become the greatest knights in the world.'

The citadel hovered above us in the pale moonlight.

We were only halfway to the top.

Gospel Mark was sitting on the ground, head in his hands. Ewan had retched himself dry and was drinking Catalan wine.

'Bring the ladder,' I said. 'Let's go.'

Gospel Mark shot me a look of pure venom. Ewan dragged himself to the sturdy steppe pony that Marc-Antonio was holding for him. But both men mounted, and then we were riding into the darkness.

The fortress was so large that it took time to ride up to the second gate. We rode for perhaps the length it takes a priest to say the prayers over the Eucharist – maybe less. I was in quite a bit of pain by then, and I wasn't thinking well. But when we reached the gate, we found it strongly held, and young Francesco had all the men-at-arms and archers dismounted.

'Five shafts a man,' Rob Stone said to me.

That was bad. The only way to clear a wall so that the ladders could be used was to shower it in arrows – to drop so many shafts into the space around the ladders that no sane enemy would try to throw them down or to hold the ladder-heads.

'We have the only other gate,' I said to Nerio. 'Couldn't we just starve them out?'

'And when a relief force comes from Athens?' Nerio said. 'We'll be caught between armies.'

'Besides,' Fiore said, 'we want to have a great reputation, do we not?'

That may seem a reasonable thing to say, but in the firelit night, with slingstones raining on us and my shoulder throbbing as if a giant was squeezing it, it sounded insane. Glory goes to all the wrong men anyway, or so it often seems to me.

But Nerio agreed.

'I have a device,' he said. 'It will only work once – maybe not even once.'

'What is it?' I asked.

'Something I bought,' he said. 'It burns like Greek fire.' He turned, so that his hawk-nosed profile showed against the fires burning behind the second gate. 'I wanted to save it for the citadel.'

The big mule was now explained.

'Ever seen one of the alchemical siege engines?' Nerio said.

I had, too, and German handgonners as well. Italy was teeming with the foul stuff – smells like hell, burns like pitch. Faster than pitch. In the summer of 1367, I had no idea that the damn things were going to be part of my profession for the rest of my days. And, to be fair, we still thought of the alchemical powder as magic, or leastways unnatural.

Two pages stripped the straw panniers off the mule and from the wicker basket came an engine, like a cauldron of bronze. It had flanges cast into the rim, or what would have been the rim of a cooking pot, and each of the flanges had a hole in it.

'Spikes,' Nerio said. He produced a handful of black iron spikes, almost invisible in the darkness.

'How many men do you think they have on the gate?' I asked.

Fiore had gone forward, all the way to the dangerous zone where the crossbowmen could hit him, and returned. 'I think it's the same men we drove off the wall,' he said. 'Slingers and a handful of armed men.'

'Why are they fighting so hard?' l'Angars asked. It was a good question, a routier's question.

'They are well-paid, or they fear their master,' Nerio said.

'Or they think we slaughtered their women,' I said.

Nerio frowned. 'You didn't?' he asked.

'No, we drove them from the gatehouse. I broke a woman's nose,' I admitted.

'Not the most chivalrous thing to do,' Fiore snapped.

'She was trying to kill me,' I said.

Nerio shook his head. 'Where are they?' he asked.

I pointed into the rocks off to our left, which rose almost sheer and lay below a rise in the inner wall.

'I suppose that you spotless knights will object if I round them up and offer to execute them if they don't hand over the gate?' Nerio asked.

It was difficult to know whether he was serious.

L'Angars laughed. It was a deep, resonant laugh, the last thing you'd expect to hear in the hellish dark of a storming action.

'I'm sorry,' the Gascon said. 'It was the first thing I thought of. I was trying not to say it.'

'No,' Fiore said. 'We will not stoop to such a thing.'

'Won't we?' Nerio asked.

'We slaughtered every armed man in the tower,' l'Angars said.

'It's different and you know it,' Fiore argued.

L'Angars shrugged. 'Threatening the women might even save lives,' he said.

'Tell yourself any story you like,' Fiore said.

Nerio looked at me. I could see him clearly because of the glow of the fire behind the wall. He looked like a mild-mannered Satan. 'And you, William?' he said.

I wanted to say, *my shoulder hurts, and let's get this over with.* But chivalry is all about who you are when your shoulder hurts and you've had no sleep.

'My whole life depends on taking this gate,' Nerio said.

I took a deep breath. I thought of the Passion of Christ. Say what you will – Christ has a lot to teach a knight.

'If your whole life depends on this gate,' I said, 'then let us take it in a manner that all of us will be pleased to remember.'

Fiore lit up. He didn't light up often; joy was not his usual way of responding, even to pleasure. But he smiled broadly, and what I remember best is that, unthinkingly, he slapped me on the left shoulder.

I cried out and dropped to one knee.

And I'm not ashamed to say that I played it for all it was worth. Oh, he hurt me cruelly, but, regardless, I whimpered a bit and moaned, and Nerio called Fiore a stupid arse, and they were all contrite, and the moment passed when Nerio might have turned on Fiore. Or me. Or ordered a massacre.

I love Nerio. We are closer than friends. But, like me, he is a very bad man working hard to be good, and he doesn't always see that the easy way is the wrong way.

'Tell us about your engine,' I muttered.

All of our archers moved forward in a spread line, about five paces between them. All of them had an arrow nocked and another to hand.

We carried the bronze bucket between us. That is, Nerio and Fiore carried it – l'Angars and I were too badly hurt to carry something that weighed as much as a man.

I was having some trouble walking by then, and I thought that the stars were dimming overhead. Dawn was out there somewhere.

Our archers kept moving forward when crossbow bolts began to skip in among us, the shafts moving like snakes, invisible in the darkness, passing with a hiss before the *snap* or *crack* of the crossbow string could be heard. Rob called out every time they slowed. Men were tired; tired men take fewer risks.

Rob kept them going.

When the wall was less than a hundred paces away, and one of ours was lying silent with a bolt through him, Rob called out for the archers to halt.

Instantly forty heavy bows came up.

I lumbered into a fast jog. I could no longer manage a run. The slope was steep, but the road was paved. The archers were out to the sides of it in the broken, rocky ground. I just powered along, my smooth, leather-soled fighting shoes slapping against the paving stone, my greaves biting into the top of my feet despite a near-perfect fit, my padded hose weeping sweat, my brigandine weighing on my shoulders like a man's life of sin, my basinet a demon on top of my head.

A bolt struck the top of my helmet, and *whanged* off into the darkness. I didn't fall. I was, if it makes sense, *too tired* to fall. I jogged on.

I can't really imagine what it was like for Nerio and Fiore, carrying the whole weight of a church bell between them.

Slingstones began to strike me. One hit me in the chest and only my shambling run saved me; I had my weight well forward.

Another struck me. Those slingers were excellent. I got a stone in my left shoulder and I roared in anger and in pain, and managed a burst of speed that was more like the gallop of an old horse, and then I was in the shadow of the huge gate: double doors, ten layers of oak boards almost perfectly sheathed in iron bars.

Despite my injuries, I was first. Nerio and Fiore came in behind me, and l'Angars was down.

'Fuck,' I said, and went back into the dark.

I was hit immediately. I was hit three times like an armourer hits a rivet: *bang bang bang*. They knew we were going for the gate and they were afraid of us. After all, so far we'd beaten them like a drum.

I couldn't see. My visor was closed and everywhere was dark. I remember moving my whole head back and forth, looking for some point of light to orient myself, it was that dark.

My basinet had a high back point, a little like an onion, and it shed blows well, but the rock that hit me next knocked me to my knees and jammed my basinet down around my throat. I had heavy padding in there, and the stone drove my helmet down on my head, bounced off the back plates of my brigandine and rolled away. I was on my knees, and I thought my neck was broken.

I lost a few minutes. I remember nothing but darkness, and the smell of blood. And then I was moving again, getting hit by slingstones. I think that the crossbowmen were afraid to come to the wall; no bolts hit me while I was an obvious target.

Someone threw a torch down, and then another, to light me up.

I saw l'Angars. He was crawling, and his left leg was bent under him.

'Got you,' I said. My neck was odd; my head didn't want to turn. I wanted my helmet off. I was having trouble seeing, and I was sure something was wrong with the helmet or my head or both, but what mattered was l'Angars. I got his hands and pulled. I was probably hit by more stones, but I don't remember anything. I dragged him about forty feet, from where he lay in the fire-shot darkness to the base of the wall.

I heard a loud hammering.

'Help us!' shouted Nerio, and turned into the gateway.

They were using the iron spikes to nail the bronze cauldron to the gate.

It was a brutal job, because so much of the gate was covered in iron bars and nail heads that it was impossible, or nearly impossible, to find purchase for a spike on the gate, and the spikes had to be driven home tight, or so Nerio shouted.

Really, we were saved by the men on the wall, who were throwing more and more torches, looking for us.

I plucked my little war hammer off my plaque belt and managed to grasp a spike with my armoured hand.

'Low,' I growled.

'Low?' Fiore asked.

'We don't need a hole four feet in the air,' I panted. 'Put it on the ground.'

Fiore complied immediately; he had been holding the cursed thing up on the gate. He pressed the mouth of the bell against the gate, and I probed with my good hand, running the head of the spike back and forth . . .

I found something soft, and swung my hammer. My left arm shot pain from shoulder to wrist, but I had other concerns, and I got the spike in.

Nerio was no laggard and he got a spike in on his side, and then we were kneeling in the dust of a big gate. I remember noting that there was a pat of horse dung right where the gates closed, under my knee, and thinking that Marc-Antonio was going to hate me, and then the last spike was in the gate, and we stumbled back.

'Oil!' l'Angars shouted.

I got out of the gate in time to see the stuff being poured down the wall. I got him under the shoulders, dragging him into the shadow of the gate. His heels were just ahead of the spreading, dark, inky stain of the stuff, and smoke rose from it.

'Loose!' called Rob Stone in the darkness, and there was a scream above us.

'Now!' Nerio said. 'Outside, now!' He took a sputtering torch from the ground and pressed it to the dangling string of nitre-impregnated thread that coiled from the bronze engine's apex, and fire raced up the thread even as I dragged l'Angars back from the arch of the gate. I stepped in the oil; it was scalding hot, but not deadly.

To the left of the gate, a fallen torch caught a pool of oil and the flames leaped up.

I was going to shout a warning when the Hell Engine exploded.

I have no idea what it did. I've used them since, so I know what a petard is now, but at the time, I was unprepared for the sound, the incredible burst of flame and heat, and I had a stone corner between me and the blast. Fiore was knocked flat, Nerio lost all one side of his beard, and none of us could hear for minutes.

My left foot was on fire. The oil had caught. I stamped, and l'Angars, on the ground, got his hands on it and put it out. Everything happened silently.

I was stunned. I couldn't think; putting out the fire on my foot just about used up my reserves.

Fiore rose like Lazarus. He had his sword in his fist, and he pointed at the gate. He opened his mouth, and I could see his tongue and his teeth; perhaps he was shouting.

He ran.

I followed him. I had enough sense to guess that he was telling me that the gate was open.

And it was. The force of the engine had blown a six-foot hole in the gate. Behind should have been a second gate, or a portcullis. But the inner gate was open, wide open, and we were inside, stumbling in deafened silence up the stone steps.

The garrison ran. They ran along the walls to the right and left above us, and as our archers poured in behind us, they began to chase the enemy down, or at least to push them to run faster.

Nerio and I got the wrecked gate open.

Young Francesco burst through the gate on horseback, and behind him were Giannis and Giorgios and twenty other armoured men. They went straight up the hill to the citadel, still two hundred paces above us. Marc-Antonio brought me Gabriel, and I mounted. That is, Marc-Antonio and my Greek boys pushed me into the saddle and acted as human mounting blocks. Marc-Antonio handed me my war hammer, which I had lost in the scuffle, and tried to tell me something, patting his head.

The citadel was above us. Between the second gate and the citadel was a small town: a fine church, an Italianate palazzo of some quality, if a pain-shot glance in moonlight can be any judge, and forty or fifty good stone houses. Everything was dark, but there were cressets burning in baskets on some of the buildings and on the walls of the citadel.

I was behind Francesco, but I caught him up easily. He was cautiously moving our knights through the town. I couldn't hear him, so I played no part except to motion for him to continue giving orders. I was still getting over the stunning nature of the explosion; I couldn't hear, but I could feel pain from all my little wounds and abrasions, and, to add to the scene, the charred remnants of my fighting shoe came off my left foot in mounting, so I was fully armed except for sabatons, and yet my left foot was bare. My head was pounding and my visor wasn't quite right, but I didn't have time to fix anything.

Well. The things you remember.

We felt our way through the town, men facing every street. This is another skill practised only by routiers – covering streets as you move, so you do not get surprised. Town and cities are terrible traps, worse than canyons and gorges.

But the town was small, and in a few minutes we were on the last switchback, past the palazzo on the right, and a stone barn or warehouse on the left. Above us towered the three turrets of the citadel, a thousand paces above the sea far below.

Francesco was trying to speak to me. I pointed at my ears and he shrugged.

He ordered all the men-at-arms to dismount. I only knew that when I was the only one mounted. Above us were about a hundred steps, and on the steps stood a huddle of Catalan men-at-arms. I think there were only three. At the time, they seemed like a hundred, and they were above me.

Spirit is everything in battle. If this had happened earlier, I might have hesitated, but by the Virgin, I was a hundred stone steps from the top.

I dismounted, took a spear – a short one – from Marc-Antonio and, barefoot and all, I went up the steps. There were no slingstones or bolts flying, and we were in range of the gate. That was a good sign. They were out of crossbowmen and slingers.

Fiore was commanding men lower in the town, and Nerio was nowhere to be seen. L'Angars was wounded. I had young Francesco Gatelussi, Sir Giannis and Marc-Antonio.

We all had spears, and we started up the steps. The Catalans didn't come down to us, which I think was an error. They waited, and we climbed, and I can't remember how often we stopped to rest, but we did. I did. I remember stopping just four or five steps below them. I suppose they said things, but I couldn't hear, so I just stood there, panting, my bare foot curiously cold on the stone.

Then I turned and gave Francesco and Marc-Antonio a little shove, spacing them out, so that I was in the middle, one step above them, and they were on the outside of the steps. The steps had been built into the steepest part of the rock; the citadel above us was lit in the grim grey of a false dawn.

Both of the Catalans in front had poleaxes.

Behind them, the other two had spears. They all wore armour that was a little antiquated – double maille with some heavy plates, leg armour that was more modern, Milanese or Brescian maybe, and kettle helmets.

I tell you this because Fiore had taught us that the first thing you do in an armoured fight is evaluate your opponent's armour.

I held my spear high. It's not a good *garde*, but when you fight on steep stone steps in the dark, there aren't really any good *gardes*.

I went up the steps. I went up against the two men in front and the two in back because that's how I wanted it; I trusted my squire and Francesco to cover my shoulders. I wanted space.

I knew we were better, man to man. Fiore gave us that. And like fear, fatigue and injury fell away as I saw his axe-head come forward. In that one move, taking a guard with his heavy weapon head forward, my chosen target forfeited all his advantage of height and strength of weapon, and showed me how little confidence he had.

My spear had lugs below the head, like a crossbar. A *ghiavarina*, they call it in Italy. I got my bare left foot up one step, my spearhead shot forward, my opponent tried to cross and my crossbar caught his axe-head.

In a breath, my spear-point was buried in his forehead. I cleared it by swinging the butt up into his mate's axe. It was clumsy, but I tied his weapon and Marc-Antonio killed him with a flick of his wrist, putting his spear-point through the maille under his arm and into his lungs.

The spearmen on the upper steps were hampered by their own friends, and as my first victim fell off my spear-point, I swung my spear into the shin of the next man. Foolishly he tried to parry my cut; he had leg armour that would have done it for him. Francesco killed him over my shoulder.

I went up a step. There were two more men, now, just hurrying down the steps – one in full harness, and one still struggling with a big gorget, or neck guard.

The second spearman tried for Marc-Antonio. I put my butt-spike into his hip, inflicting little damage, and then I pushed with all my weight, collapsing his body structure so that he sat back on the stair above him. He lost his spear in the fall and I was up another step, my spearhead buried in the thigh of the man with the gorget, who screamed and fell, fouling my legs. His mate above me had a longsword, which he swung, grabbing for my spear with his other hand.

I shortened my grip until I had the spearhead in my right hand, the haft of the spear like a long tail behind me. The Catalan with the longsword tried a thrust and I turned it; he raised his arm for a heavy cut and I popped his elbow with my left hand, turning him. He backed a step and then another and I was on him, clambering over the man I'd dropped with a stab to the thigh. This one was the last. He cut, and backed, and cut, and I thought he must be someone's squire – brave, and not very good, cutting from out of distance and giving ground when he didn't have to. I followed him like a wolf follows a wounded sheep. At some point I'd caught my spear up in both hands, point up and back, butt-spike a little forward. Behind me, the man down on the steps surrendered to Marc-Antonio.

Perhaps we climbed six steps.

Then he was on flat ground. He had nowhere to run. He put both hands on his sword hilt and attacked.

My counter broke his arm and threw him to the ground, just as Fiore taught us. I didn't even kick him in the head. I was at the citadel.

The gate was closed. There was a postern, a smaller gate, set in the main gate. It was locked. I know; I pulled at it, because we needed a miracle. I thought the last man out from the garrison might have left it open.

Still, no one was shooting at us.

'Take him,' I said to Marc-Antonio. I guessed him to be someone worth a ransom. The squire, I mean.

The walls were about twenty feet high. Our ladder would make it to the top of a wall, but the man climbing it would be under fire from all three turrets.

I walked back down the infernal steps, my greave pounding my bare instep, got back on Gabriel, which was as hard as anything I'd done all day, and rode back to the second gate. I found Gospel Mark; it took me so long that the sun was rising. I could hear a little by then, and I managed to get him and Ewan to bring the ladder. The bloody thing weighed a ton, but the archers were full of spirit; after all, we'd almost done it.

We were like hounds that have scented blood.

By the time I returned to the gate, Nerio was there with Fiore. They were mounted, looking up at the gate, the three towers, and the lit window.

The sun was just cresting the horizon.

Nerio pointed at the ladder and spoke. I couldn't hear him well, but he was clearly delighted. Marc-Antonio spoke a bit, and then took a horn off his belt and sounded it. I heard it distantly, as if Marc-Antonio was far away.

The archers erected the ladder.

There was no one shooting.

I was damned if I was letting Fiore be first on the ladder, or Nerio. But Nerio insisted. Marc-Antonio sounded the horn once more; high above the gate, a shutter opened, and Nerio started up the ladder.

I got my foot on the bottom rung, ignoring Fiore's hands on my back.

A woman's voice shouted out. Isn't it odd? I couldn't hear what she was saying, but I knew it was a woman's voice from the timbre.

The voice came again, and Marc-Antonio shouted back.

Nerio was almost at the top, and I started to climb. It was terrible – like climbing up into Heaven with the burden of your sins on your back. Thighs, calves and hips all burning, left arm almost useless, bare foot and all …

I drew my arming sword, one-handed, at the top of the ladder. Nerio was still at the head of the ladder, leaning on the stone.

A Catalan man-at-arms stood a horse-length away with a spear. He was in full harness, and he had the spear in a very competent *garde*, point down, butt high, and he looked relaxed and capable and awake.

But he took a step back.

I could hear a woman's voice, shouting in Italian, a Tuscan dialect that I knew well, and Nerio laughing, again at a distance. I leaned against the stone of the parapet and struggled with my visor, and I took some deep breaths. The visor wouldn't stay up or down; it was bent on its hinges. Something was wrong with the whole helmet, in fact.

The Catalan knight stood there, relaxed, his spear now at his side.

'You are lucky to be alive,' he said in fluent Tuscan Italian. I only understood a few words, but I got the message well enough. I was hearing better; indeed, I remember crossing myself and thanking the Virgin for the restoration of my hearing. At any rate, I thought he was boasting about how tough he was. I was too tired and my body hurt too much to do any bragging, so I continued to lean against my stone wall.

Fiore opened his visor and glanced at me. His eyes widened.

'Oh, Blessed Virgin,' he said.

Fiore was ignoring the Catalan knight, and both of them were staring at me.

Nerio laughed again. 'Done!' he called, in Italian. 'Stop fighting!'

The woman called out, 'We have surrendered and we will all be ransomed by Lord Renerio of Florence.' At least, later that's what Marc-Antonio told me. At the time I heard her as a sort of braying sound. I knew it was Italian but I was having trouble with words.

The Catalan glanced at me. 'This is true? If I put up, you will not kill me?'

I bowed. So did Fiore. Fiore made a long speech and the Catalan relaxed. Apparently, he said, 'You have my word of honour that no harm will come to you so long as you do us no harm.' Fiore says that his careful phrasing was 'because you need a long spoon to sup with the Catalans'.

Our knight nodded. He looked down into the courtyard, and gave a half-smile. Then he laid his spear against the wall. 'I'm the only one here,' he said. It was the first phrase that I understood in its entirety. My ears were clearing. 'I hope you didn't kill my squire. I like him.'

I nodded, but Fiore started. 'Where is the rest of the garrison?' he asked.

'Out there, fighting you,' our Catalan said in his accented Italian. He seemed very pleased with himself, and I didn't blame him. A brave man. At the same time, he seemed curiously unconcerned with the fate of his comrades.

I was sagging. I could barely keep myself upright, and I had to rest my head on the stone of the wall for a moment. And then I looked down. There was blood all over my brigandine, and I *had* to get my basinet off.

It would not budge.

Fiore came over to me, and held my arms. 'You will do yourself a mischief,' he said. 'Stay. Stop, William. You are hurt badly.'

I didn't feel as if I had been hurt badly. That is, I hurt all over, but I did not have that feeling I knew too well, the feeling of getting badly cut, or worse, stabbed. Thrusts are the most terrifying wounds. I didn't have that feeling, the sticky feeling when your muscles don't work right that comes before the pain of the wound.

But something was wrong. I felt light-headed, and Fiore was watching me the way a mother watches a sick child.

We tried to get the basinet off. If you have never worn one, basinets have aventails, a hood or cloak, if you like, of maille that keeps lances and spears and sword points out of your throat and chin. Basinets do not have metal under the chin, so they are fairly simple to remove.

Not this one.

Before the sun was up, I was on my knees, and the Catalan knight was helping Fiore, a knee against my shoulder. The pain was intense, and then the basinet came free.

My helmet liner was black with blood, and the whole top of my helmet was crushed. My left ear was partly torn from the flesh of my scalp and now dangled painfully. The removal of the helmet tore open the new scabs . . .

And I was gone.

I've had worse wounds, but I've never had any more annoying. I was only out a day, and even then, Albin told me later that I'd passed from faint to sleep very quickly and he'd never worried about anything but infection.

I awoke in a bed. It was a good bed, and my linen sheets all but sparkled in the light of a new day. Father Angelo was by the bed, reading from my Vegetius.

He glanced at me and smiled. He was unshaven, and he'd clearly sat with me all night. Want to know what men think of you? Take a wound.

Regardless, he gave me a cup of small beer, and I drank it greedily and then two cups of water. My head swam every time I raised it, and it was wrapped in bandages like some sort of tight turban, but I was quite expert at being wounded. I worked my various limbs and muscles, and everything seemed good except my left shoulder and my left hip. The hip was stiff and cold; the shoulder was not broken, but was almost immobile anyway. I was wrapped in linen, prickly with heat.

'Master Albin sewed your ear back on,' Father Angelo said. 'There were quite a few wounded. He went to see to them.'

He showed me my basinet, or what was left of it. The visor still worked – the pivots were intact, a miracle – but the onion top, the long spike, was crushed in and the whole top of the helmet crumpled like vellum tossed aside by an angry scribe.

I had a new helmet, which I had commissioned in far-off Brescia. I'd tried it on but never worn it. 'I'll need a new helmet,' I muttered.

Father Angelo was glaring at me. Glare is too strong a word. He was watching me with a look that held a reprimand. 'Is that all you think when you see this?' he asked. 'L'Angars says you were hit in the head by a stone as big as a house, and you lived. He thinks it's a miracle from God.'

I laughed. 'He's lucky it didn't hit him,' I joked.

Father Angelo shook his head. 'The word that comes to mind is "thankless",' he said. 'God preserved your life.'

I thought that my friend Jiri, the armourer in Venice, had preserved my life, but I understood, and the crumpled basinet stood on the sideboard in mute testimony to God's mercy. I prayed, and Father Angelo prayed with me.

'What happened to the women?' I asked.

He nodded. 'I found them, with l'Angars. They are in the hall, making food.'

'The rest of the garrison?' I asked. 'Our own casualties?'

'Lapot is wounded, of the knights, and l'Angars. Lord Renerio's squire, Achille, is in a bad way. Ricardo 'All, of the archers, is dead, and four others wounded badly.'

Ricardo 'All was Dick Hall, who'd joined us the summer before. He was English, from Lincoln. A hard-drinking man, and now dead.

I said a prayer for them.

'Master Albin is with the wounded,' he said. 'The garrison is mostly intact, and outnumbers us; we have over a hundred prisoners.'

Nerio pushed into the room, carrying a tray. 'So as soon as you are done malingering in bed,' he said, 'I'm going to need you on your feet.'

On my feet proved a bit of a misnomer; my hip was in a bad way, and I couldn't bear the weight of harness or walk well, but I could sit in the hall and give orders. So I did. Nerio was securing the lower town with Lachlan, and then he was out with the Kipchaks, and then he was engaging local *stradiotes*.

It turned out that one of the reasons our surprise had been so complete, at least until the slingers heard us on the hillside, was that Nerio's uncle, Angelo, the bishop of Patras, had died just a week before. The Catalans had been ready for weeks, waiting for Angelo to attack them; they relaxed when they heard of his death.

His death had another effect that Nerio had never anticipated. Angelo's men-at-arms appeared on our third day in the fortress, and assumed that Nerio would take them on. There were about sixty lances, most of them men I remembered from the year before, when Angelo Acciaioli had hosted the Green Count and negotiated with him. They swore to Nerio on the spot, and so did most of the Catalans who'd survived our attack; that was life in Morea. Or Italy, really.

Let's discuss the benefits of chivalry for a moment.

We'd killed about twenty of them – mostly the crossbowmen in the tower. We didn't rape their women, and we took prisoners, like the man on the stairs I put down and the squire I dropped at the top. Consequently, the Catalans had no reason to hate us; it was all business.

See? Chivalry. If you must kill people for your living, best do it with grace and honour. And rules.

By the time Nerio had been in possession of Corinth for a week, a Venetian merchant round ship came across from Naupactus, and sent a longboat in cautiously. I sent Marc-Antonio aboard, and he came back with the captain, who climbed all the way to the top of the Acrocorinth to visit us, because he was our old friend Carlo Zeno.

By then I could stand without too much pain, and we embraced, although even that hurt my shoulder.

'It is the greatest feat of arms of the age,' he said. 'I confess I'm jealous.' He looked out over the Gulf of Corinth. 'This could be a great port,' he said thoughtfully.

'That's what I intend,' Nerio said, and the two of them spoke almost without pause, from afternoon through Vespers, about how to improve the warehouses and the port facilities. To me, it was all wishful thinking; Corinth was a pleasant, backwards town with small houses and nothing to ship, that I could see, but the two of them seemed afire.

After Mass, I asked Zeno if he had space in his huge ship to take twenty lances to Venice.

He smiled. 'And here I thought there was no cargo,' he said.

We haggled and haggled. I'm not particularly good at haggling, but luckily, Marc-Antonio filled my need, arguing that we could ride over to Patras and use any hull that came in, or even return to Thessaloniki where Genoese shipping touched. But, in the end, we settled on a sum that seemed a fortune to me, but which everyone proclaimed fair. And, although I was leaving the wild Irish and, to my great sorrow, the Kipchaks, with Nerio, I still had seventy men and hundreds of horses to move. The round ship could take all the men, but only half of our horses.

It took us another week to find another ship, a horse transport that was sitting at Negroponte, just down the coast from Corinth, left behind by the Green Count. I hired her, and her captain, another Venetian, and brought her up to the south beach at Corinth. Now I relate this purely for your amusement, but the two ships could see each other, and my little company loaded into both ships – most of the men into Zeno's round ship on the north beach, but l'Angars and the pages and Gascon men-at-arms and the rest of the horses into the horse transport. Here's the jest: the two ships were perhaps five hundred paces apart, but the horse transport was hundreds of miles farther from Venice, because she had to sail all the way around Morea to get into the Adriatic, whereas Zeno's round ship was only five good days from Venice, because we were in the Bay of Corinth. That tiny stretch of land separates two great seas. The Romans attempted to cut a canal through. You can see the gorge they cut – it's incredible. I assume they used slaves. But they gave it up, or the Emperor lost interest.

Zeno filled his holds with our baggage, and then he loaded currants, which were the best export that Corinth had: dried, sweet fruit. He also loaded a dozen heavy tuns of malmsey, a rich, sweet wine, and some Turkish silk.

It was hard to leave Nerio. I'd already lost Miles Stapleton; I'd sailed away from Emile. Now, on a beach at Corinth, I was going to leave Nerio, who, of all the friends of my youth, was perhaps the most like me. I admired him, most of the time; I emulated many of his little mannerisms, because he was such an effective nobleman, in ways that I had never learned as a boy. Being a cook and being the son of the world's richest man are two very different lives, I suppose.

He paid for both ships. He did it on the sly; I didn't know until we reached Venice that, in addition to paying our wages and the success bonus for storming the Acrocorinth, he *also* covered our ships. But I know he wept on the beach.

'I feel that when you sail away, my youth is gone,' he said. 'Without you and Fiore, I will be a much worse man.'

Then he handed me a contract, which I still have. At that time I was relatively new to being a contractor, in military terms. I'd served with Hawkwood, but I had little experience of contract law.

Nerio, on the other hand, was the only knight I ever knew who would draft his own legal documents.

'This is a new form of contract,' he said. 'It is a *condotta in Aspetto*.' He shrugged. 'It means I am offering you a stipend to be available to me in the future. I will pay to bring you here.'

I nodded. 'Of course,' I said.

'How much?' Marc-Antonio asked, and we all laughed.

PART II

ITALY

August 1367 – March 1368

We landed in Venice on a sunny August day with the haze so thick that you felt as if it weighed on your shoulders like armour. The sun pounded through it like boiling water pouring through a cloth. Zeno's round ship entered the Lagoon on a breath of east wind and had to tack back and forth; our five-day journey had taken ten days, and we hadn't even had a storm to distinguish our trip – just blasts of African heat so intense that tar dripped from the standing rigging to stain the holystoned white oak deck. Our horses were deeply unhappy, but alive, and Zeno, a good friend and an excellent captain, put us at Pellestrina on the Lido islands. We slung two sicker horses onto the wharves, while the healthier chargers followed Gabriel straight into the water and swam ashore.

But I'm out of order, because first we had to be checked for plague and fever, and we docked at the Lazzaretto. That was sad, mostly because there we heard that a great many of the Green Count's knights and men-at-arms and servants were recovering, or dying, from a malignant fever. One of them was Guy Albin, the count's English physician, and Peter, his nephew, went ashore to tend him, thus condemning himself to forty days' quarantine on the island. The officer of the city, who knew Zeno well and gave us a clean bill of health, said that the count had only passed with a dozen followers and was still in the city, and that he had paid for chirurgeons and physicians to come and attend his people.

All this mattered a great deal to me because I had come to fulfil my feudal duty to the Green Count. I had promised his herald that I would meet him in Venice, and I knew I'd have to pass through the city anyway; it was the gateway to Europe. And Emile had, of course, promised to meet me. I rather hoped Hawkwood might have taken work with Venice, too.

I was no great lord like the Green Count, but I knew what it was like to be missing trusted people. My two Greek boys, Stefanos and Demetrios, were good at laying out clothes and bustling with self-importance, but boiling water was sometimes too hard for them and they had only the vaguest notions of horse care. Gregorios, the shepherd boy, had chosen to remain with Nerio.

I already missed John the Kipchak. He knew more about horses than anyone I'd ever known, and my two Greek boys were no substitute for him, even though they were far better servants than John had ever been. I hadn't even got a decent goodbye from him, as he had been watching a Turkish raiding party with some of Nerio's Greek cavalry south of Hermione when we sailed.

To my surprise, Sir Giannis and his *stradiotes* had come with me, while Sir Giorgios stayed with Nerio. Giannis, it proved, had orders from the Emperor, and was to contact Philippe de Mézzières in Venice and then to find the Pope. He took with him our two Jews, who had, at last, chosen to travel to Venice. I embraced them, and by then I'd even managed to like the obsequious Isaac. His brother the rabbi was above my likes and dislikes; less outwardly warm than Father Pierre Thomas, he was still very much of the same thoughtful, holy stamp.

Where was I? Oh, horses. We left our horses on the Lido, because Venice is a huge city without a stable or a blade of grass. I exaggerate, of course, because there are orchards and fields on a few islands, but for the most part, Venice is a terrible place for horses. I was not new there, however, and neither was Marc-Antonio. He made the arrangements with a pair of farmers for our fodder, and then we took our lances down the coast to Chioggia, where the Corner family found us lodgings for a song, at least by Venetian standards. Sir Giannis went straight to Venice to find de Mézzières. I asked him to take a letter to my lord, the Green Count, whom I still thought of then as a touchy aristocrat who needed careful handling.

Chioggia is a noble town, or was then. I have many happy memories of it and, of course, Marc-Antonio was a 'natural' son of the merchant Corner, and he received a hero's welcome. I had a fine room with a chimney and a fireplace all to myself, although I feared that one of the Corner daughters had been exiled to the attic under the roof tiles to make space for me; certainly, all the icons on the walls were of women saints, and the walls were a beautiful pale blue with silver-gilt accents, very feminine. But the bed was comfortable, two feather mattresses, and as my hip and shoulder knitted and healed, I found myself often tired and fond of sleep.

But what I remember best is having to function in a sort of numbness, because there was so much to be done before I could fall into that bed. My lances had to be found good billets, and I had to oversee Gospel Mark and Rob Stone conducting a distribution of about a quarter of the pay the archers had coming. Then I tottered away towards sleep, and even then I was not done. Fiore was human enough to want to go home to Udine, and we had to discuss a hundred small matters – and it was only after I'd had an enormous dinner with the Corners that I was finally allowed to fall into that marvellous bed.

I slept for ten hours, rose to eat, wrote a letter to Emile and another to John Hawkwood, and slept again. My third day in Chioggia was Sunday, and that was the first day I felt like a man. I rose early, ate good warm bread in the kitchen, flirted somewhat automatically with the cook who was twice my age but had a noble twinkle in her eye, and dressed in my faded and unpressed best to accompany the Corners to Mass. We went to the church of San Domenico, a very fine church, and the Mass was magnificent and the priest's Latin excellent. Afterwards, people pressed around and I found that Donna Corner had, as usual, been name-dropping. But it gave Marc-Antonio time to play the great man, which he enjoyed as much as anyone.

We were standing in the square, a beautiful one, paved in brick and stone, talking about the Turks. That is, Marc-Antonio was discoursing on the Turks. I was selling Matteo Corner a third of my remaining saffron. This gave me a healthy roll of gold and silver.

I noted the herald immediately. He was finely dressed; truly, he looked more like a famous knight than I did myself, as his good clothes were not a year old nor had they travelled five thousand miles. He had fine manners, and I knew him from somewhere, and while I searched his face it came to me: he was one of the Green Count's pages.

I inclined my head, and he came forward, murmuring apologies in stiff, francophone Italian as he passed through a crowd of rich merchants to reach me.

'My lord,' he said. It is funny, but almost no one had addressed me as 'my lord' before then, except Jean-François, that is, but he only did it to mock me. Anyway, I almost looked around to see who he meant.

'May I be of service?' I asked.

He bowed. It was a deep bow, the kind of bow you make to a superior.

The depth of his bow silenced the crowd. Men took their wives by the elbow and backed away. They were merchants. They didn't meddle in the affairs of the fighting class.

'My good lord, the Count of Savoy, requests that you join him in Venice,' he said softly.

Such a request was a politely framed command.

'I have other obligations,' I began, and then realised that this was my new life, as a 'gentleman' who had feudal obligations. So instead of continuing, I bowed deeply; in fact, as we both knew, I was bowing to the absent Green Count. 'But please tell my lord I will respond instantly to his summons. I will be with him tomorrow, or possibly the day after.'

The page smiled. 'I will tell him, my lord,' he said, 'and he will be delighted to see you.' He leaned closer. 'It is an urgent matter, my lord.'

My first thought was that I couldn't go. I had an obligation to Sir John Hawkwood, virtually a *condotta*, or contract. But my second thought was that, realistically, my horses needed a week to recover from the sea travel and the heat, and until they were ready, I couldn't go anywhere; that beyond that, I really needed l'Angars and my pages, and they were *another* week away. All of this crossed with the unworthy, but real, thought that I needed a new harness, new clothes, and that I had money in my purse and Venice was the greatest place to buy ... anything in Christendom. In fact, I was as eager to spend money as the newest archer.

Fiore wanted to go home to Udine. My archers had seen too much action. They needed a rest, and Chioggia was perfect: waterfront taverns with good wine and tough fishermen. They'd drink, they'd carouse, but they wouldn't make too much trouble; the podestà had soldiers, the fisher folk were solid enough. Altogether, I realised that I had time in hand, two or three weeks, even.

I explained all of this to Matteo Corner as we walked back to his tall house, and he slapped his head and admitted that Emile and 'Messire Iasson' had stayed a night with him three weeks before and he had a letter for me. So while Marc-Antonio and my two pages packed my valise, and Matteo engaged a fishing smack to run me up to Venice, I read Emile's letter. Once I read it, most of my fears for her fell away; she'd arrived ahead of Count Amadeus, but not by much, and before she was ready to travel on, he'd arrived and she'd heard his news, and also heard, from him, that Prince Filippo had engaged the Bourc Camus as a captain. You'll remember from my stories on previous nights that Camus is the very spawn of Satan, a man-at-arms committed to atrocity and the rule of the sword. He and I had crossed each other too many times. What was worse was that he had some history with Robert of Geneva, who was my former master's – that is Pierre Thomas's – sworn enemy, and he also had some reason to hate my Emile. So it comforted me greatly to know that she was aware that he was about, in Savoy or near enough. I could fear for her without having to change my own plans; she had an escort of fine knights, as you have heard, and more loyal retainers on her estates. She did not need me riding to her rescue. Which was a relief. I'd spent days trying *not* to worry.

I kissed the letter and made my preparations to leave for Venice with the count's page and a clear conscience. I did take a moment to send John Hawkwood a carefully worded note, explaining that I had feudal duties I could not avoid. I sent my note to his camp. He was away in the west, serving Milan, or so rumour had it. I also scribbled to Emile, a lot of nonsense, most likely, but my hand cramped and I sealed it hurriedly and gave it to Matteo because he had goods going upriver to Padua and said he'd see my letter delivered. I hugged Fiore, too. He was going with the letter, at least as far as Padua. I wanted him to come to Venice, but he was determined to go overland.

When he rode across the causeway, I was alone. I hadn't been without my friends for years.

Venice is, without a doubt, the noblest and most beautiful city in Christendom, and indeed, in the world. The canals keep the city cleaner than London or Paris or Milan will ever be. The churches are magnificent, and every *calle* or canal side seems to open into another tiny square with another fine church, endowed by another family as rich, or richer, than the wealthiest merchants of London. Every house is of stone, and some, like the 'Palazzo Donà', are palaces that rise above the canals. Rows of palaces, in fact, so that it seems as if every sailor and *Arsenali* man in the city has a palace of his own. If

I have not explained before, the city is incredibly rich, and is not like any other city I have ever visited, in everything from cleanliness to government. The government has nobles and commoners, like any country, but the commoners, and most especially the men who work in the *Arsenale*, the shipyard, have unique citizen rights greater than any London apprentice. The nobles compose the government, yet many of their offices, including the Duke, or Doge, are elected. The systems of election are complex and labyrinthine and sometimes exceptionally clumsy, but they work, and Venice has been that oddest of states, a republic, for a thousand years.

The houses and palazzi are worthy of comment, as they are unique. Venetians tell me that they are based on the houses of Constantinople, but if that is true, the changes are greater than the originals, because I never saw a palazzo as elegant or as clean in Constantinople, for all its beauty, as in Venice.

The form of the finest is as follows; they front on a canal the way a London house fronts on the street, and there is a little dock there and an entrance at water level. Often there is a colonnaded walkway that connects, like a pathway, to the palaces on either side along the waterfront; indeed, these waterfront walks, often covered and embellished, are one of the most beautiful elements of canal-side life in Venice. The canal-side loggia gives access to the house itself via the entrance hall, and behind that are often kitchens and storage, because the ground level is often filled with water at *acqua alta* or high water, a condition that depends on tides and winds and weather and the will of God.

Above the ground floor colonnade is the enclosed balcony (another loggia, if you like), and behind that, the piano nobile, or grand room. But the great gothic halls, stacked one atop another, are not the whole of the palaces, and behind the first set of rooms there is a courtyard, surrounded by gothic-arched colonnades on all four sides, usually with a gatehouse onto the street. This is a palazzo I'm describing; but a merchant's house is often very similar, if without the courtyard. One feature that remains the same from Venice to Chioggia, and even in Venetian Greece, is the shape of their chimneys, like Turks' hats, and built outside the houses for fire safety; but unlike England, where most private houses have an open hearth and the smoke must pass through a dormer in the roof, in Venice, most houses have fireplaces built into the walls, cleaner and neater in all weathers, and allowing smaller rooms to be heated. I have seen the chimneys in Constantinople and Corinth, and I will confess that in this, at least, the Venetians seem to have followed the style of the Greeks, and a fine style it is.

At any rate, Venetian places are both magnificent and comfortable; the canals keep them clean and sweet except when the water gets rough, and the fireplaces keep them warm in the mild winters.

But, like the very core of London, land is at a premium and so building sites are very valuable, and the buildings, even the palaces, are, for the most part, crushed together more closely than anywhere else I've ever been, and all built of stone. Remember that Venice is not really dry land, but a set of marshy islands, and that to build houses, the Venetians have to drive huge pilings, whole oak or alder trees, straight down into the muck – not just a few, either, but hundreds of pilings for a single house.

I say all this so that you can understand, if you've never been to Venice, that it is a city of close-packed stone buildings, magnificently built and decorated, but packed like Hawkwood's armoured spearmen, and the alleys they call streets are narrower than anything in London. There are passages that go *under* houses, and others so narrow that two men may not pass at the same time. The street of swords, *Spadaria*, is so narrow that it can be difficult to raise a sword to examine it, yet some of the finest cutlers in Christendom line both sides.

The other thing I feel you must know about this magnificent city is that it is surrounded by ships; every street ends at the water, and every street end is a wharf. Sometimes it can be difficult to see the houses for the masts. Venice has galleys and round ships by the score, as well as foreign merchants permitted to trade: ships from Portugal and England and Aragon and France, although not so many of the last. Viewed from a distance, the city looks like a wooded island that has been struck by frost – a veritable forest of masts, with the steeples of the churches rising above them. And there are not just great ships and warships, but small coastal luggers, fishing smacks, and hundreds, if not thousands, of smaller craft that are like Thames wherries – they will carry a gentleman anywhere he needs to go, out to the Lagoon or just around the next bend to church. The boatmen know everything, and have special privileges, and are not to be crossed.

I had lived in Venice for months, waiting for the crusade of Alexandria to finish its preparations, but I still got lost easily.

But I love the place. Venice, with its waterfront forest of masts. Venice, with the constant smell of fish, and the sea. Venice, city of outspoken women and argumentative workers and fine crafts and magnificent display.

I'm biased, I admit it. I have fought and bled for the Lion of Venice, and to me, the place is home. But in the late summer of 1367, as the odd weather blew up the Adriatic, the place was still a little alien to me.

My fisherman landed me almost on the steps for San Marco and then poled off before angry local boatmen could bury him in insults. The men of Chioggia account themselves Venetian only in matters of state; otherwise, the Lion of Saint Mark is a distant lion, and Chioggians go their own way and fish their own end of the Lagoon and they hope the Lion isn't looking too closely at their taxes or their seamanship.

It was Sunday evening, and no one expected us, so the herald and my two pages and I carried our baggage up the salt-stained steps ourselves, and then hailed a small boat rowed with a single oar. Again, in Venice, all traffic moves by water. Our waterman used his oar from the stern on a low, sleek boat with a rising bow; he pushed us out into the chop of the main channel and then, with a few comments exchanged with the Green Count's man, he understood where we were going. We went up the main channel and into a side canal to the count's lodging, a palazzo hard by the old church of Sant'Agnese, and landed on a loggia, or water-landing, so old that I imagined it might have been built by the Romans. The whole palace looked like something from the ancients; coloured marble adorned the exterior, and there were statues in niches far up the sagging facade. A noble building, but long past its best.

Still, we were well received, and in moments I was embraced by Richard Musard, and Mayot, of all people, clasped my hand. I felt at home in a way I had never expected to feel with the Savoyards.

I know that Chaucer will nod, but while most of you imagine that great nobles like the Count of Savoy live lives of unequalled splendour, the truth can be very different. At the Ca' Lorimer, off the Grand Canal, the entire command of the Savoyard crusade was sleeping in one building, knights and men-at-arms and squires and pages. The ground floor smelled a little like a good barn, with bundles of new hay littering the floor as sleeping pallets – so much hay that Marc-Antonio began to sneeze. On the upper floors, the grander apartments, it was clear that the building was rented. Some furniture, no tapestries – the count's only privacy was a closed bed by a series of magnificent Gothic windows.

They all fitted there because they were so few. I counted perhaps a dozen gentlemen and as many young men.

The count sat on a camp stool, almost unattended except for local men of business: a Venetian merchant by his dress; a pair of Jews with long beards and high hats of fur. Behind them stood a party of Greeks; I had heard that at the last moment the Emperor had sent an embassy to the west, but I had not met the men. As the count was clearly engaged, I bowed to the Jews, and greeted them; my Order has made it a policy to befriend and protect the Jews, as I have mentioned, and while I once believed otherwise, my experiences, especially in the East, have taught me that they are a fine group of people, much given to disputation, like Greeks. And I think that their reputation for ill-doing in London and Lincoln is utterly false and based on their not accepting Christ in countries where every man and woman confesses Christ twenty times a day. But when you travel to Jerusalem or Alexandria or Constantinople, or even more, travel into Turkey, you find that you are the only one who confesses Christ, and you are surrounded by men who love Mahomet or Abraham, and the shoe is very firmly on the other foot, or so it seems to me.

All of which reminds me that I have forgotten Benjamin and Isaac, who we took from Didymoteichon to Corinth and then to Venice. They had vanished into the Jewish community of Venice. I mentioned them to the two merchants, and their careful dignity cracked, and the man with the richer beard bowed.

'So you are the famous brigand William Gold,' he said, pronouncing my name in good English, so that I knew he'd heard of me from either Isaac or Benjamin. But then they both unbent, and we chatted about horses and grain prices, and the smaller man offered me a scrap of paper with his address.

'Can you read?' he asked. His tone suggested that he didn't expect me to be able to read. I thought to bridle, but then, we all make assumptions about other men, do we not? I took the offered paper and I'll note that I saved a good deal of money on grain because of it.

I went on to speak to the Greeks, who were, if anything, more out of place – ill-dressed and ill at ease – and I spent some time using my poor Greek and my knowledge of their country to try and make them more comfortable. Marc-Antonio, whose Greek was better than mine on account of his endless habit of lechery, managed a small joke and made them laugh. All of them were priests and monks, and I could see that they were going to be trouble. I couldn't exactly ask them where they stood on issues of theology, but I had, as my lord of Mytilene had suggested, managed to do some reading on the issues that separated the two churches, and I did not need to be a priest or a scholar to know that these men were not happy to be in Venice and were, perhaps, unlikely to be supporting the union of the two Churches. I wondered why the Emperor, who was no fool, had sent a dozen angry monks instead of just a few monks and some soldiers, men who could speak to westerners, like Sir Giorgios and Sir Giannis.

Richard came and took my arm and I made my bows and escaped.

'They are very difficult,' Richard muttered.

'They see us as the enemy,' I said.

Richard made a face. 'The count would like to see you on the loggia,' he said. 'In private.' He looked me over. 'You need some new clothes, brother,' he said. 'You look like a rag-picker.'

I was stung by the accusation and delighted that he had called me brother, as we used to call each other when we were routiers in France. And I confess that my doublet, my best red one, was out at the elbows and had been patched; it was missing many buttons on the sleeves and front, and the once brilliant red had faded to a sort of russet brown, and not very evenly. My half-boots were shapeless, and my hose, once black, were now a sort of blue-brown. Only the good spurs on my heels, the belt at my waist and the Emperor's sword gave me any sort of distinction, and when I looked around, I realised that I was shabby, or worse, compared to the Savoyards.

Richard took me out into the pounding sunshine of a clear August day. The sun seemed as strong there as it was in the Holy Land, but the cool air off the canal made it more tolerable.

I had quite a long time by myself. I thought of Emile and of her trip home, over the Alpine passes. I had time to consider how little, really, I relished the prospect of joining Hawkwood. Fighting for its own sake was less appealing to me than it had been. And I found that, unlike most routiers, I was forming opinions. I had an opinion about the Union of Churches, for example. I had a notion that the papacy was at the root of the disorder, and I wondered how I might feel if I was called upon to fight for the Pope. A French Pope who was, by all accounts, returning the papacy to Rome from Avignon.

And I worried about my clothes. There, I admit it.

Regardless of my sartorial failings, I had time to think about employment. The rumour was that Hawkwood was fighting for Milan against the Pope. It was also whispered, in confident tones, that Prince Lionel was going to marry the ruler of Milan's daughter. It looked to me as if there was a change in diplomacy going on: Milan was deserting the French. Years in Italy and Outremer had caused me to shed my way of thinking of England as the centre of the world; there were so many irons in the fire of diplomacy that no one could really point at one faction and understand it in isolation. In the old alliances, France and Genoa and the papacy had stood together, with Milan on the periphery. Venice had gone its own way; England had been too far away and too weak to play in the south. Naples and Aragon had resisted the papacy and the Holy Roman Emperor. But now, it appeared that all the players were changing sides, and King Edward III of England was as able in the council chamber as on the battlefield. England was a great state, and so, suddenly, was Milan.

It was a completely new game, and it was being played for the highest stakes imaginable: possession of the new trade and the new ideas; perhaps even the overthrow of the papacy. All that flitted through my mind as I waited for the count. He came out onto the loggia reading from a wax tablet a short time later. In his other hand he had a roll: some sort of accounting. This is not how we tend to imagine our great lords, but a great lord, if he wants to play on the grand stage and fight wars and garner fame, must also cast careful accounts, pay his soldiers, and make sure that everyone is fed. So Amadeus came onto the sun-dappled porch with his documents and stood for a moment in the dazzle of sunlight that reflected off the canal below us and up onto the whitewashed ceiling of the loggia.

He looked up, and smiled. Again, a little thing, but he was clearly happy to see me, and I confess it, I was happy to see him. A great deal had changed between us. I confess that I had resented his summons, but now …

'Sir William,' he said.

I made a full *reverentia*, down on one knee, as if to a king. He was, to all intents, a king. 'My lord count.'

He grimaced, walked a few steps, comparing the scroll in his right hand to the marks on the wax tablet. He shook his head.

'You came with some dispatch,' he said. 'You have my thanks, Sir William. You are a good vassal.'

I bowed.

He waved the scroll over his shoulder and a page came out from the hall and took both it and the tablet. This is the real difference between a great lord and a knight: forty servants. But I could tell that his staff was thin.

He turned to face me. 'I have a matter of some import to propose,' he said. 'Listen: do you have a contract with John Hawkwood?'

I tugged at my beard. Somewhat unwillingly, I said, 'No. There is an understanding …'

He nodded sharply, as if to say that understandings between routiers were no concern of his.

'Any other contracts?' he asked.

'I have a sort of waiting *condotta* with Lord Renerio for Morea,' I admitted.

Again he nodded. 'Would you consider serving me, at my expense, until spring?' he asked. 'And perhaps right through the summer?'

I took a breath. Why do these things always take me by surprise? In retrospect, I confess it was virtually the only reason he would have summoned me, but I had no idea …

I nodded. I thought of my answers, and chose the best. 'My lord, I would consider it,' I said.

He smiled. For all he was a great lord, he was also a man of the world – a paragon of chivalry who also knew how to play the game. 'I could pay you for thirty lances,' he said. 'I would pay fifteen florins a month per lance.'

Fifteen was below the market. Venice was recruiting at eighteen. Everyone on the Italian peninsula was recruiting; the cold war between Milan and the Pope was warming up slowly, like a posset of wine placed close to the fire, but the players were still recruiting. And as I've been hinting, they bid fair to draw in every state in Europe, from England to Hungary.

I bowed. 'My lord, it would never do to bargain with one's feudal lord.' I made myself smile when I said it. 'But the Venetians are paying eighteen, and Milan is rumoured to be offering twenty.'

He barked a laugh. 'Monsieur, I am so glad we are not actually haggling,' he said. 'And since we are not, I will point out that you will be home with your wife, and I will feed your people – so perhaps I might be as generous as sixteen. All I require is escort work.'

Then I had to reckon quickly. Who knew that life as a knight required so much attention to numbers? But if he was to feed my people, and our horses, then he was paying very well indeed. Usually the wage included money for the soldiers to feed themselves.

It really took very little calculation. 'I accept,' I said. John Hawkwood would have to wait.

He nodded, as if he had known this all along. 'For yourself,' he said, 'I will offer you wage as a paid captain: three hundred florins a month. Or you may serve me as a vassal, for nothing.'

For nothing, but as a vassal I would be included in councils, and I would have rights, and frankly, at the ripe old age of twenty-seven, I needed reputation more than I needed money. I had estates, and Emile was rich beyond any wage I could collect. Nerio had paid me for the attack on the Acrocorinth, and I'd sold my saffron – that is, most of it – and the rest was going to a Jewish merchant...

'I'll serve as a vassal, my lord,' I said.

He flushed with pleasure. 'Musard said you would,' he agreed. *He* had not thought so; that much was clear. He waved for me to come close. 'I will include you in my thoughts, then, vassal. I have an insurrection on my hands ...' He glanced at me and our eyes met.

'The Prince of Achaea?' I asked.

'The very same,' he said. 'So Richard told you?'

'No, my lord. Nerio told me,' I said.

I made nothing of his grimace. 'Ah. No surprise there. Very well. Prince Filippo is determined to ... let us say ... expand his inheritance. I believe that he is being encouraged by the Archbishop of Geneva and perhaps even by my Visconti brother-in-law in Milan. I am sending most of my knights under Sir Ogier, one of my best knights, into the affected areas to strengthen the garrisons there. Too many of my people are on the Lazzaretto; I have more knights sick out there than attending me here. I will need you and your lances to escort me to

Rome, and then home. I suspect that I should go straight home; it is my entire inclination. But these Greeks must see the Pope. We are close to a union – so close that I cannot let it go.' He glanced at me.

Well. All of Italy was at war, or near war, and here was one of the richest and most powerful princes in Christendom proposing to ride the length of Italy with twenty lances. 'And then home?' I asked.

'Chambéry for Christmas,' he said. 'I have promised my lady, and you may write to Emile and promise her as well.'

'How soon, my lord?' I asked.

'I can't escape Venice for a week, at least,' he said. 'But I must leave no later than the first week of September.' In a more human tone, he said, 'I'd like to wait for some of my people to recover.'

He dismissed me with a wave. I spoke at length with Richard Musard, and we agreed that most of my lances would stay at Chioggia until the count was ready to ride south. Richard put a hand on my arm. 'He is a great lord,' he said. 'He is beginning to value you. Please ...'

I smiled. 'I'm beginning to like him, too,' I said. 'But he's like an actor, always on stage ...'

Richard ignored my grudging praise for his master. He looked both ways. 'This Prince of Achaea ...' he said. 'He is not to be trusted. Get me a half a dozen swords, William. We may need them.'

'In Venice?' I asked. 'Really?' I looked around too. 'He's not just looking for window dressing?'

'Really,' Musard said. 'Trust me.'

I shrugged. I did trust him, despite everything.

'He can be a great leader,' Richard said. 'Right now he needs a little cosseting.'

I made a face, no doubt. I was coming along with the count; Richard didn't need to caress me so.

My thoughts must have shown in my face, because Richard laughed, very like my old friend. 'Jesu, I'm like a man trying to get his mother to like his girl,' he quipped, and we parted with more smiles than had been our wont, of late.

I walked across the city to the Hospital and there reported to the prior, who I knew a little from Alexandria. I got a fine meal and some good wine; I reported on our spring campaign and the diplomacy I had seen with the Turks and then on Nerio's storming of Corinth, which was news to them and caused some rejoicing.

My period as a 'donat' was at an end. I had volunteered with the Order for more than a year and made a caravan and a complete military campaign; no one treated me like a neophyte, even though I was not a 'Knight of Justice' like the men sworn to the Order. But I meant to keep my ties with them, and they seemed happy to have me, and when I explained that I would be escorting the Greek dignitaries to Rome, the prior suggested that I wear my surcoat.

'I do not have a single knight to spare,' he said. 'But nothing is dearer to us than the Union of Churches. Wear your red coat with my blessing; be a Sword of Justice for us.'

That was unexpected, but it was a day of unexpected benison. Of course, the coat of the Order would be helpful in Rome, that cesspool of politics. Instead of being a mercenary captain, I'd be treated as a son of the Church.

'Sword of Justice' is an odd title in the Order. Some day, when I have time, I'll look into it, but I assume that it's a remnant of the days when knights rode abroad, dispensing justice, as you see in the writings of Sir Ramon Llull. Regardless, it was a high honour for a mere donat; it made me, in effect, the Order's legate to the Green Count. And to the Pope.

'Don't let it go to your head,' the prior said with a raised eyebrow. But he gave me a silver sword to pin to my surcoat, and I had a limner repaint my shield, later. The important point is that it made me an officer of the Order. As the title has never been rescinded, I continue to use it; I remain *Spatharios* to the Emperor and Sword of Justice to the Knights of Saint John.

From the Order at Venice, I got some sense of the Pope's movements, and I gathered that he was not at Rome yet, because he feared the city's politics and factions, but was somewhere in Tuscany, or perhaps Viterbo or Orvieto. He had landed a month before; he was moving down the coast, distrustful of the Visconti of Milan and their allies.

The prior allowed me to copy some itineraries, and I agreed to return the next day.

My evening was capped when the brethren offered me rooms. Lodgings in Venice are more precious than gold, as you may remember from my other stories, and I found myself, with Marc-Antonio and my two pages, in a high-ceilinged room at least as good as the Green Count's. The Hospital is a hundred paces from the nearest canal and gives the impression of being somewhere else; it has a small orchard, for example.

The next morning, I wrote a long note for Prince Francesco Gatelussi, and another for Sir John. Truth to tell, I doubted that Sir John had much need of me, but I didn't want to offend him. I felt foolish sending so many letters, like a lovesick swain, but I was new to command and didn't wish to offend the great man.

I sent Marc-Antonio with orders to look at our horses as he went down the Lido, and to report back as soon as he could on our people in Chioggia, bringing Sir Giannis and a handful of other men-at-arms for Musard – whoever was available.

I told him to check on the archers. I suppose I feared what they might be up to in my absence.

Neither of my young Greeks could do any clerking at all, so I spent the morning writing. A pair of scribes, both civilian employees of the Order, sat with me, eyeing my longsword leaning in the corner, and while they copied at ten times my rate, chattered like magpies about courtesans and wine shops and political gossip about the Bishop of Aquila.

I kept copying. I was out of practice, and my Gothic lettering all leaned, but I could read it well enough, and as I wrote the town names, I tried to imagine the road south. Maps were far rarer in the sixties than now; the Italian cartographers have begun making pictures of our world instead of using words to draw the pictures, but twenty years ago, we still used itineraries for everything. If you've never used one, it's really just a list of town names, from Florence to, say, Rome, with the name of every village between, and sometimes alternatives. No picture: no mountains, no rivers, although a really good itinerary will include some 'stages' with descriptions, like 'this day you will cross the Po, which can be difficult in flood', or 'on your left rises a great mountain, often infested with bandits'. The odd thing is that some itineraries were originally written for pilgrims more than five hundred years ago; the bandits may well have moved. In extreme cases, bridges have been erected, or the rivers have been diverted. Sometimes villages change names.

Still, a good itinerary will keep you moving and prevent you getting lost, although for cross-country travel you always want a guide. As I have said before and will say again, a good guide is worth his weight in gold.

It was well into the afternoon when I finished. My fingers were cramped and none of my recent injuries were fully healed, and so a day sitting on a high stool and leaning into my writing (my hand is too heavy) had tired me; my shoulder burned, and my hip was cold and ached as if I was at sea.

I got up from my seat, sanded my wet ink, and, while I waited for it to dry, I stretched. First my arms and then my legs and hips, which scandalised the two clerks. I was sure they'd be gossiping about me for many days to come.

When the ink was dry, I rolled the parchment carefully, fitted it in a scroll tube, and buckled my sword over the gown I wore for comfort. It was hot in Venice, and my plain brown robe was as much clothing as I really fancied; in addition, it went well with all the clerks and monks that worked in the commandery. I ate a bite with Stefanos and Demetrios, my Greek pages, and then set off to spend some money.

I hadn't had anything new since Famagusta, and one of the reasons for my plain brown robe was that almost everything I owned was worn, salt-stained, dirty and, in many places, coming apart. My arming coat, once the pride of the company, was as tenuous a collection of fabrics as the Holy Roman Empire was of princes, and my hose were all through at the heels, the knees. My toes stuck out, too, and I couldn't take my boots off in public.

Besides, my two Greek boys needed clothes. Their Greek padded hose and uncut cotes stood out in Venice, and might cause trouble in Rome.

The three of us took a boat across the city. The Hospital is in the richest part – the tailors and cloth-cutters I wanted were *not.* We went over to the landward side of the city and spent two hours wandering through streets so narrow that at times Stefanos could touch both sides at the same time. My sword drew stares: no one but Arsenali – the carpenters and caulkers who built the city's warships – wore swords in the streets. Finally I stripped it off and gave it to Stefanos to carry, while Demetrios carried the purse.

I remember the pleasure of the shopping, if not the actual purchases. The boys were happy, and I dressed them in my red and black livery as if I were a great lord, and bought them *zepole*, a Venetian sticky treat made with pure Cypriote sugar. I saw a jeweller at work, a woman with her head bent over her craft, at a booth on the street. I watched her carving wax, and I bought from her a reliquary cross. From another jeweller I purchased a set of beads, ivory and coral in colour, and fashioned a rosary from them. It was the most precious thing I had ever owned. I saw a gold-hilted baselard and thought of Fiore's wager before the assault on Corinth. It was a pleasant afternoon.

I didn't see the count that evening. Instead I had dinner with Carlo Zeno.

He looked at my brown gown. 'You have to dress better than that in Venice.' We had met in a small square by his neighbourhood church, and he took me to a tavern for dinner. 'If my father invites you for dinner,' he said, 'and he will, you'll need better clothes. The rosary, on the other hand, is quite nice. Local?'

I told him I'd spent the afternoon shopping. Then we whiled away a few happy hours arguing about politics and war. Zeno was Venetian through and through – to his fingers' ends, as the French said. It was almost refreshing to hear such a biased account of the events of the world. To Carlo Zeno, the Pope, the Turks, the Mamluks, the Byzantine Emperor, the Holy Roman Emperor, the kings of England and France and the Count of Milan were all to be viewed through the lens of Venice, and they were good or bad as suited the needs of *La Serenissima*.

I trudged back to the Hospital after Zeno left me to visit his mistress. I missed my friends. Fiore was headed for Udine, or there already; Nerio was in Greece and Stapleton was in England, and I felt their absence. I felt the lack of Emile as well, make no mistake, but visiting her was always by way of a holiday. I used to have Nerio and Miles and Fiore by my side every day.

I was lonely.

Venice is a city that stays awake late, and I wandered a bit around the Hospital along the Fondamenta dei Furlani and through the streets crowded with newly built tenements, mostly full of Greeks. My two pages found cousins, however distant, within an hour, and I found myself drinking sweet wine with a shipwright from Constantinople. He was good company, and knew more about the applications of mathematics than I had ever heard from anyone. His Italian tried me, but the conversation ended my evening well enough, and I walked back to the Hospital before the doors were locked.

The next day, I had a note from the count, bidding me attend him later in the day. I started my morning early, in a street of merchant venturers, bankers and moneylenders. Some were Jews, some Christians, but my man, David – the merchant I had met at the count's palazzo – was prepared to buy the remaining third of my saffron. I got from him a fine price, the highest I had been offered yet. I probably could have had more, but he was so polite that I lost interest in haggling, and instead we shared a small glass of white wine and some cakes at his stall, and Marc-Antonio handed over all our remaining saffron, including his own. He was not just a good squire, but a good Venetian; he'd bought his own saffron.

'But I haven't paid you,' David said. 'And I cannot until I raise a little money …'

I shrugged. 'I am at the Hospital,' I said. 'Send me a boy when you are ready to pay.'

Then he smiled. We clasped hands, and Marc-Antonio raised an eyebrow at me as we walked away.

'You trust him?' he asked.

'Yes,' I said.

Then I sent him to the count and took my pages to the street of the armourers, which wasn't far from the Hospital. I bought daggers for my two pages and belts to hang them on, and then I went to see Jiri, the northern armourer who kept his shop in Venice. By a stroke of bad luck he was in Brescia, so I had to talk to his assistants instead.

They assured me, however, that I could be fitted quickly. It may seem odd to you, given how poor I had been, but it was only visiting the shop that recalled to me that somewhere in my baggage I had a new helmet, one that I had never worn in tournament or combat. I had to hope it would arrive with l'Angars and the horse transports. Otherwise, I commissioned a new harness entire, cap-à-pie, or perhaps neck-à-pie, so to speak, in the new Brescian style, with a hard ridge down the centre of the limbs and some latten edging for show.

'Brigandine?' the assistant asked. 'Or a multi-piece plate? Or even a single plate, master, if that suits you?'

The two assistants convinced me that all-white armour was the coming thing: that a solid breastplate was worth the money. I didn't mention that I'd owned one, second-hand, after Poitiers. Boucicault ruined it, I think, or maybe I lost it when I was arrested by Camus; I can't remember.

'Maestro Jiri will be back in eight days,' Davide, the older assistant, promised, 'after the feast of Saint Eusebius.'

I admitted that I had never heard of Saint Eusebius.

Davide shrugged. 'A saint. Doubtless a very holy man.' His shrug was Venetian. 'But *Milanese*, you know?'

I laughed.

My two pages were proud as Pontius Pilate with their daggers and belts and matching cotes. Meanwhile, there *I* was in my frowsy old brown gown, ruined low boots and hose so frayed that there wasn't any part of them I could show with decency. It was too hot for a hood, and I was wearing a straw hat I'd picked up in Greece. I confess it, I looked anything but a successful *capitano*.

That day we went to the shops behind St Mark's Square. The first shop I entered had a dazzling array of good English and Flemish wools, and lost my custom because they ignored me not once but twice for better-dressed potential customers.

The second shop, on a *calle* that ran north of the square, was not so choosy, and the tailor came out in person to wait on me. We found a fine piece of scarlet, as supple as doeskin and almost as thin as silk, brilliantly dyed in cochineal. We haggled for a hood and hose and a cote-hardie. I had planned to buy a pourpoint in the French fashion, cut and padded and stuffed, but in that year, in a Venetian summer, men were wearing unpadded garments, cut very tight and a little long. The tailor produced a nice piece of black wool, Flemish, almost like a velvet, for my cote-hardie and offered to put on long tippets, which is to say, hanging sleeves like leading strings for an infant. They were all the rage in Venice.

In the end, I bought three of everything, and he sent me up the *calle* to a middle-aged woman who measured me for underclothes, that is, shirts and braes.

I remember her well, partly because she was a jolly woman with a fine loud laugh, but mainly because she made me strip naked.

'Don't make me guess,' she said. 'I've seen the Doge as God made him, and the archbishop too.'

She looked at the braes I took off. 'You have been in prison?' she asked.

'No, *Siora*,' I answered, one of my few words in Venetian. 'I am a soldier.'

'Oh, Christ be with us,' she muttered. 'At least you smell clean.'

I noted that my braes were, indeed, well-stained; and wet saddles had ... well, left them looking as if I had been very ill, many times. Brown. Laugh if you must; when you are in the field, with a company, you cease to think of such things.

I was glad for my long gown. Perhaps it made me look old, but it covered all my other shortcomings.

'You want five sets,' the woman said. 'Not three.' She nodded emphatically. I never had a chance.

I went back to the tailor, who measured my arms again. I have very long arms, as all of you will allow, and all my life, tailors and armourers have had to re-measure me to reassure themselves.

'Day after tomorrow,' the tailor said. I paid him half of his outrageous price in advance. Everyone must be a little profligate once in a while; indeed, I enjoy spending money far too much.

The tailor's attitude, which had been pleasant all morning, became downright obsequious when I produced hard coin. He became my informant and my guide to all the luxuries of Venice. He sent me to a cousin, who made fine shoes and boots, and then he sent me to a jeweller's, but the man didn't do the kind of enamel work I had in mind. I had seen the sort of belt that I wanted; all the Savoyards had belts in gold or silver, with their arms in enamel on the plates. I'd seen them in Constantinople, but in Greek styles, and I was determined to have one, but I had to walk about, take a boat, and try three jewellers before I found one who could do the work.

The price made me blanch. Two hundred ducats for a belt seemed like a terrible waste of money – almost the cost of my new harness, or of Gabriel, my destrier.

I paid. I was determined to be fine; if I was going to accompany the Green Count to Rome, I needed to look the part of a prosperous captain of lances, or so I told myself.

And finally, I went to a scabbard maker and left my beautiful longsword. The scabbard fittings were still beautiful – gilded bronze and enamel work, almost as good as new – and the hilt was still fine, although the cross guard had been hit quite a few times and the gilding was almost gone. But the leather of the scabbard was worn through to the wooden core in places, and constant wear had bleached out its original, vibrant red to a pinky-tan that looked uncomfortably like rotten meat.

Then I took a boat to the chiesa di Sant'Agnese and walked to the back of the count's palazzo. I left my pages in the kitchen and went up into the *appartamento*, where I found Richard.

'I thought …' he said, looking around, 'I thought perhaps you'd … be around more.' He shrugged. 'Anyway, the count is entertaining a Foscari, and you can't be seen in that gown.'

'What's wrong with my gown?' I asked. But I knew.

'You used to dress so well,' Richard said.

I was tempted to say 'we used to rob nuns for the money', but Richard didn't appreciate that kind of humour. 'Why does he want me?'

Richard led me into a corner. There was no privacy at all in that house except out on the balcony, and I thought of suggesting that they all move to the Hospital. 'There are rumours,' he said. 'The Prince of Achaea is coming here, to meet the count. My lord sent most of his people away yesterday; we're thin on the ground.'

I nodded.

'You need to be here,' Richard said. 'Where's your company?'

'Chioggia,' I said. 'I sent Marc-Antonio for half a dozen of them yesterday.'

Richard nodded.

'You fear an attack? In Venice?' I asked. I was, frankly, baiting him. He was always a little more cautious than I, but this seemed foolish. No one attacks *anyone* in Venice.

He shrugged. 'The Prince of Achaea is like something from pagan times. My count's death would solve most of his troubles.'

I pulled at my beard. I knew that Richard was serious, but I found it difficult to really value his worries.

He changed the subject. 'You have ordered new clothes?'

'Why? Should I?' I asked, baiting him.

We played cards until the Foscari was gone, and then I was summoned to the loggia by the count, who didn't seem to notice my fusty brown gown. 'You have sent for men-at-arms?' he asked.

I nodded.

He waved at a page; at Roger, in fact. I was getting to know the household, and his favourite page was Roger de Lors. The boy was fifteen and ready to be a squire. He is a knight now; I saw him in Italy last year. In those days, he had the hardest head of the count's servants and he usually carried the purse.

'Give Sir Guillaume fifty ducats to clothe his men in a way that is suitable,' he said.

'Green?' I asked.

The count glanced at me. He had a document in his hand, and there was someone in a magnificent squirrel robe, five hundred ducats worth of 'vere', standing in the entrance.

'Emerald green or Savoyard scarlet,' he said. He smiled – the smile of the busy man going through the motions of leadership.

I bowed and withdrew as the man in the squirrel robe entered. I didn't know him.

'I came here to get money to buy surcoats?' I asked. I was unused to having a master, and Pierre Thomas had only summoned us in real need.

'You should attend him every day,' Richard said. 'I made excuses for you this morning. Where were you?'

'Copying itineraries and making plans to escort you south,' I said.

Richard nodded, mollified. 'I was sure—'

I raised my hand. 'Richard, you are an accomplished courtier and I am a plain soldier. This is Venice! My little company has been in the field all summer. I need to buy things, fix things, write orders ...'

'You need to do all that *and* attend your lord every morning and evening,' Richard said.

I knew in my heart he was right. We'd been courtiers before, with Prince Edward. You, Chaucer, have spent half your life in courts, so you will allow that Richard was perfectly correct. But I resented it; I wanted to roam Venice and see everything. I wanted to visit all the islands I hadn't seen when I was recuperating from the beating d'Herblay gave me.

At any rate, I drank a cup of wine with Richard and we read over my itinerary for Rome. He took it in to the count and returned with some notes on a wax tablet. I copied them out; the count wanted to visit Siena. I ate with Richard and Georges Mayot and we went off to church together to see the elevation of the Host. I prayed on my new beads. I was the worst-dressed man in the church, and women looked away when I was close. Oh, vanity.

It was still light out, and the canals caught the pink light of the sunset and reflected it. All of Venice looked pink and healthy and glorious, and I decided to walk home, across the great square. I love the square of Saint Mark's; it is like nowhere else in the world, especially at dusk, and so I gathered my pages and we took a boat across the Grand Canal and then we walked, like Venetians. It was so beautiful, so otherworldly; I had just heard Mass, and I was, I suppose, on a spiritual plane.

We were speaking in Greek, and I was explaining the Latin rite to the two little heretics when we entered the great square from the east. There, as we were walking in under the great arch, stood the Bourc Camus. He stood with his back to the cathedral, its brown stone rising above him like a storm cloud and casting a dark shadow across him and his brigands.

I hadn't seen him for years, and those years had not been kind. His face was heavier, and redder, as if he drank too much or lived outdoors all the time, and his hands were rough and crimson, as if stained with the blood of his victims.

He was well dressed, in a fitted French pourpoint in scarlet and azure. Not his usual stark argent and sable, either, and thus almost certainly his new employer's livery, with matching stockings that had gold tips on the ends of the garter straps, and he had half a dozen bravos at his back. They slouched around a tall, thin man in the best French fashion, a silk doublet cut to reveal a second silk doublet beneath it. He was as thin as a rake and looked a little too hungry to be well-off. The gangly man was sniffing from a pomade ball on a finger ring.

I have no idea what they were doing or where they were going, but suddenly Camus stopped, and his eyes locked with mine. He knew me in an instant.

'Get behind me,' I said to my Greek boys.

Camus said something and his men began to spread out, to the right and left.

I went straight at him. I just kept walking. The arch is only twenty feet wide, and I didn't actually think that Camus would murder me in front of half of Venice. The square was crowded with people out for an evening stroll, or just coming from Mass at San Marco. Indeed, there were a dozen other men under the arch itself.

'William Gold,' Camus shouted. His anger rang at me inside the arch, like thunder against a mountain.

I kept walking at him. I had no sword, but I had two boys to protect. And I knew that Camus knew no rules; he just might try to kill me in public.

'You have seen better days, I fear,' he said, his eyes roving over my tired clothes.

I was ten feet away. Heads were turning.

'Good evening,' I said. I sidestepped a large Venetian, round as a cheese, and I was past Camus. I looked back, and the tall man had a hand on Camus's shoulder. He had a louse crawling out of his high, tulip collar, and the face of a stoat. I marked him – he had to be the Prince of Achaea.

'You are a dead man,' Camus shouted suddenly.

I kept walking, although my back was burning. I heard 'Count Amadeus' mentioned.

'My lord, two of them are following us,' Stefanos said. His voice wavered. His brother's head went back and forth like an owl's.

I nodded and walked towards the Doge's palace. Looking back, I saw two men in the Bourc's red and blue, close behind us.

The *fondamenta*, the street or path along the waterfront, was packed with people visiting, taking the air, or shopping in the open-air market that stretched away along the waterfront from the palace to the Arsenale. I walked along with my pages, all the way to the edge of the Dalmatian market, and then I realised that I was thinking like a landsman and not like a Venetian. I turned and walked down one of the dozens of low wharves and hailed a boat. I asked the boatman to take us to the Ca' Zeno, and he obliged, rowing hard with his single oar. My pursuers stood dumbfounded on the waterfront, watching us row away.

I paid a call at Ca' Zeno and asked for Sir Carlo, who came down, a little out of sorts.

'The Prince of Achaea – you know him?' I asked.

'I know of him,' Zeno allowed.

'He is here, with some bravos. He means trouble for the count.'

'Foreigners and barbarians,' Zeno spat. He raised his eyebrows as if to suggest that perhaps he didn't mean me. 'I'll look into it, or my father will.'

I had a glass of wine with him – indeed, it was a fine glass – and he talked to me of mirrors and goblets and the luxury trade out of Venice. I asked Zeno to send a boy to the count and tell him of my meeting with Camus, and then, when it was dark, we left out of the landward side through the magnificent courtyard.

I got lost on my way back to the Hospital; it was closed and locked when I reached it. The porter was none too pleased to be wakened, but eventually, dry and warm, I tumbled into my pallet and went to sleep. I dreamed of France, of burning monasteries and the tavern we ran, and the Bourc's men-at-arms in their white and black livery. I dreamed of men with the plague, and a boy with half his face flayed away.

All that, just from seeing the Bourc.

In the morning, I left my boys at the Hospital with orders to stay put, and I went by boat to the count's hotel. I crossed the square by the chiesa di Sant'Agnese and I knew one of the men there. One of Camus's men in the Prince of Achaea's colours, he stood near the well head, picking his teeth and looking like a feral rat in fine clothes. I ignored him and went into the palazzo where, as soon as I was admitted, I explained the Bourc's man to the count and Georges Mayot.

'I only have the four of you,' the count said.

'Sir Giannis will come today,' I said. 'Tomorrow at the outside. And my lord, despite my little altercation, it would be incredibly foolish of this Prince Filippo to attack you here.'

'He's a very foolish young man,' the count said. 'I need to see the Doge today; it is an official appointment. Other than that ...'

Roger the pageboy appeared. He was flushed.

'A messenger,' he said. 'My lord, there is a messenger from Prince Filippo.'

The count snapped his fingers and a pair of servants came and brought a heavy chair. He had it placed at the head of the loggia, the east end, and Richard sat by him.

'Show him in,' the count said.

The young man who came in looked as if he might have been cast to play Satan in a passion play. He had a black forked beard, florid skin, the nose of a drinker and a paunch, but he was meticulously dressed and wore a remarkable surcoat cut magnificently of heavy silk, bearing a coat of arms mostly unfamiliar to me. But, as it bore within it the arms of Savoy and Jerusalem, I could guess that it was Prince Filippo's.

The man made an unsteady bow. Up close I could see that he had grime under his nails … and he stank.

The count's eyes narrowed.

'You can't hurt me!' he said, drunk as a lord. 'I'm a herald!'

The count sighed. 'Yes,' he agreed. 'State your business and be gone.'

'Mosh grashioush lord,' he said, his voice tight and high. The man was terrified, and drunk.

Amadeus passed a hand in front of his face.

'My own lord, the grashioush lord Filippo of Achaea and S-s-savoy, deshiresh a meeting, ash your lovink … lovink …' The man's fear, and hiccups, overwhelmed him.

'Nephew?' the count finished. He looked at Richard. 'This is a calculated insult.'

'He wishesh to meet with you today, lord, in a way that might be …'

'Is this really a message? I do not think this man is really a herald.' The count was not amused. 'Throw him in the canal.'

'No, great lord!' the herald cringed. He tried fawning. 'Grashioush lord! My prince sheeks only peash … A meeting to your mutual benefish …'

'I can't understand a word,' the count said.

Perhaps I'd listened to more drunks than he had. 'My lord, he says that the prince wishes a meeting, to your mutual benefit,' I said.

'No,' the count said.

'You mush!' the herald whined.

'Throw him in the canal,' the count said.

'You cannot harm me!' said the herald. 'My pershoun ish shakred!'

'Harm?' The count smiled thinly. 'You need a bath. Take one, at my expense.'

I didn't need to move. Richard grabbed the man by the shoulders, Mayot took his feet, and they threw him from a third-floor loggia into the canal. He screamed all the way down and he floundered about a bit in the water, but he was a Venetian. He hauled himself out of the canal on the far side, pulled off the surcoat and threw it on the pavement.

I hoped that he had been well paid.

The count looked at his hands, as if considering cutting his nails. He glanced at me.

'As I was saying,' he said, 'I have to visit the Doge. Do you have other clothes?'

'They should be ready, my lord,' I said. 'May I ask why we are going to the Doge?'

The count smiled, as if this was the right sort of question. 'I'm not precisely sure, although it is always an honour to wait on the Doge, who is, let's be honest, the most powerful prince in Christendom. But I believe we will discuss the Union of Churches, and by God, Sir William, with God's grace and a little *fortuna*, I will win Venice as an ally.'

I nodded. 'I will collect my new clothes, my lord.'

He nodded. 'Kindly do, and attend me to the Doge.'

I left Richard to tidy up and I went out in a rented boat – first to fetch my sword, which had been cleaned and sharpened by a cutler while the new scabbard was being made. It looked very fine. I carried it, with the sword belt wrapped about it, and went to fetch my clothes. My seamstress had a set of braes and a beautiful new shirt for me, and she poured me a bath with her own hands and gave me a screen, as well as a suggestion that I could leave it open.

Only one cote-hardie was done, but that was enough, and I was clean and neat in new wool and linen as white as snow, head to foot, when I returned to the Hospital, where three pairs of fighting shoes and two pairs of boots had been delivered. I put on a pair: too tight. Annoying, but I was in a rush and I wet them in my washbasin to stretch them and then went out, a half-cloak over my arm. I picked up my pages, and we made a good show, all red and black and black and red. My hose were cut and panelled in the latest fashion so that stripes of red and black were set vertically on one leg; I had had time to put on the chain and badge the count had given me. I lacked gloves. I missed Fiore – he always had gloves.

Have I said it yet? I missed my friends.

At any rate, it was not yet noon when I returned to the count's lodgings. Richard and Georges clucked with approval at my clothes.

'Very Venetian,' Richard said, eyeing my cote-hardie.

He himself was in unrelieved green, with the same chain I wore and then a collar of the Order of the Swan, the count's knightly order, at his throat. He too had a sword.

'Who are we leaving here with the servants?' I asked.

Richard paused.

'We have to leave a sword or two here,' I said. 'Richard, you *know* Camus. He'll kill the donkey, the cat, the dogs, and eventually the linkboys to make a point.'

Mayot raised an eyebrow.

Richard nodded. 'He's right,' he sighed. 'Damn. This is not the homecoming we expected, and Filippo has stolen a march on us.'

'Camus only had six bravos that I saw,' I said. I wished I had Fiore, or Nerio – better, both of them. Even Marc-Antonio, who was, by then, a truly expert man-at-arms.

But I had only my own blade. I was confident that I could take them; three years of fighting alongside Fiore had made me something of a sword.

'Send to the Doge,' I suggested. 'Ask for an escort.'

'Then we appear weak,' Musard said.

I shrugged. 'Better than a fight in some *calle* and one of us wounded or dead,' I said. 'What are we playing at? The drunken herald, the man this morning? It's as if this is a game.'

Richard glanced at Georges Mayot. 'They hate each other,' he admitted. 'It's mutual. And the count has done what he can to Filippo, too.'

'All the more reason to get a guard from the Doge. If not the Doge, send to the Arsenale for a dozen of your oarsmen.'

'That contract is over,' Musard said.

I shook my head, frustrated. 'This isn't a game, Richard,' I said.

He shrugged. 'I feel that you are new to us. Things for the count must be done a certain way – the count must not ever appear hesitant or weak.'

I threw my hands in the air. 'Then the count is playing at being God,' I said.

Naturally, at that moment Count Amadeus walked into the hall. 'Monsieur?' he said to me. 'In what way do I play at being God?' He was not amused.

I made a deep *reverentia*. 'My lord, I am arguing that we need to send to the Doge or the Arsenale for an escort. Monsieur Richard says that you will not accept such an arrangement.'

'Monsieur Musard is correct. I will never accept such a subordination.' The count's eyes were afire with anger. 'Perhaps I should reconsider having you command my escort.' He looked me over like a farmer eyeing a prize ram at the fair – a prize ram with a bleeding ulcer. 'You look much better,' he said, pleasantly enough.

I was still on one knee. 'My lord,' I insisted, 'if I am commanding your escort, I have the responsibility for your safety.'

'And of my honour,' he said. 'You must take care of my safety and my honour together.'

I wanted to slap him. His honour, indeed. He was a great lord, a successful crusader, a man of nearly equal status to the Doge and the lords of Milan. No one would ever even remember that he engaged an escort to protect him one rainy afternoon in Venice.

Musard was doing all he could with the weight of his glare to silence me.

'Very well, my lord,' I said. My teeth were no doubt clenched. All in all, I have served lords with far more vanity and outward display than the Green Count, but after Pierre Thomas and Francesco Gatelussi, he seemed like the most arrogant popinjay ever to walk the earth.

'Good,' he replied with a mild tone that implied that any attempt to question his will had been a waste of time. And perhaps it was.

And you can say that I'm an arrogant ninny myself, and I confess it: pride has often headed my list of sins. But I had no trouble taking orders from Gatelussi, or Percy, or Fra Peter Mortimer.

Bah, never mind.

We walked across the smaller island from Sant'Agnese to the Grand Canal. Richard had his squire, Roberto, and Roger, the page; I had my two pages. I paid a boatman to carry us up the canal and right to the steps below the Doge's palazzo, and we landed in the full heat of the day, a damp day that made even the lightest wool stick to your skin. The horizon beyond the Arsenale was so dark as to be black, or at least slate grey, and there was lightning off over the Adriatic.

'Heavy weather coming,' I said. I made sure of my sword.

But there was no secret ambush waiting for us, and we went into the main portico and made our prayers at the little shrine to the Virgin, and then we saluted the Doge's men-at-arms and went into the courtyard, which was larger even than the Ca' Zeno courtyard. The walls appeared at first glance to be frescoed, but closer inspection showed them to be decorated with inlays of different-coloured marble and other stones – a marvellous coup d'œil and very beautiful. We were taken up to the apartments of the Doge, and then Musard and I cooled our heels while the count went straight in to the Doge.

The apartments of the Doge and the offices and rooms of state were magnificent beyond anything I had ever seen in London or Paris or Prague or Alexandria. The wall sconces, for example, were of gilt bronze, cast in fantastical shapes like dragons and griffons and gargoyles, and every sconce held either two or four wax candles as good as candles in churches; silent servants bustled in and replaced them when they burned low, as efficiently as any altar guild. The state rooms were also hung with many small mirrors of steel and bronze that reflected the candlelight and the light of the great windows. Glass was one of the industries of Venice. The city produced window glass so good that we use it in London, and the windows of the Doge's palace had a thousand panes of glass.

We were waiting in the 'Scarlet Chamber', which was hung in red silk. Even on a dark day with a storm brewing over the Lagoon and the air as heavy as lead, the room was splendid. I found myself examining the tiles of the floor, the cherubs supporting the fireplace, the icon of the Virgin …

After we had waited half an hour, there was movement on the staircase from the great courtyard to our right, and the Bourc Camus and a dozen men-at-arms in court clothes came up the steps.

They were not wearing armour, and none of them wore a sword, only daggers. In their midst was the tall, gangly man with the lopsided smile.

A pair of Venetian equerries, or squires of the Doge, opened the door to the Doge's apartments to him. They bowed deeply to the newcomer, and he swept by. I suspected that this was the famous Prince Filippo, and the ushers confirmed it by announcing him by his titles.

His titles rolled on and on, and included, apparently, 'Count of Savoy' as well as 'Prince of Achaea' and 'Duke of Athens'. I listened attentively, my eyes on Camus. He was as surprised to see me as I was to see him, and we eyed each other like cats on a fence. Thunder rumbled out over the Adriatic. A storm was coming.

Camus was wearing a black and white cote-hardie, and fine black hose. He looked smaller than I remembered him, but his eyes were still mad.

I decided not to lock eyes with a madman and follow that path to the end: glares, posturing, violence. Listen: I had learned some things from Pierre Thomas and the Holy Sepulchre. I could slide back into being a simple brute, when required. But I had other weapons. And I knew, then, and I know now, that nothing separated me from Camus but the grace of God.

So instead of meeting his eye, I took my paternoster off my sword hilt, where I had hung it, and began to pray at the icon to the Virgin. There was a small prie-dieu with a kneeler. I knelt.

Camus's face registered something – shock, anger, rage. He strode across the Scarlet Chamber.

I thought he was going to strike me, so powerful was his stride.

'Prayer?' he said. 'You pray, Gold?'

He always surprised me. I took a breath, thinking of the Passion of our Saviour, using the image of the crucified man on my new cross to focus my mind. I clung to the image of the Passion for a moment, and then I let go of my attempt at meditation.

'Yes,' I said.

'You fucking pray? To what? The god of hypocrisy and torture?'

Even his own men-at-arms looked uncomfortable.

'I was praying to the Virgin,' I said mildly.

'Don't you think she was just some little *putain* who spread her legs for the wrong man and lied about it? Eh, Gold?' He was close to me, and his breath smelt of cloves.

It was odd that his blasphemy had so little effect on me. Camus was evil; I had known him to claim he was Satan's own knight. But the foolish blasphemy he spouted was more like boys' banter than something evil.

'I think everyone must consider that, from time to time,' I said. 'It's an absurd story.' I smiled, not because I was unafraid of Camus, but because that was one of Pierre Thomas's phrases – that Christ's story and Passion was so impossible that it must be true.

He didn't like my smile. 'We kill people for money,' he said. 'I think I'll kill a couple of yours, so you remember we're whores, not nuns.' He glanced past me, at Musard. 'I know Blackie, there. What about those two boys. Lovers? I could geld them for you.'

Musard walked towards me, and three of Camus's red and blue bravos stepped out to meet him.

We didn't have any more cards to play, either. We were very short on swords.

'You went and got famous,' Camus said very quietly. 'I hate that. I hate that men know you and don't know me.'

'Perhaps you should change your life and be a better knight,' I said.

'You fucking pious whore,' Camus said, as soft as a lover. 'Do you think that you are a better knight? Because you can kill Saracens instead of, say, nuns? Are you an idiot? It's all the same. Sacks of meat, and blades to let out the blood. All the fucking same.'

'Is this how you lead your men?' I asked. 'With talk of sacks of meat?'

'Is this how *you* lead *your* men? With pious crap about your fake god and your righteousness?' he asked, his voice sing-song with contempt. 'I kill, and I like it. I make men grovel, and I like it. I am strong, and they are weak. That's all there is.'

'You must be very popular at court,' I said. 'All the best parties ...'

There are many moments when your life changes – when you change yourself, or someone changes you. That was one. It is, perhaps, difficult to explain, but something left me, and something entered. It was not that I was no longer afraid of Camus; he made me afraid every moment. But I was afraid that I *was* him – he had me down in that respect – not *of* him. I was afraid I was a pious hypocrite. You cannot kill men with a sword and not wonder. I knew what he meant; in many ways, we were very alike.

But I didn't find him as ... intimidating. I found his anger childish and his antics a little overdone. Perhaps Alexandria burned something away; perhaps two years with Pierre Thomas taught me something about good and evil. I had seen evil that rendered the Bourc Camus ... banal.

'You mock me!' Camus spat. 'I dream of killing you.'

I shrugged. I admit that my disdain was largely feigned, but just two years before I could not even have feigned it.

I said, 'You dream of killing me? I don't even think of you. Go away and plot, or whatever you do. I wish to pray.'

And then, in one of the bravest acts of my life, I turned my back on him. He had spittle flecking his lips and his eyes glittered and his hand was on his dagger, but I turned my back on him, raised my little paternoster, and knelt at the prie-dieu below the icon.

Pater noster qui es in caelis ...

'I will kill you,' he said.

Sanctificetur nomen tuum

'I will kill the people you love. All of them,' he said. 'Turn around!' he shouted suddenly.

Adveniat regnum tuum

Fiat voluntas tua

Sicut in caelo et in terra ...

'You will turn around!' he roared. He was very close. I could hear footsteps, but I was committed. It was curiously like the time I was kneeling and waiting to be recognised by Peter of Cyprus last year.

I finished my paternoster and began *Ave Maria.* A bead passed through my fingers. I realised I had started without a *Credo,* because I was, in fact, deeply afraid, but I went on anyway.

I could hear a man with a Venetian accent speaking insistently in French.

'You are hiding behind the Doge,' Camus said behind me. 'You think I won't kill you here, and that's smart of you, isn't it? But you have to leave here eventually, Gold, and I'll find you. Or your nice little Greek boys, or your wife, or your children. I fucking hate you all.'

'You must not speak this way, messire,' said the equerry.

I went on praying.

'I will get you,' Camus said. 'I will get you and strip away everything from you. Everything!'

'I will report your behaviour to the Doge,' said the equerry.

'Go and tell him, little puppy,' Camus snapped. 'Tell him I pissed in the milk, too.'

'You are absurd, messire,' the equerry said. 'I must ask you to leave.'

'Or you will do what, pup? Lick me?' Camus laughed his terrible high-pitched laugh.

Musard was near me. I could feel him; I knew his breathing. He spoke in good Venetian-accented Italian. 'If you want him gone, I'll be happy to help you move him.'

'I have nothing against you, Darkie. Don't cross me,' Camus said. 'Although I see you and Gold are butt-buddies again.'

'You are a foul-mouthed fool, Camus,' Musard said. 'I am a knight, and you are a criminal. If I run you through right here, no one will complain about anything but cleaning the floor.'

'Dream on,' Camus said. 'I am the captain of the Prince of Achaea. We will take your Green Count and make him nothing. My master will be Count of Savoy. And you can go back to sucking cocks in Avignon.'

As prayer, it was worthless; my mouth formed the words, but my entire attention was focused behind me, and I was ready to roll to the right and draw in a heartbeat. Yet I had decided to kneel and pray rather than engage in precisely this wordplay. Camus was mad – as mad as any inmate in Bedlam. And bad, right through. There was no point in talking with him.

I heard Richard's indrawn breath. His hand had been on my shoulder and I felt it go to his dagger. As he was not a Knight of the Hospital, he didn't have the right to wear a sword; no doubt his squire had it, further down the room.

I rose and turned, raising my paternoster.

Camus was surprised, and he backed a step, so that it appeared that he fell back before the image of the cross.

He stepped back into a huddle of his own people. He had flinched.

'Fuck your God!' he shouted.

I turned to the equerry. 'He is mad. Forgive him.'

'You know what comes next,' he shouted. And then it was as if, between one breath and the next, someone else was in his head. 'The jolly part.' He nodded, suddenly calm. He bowed to the equerry. Then he leaned over to one of his liveried bravo's and whispered in his ear, and the man bowed, clearly afraid – who could serve Camus and not fear him? But he turned and ran for the stairs.

'I was going to kill him,' Richard said. He was red with fury.

'And that would have made trouble for your master. Our master.' I smiled. I was feeling fairly confident, by then. And I was thinking of the next move. Whatever happened was going to be bad, I could tell. Thunder rolled in the south. I thought of the storm coming up the Lagoon, and the heavy rain, and the narrow streets.

The count thought that he had been summoned to the palace to discuss high policy with the Doge: Milan, the Pope, the Union of Churches. As it turned out, the Doge, Marco Cornaro, another member of the endless Corner clan, intended to affect a reconciliation between the prince and the count. Perhaps he had been bribed, although I find that difficult to imagine; instead, it seems to me probable that he didn't know the depth of the quarrel.

Camus was standing there with his smile and his sudden accession of good humour, and I was just considering how vulnerable we were, when the candles seemed to flicker and there was a levin-flash that illuminated for a heartbeat the corners of Camus's mad eyes. He turned, and the first crash of thunder hit. The panes of glass rattled; the walls vibrated. Then, as quick as thought, another flash, followed too closely by another peal of thunder, and a series of flashes off to the east, fast and bright orange, and a long snake of forked lightning visible in the sky through the upper windows of the chamber.

The doors to the Doge's inner apartments opened.

'I would ask you to reconsider, as a friend of Venice,' Doge Marco Cornaro said. He was seventy-five or eighty years old, wearing a long gown edged in miniver, and he had a rod of office in his hand, but he was not wearing his cap of state.

I could tell at a glance that the count was angry – deeply angry.

'Serenity,' the count replied with a barely civil inclination of his head, 'I beg to be excused. I wish to be back at my house before the rain hits.'

The Doge tried again. 'If you would just allow me ...' he said.

'This is not your business,' the count said icily. 'This importunate young man needs to submit his claims to my justice, not yours.'

'I'm not your vassal, cousin,' the prince said. He had a high-pitched voice – high without being melodious, so that it almost grated on the ear. 'I cannot hope for a fair hearing in your courts; everyone knows how corrupt you are. His Serenity has graciously agreed to act as—'

'His Serenity has no business whatsoever in the law courts of Savoy,' the count said. 'Your father made a will. You were not included in it.'

'Because my mother died and my father married a whore, a low-born slut ...'

The Doge froze, his face changing.

'My father disinherited me because of that witch. I am the prince, not her little bastard ...' He smiled nastily. 'Any woman like that is a witch and a whore.'

The Doge stepped back from the Prince of Achaea.

'This is not the situation you described to me,' the Doge said. Dignity and age failed to cloak anger.

Camus was standing his ground, and his bravos were all around him. But luck, and the prie-dieu, and perhaps God, had placed me nearer the doors to the Doge's apartments, and I was virtually at the count's shoulder.

'Foolish old men lose their wits and marry smooth-skinned whores all the time,' Prince Filippo spat in his contralto. 'It is common knowledge.'

'This audience is at an end,' the Doge said suddenly. He turned, his face deeply flushed.

'But can you not require him ...' Prince Filippo said. 'Listen to me!' he roared, when the Doge turned his back. 'I paid for this meeting, God's curse on you! Require him! Force him!'

With slow dignity, the Doge vanished into a crowd of his own officers and courtiers.

Lightning flashed, three pulses, and then thunder rattled the windows again, closer now. I could see, out of the south windows, the Lagoon beaten to a froth by the wind. I'd never seen anything like it, not even when I lay watching the Lagoon for a month, recovering from d'Herblay's beating.

But the violence of the surface of the Lagoon was nothing compared to the prince's face; his cheeks were mottled red and white, and the muscles of his mouth were moving like rollers on the deep. His right hand was spasming open and closed like a dying man's hand. He was not privileged to wear a sword there, and it was as well, as that hand was looking for a sword hilt.

I took the count by the shoulder.

'Now, my lord,' I said sharply, and Roger, the page, threw the count's cloak about him. We put ourselves between the count and Camus and moved to the head of the stairs, while Achaea stood stupefied and lightning flashed again. I passed Camus, so close that I could have touched him. In a levin-flash, his face was stark and white, and his eyes wide and glittering. He reached for his dagger. Perhaps he hesitated; perhaps I was faster. I didn't go for my own, but for his, and I threw it towards the fireplace and backed to the head of the stairs. Thunder cracked, closer, and his words were drowned in an explosion as loud as the petard at Corinth. We were down the staircase in a moment.

'My lord, that man means us harm,' I said.

Amadeus glanced at me. 'You cannot be serious,' he snapped.

I didn't answer. We emerged into the courtyard, and even there the wind was high. The sky overhead was dark and getting darker, and lightning shot across it from side to side, a brilliant fork of a malignant red-orange such as I have seldom seen.

'He is a fool,' Amadeus said. 'But not such a fool that he would attack me in Venice.'

I shook my head. 'My lord, my mother used to say better safe than sorry. Let us be safe, and move.'

'I feel that I am running from ... Jesu!'

A flash and deafening crash of thunder. We were in the short tunnel between the courtyard and the guarded portico, and I saluted one of the guards.

He shook his head. 'You should wait,' he said. 'Something is happening on the docks.'

I ran out into the wind, leaving the others in the tunnel. I wanted to hire a boat before the weather got worse.

There were no boats. As I emerged, the first rain hit, and in a moment it was raining steadily. The rain might have explained the absence of wherries, except that I saw a boatman trying to land off to my left, down the wharves, and an unliveried man forcing him away.

I ran back to the gate of the palace. 'Someone is paying the boatmen not to land here,' I said to one of the guards.

He shrugged. 'In this much rain, boats are difficult to find,' he said.

I cursed. I probably tried some blasphemy, and perhaps even a prayer.

'Could the Doge provide a boat?' I asked. 'Or an escort?'

The man shook his head. 'Not today, in this kind of rain,' he said. 'Pierrot and I are all that there is in the lower hall.' He clearly thought I was an excitable foreigner; his next comment confirmed it. 'This is Venice,' he said, with kindly contempt. 'You may get a soaking, but the streets are safe.'

That's what you think. I remember feeling that I owed Richard Musard an apology; clearly Camus was willing to use violence. We were being set up to walk, and I could feel the Bourc's malevolence. He *wanted* me to know that we were to be ambushed, and he wanted me to feel terror.

Thunder rolled outside.

'Perhaps we should wait out the rain?' I suggested to Richard. I made a motion with my head at the guards and he clearly agreed.

He made the suggestion to the count, but the count would not hear of it.

'We are soldiers,' the count said piously.

'There are no boats, my lord,' I said. 'We will have to walk all the way to the Rialto Bridge.' The Rialto is another landmark of the city – built of wood, and quite ancient, with shops all along it.

I could see men coming down the Doge's stairs into the courtyard at our backs.

'Do you know a good route?' he asked me. 'I really only know the ground around our "hotel", and the square of San Marco.'

I was thinking. 'Yes,' I said. 'If you are determined to go now.' I caught Richard's eye. 'Now,' I said.

We walked out of the portico, all of us close about the count, and we had to lean into the rain, which hit us like hail. I turned them north, and we walked along the magnificent front of the ancient cathedral of San Marco, and then across the tail of the square and into a street. I saw movement behind us in the rain, but I hoped that if we stayed closed up, we wouldn't be a target. In a narrow alley overhung with houses as big as those in Constantinople, I stopped them all.

'Everyone stay close,' I said. 'We're being followed. Do not get lost. Don't trip over your feet and fall. Keep your dagger to hand.'

The count's green eyes seemed to bore into mine.

'You really think we may be attacked?' he asked.

'Yes, I do, my lord,' I said.

He nodded. 'Well,' he said, 'we have faced Saracens and Bulgars together. I do not expect much from the Prince of Achaea.'

It was well said, and he went up a little more in my estimation.

We set off north and a little east. I knew a route, on a sunny day, with the shops open, but I was less confident in a downpour in the dark, with all the lanterns out. I thought that the next alley was the *Spadaria*, the street of sword makers.

I was wrong.

'Are we not walking north instead of east?' the count asked, mildly enough.

'Men ahead,' Richard said.

A flash of lightning. Richard's eyes must have been sharper than mine, or I wasn't paying enough attention – a huddle of men in the rain, all standing together to avoid the flood of water coming off one of the tall buildings like a waterfall.

They had swords and cudgels. The flash spun off the swords and glittered on the wet wood of the clubs.

I pushed the count back into Richard's arms and drew. The Emperor's sword caught a flash of lightning in the sky above and burned orange-red in my hand.

I walked forward at the six of them. The obvious leader was a bandit or a routier; he wore maille and had a black silk scarf around his head. But he wanted no part of me after his bravos flinched. I saw his face in the flash of a levin-bolt; he was more angry than afraid, but he wasn't coming for me alone.

When I reached the corner, they were gone.

In that moment, I made a new plan. Camus had to assume we were making for the Rialto; there were only a few routes, and he could cut us off.

But if we didn't make for the Rialto ...

'This way!' I called, and led them west, towards the Greek neighbourhoods.

We crossed two little streets and a very small canal.

'You have a plan, messire?' the count asked me.

'Yes, my lord,' I admitted. 'I have a plan.'

The rain began to fall on us as heavily as following waves fall on ships in a storm. I was soaked through my half-cloak and my new hose; my new black shoes were wet through, and I had no pattens. The rain fell heavily enough that the count put up his hood, which was largely decorative. I did not, because I needed to see and hear, but it was hard to hold your head up in so much water. I could only see the length of a church nave, or less, and the streets twisted and turned, and it was hard to know exactly where I was, even with tavern signs and shops I knew. I knew that I was lost when we came through the *Spadaria* the wrong way, but perhaps that saved us. I knew where we were, and perhaps, when I think of it, we had doubled our scent, like a wily old fox.

The shops and houses overhung the street enough for us to stay dry for a few moments, and I looked both ways. There were people behind us; I was tempted to go for them because I didn't fancy being taken between two parties. I had to assume that if the Bourc was paying boatmen to stay clear of the wharves, then we were the target of a real attempt.

It still didn't make much sense. How many men could the Prince of Achaea have?

'We are going west, away from our house,' the count said.

'Yes, my lord.'

Musard looked like a half-drowned cat. He glared, his hood up; was it possible, I wondered, that he thought me false?

'My lord, we are being followed by men who mean you no good,' I said. 'I am taking action to keep you safe.'

The count nodded. 'Carry on,' he said, and we turned right, passed over a bridge and then emerged onto one of the narrow canals.

A crossbow bolt shattered into a thousand splinters right next to the count's head. It had struck a little pylon that in turn held a wall sconce, and the whole sconce tumbled into the street.

The count whirled, his sodden cloak flying.

There was a small bridge less than ten paces away, and on the bridge stood two men, soaking wet. By their postures, I assumed they were not men of violence.

'Roger, see to the count!' I shouted, and pushed the Count of Savoy towards the low bridge with what could only be described as a shove.

Roger understood. He had his dagger in his hand, and he pulled at his master's cloak and kept him moving.

I ran back, to where I could see steel in the darkness behind us.

If they had a second archer, I was a dead man.

I splashed through the alley and, this time, three swords rose to meet me. Behind the two swordsmen was another group. One, I thought, had his foot in a stirrup, trying to span his crossbow.

I slowed, reached my distance, and threw a hard cut, straight from the shoulder, at the first man with a sword. He was soaked as badly as I; his hood slowed him, and my cut went right over his *garde* and into his head.

The other man was the bravo in the silk scarf. He had a coat of maille, and he was fast. I still had the last four fingers of my sword caught in a dying man's skull, and I couldn't really see in the rain and dark, and I raised my hilt.

I got the other man's cut on my cross guard without losing a finger, and went forward with my cover, collapsing the bravo's arms against his chest, slamming him into the alley wall and bouncing his head off the stone. Then I kneed him in the groin ruthlessly, and turned away, wrenching my point out of the skull of the first man, who was already on the ground, his blood fairly pouring out into the water, a terrible sight.

Richard Musard went past me like a bolt of lightning, and his dagger took the next swordsman in the hand, a pretty blow, and then I couldn't watch more. I had my blade up, got my left hand on it in at the half sword, and I went forward into the press of brigands like a boatman poling in a heavy current – point, pommel, point, pommel. I probably pinked or bruised five of them, but they were already running, and the crossbow was left in the torrent of water at our feet. Richard took it, along with the dead man's arming sword.

Black Scarf was gone. He was a tough bastard and no mistake.

We ran back towards the little bridge.

The two men on the bridge proved to be Armenian monks, soaked to the skin and lost, and there ensured a moment of comedy, as we, the hunted foreigners, paused to give them directions, because we were all Christian men and we couldn't see them so miserable. And then we were across, and I relaxed, although the rain fell with renewed ferocity, so that we bent into it as we walked, and the wind rose. I looked back, ready to hold the bridge if I had to.

'Where are we going?' the count asked me.

'The Hospital,' I said.

He nodded. 'Good,' he said, and we made another turn to the right. I thanked God I had spent months in Venice before the crusade. I knew this route like I knew my own hands, and even in a high wind, with rain rattling off the glazed windows like arrows on good armour, I could find my way. The street had become a sewer, and water rushed past our feet, ankle-deep, with a current that could unbalance an unwary man, but we stumbled along to the Fondamenta dei Furlani and crossed the little bridge to the Hospital. If we were followed, our followers were as wet as we and far behind. When the porter opened the door, I have seldom been so relieved.

The knights made much of the count. The only knights of the Order actually present in Venice at the time were older men, who had seen many years of service; still, the count had just commanded one of the most successful crusades in many years, and he was much admired. They brought him a dry robe and shoes, and did as much for the others.

I took the porter aside. 'I had hoped that there would be companions here waiting for me,' I said. I explained having sent my squire to Chioggia.

The porter shook his head. 'Even the fishing boats stayed put today,' he said. 'This is terrible weather for August, but it cools the city.'

I asked him to keep an eye out for malcontents. He dismissed my fears as unworthy of his great city, and told me that there were no assassins in Venice.

'We were attacked,' I said. 'A killer shot at the count with a crossbow.'

The porter looked as if I was telling him that incarnate devils had danced in San Marco's square.

'I give you my word,' I said.

He just looked blank.

I had another idea. 'Do you know where the Lord de Mézzières is residing?' I asked. Philippe de Mézzières was not really a friend, but he was a famous crusader, the chancellor of the King of Cyprus and a friend of the Knights of the Hospital. Most importantly, he was the destination for my friend Sir Giannis, who had ten good Greek *stradiotes* at his back.

The porter nodded. 'Of course! Monsieur de Mézzières is not so far. But you cannot go out in this rain!'

I went back to the count and dripped on the parquetry floor. 'I'm off to get help,' I said. 'I want to strike while they are still in disarray.'

'You cannot imagine that a pack of bravos will lay siege to the Hospital,' the count said.

I shrugged. 'Better safe than sorry,' I said. I had a hard time imagining myself as the voice of reason, but there you are.

I went back into the rain as willingly as a cat might have, but in the end my fears were for nothing. I found de Mézzières' house easily enough, not far from where I'd dined with the Greek boat builder. One of Giannis's soldiers opened the alley door for me, and in a moment I was dripping on de Mézzières's wooden floor and explaining our plight to him.

He just shook his head. 'Assassins in the streets of Venice?' he asked.

His servant handed me a cup of warmed wine full of honey, and it was the most delicious thing that I had ever tasted.

'I need you and all your *stradiotes*,' I said to Giannis.

'Of course,' he shrugged, as if this sort of thing happened every day.

I went back into the storm, but this time with ten very hard men at my heels. The Greeks followed me at first, and then ranged into the streets on either side. Close to the Hospital we found two of the prince's men; Giannis's *stradiotes* beat them and threw them in the canal.

And then we were in the Hospital, with the *stradiotes* as a garrison. The old commander was as happy as a man can be, and he sat up late with two of the older *stradiotes*, swapping stories of fighting in Outremer.

I saw to the count and then staggered to bed.

The next day dawned to a clean city and an almost cloudless sky, and Venetians told me that the very best reason to have such a storm was to wash all the dirt off the buildings and the streets. Indeed, the combination of the seasonal high tide and the high winds and rain had brought on an *acqua alta*, my first, with water up to your groin in the streets. Shopkeepers laid boards on old stools along the alleys; sometimes you'd see a boat handing hot rolls through a window, because some houses didn't have a ground floor in high water.

The water went down very quickly, however, and we went back to the count's lodging in two boats, well guarded by armed Greeks. Afterwards, I made the time to visit de Mézzières, once I had collected the rest of my clothing.

De Mézzières was a fund of information about Venetian politics; he accompanied us home and spent some hours talking with the count about the state of the world, I suspect. I know they called me in to ask me about conditions in Jerusalem. De Mézzières treated me with every consideration, as if we were old friends, which was odd enough, but I was present when he explained one of the small mysteries of the day before.

The count was relating what had happened in the Doge's audience. De Mézzières shook his head ruefully.

'Cornaro is a busybody,' he said. 'He's not a bad man, and not a bad Doge, but he seeks to please all factions, to placate. That is why he's losing territory to the Genoese and the Pope.'

'He was a compromise candidate,' the count agreed.

'Next time it will be Contarini,' de Mézzières said. 'And then ...' He sat back. They were both sitting, and I was standing, which neatly expressed my social status.

'And then?' the count asked.

De Mézzières shrugged. 'I have given my life to the idea of taking back the Holy Land,' he said. 'For that to happen, Genoa and Venice must be at peace, and ready to lend their fleets to war on the Infidel.'

Count Amadeus nodded.

'If Contarini is Doge, then he will make war on Genoa,' de Mézzières said.

'That would be a terrible war,' the count allowed.

There was a little silence, and then the count went back to relating his interview. He was just repeating the prince's slanders against his father's second wife when de Mézzières shook his head again.

'*How* can the Prince of Achaea not know that the Doge is married to a second wife half his age?' he said with real incredulity. 'Indeed, he was a compromise candidate, as you say, and men tried to use his wife's low birth against him, and his foolishness in choosing to marry a low-born girl.'

The count looked at me.

'I was too angry to notice,' he said. 'Messire Guillaume, did he seem offended to you?'

'Mortally so,' I said. 'He stepped away from the prince and declared the audience at an end. The prince was deeply angry.'

De Mézzières nodded. 'Achaea may just have crushed himself,' he said.

I'll confess that I had already begun to wonder if I was going to be in a position to do Nerio a favour, by helping the Prince of Achaea to end up in an early grave. It was not, perhaps, a very chivalrous thought, but some aspects of war and rulership can be deeply ugly. And anyone who employed Camus was not likely to be much of a paragon.

At any rate, the next day, Marc-Antonio returned with Francesco Gatelussi and another half a dozen men-at-arms. Gatelussi received a very cautious welcome from our hosts, and, indeed, claimed he was the first member of his family ever to set foot in Venice. But the Hospital gave him a fine welcome, as did de Mézzières, and we heard on the same day that Prince Filippo, his men-at-arms and bravos had taken boats across to Mestre and ridden north.

I wasn't so sure. I went across myself a day later with Marc-Antonio and a pair of Giannis's stradiotes, and we rode west along the shore. I asked at several inns, and it seemed to me that the prince had gone to Padua, possibly on his way to Milan and Savoy, but other possibilities suggested themselves.

The count had several audiences; he visited many of the great families of Venice and he was, as I discovered later, on fairly intimate terms with the very same Contarini of whom de Mézzières had spoken. He went there the day I went to Mestre, and then again, on the feast day, when he took me. I discovered that the great Contarini was the same one-eyed old bastard who had won the naval action in the Aegean. And who had taught me to steer a galley – or taught me better.

He surprised me, not just by remembering me in the portico of his great family palace, but by wrapping me in a velvet embrace.

'Guglielmo le Coq,' he said. 'I have told the story of you leaping into the water a hundred times.' He actually held my arm as he ushered us up his broad steps to the piano nobile, and he seemed pleased to see me, which was kind.

It was a very pleasant evening, full of food and music. I met his wife and his family, which was extensive. Carlo Zeno, who was about to be employed in a military capacity, and Vettor Pisani, who had been our *capitano* in the expedition and who had led the Venetian ships at Alexandria, were there. Philippe de Mézzières was there, too, and the conversation, naturally enough, went to the taking of Alexandria. We discussed Jerusalem and de Mézzières held forth, not without persuasiveness, about how easily the chivalry of the west, if harnessed to the fleets of Venice and Genoa, could restore the Holy Land to the Cross.

I could tell that my lord the Count of Savoy was ill-pleased. I think that he felt unrecognised; I think that he felt that his own contribution was undervalued. Certainly, de Mézzières was not an ally of the count, and had a way of flattering the Venetians. And the count had contracted a mild fever, or an ague; his nose dripped and he had a cough, and illness made him darker than usual. So he sat and sniffled, and glowered.

I could see that this wasn't going to benefit anyone, and with a whispered prayer for aid in diplomacy, I tried to steer the conversation. Let me just say that when a dozen truly great men are having a loud conversation about an event in which they all participated, it can be very difficult to turn the ship, so to speak.

I had a notion, though.

'Do you think that any crusade can prosper without the support of the Emperor of the Greeks?' I asked de Mézzières, but in such a manner than anyone could answer.

The count looked at me.

De Mézzières sat back and frowned. 'The Emperor at Constantinople does not have a tithe of the sea power he had when I was a boy.'

'And yet . . .' I said, and Contarini sprang to my aid.

'The Emperor is not much of a friend of Venice,' he said, 'and yet, I'll say to any man that it is our duty to support him. The walls of Constantinople are the bulwark of Christendom. It is not just a centre of trade – it is the very presence of Christian power at the edge of Asia.'

Pisani nodded. 'Indeed, if the count here had not rescued the Emperor last autumn, we would be in an even worse state than we are in now. As it is, despite my opposition to the attack on Alexandria, the Sultan and the various beys and pashas know we have teeth.'

There followed a barrage of questions to the count about his operations in Bulgaria and in the Dardanelles. I rose and congratulated the musicians; there was a young man singing, probably a castrato, as he had a remarkable, clear, high voice like a woman. He pointed out a young man, who was playing a small organ, and who one could see was quite blind.

Old Contarini joined me. 'Florentine,' he said, indicating the organist. 'Brilliant, like all Florentines; he's already built two new organs here.' He introduced me, and I saw another side of Contarini – not just an admiral, or a man of business, but a serious patron of music. I shook the blind man's hand and thanked him for his music, and he flushed with pleasure.

'Tell us about Corinth,' shouted Pisani. He was waving at me from the table.

'You are French?' the blind man asked.

I allowed that I was English.

He nodded to himself, I think. 'Ah. If you were French, I would ask if you had met Monsieur Machaut.'

'But I *have* met him,' I said. 'My wife admires him enormously.'

Now the blind man's grip on my hand became ferocious. 'You have met Machaut?' he asked.

'William!' Zeno shouted.

'My apologies, messire,' I said to the blind man.

'Another time,' he said.

I went back to the table and told the story of the storming of Corinth and then, after dinner, Pisani and Contarini took me aside, together, in the loggia of the palace.

'Venice is always hiring men,' Contarini said. 'You are a lord and captain in your own right, but by God, sir, you have shown yourself a friend of Venice and a good soldier in the east. I could find you a contract ... The Council of Ten has funds ...'

I bowed deeply. 'I am very fond of Venice,' I said. 'Sadly, my lords, I have promised myself, first, to my lord of Savoy, and second, to Sir John Hawkwood. And third, or perhaps before all, to my friend Nerio.'

Contarini nodded, a very man-of-the-world smile on his old face. 'Ah, Nerio,' he said. 'Another promising young man. Well-disposed to Venice, would you say?'

I thought that Zeno was going to explode, but Contarini raised his hand. 'Let Le Coq speak,' he said.

I nodded. 'Nerio has fought under the Lion as often as I have myself,' I said. 'And he needs Venice to make Corinth rich. I have heard him say it.'

Contarini nodded, obviously pleased. 'And the current so-called "Prince of Achaea" blows with every wind,' he said. 'Listen, Guillaume. The war is coming. Not just any war – the great war we have all avoided since the plague fell on us. Venice will need allies.'

'Nerio is your man,' I said. I was over my head, but I had heard Nerio talking with Zeno. I had to hope he meant what he said.

They let me go with many professions of goodwill and future service. It is always pleasant to hear praise from men you value, and I rather liked the idea of fighting for the Lion once more.

Well, my time was yet to come.

I tell you all this so that you will know that, by the time that I heard that l'Angars had finally landed with all our horses at Pellestrina from Corinth, by the time that I knew he had brought fever and plague and all of my people with him were held on the Lazzaretto, by the time my new armour was ready and a company banner had been embroidered, by the time all these things had come to pass, I had convinced the Count of Savoy that I was more than just a sword. A little.

Which was just as well, as it was to be an autumn of daggers and diplomacy.

I sent money to the Lazzaretto and went myself to the receiving house, where I sat for a while, thinking of Emile, and then spoke to Peter Albin.

His eyes were red, and he looked terrible. And he was the healthy one, the doctor.

'My uncle died,' he said very quietly. 'A great many of the count's people are sick – a dozen are dead.'

It took an act of courage to breathe the same air, I promise you. They had plague, that summer, and we all feared plague like we feared God's punishment. More, to be honest; there are men who do not believe in God, but there are no men so foolish as not to believe in the pestilence.

The men who were sick were among my best: l'Angars, Pierre Lapot and Gospel Mark.

'I don't think they have plague,' Albin said, rubbing his face. 'I'm sorry. I am so tired.'

'Who does have plague?' I asked.

'The count's people. But most of the ones who had plague are dead. My uncle was among the last; he probably caught it from them. Do you know that there are fools in my profession who do not believe that plague can be transferred from person to person?' He shook his head. 'My uncle was a famous man. He is dead, and the count has done nothing – no burials, no extra food …'

'I will see to it that the count is informed. Things have been difficult.' The truth was that my patron had apparently forgotten; he was sick himself. And he was short on ready money. Twice he had borrowed small sums from me, and I knew I'd never see that money again.

Despite which, I handed over about forty ducats in gold and silver, all I had on me, or rather, all that Demetrios, the braver of my Greek boys, had in my purse. Stefanos stayed with the boat, being too afraid of sickness to come into the entry hall.

I didn't blame him. Have you ever had the experience of hearing someone describe an illness and feeling your skin prickle, or itch, in response to the description? Listen, then. I sat there in the entrance hall of the Lazzaretto, talking to Peter Albin through a grille as if he was a priest hearing my confession on a holy day, and I felt as if I could see the miasmas in the air around us. My skin burned, and my breathing was odd, and my heart raced.

I was perspiring freely.

I was afraid.

'Venetian doctors are the best in the world,' he said. He shrugged. 'And there are three very good ones here. But everything costs money – every medicine, every cup of wine.' His eyes went to a boat just landing at the side pier.

Half a dozen women came off, laughing and joking with the boatman about his pole. I could not understand much of their Veneziano, but enough to know a saucy joke when I heard one.

They were hard-looking, those girls, and none was what I'd call a great beauty, but they were well dressed and they could laugh. The prettiest one, who'd made a quip at the boatman, saw me looking at her and she made a little bob, a sort of abbreviated curtsy, and jutted her chin at me.

'See something you like, sailor?' she said in fair Italian.

I gave her a smile; her spirit was as pretty as her face. I got into our boat to go back to the Rialto, and after we were away from the Lazzaretto and Stefanos was crouching in the far corner of the boat from me, I asked the boatman.

'Whores?' I asked, pointing back at the landing stage.

He nodded. 'Salted,' he said. 'Girls who have had plague as children, or marsh fever, or both.' He shrugged. 'Sometimes they get sick and die anyway.'

I crossed myself. 'Jesus and Mary,' I said.

The boatman looked back. 'They are brave,' he said.

I nodded. 'By Saint Mary Magdalene,' I said, 'if I were dying, I'd rather one of them holding my hand than some bony-handed doctor.'

The boatman smiled with a world-weariness often found in Venetian boatmen. 'And if you could pay, one would hold your hand,' he said.

The next day, I took more money from the count to the Lazzaretto, and then I went along the Lido to look at our horses, which had been landed by strangers. Thankfully, none of them were missing. We had a fine herd, the best horse herd of any *compagnia di aventura* I have ever known – more Arabs, and better, taller, and in good condition. I talked to a farmer, paid a terrible price for another week of his pasture and grain, and pondered insolvency.

I sent Marc-Antonio back to Chioggia with orders for our people to be ready to ride to Padua on the fifth day of September, which was the count's projected day to leave Venice, but he continued to be busy. I will note that he gave Guy Albin, who had been his personal physician, a very good funeral and burial, and Masses were said for him at Sant'Agnese. He arranged funerals for a dozen more men.

'I lost more of my knights to this fever than to the Saracens,' he said. 'And I may miss the doctor most of all.'

I'm not telling this well. This was just after Master Albin's funeral, and we were both dressed in our best; the count went in person, which was quite an honour, and Vettor Pisani came.

We were perhaps ten days after the attack in the rain. I was almost constantly in attendance on the count; I was getting to know him quite well. He was very reserved, as most great lords must be, and he needed to be right on all subjects, which is tiring for servants. Even attendants require a certain spirit, and leading can be fatiguing. Mostly he issued orders in a direct way, affable enough, but leaving no possible room for converse or question. So his comment about Master Albin was curious – almost an invitation.

The count was sitting in the shaded end of our loggia and he was looking out over the canal. The fever had not left him, and he looked drawn.

Across the canal, a boat was unloading furniture, coffers and what appeared to be rolls of tapestry.

'He was a most engaging man,' I said.

'You found him so, did you?' he asked.

I wasn't sure what the count wanted. So I shrugged and spoke directly. 'It was a pleasure to speak English,' I said.

'What did you two talk about?' the count asked. 'I saw you speak at the rail, often enough, while we were cleaning up the Dardanelles.'

'The gospels, mostly. And medicine.' I smiled and tried not to tell the count, who seemed to me very pious, about Guy's pleasure in a little bawdy.

The count was looking out, not turning his head. 'I miss him,' he said quietly. 'You have commanded a company, messire. You know what it is to always keep up your face?'

'I do,' I said softly.

'A physician …' The count took a deep breath, and recollected himself. 'You will not repeat anything I say to you, monsieur?'

I sighed. It would be so easy to be offended by the count, or really, any of the other 'greats'. I found Prince Francesco very much of the same cloth when I served him as a young man. 'Never, my lord,' I said, although, of course, I'm repeating it now.

That was the first time I saw any sign he might actually like me, or favour me as anything but his available sword. He had never confided in me before, and while I knew he had repeated meetings with de Mézzières and with the Doge and his officers, I had no idea what they were cooking up. I just sent my messages, looked after the horses, and made sure that the count was constantly guarded. Just after our conversation, if I can call it that, his fever took a turn for the worse, and he went to bed. He stayed there for several days.

August gave way to September, and I was falling into the pleasure of living in Venice. I wrote to Emile almost every day; in fact, I associate that time in Venice with writing as much as with Camus, because I spent so much time at it. When the count discovered that I could write a fair hand, he had me copy confidential letters from his bedside, through which I came to know that affairs with the Prince of Achaea were worse than I thought. There was insurrection in Savoy, and some garrisons had betrayed the count. The deaths of a dozen of his leading vassals, in battle or from fever or plague, had left important lordships in the hands of minors, or even rivals.

His wife Bonne was dealing with the crisis cautiously. I was given one of her letters to copy, and while she showed all the outward submissiveness that one would expect in the daughter of the Duke of Bourbon, she also wrote clearly and seemed completely at ease with the reins of power – also to be expected from Bonne de Bourbon.

I also made the tour of libraries, and my itinerary of Northern Italy grew in complexity as I mapped out – literally – the optional routes south from Padua and Verona. The worst of the heat was passing; there were no new cases of plague, and all of our people on the Lazzaretto were healing, but the count was no better. I had a letter from Emile, who had been home, rallied her vassals, collected some taxes, and gone to court, where she was supporting the Countess of Savoy, Bonne. It was a letter full of news, pleasant and cheerful, and it hid all sorts of anxieties, from travelling with children to recalcitrant vassals, and yet I could guess them. It held a tiny lock of wispy blonde hair, from our daughter Cressida, and I still have that. I kissed that letter a hundred times, for all that it was bereft of love talk. It had something better. Emile was pregnant. She was due in December, or so she guessed. I let out a whoop like a war cry.

There was even an enclosure from Sister Marie, containing specific reassurances about Emile, about politics in the county, and some suggestions for my prayers and soul, which she felt was somewhat neglected. At any rate, my wife was in good hands, and happy. She liked ruling; she had Jean-François and Jason and Bernard. And she liked being pregnant.

And then there was a letter from Sir John Hawkwood. I feared that letter, I confess it – it sat unopened. I was busy; I had a boatload of supplies to take out to our people on the Lazzaretto, and I had hired a new pair of men-at-arms. I had a dozen little concerns, but the flat truth was that I feared I had done ill by Sir John in taking service with the count.

I went back out to the Lazzaretto with the count's boatman, Ambrogio, and Marc-Antonio. Most of the survivors of the fever and the plague from the count's household were ready to be released, and I was to fetch them. The men-at-arms looked like well-dressed scarecrows, and I had a long conversation with Peter Albin through the grille. I gave him more money, and told him of our travel plans.

'I will need you, and l'Angars,' I said. 'Can you take ship here for Ancona?'

Albin looked much better; he'd had sleep, and he was recovering from his uncle's death. 'Venetian ships don't land at Ancona,' he reminded me. 'We'll be clear in ten days. I'm not a soldier, but I'll guess as a physician that twenty men with good horses will double the distance the count makes.'

I thought about that. 'Make for Florence, then, and the Via Francigena,' I said. The Via Francigena, or Frankish Way, was the old pilgrim route to Rome. I explained about Camus and the Prince of Achaea.

Albin managed a laugh. 'After the plague,' he said, 'I'm finding it difficult to be afraid of a mere man.'

I sent my regards to l'Angars and Lapot and went down to the boat. The count's people were just coming out onto the landing stage, and our boatman was putting them aboard. We had a larger boat than usual, with four oars and space for a dozen passengers.

One of them looked better than the rest. It was Antonio Visconti, the scion of the Milanese family. He was a famous *condottiere* in his own right, and I had rescued him the year before in Bulgaria. He hooked his thumbs in his knight's belt and shook his head, looking over the Lagoon.

'I don't want to go to Venice,' he said, catching sight of me. 'Can you drop me on the Lido? And loan me some money?'

It was a bold request, but we knew each other, and I certainly knew he was good for money.

I motioned to Demetrios and he came out of the boat and handed over our purse. I counted out twenty ducats, mostly in silver soldi.

'You are a good friend,' Antonio said. 'My brother Ambrogio is fighting in the south, and he wants me. I don't need to linger here.'

'The count will leave for Rome in a few days ...' I began.

Lord Antonio shrugged his eloquent Milanese shrug. 'Messire Guglielmo,' he said, with a deep and somewhat sarcastic bow. 'The Green Count will take twenty or thirty days to cover what I can ride over in five. And if I never see your pompous count again, it will be too soon.'

Well. I once thought as he thought. On the other hand, I had rather counted on his sword for the trip south, the more so as he didn't seem as reduced by illness as the other Savoyard knights.

'My brother is fighting against the Pope in the south,' he said again. 'It is finally starting. All my life, my father and uncle have talked of luring the Pope to Italy where we can finish him.'

'Milan is at war with the Pope?' I asked.

Antonio looked around, afraid to be overheard. 'Of course not,' he said. 'My brother is deniable. I am deniable. We are by-blows – mercenaries.'

I may have rolled my eyes. I did not yet know the Visconti the way I would come to know them over the next year, but I knew them well enough to know that they hung together; their family was their creed. I doubted that the Pope or anyone else was fooled.

It concerned me, as I knew that the Count of Savoy was a close neighbour of Milan, and yet was trying very hard to work with the papacy.

'I hear you have many excellent horses to sell,' he said. There are no men in the world more confident than Italians and, in particular, the Visconti. Antonio stood on the landing stage of the Lazzaretto, penniless, thin, and lacking everything but will, despite which, he burned with confidence.

'You mean, you'd like me to sell you a horse and then loan you the money to buy it?'

'Four horses,' he admitted. 'The best.' He leaned forward. 'No one in my family will forget it,' he said. 'And we are a good family to know.'

'Antonio,' I said, because I don't like to be snowed, 'I saved your life last year, as I remember. I am not sure I need to give you my best horses to win your family.'

He had the good grace to grin. He bowed. 'I suppose what you say is true,' he said. 'But I still need those horses.'

I did make him sign a little scrap of parchment, as he now owed me almost five hundred ducats, and I was running out of money.

He arranged a boat to the Lido, and I helped him with his harness and his squire's harness, and then he rowed away, headed towards a war in Naples that I might have been fighting in myself.

I was coming back up the pier when I saw the pretty whore sitting with her bare legs dangling almost in the sea. She was fishing, and as I watched, she caught a fish. I rather enjoyed watching her play it; she had her tongue between her teeth like a cat, and yet she knew her business, and she brought it in deftly.

Marc-Antonio, who was always eager to serve a lady if there was a chance he might come to her favours later, got down and hoisted the fish from the water – a good three or four pounds.

She took the fish, but not the casual hand that Marc-Antonio tried to place on her breast, and she laughed and kicked him as she went up the dock.

Marc-Antonio tripped her, quite casually, and then ran a hand up her leg as he caught her. The boatmen laughed. She kicked again, almost helpless now.

I caught his shoulder. 'Let her go,' I said.

'She's a whore, common to all,' Marc-Antonio said. 'I'll have my turn, my lord, will she, nil she.'

'No,' I said. 'You will not. Go to the boat, if you please.' Perhaps I was so firm because I fancied her.

The girl, on the other hand, was sheathing a small knife in her hair. She gave me a broad smile. 'Eh, Signore. I like the way you give orders.' She blew me a kiss and skipped away quickly.

We got into our own boat and were rowed across the Lagoon, past San Marco and into the Grand Canal. I spoke gently to the men who had been sick; most of them still looked terrible and I realised that none of them were going to be any help in the ride south. I had counted on a dozen more men-at-arms. I will admit that, after a fortnight of the Green Count, I liked him better, and yet I would have been content to have Musard take charge of his escort while I rode south to Hawkwood. I regretted that I hadn't read Hawkwood's letter yet; I suspected he'd be in the south, with Ambrogio, as they had served together before.

Marc-Antonio was sullen. He resented my action, and he was considering saying something really unforgivable, as young men sometimes do. Marc-Antonio often made me feel old. I was thinking all these thoughts as we turned into our own small canal. The boat we were in was considerably larger than the usual canal boats, and the count's hired boatman was yelling some surprising imprecations at a heavy cargo vessel that was unloading opposite our fondamenta on the narrow Calle del Ponte Storto.

I was still trying to understand what he had just yelled. Something about a pack of hyenas?

The rival boatman snarled a reply, and I realised a great many things in a sort of crescendo, like the moment when all the choirs come together at San Marco in the elevation of the Host.

I realised that this cargo boat had been unloading now for two full days. That was not possible.

I realised that it had rained the night before, and that the boxes and carpets rolled on the cargo boat's deck had been left out in the rain. No sane working man would do that.

I realised that the angry boatman yelling at us was a man I'd seen in the rain: a man who had been wearing a black headscarf when I had seen him abandon his friends and run …

And, of course, Black Scarf knew that I knew. My face, no doubt, gave me away. That or my hand going to my dagger.

My sword was twenty feet away, being held by Stefanos in the stern. I was in a boat full of virtually defenceless men. And I had to wonder if they'd already killed the count. There was no other reason for them to be there; they were watching the little palazzo. All this, as our boat glided towards theirs. Ours was lower in the water, but not enough to make much difference; the two boats were much of a size, and there was no way they could pass each other on the narrow side-canal.

Black Scarf was turned away from me, bellowing orders.

'Those men mean to attack the count,' I said to Marc-Antonio and the Savoyards nearest to me.

Thank God, they all believed me.

Black Scarf appeared with a crossbow – a light one, the kind you use for hunting birds.

I didn't even have a stone to throw.

It is a terrible thing, a fearful thing, to stand and wait to take a lethal bolt. I can't describe it: the boats moving together … the sheer terror of the crossbow. He was aiming at me, the bastard.

God saved my life. God, and an unseen boatman coming down the canal the other way, asleep at his oars, or perhaps flirting with his passenger. His little gondola struck the cargo boat just as Black Scarf pulled the trigger on his weapon. The bolt passed between me and Marc-Antonio and killed a Savoyard who had just survived the plague.

Our bow ground into the cargo boat and I leaped over the gunwale, armed only with my wits. I had a dagger in my belt, but I was not so handy on boats that I could spare a hand for a weapon yet.

Marc-Antonio came with me; I felt him land on the cargo boat. Now don't imagine a great round ship. This was a boat smaller than most fishing wherries, capable of carrying four passengers or a lot of rolled carpets. I went over the cargo, and the boat threatened to tip. The next bolt ripped along my inner thigh like a hot iron on my flesh. The pain was so intense that I fell, bounced, and caught my feet on the opposite gunwale, saving myself from an unwanted swim.

Black Scarf had an arming sword, a hand's width broad at the grip and narrowing to a needle point. He cut at me, and he hit, slamming the blade into my shoulder and back and catching a little of my scalp. It all hurt. Then I turned, facing him, my feet still on the gunwale, and I got my dagger in my right hand – a long dagger with a heavy backbone. I'd drawn right-handed, with the blade down, and I covered his next blow with a sweep across my body, so that his cut came onto the backbone of the dagger, but he was too fast for me to accomplish anything. Anyway, I was balanced on the edge of a boat and had no place to put my feet.

I considered going into the water.

He tried a deception. He wanted me dead, but he was in a hurry and he was afraid. All men are afraid in combat, I suppose, except the stupid ones, but he was functioning and not thinking, if that makes sense, and instead of just pushing me into the water, he did something complicated.

You can't deceive a dagger. I mean, I suppose maybe Fiore can, but not many other fighters. I didn't have to think; the point of my dagger went into his sword hand while he rolled it left and right, trying to open my centre, I suppose.

Then I had his sword and he was dead. I went over him into the stern of his boat, and his other three bravos were running. But I was not alone; one of the Savoyards had got himself all the way onto the fondamenta, despite a month of poor food and no exercise. He picked up a candlestick and attacked one of the crossbowmen. And got him.

Marc-Antonio vaulted over the cargo and came down feet-first on another, breaking the man's shoulder.

The third man dived into the canal.

What was I doing?

I was standing, as the wave of pain began to hit me. Black Scarf had landed a good blow. His cut hadn't gone through the good wool of my old doublet, but it had gone into my scalp and everything hurt, and my left side hadn't been working all that well to start with.

I sat suddenly, and it took an effort of will for me to stand up.

Our boatman slammed his steering oar into the swimming man's head before I could demand that the man be captured.

It was a stout blow – the oar splintered, and the swimming man sank. He never came up.

Marc-Antonio had the only prisoner.

But an hour later, in the wet lower rooms of the palazzo, the prisoner, clearly terrified and badly injured, had admitted nothing. He claimed we'd attacked him, that he had been unloading furniture, and he claimed it with a conviction and a steadiness that made me doubt.

Vettor Pisani came with a dozen Arsenali. They took the man away and, before he'd left the room, Pisani reassured me.

'He's not Arsenali,' Pisani said. 'Not one of mine. And no one but an Arsenali may walk armed, much less carrying an arbalest.' He had both of the weapons. 'This one will swing, even if he talks.'

'Not much incentive,' I said.

Pisani shrugged. 'He's not Venetian. Can't you hear him? Milanese.' He shook his head. 'You're bleeding, young man,' he said.

That evening, I moved the count to the Hospital. His boatman helped us. He was a Roland or Galahad among boatmen. He accepted that hiding the count from enemies was part of his duties, and we delivered two boxes of new glass panes – a real order from Murano – which our boatman went and fetched to give his errand complete verisimilitude. He smiled the whole time.

'My father was a smuggler,' he said. 'I enjoy defying authority.' This seemed an odd attitude for a man employed by the Count of Savoy. But I was not in a place to complain, and when I saw the count to a Hospital bed, with Musard there to guard him, I went to my little chamber. Sir John's letter was there, waiting for me.

It is hard to explain. I had been afraid of it, and now I was not; or perhaps I was beyond fear. The blow to my head and shoulder had been as close to mortal as I ever need to come. It scared me every time I thought of it – made my insides turn over, made my hands tremble.

I popped the hawk seal on the letter with my thumbnail and unwrapped the outer layer, which was oiled linen, and then pulled open the inner parchment envelope which, I noted, was an old itinerary with numerous wormholes.

It was addressed to 'Guglielmo d'Oro, Miles,' which made me smile.

'To my gracious and puissant lord, Guglielmo d'Oro, Lord of Methymna, Baron of Gorytos, greeting,' it said. I smiled wryly, even with pain. The light was bad; I was allotted one taper to get myself to bed, and I needed more light. I went out into the corridor and there was a serving brother with a towel over his arm, clearly on his way to bed.

'Brother,' I said, stopping him, 'do you think I could use the library at this hour?'

He grinned. 'Prior is still up,' he said. 'He won't mind.'

I went down the curving stairs from the monks' hall and then crossed the little bridge to the library. Sure enough, the Prior of Venice was sitting in a fur-lined robe that had seen many better days, his bare feet up on a stool, reading from a scroll.

'I have a perfectly good house,' he said when he looked up. 'But there are more candles here.'

I was meant to laugh, so I did. He waved me to a seat, and I pulled one up at the reading table, lit by two big oil lamps and a pair of candlesticks that would not have looked out of place in a great cathedral, all silver gilt.

'There's wine, if you want it,' he said. 'A good year, out there in the Veneto somewhere.' He pointed at a pitcher on the sideboard, which by chance sat almost exactly below a small sign in carefully lettered Latin that demanded that neither food nor drink be consumed in the library.

I poured myself a glass. A real glass, as good or better than Bohemian glass. It was a pale green and very clear. I sat down at the table, wine in hand, and went back to Sir John's letter.'

'It is with every joy that we hear you are safely returned from Outremer and many deeds of arms conducted in the very face of the enemies of our Lord,' he said. I smiled, as the Pope sometimes referred to John Hawkwood and mercenaries as the enemies of our Lord.

'And we understand with pleasure that you continue in the service of that estimable and noble lord, Count Amadeus of Savoy, of noble fame! The count has never been our friend, and yet we hold him in the very highest estimation.'

I wasn't sure exactly how to take that last. I drank wine.

'I myself am not in service to any lord, great or humble, but lead a Free Company now; many men well known to you. We have elected to act together to protect ourselves from the depredations of our many enemies.'

That made me smile.

'It is possible that in the spring we may be in a position to offer employment to all of our friends, but at this time, we fear that we cannot honour our obligation to you, which makes us all the more joyous to hear that you are in service to that noble Lord of Savoy. And we understand that you intend to accompany him to Rome, which service you may find arduous, so we recommend some caution. Even in the south, where we are now, we have heard of certain men who seek to harm the noble count.

That was bald enough. And if John Hawkwood, ten days' ride away, knew that the Prince of Achaea was attempting to kill the count, I needed to be even more cautious.

The truth is, the first attempt in the rain had been so haphazard and so like the temperamental, mad Camus, that I had assumed it was delivered in a rage. I had not yet assimilated the second attack, and the preparations they must have been making. Indeed, for the first time – and call me a fool if you will – I realised that nothing but the count's sickness must have saved his life. They had been ready to murder him if he left the palazzo by water. And if Hawkwood knew enough to send me a warning … And the warning was, by then, ten or twelve days old.

The Prince of Achaea must have come to Venice intending to kill the count.

I sat back suddenly, and the prior looked up.

I shook my head and went back to the letter.

There was a flowery ending, full of empty Italian praise, done by a professional notary. Indeed, the whole letter bore the stamp of a scrivener: elegant Tuscan Italian and well-practised flourishes.

There was an enclosure. It was a small slip curled inside – paper, not vellum. I opened it and saw it was from Janet, whom I hadn't seen in two years. I had requested that she send me something for Richard.

It said: 'Guillaume — We are north of Naples, facing Albornoz. Sir John is afraid that everyone will know we are serving Milan in this; I think that everyone already knows. We are serving under Ambrogio; he can't find his arse with both hands, and you should not come. And as to Richard, tell him I am not for him. And that I'm sorry. Show him this if you like.

'Hawkwood says you are both serving Count Amadeus. I knew him as a child; you are fortunate. Stay with him. Do not come to Naples; it is like Hell come to earth.

'Janet

'P.S. And now I am reduced to writing letters and watching the money.'

I put the letter into my purse, finished my wine and crawled off to bed. The prior didn't even raise his head. The hospital's cat was an old, well-fed tom; he raised his head and gave me a look.

My shoulder hurt like fire in the morning, but the count was better, and announced that we were leaving in two days.

We left Venice on the eighth day of September. I was still recovering and, for the first time in a long time, my wound had become infected – the scalp wound, that is. I was lucky that Black Scarf's cut hadn't been delivered better, or I'd have been dead. Instead, I merely suffered from a fever and headaches.

Musard did most of the work. But he did it well; he knew how to lead a company as well as I, and although most of my men didn't know him that well, they knew of him. We stayed a night in Chioggia and my hosts, the Corners, were amazed and delighted to host the Count of Savoy.

The count didn't go anywhere, even Mass, without four armed men in maille attending him. We learned to be very close. I made them accept that the threat from the Prince of Achaea was real – that a murder attempt was possible. We used tasters, and we planned deceptions.

I left half the horses and a power of attorney with Matteo Corner, with instructions to pass it on to l'Angars when he was released from the Lazzaretto. To ride with the count I had six of my own lances, as well as half a dozen more archers under Rob Stone, all mounted on fine horses and with spares just as good. In addition, we had Sir Giannis and his *stradiotes*, or at least the eight who remained, as one had died at Corinth and one had just married a Greek girl in Venice. We also had Richard Musard and his squire, Georges Mayot and his squire, and a dozen pages and servants; altogether about forty men and eighty horses.

Most men turned north at Chioggia, rode across the causeway and then followed the river Adige northwards to Padua. Richard sent Sir Giannis and our horses that way, and the rest of us took a flatboat up the river. It cost a mint, but it was pleasant and fast. It allowed me to keep the count under cover.

We made Verona on the second day, and found Sir Giannis there before us, staying in a fine house in the countryside. I knew the town, and so did the count. He had good friends there among the della Scala – we had no need to hide him.

Father Angelo came into his own in Verona, as he was a della Scala himself, albeit of the cadet branch, and he knew everyone, and everyone knew him. He arranged lodgings for us all. Thanks to him, and to the count's reputation, we stayed in the magnificent *castello*, all brick, almost new, where I had once almost been captured or killed. This time I was well received, or perhaps they didn't know me at all. We were all fed by the tyrant, and he gave a fine feast for the count, although I suspect it had been intended for a religious festival, and our arrival was not as surprising as he suggested. Regardless, it was a fine fête, and we ate until we could barely walk.

I think I have said before that Verona is a beautiful city. Perhaps the fairest thing about it is its squares; there are several, and each leads on to the next through fine arches of worked stone. There are magnificent outdoor staircases, and balconies and porticos and colonnades at every level; it's a little like Venice without water. So we dined in the square of the city hall, and then walked through a magnificent arch to where there were musicians outside a building with a magnificent facade, all frescoed, with a lower line of fretwork. And in that square we danced – fast Italian dances, unlike anything from England. The count led almost every dance, at the invitation of the della Scala, and we were not bereft of partners. Indeed, the women of Verona are second to none in beauty or dress. I danced with a Giulia and a Beatrice and an Esperanza and a Bianca and a Sabina; all five were clever, witty, and kind. Even Father Angelo danced, which surprised me, but he was at home, and these were his people, and through him I met many of the local gentry.

I was too long away from Emile. I should be ashamed to admit it, but I am a lovesome man, and I do like women. I like to dance with them, and I like to look at them, and months riding around Greece without women, and living with the Order's monks in Venice, had not shown me the charms that Sabina showed in a single elegant turn of her head, or Giulia in a wave of her hand and a laugh.

I'm sure it's all a sin, this admiration of women, but I will crib the great Aquinas and say that as women are God's creation, the admiration of them can hardly be a sin.

Sadly, Marc-Antonio failed to keep his hands to himself and was almost killed. He was an aggressive lecher – we'd had words about it in the past – but at Verona he got a hand under someone's kirtle and she was not agreeable.

I pulled a young man off my squire, and then had to take his dagger away from him and not break his arm. The girl was obviously shattered.

'You will apologise,' I said. 'Get up.'

'She …' he began. 'She invited me …'

Somehow this incensed me. One look at the girl and I could see that being groped by my squire had never been her intention.

He looked at me. My squire – my right hand. My trusted man, my friend. But he had done this before. I had not made a stand then, when I'd seen him grope the whore at the Lazzaretto …

'You completely misunderstood her, you are an idiot, and you must beg her mercy,' I said in Greek.

He flushed. He was angry, and he'd been hurt when the young man attacked him.

He managed a pretty good bow. 'Madonna, I am devastated that I have been such a boor. I beg your pardon.'

The girl was crying. But she steadied herself. 'I never …' she said.

I looked around. We were under the loggia, the row of colonnaded arches; no one was looking.

I managed to catch the eye of Siora Giulia, who had just been my partner and who, I admit, I had abandoned. She was … cautious … about joining me in the relative darkness under the arches. But she came.

I turned her away. 'My squire has made an arse of himself,' I said. 'This poor lady …'

Giulia shook her head. She shot Marc-Antonio a basilisk glare and passed him as if he was carrion or dung and put her arms around the young woman. She walked the girl out from under the stairs, leaving us with the angry young man.

'I want to fight him,' the young Veronese said.

Marc-Antonio was no longer an overweight accountant trying to be a fighter. He was a man who'd been in twenty actions; he'd probably killed ten times or more.

'No,' I said. 'He'll kill you.'

'I'm not afraid!' shouted the young man.

'Calm yourself,' I said.

One of the della Scala officers appeared as if by magic. Later I learned that he was Lady Giulia's knight; at the time I was delighted at his forbearance and rapid Veronese Italian. He took the young man away almost as efficiently as Siora Giulia had removed the young lady, with an admonition that we were preserving the young woman's reputation.

When the man was gone, Marc-Antonio glared. 'You didn't even hear my side,' he said.

'You have no side,' I said. 'You attacked her.'

'She was willing enough—' he began.

'That's weak,' I said. 'She's young enough that she hasn't ever met a bastard like you. Now she has, she won't go for walks ...'

'Most girls—'

'I will kill you myself,' I said. 'Shut the fuck up.'

Yes, I was very angry. He was my squire, and I was responsible for him, and here he had very nearly committed a rape. I had to wonder how many other women had been as unwilling.

'She didn't say no!' he said.

'Did you let her say anything?' I asked. 'Don't tell me.'

'Even when they say no they mean yes—'

I hit him. I'm not particularly proud of it, but I'm not altogether ashamed either. Sometimes a blow does more than words to convey disapproval, especially to young men.

He fell back to the same bricks from which I'd lifted him. And spat, rubbing away tears of rage and shame with his fist.

'You are my squire,' I said, after rubbing my knuckles. 'I do not expect to discuss this with you ever again.'

I walked back to the torchlight, had a cup of wine, and returned to dancing.

Perhaps you will think me a great prude. Perhaps I am. I am a lovesome man myself; I have made love to women against the laws of God. But, by the risen Christ, I have never forced a woman, even by word or manipulation. It is the exact repudiation of what I believe in knighthood.

I was prepared for him to leave me. I was angry, but not so angry that I couldn't think. I was level enough to know that he might just collect his horse and arms and ride home. His family was only a day away.

And that is exactly what he did. It is a little amusing that from the ripe age of twenty-eight I could read a nineteen-year-old so well, but I could. I danced a little more, and then walked back through the beautiful streets to the castello, where I fell into bed, waking some time later to find that the count was already up, and I was short a squire.

We stayed three days in Verona. We went out into the countryside and ate in the hills above the town, Valpolicella, where the best wine comes from, and Father Angelo took us to Montorio. It was a pleasant party, and I flirted a little with various locals and thought of the pure hypocrisy of my anger at Marc-Antonio. When I was nineteen, I ran a brothel. And I had had various girls. While they had all been willing, I wasn't exactly choosy.

Bah. And yet, let us say one is a poor swordsman. And let us say one devotes one's life to a life of arms, and becomes proficient. Should other young men spurn you as a teacher because you were once a poor sword? No. Your experience and training have earned you the right to teach. I hope it is this way with sin.

Richard asked me where Marc-Antonio was on the second morning, when I was tacking up my own riding horse, whom I called Juniper, a magnificent Arab mare who I planned, if I got her alive to Emile, to make a brood mare for a line of Arabs. She was as beautiful as any horse I've ever known, and tough as an old boot, and while she was no Gabriel, I'd practised some fighting from her back and she was capable.

I digress, as usual. Richard asked me where Marc-Antonio had gone, and I explained.

He scratched his beard, leaning against the wall of my stall. 'Does it ever make you think?' he asked, toying with his paternoster.

'What? Does what make me think?' I asked.

Richard spread his hands. 'Our old life. Our new life. I've grabbed a girl or two in the dark.' He smiled sadly.

I had my saddle on Juniper, and I adjusted the girth, walking around her murmuring words of comfort, and then tightened the girth again. I leaned on her and looked at Richard. 'All the time,' I said. 'I'm no Galahad. But what he did ...'

Richard shrugged. 'I know,' he said.

'He was an excellent squire and a good fighter,' I said. 'But that's not enough.'

Richard tugged at his beard. 'Ever think that maybe we're such a pair of prudes because we lived so hard?' he asked. 'Mayot taxes me for my "morals" all the time.'

I hadn't considered it, but now I did, in the pleasant warmth of a stable in Verona. 'You mean, having started as thieves and rapists, we know why all the rules matter?' I asked.

Richard nodded. 'You know, before you came ... I just tried not to think of it. Of ... being a routier. And of ... Janet. And all that.' He looked away. 'But you came, and it all came back with you.'

What could I say?

Juniper shuffled and stamped a foot, and I calmed her.

'I guess I'm afraid,' Richard said. 'Afraid it's all a dream, and I'll find myself on a road in a rusty harness, off to kill some strangers. Or running a fucking brothel.' He looked at me. 'I want it to be far away, but it's close, every time I fight, or ...' He shook his head. 'Listen to me, I'm sounding like some sort of weak ...'

I went and put my arms around him, and we clasped each other hard.

'We won't go back to being routiers,' I said. I guess it was the right thing to say.

By the time we left Verona, my scalp had mostly healed, and Richard and I were getting along well. The count was ready to dispense with our anxious and close guard.

We rode south to Mantua. The count was well received, and the countryside was flat and ambush-proof. In Verona I'd been received as an important man in the great man's train; the Lord of Mantua treated me as a sort of soldier-servant. He treated Musard and Mayot the same; we went to barracks, mostly full of German men-at-arms, and there were no pretty maidens to dance with.

South of Mantua a day was Bologna. And if you are wondering

why I didn't go straight to Bologna via Ferrara, I can only say, ask the count. He was on a triumphal progress of sorts. Richard and I had also determined on a strategy, since the count would not travel in secret, of making dashes from stronghold to stronghold. And with forty men, we were a difficult target as long as we stayed together.

Bologna had other problems. It was a Papal city; the city itself was the very bone of contention between the Pope and the Visconti, as the Milanese laid claim to it. I had seen a crowd there, paid to kill the Papal Legate, or so it seemed to me, and I mistrusted Bologna, and the city government apparently returned the favour by mistrusting me. I spoke to a captain and the podestà, and we rode into the city under an escort. They hosted the Green Count for a single day; no one commented on how young he looked, or noticed that his eyes had changed colour, and we rode out again without being attacked. In fact, Francesco Gatelussi had played the count very well, while Richard had taken the count around the town and spent the night in the Capuchin monastery.

But there was no attack.

I will say that during this time, as my head wound healed and my fever abated, I really began to see Richard at work. The count, like most great men, took a fair amount of handling, and was somewhat given to sudden ideas that were – some of them – quite useful; others, less so.

I came to realise that Richard's handling of the count was masterful, and far more closely planned than I had seen before. The count was so formed that he had to be right, nearly all the time. He would correct me on matters of horsemanship, or etiquette, and I had discovered that it was my role, as the low-born but noble knight, to graciously accept his correction in all such things. Likewise, he was, by virtue of his birth, pre-eminent in matters of diplomacy and statesmanship and most other things, and he would correct any suggestion that Musard made on almost any subject.

For a week I writhed whenever he took his most patronising tone with Richard, but Richard never seemed to resent it. In small matters of household management – things like wines to be served with meals – Richard would present his intention and the count would correct him, a good master admonishing an erring servant. It happened every day, over and over, and it annoyed me on Richard's behalf, until we came to the matter of the route to Florence.

Florence was our next destination, and there were mountains and very bad roads between the two cities. The problem for me was that we hadn't had a sniff of an attack since Venice. And the count was no longer very interested in my precautions, so that almost every day, I had to call on Richard to mollify him. Richard and I discussed the day's travel for a quarter of an hour after Matins.

In brief, I wanted to take a series of small country roads, really like paths. I'd found a guide I wanted to hire and I intended, as Hawkwood had taught me, to pay him very well. I was afraid, however, that the count, who had been less than pleased by the deception at Bologna, let us say, would demand to travel by the main road to Florence.

My fears were increased by chance events. I am not a superstitious man, but the priest dropped the Host at the elevation that night at Mass. The endless rolls of thunder in the distant hills served to remind me of how dangerous our next stage was.

The thunder was accompanied by a fine, but soaking, mist of rain the next morning, and the skies were a solid iron-grey. When the count came down from the solar he'd slept in at the monastery, he had a simple breakfast, served by Richard, and then he waved for me to attend him.

As I walked up, Richard smiled at me. 'Messire Guglielmo would have us take some tangled trails across the mountains,' he said, sneering at my efforts. 'Listen to me, my lord. We can make the journey on the best road, and with more comfort.'

Richard and I had been getting along well enough, but at this, I thought, *you traitor*!

As if to put the last nail in the coffin of my careful planning for the count's security, Richard said, 'And the expense! He wants to hire a guide that will cost as much as a day's fodder for the horses. An unnecessary expense, I feel, my lord.'

I am not much slower than the next fellow, I hope. I met Richard's eye and it held no hint of reserve or shyness. Instead, it looked as if he was laughing.

The count glanced at me. And then at Richard. 'You rate my safety so low, do you, sir?'

Richard bridled, as he did every time the count corrected him. 'But my lord!' he said. 'Just yesterday you complained . . .'

'Messire Guglielmo works patiently to protect us,' the count said in his tone of gentle admonishment. 'Sometimes his precautions are over-elaborate, but in this, a simple deviation from the well-travelled route, I see good planning. Come, Richard, what is a little inconvenience to knights? Perhaps we will have an adventure.'

'As you say, my lord,' Richard said, with good grace, and smiling at me over his shoulder.

I probably rolled my eyes. Listen, my friends; Chaucer is already nodding. A few months later I was a better courtier, and I thought nothing of such manoeuvres to get my lord to do what was necessary, but that autumn, travelling south to Rome, I felt the count's presence like a horse feels a bridle.

I went and fetched my guide. He was a small farmer, Alonzo by name. Clean and neat, he had a scar over one eye and a long nose, and I found him a little too obsequious for my taste, but I assumed he was unused to the likes of the Green Count. I paid him five gold florins and showed him five more.

'When we enter Florence,' I said.

He bowed deeply. 'Two days,' he said, 'and you will see the new cathedral rising into the sky over the city.'

That seemed an odd thing to say, and I didn't like him, and suddenly my whole plan seemed too bold.

I sat on my riding horse in the yard. I was in an agony of indecision; it's not my best state. The count was waiting. Richard was casting anxious glances at me, and Mayot was toying with his reins in a way that suggested that his temper was fraying.

'Let's go,' I said, with an authority I wasn't sure I really felt. We rode out through the gates of the monastery and then we rode past Santo Stefano and out into the countryside, where the hills rose green and round against the blue sky, contrasting splendidly with the golden fields of wheat all around the city.

Those hills were quite a barrier.

We rode by Ponticella, a little village. An odd thing happened there: I was riding in front, with Alonzo, and a man came out of a small house. When he saw us, he flushed, and then he threw the apple he'd been eating at Alonzo. The apple core clipped Alonzo's horse and made it start, and the man himself called 'Traitor!' and ran into his house.

Alonzo turned white, but his scar flushed bright red.

Richard Musard was right behind us. He smiled affably – always a sign that Richard was on edge. 'Family?' he asked in his excellent Italian.

Mayot laughed, and I smiled, but Alonzo turned red as a beet. 'No family of mine,' he said. 'His fool of a son went and got himself killed. He is nothing to me.'

After Ponticella we turned due south, into the hills. The road became a track, and the track became a trail, and by mid-morning we were leading our horses and thanking our maker we had pack animals and not wagons. We climbed steadily until it was time for lunch, and then we passed Casa Grandi, a well-deserved name for the fine castle there, and travelled south along the valley floor. We made good time, amid the oak and beech and silver fir. Small streams wound along our path, and the count declared himself delighted; indeed, we were all of a mind to see a unicorn in such beautiful surroundings.

The Lord of Mantua had given the count a hawk, and he decided to fly it after partridges then. Although he was a fine hawker, he had to cross and recross the little brook that rolled along to the west of our track, which slowed us considerably, and then the hawk settled in a tree. The count cursed, and all of us spent an uncomfortable hour trying to rescue the belligerent bundle of feathers.

The day was passing and our guide was growing increasingly disturbed.

I didn't watch the hawking much after that, because I was watching my guide. I'd chosen him, with the help of the monks at the monastery and with the approval of the podestà. I couldn't imagine that he had been planted on us.

But I couldn't like him. He started at everything and he was clearly affected by our delays.

'Can we not . . . convince the count . . . to ride on?' he asked me, finally.

'No,' I said. 'Are you in a hurry? The count is not here for our convenience.'

He mumbled something.

I wished that I had Marc-Antonio. Even more, I wished for John the Turk.

I had to settle for Rob Stone. I rode back to him.

'I need you to scout ahead,' I said. 'I don't trust our guide.'

'That's not good,' he said. 'Give me Lazarus and Ewan.'

An hour after the bird was found, my archers had cantered off down the road. No sooner had they ridden away than I lost my nerve.

I turned my horse and bowed to the count. 'My lord, there is something I do not quite like. I wonder if you would allow me to ride ahead a little, while you take your ease.'

Musard shot me a look, and I nodded to him.

'My old friend can be an old woman,' Richard said. 'And we have already lost time.'

The count favoured me with a smile. 'If Messire d'Oro is cautious, let us benefit from it. This is a pleasant place – let us eat a bite here.'

I probably rolled my eyes.

I took Francesco and his friend Alessio, and we cantered down the track. We caught the archers at a stream crossing. The ford was muddy; Rob Stone had dismounted to look at it.

'Hoof marks,' he said. 'Shod, military horses, at least …' He shrugged. 'At least one,' he said, and Ewan laughed.

'One busy horse or five moving in a line,' he said. 'Or ten.' He looked up. 'My lord?'

I shrugged. 'I don't trust the guide and I didn't like sending you three alone,' I admitted.

Stone sighed. 'That's good, my lord, as we didn't really like being out here alone, either.'

Across the stream, the beech woods were open, rising to a low plateau up ahead of us, but the trail switched back, climbing the ridge. A deep cover of leaves was killing the undergrowth, and only the occasional fern gave it a touch of green. It was quiet.

'A perfect ambush site,' I said.

Stone shrugged.

Ewan nodded. 'Yep,' he said.

The archers expected me to go first. I had armour and the best horse. If there was an ambush, Francesco, Alessio and I were far, far more likely to survive it than Ewan or Stone.

'If even a single bolt flies,' I said, 'we ride away.'

Francesco nodded.

'Visors closed,' I said.

Alessio slapped his shut. Just then, I loved him; he asked no questions, and he wasn't really one of mine. He just closed his visor.

We crossed the stream and picked our way up the far bank. Juniper had to give a mighty spring of her haunches to get us up, and I am not a small man. I almost lost my seat. I was still recovering my right stirrup when the first crossbow bolt whickered past me.

Alessio was down before I knew what was happening. He was pinned under his horse, which had taken three or four bolts. All this happened in an instant, while my head was down.

I put spurs to Juniper and we went forward, past Alessio. He was hit, too. I had an impression of blood, and his left leg was trapped under his dying mount.

I couldn't see anyone.

A bolt *thudded* into a beech tree, a few feet to my right. My eyes were turned the right way, and I saw a crossbowman, wearing a dusty green, lying behind a downed tree.

I turned Juniper and went at him.

He was trying to span. When I was a few paces away, he gave up and tried to draw his sword. He died in the attempt, and I was through their line. Juniper powered her way up onto the road. I'd passed straight up between two switchbacks, and now I could see a dozen men below me, and more to the right.

Francesco raced along the road, caught a man, and skewered him with his sword, stabbing deeply between the man's shoulders like a man killing a bull from horseback. The man slid off his blade, and Francesco wheeled his mount, turning her on her back feet, just as a bolt clipped his visor.

It was the last shot of the action, though, because our ambushers were running. They had horses in the woods; they were not *banditti* but professionals, and they didn't intend to stay around and fight knights.

I wished for my Kipchaks. I wished that I could run them down.

Instead, we got Alessio out from under his dead horse and made him comfortable. He had a nasty wound on his neck. There was a lot of blood and he couldn't speak; it looked bad.

I left Francesco with him, and I sent Ewan for the rest of the party while I pushed up the hill, but the *banditti* were gone. The count came up quickly, having already started for us, and by then we knew that, despite the blood, Alessio's wound was not as bad as we'd feared. He was, with God's mercy, going to be fine.

Our guide was gone. Of course he was gone, the false traitor.

The two bandit crossbowmen were dead. We had no one to question and we were in the middle of the Apennines with night falling and wolves howling.

Luckily, we were a strong company and well supplied. We built a camp at the stream-side, made Alessio as comfortable as we could, built three big fires, and Ewan brought down a deer. He killed it almost a mile away, and we had a bit of an adventure dragging the carcass through the darkening woods with the wolves pacing us, but the cooks made a risotto and the archers toasted the best cuts of the deer, and the count showered Francesco and Alessio – and me – with praise.

'Ah, Messire d'Oro, the next time you see adventure looming, please do not ride off and leave your poor lord to his hawking,' the count said.

'I will remember,' I promised.

Later, over wine, I brought up the organised nature of the attacks. 'These were not mere brigands,' I said. 'Italian *brigandi* do not have arbalests and horses and swords.'

Francesco nodded. 'My lord, I have not been in Italy since I was a boy,' he admitted. 'But I think those were professional soldiers. Genoese.'

'Hired killers,' the count scoffed.

'My lord, someone is trying to kill you,' I said. 'It is not my duty to speculate, but—'

'Then do not speculate,' the count said. 'What do you intend tomorrow?'

'Straight up the hill at dawn,' I said.

And so we did. We went up that hillside when it was still dark under the trees, for all that the sky was pink. We spooked a good stag halfway up the hill and we all laughed, because, even though we were not all old huntsmen like Ewan, we knew enough to know that a stag of twelve tines had not got that old by wandering past a bunch of armed men. That is, if the stag was there, the Genoese were not. We made the top of the ridge before the sun did, and we had the whole camp moving an hour later, and it was an adventure, a good adventure. Mayot rode with Alessio now, and the two chatted amicably, and the count was in a fine mood, praising the day and the countryside. Alessio was armed but could not wear his helmet and aventail; instead, he had a thick gorget of cloth wound round his neck. He claimed it did not hurt.

We went up and then we went down, and late the second day from Bologna we reached the shores of Lake Bilancino and made camp again. We didn't have the luck to poach a deer the second night, but on the other hand we hadn't been attacked, either, and we set watches and drank water and told some stories, and listened to the chorus of wolves on the hillsides above us. In the morning, a shepherd offered us a six-month-old lamb, and we took her, and his directions as well, and fifteen minutes later we began to cross an arm of the lake on a small ferry. It took the boat ten trips to get all of us and our horses across, and most of the horses had to be untacked and swim, but we made it. Then we were moving well, and we were at the monastery of San Marco in Florence before Vespers, descending out of the hills, and without the loss of a man. Our only loss had been Alessio's riding horse.

Of course, Florence was itself a possible source of danger, but there, the count took over. If I have made him sound foolish, or tyrannical, he could be both of those things, but in truth, he was, and remains, a fine lord – bold and *preux.* He demanded an escort from the Florentines, and we received one and we entered the city from the north.

Florence may be the most beautiful city in the world. Surely hundreds of men have told me that it is, and if they ever finish their Duomo perhaps it will be, but I look at Florence the way a man may look at the beautiful wife of a good friend; she is beautiful, but she is not for me. The streets are clean, and the sheer wealth of the place seems to flow like a river of silver through the heart of the town – and Florence is huge, larger than London. Indeed, and I think I have said this before, Englishmen may count themselves prosperous and fortunate, but Florence, Milan, Venice and Genoa are each richer and larger than London. Or Paris.

The count didn't exactly have a triumphal entry, but our escort was of city knights and cavalry and we drew crowds, and the count, given a night to prepare, was in his emerald finery. He stayed in one of the magnificent public buildings. I was taken to a private home of a rich notary from the town council, because the Order of Saint John had no priory in Florence, which seemed odd to me. The notary was Brunellesco di Lippo; his wife, Signora Giuliana, was a distant relation of the Cornari in Chioggia, and despite the different accents, they were very fine hosts and they listened to all my stories with apparent delight. I admit that sometimes I fear to be a bore, but children do not lie, and when children listen to you open-mouthed …

Listen: I don't tell children tales of Alexandria, and I can curb my manners to my audience, I promise you. At any rate, I kept them entertained, and I was in turn told a dozen tales, each funnier than the last; indeed, Signora Giuliana knew Messire Boccaccio and might have inspired some of his tales. She had such a fine laugh you had to laugh with her, and we had a delightful dinner.

In the morning, I attended the count and prepared to travel south for Siena. I met with the Council, briefly, to testify about the attack on the road. Then, with Francesco and Musard, I wandered the city's shops and markets. I bought gloves, including a pair of white doeskin for Fiore, if I ever chanced to see him again; I knew he, who had little care for anything material, would adore them. I bought a small icon of Saint John from a goldsmith, and I found that I could negotiate a bill on Emile at a much better rate of exchange than I could do in Bologna, and I took another two hundred gold florins based on her and hoped that my wife would forgive me. The count had not mentioned money, and Emile had warned me, several times, that he was not the best lord for paying his bills.

I wrote several letters from Florence, and was sorry not to receive any. But too much of my time was taken attending to horses; I missed John, I missed Marc-Antonio, I missed l'Angars, and I was doing all the work myself – the command work, that is. I had to direct the military elements of the count's household, because Mayot didn't know the job, and I had to direct the squires and pages and make sure the horses were fed. I was, in fact, the constable in all but title, and Richard was steward, and between us we maintained the count's household in a great city.

Our second full day in the city we all went to Mass, and afterwards the count summoned me and told me that we were going to Viterbo, south of Siena, where the Pope was.

'Do you understand what is going on here, Guillaume?' he asked. 'Get the Baron of Methymna a cup of wine,' he ordered his page.

A seat was brought. Richard sat too – an uncommon event. I got a cup of wine.

'In what way, my lord?' I asked.

The count looked out over the city; we were sitting on a balcony. The great doors were open, and the autumn breeze carried a scent of pine from the hills. He looked at Richard. 'All Italy is like a tinderbox waiting for a spark,' he said. 'And we are riding through it.'

I could see that I had come into an existing conversation, but it was similar to one that I had had the night before with Messire di Lippo.

'Yes, my lord,' I said. 'Genoa and Venice, the Pope and Milan.'

The count favoured me with a smile. 'With Florence trying to stay neutral while she bullies Siena, with the Kingdom of Naples virtually in the hands of Cardinal Albornoz and the Pope. The Greeks need a unified west to face the Saracens; the Pope needs a victory over the Greek Church; England and France are edging back towards war …' He shrugged, and I wondered if he was a little drunk. 'The Florentines say that they cannot guard me, or guarantee my safety south of their border,' he went on.

Musard nodded to me. 'The Council has just tried to prevent us from going south at all.'

The count drank. 'I'd have done better to bring an army,' he said. 'And they say that the Emperor is coming.'

'John Palaeologus?' I asked.

The count laughed. '*Par dieu*, monsieur, the next time I see my Greek cousin, I'll tell him you said that. No, more's the pity. I wish he was; if he abjured the Greek Heresy here, we might do something. No, I mean Charles of Bohemia, the Holy Roman Emperor.' He glanced at me. 'You know him, Musard tells me.'

I bowed in my seat. 'Yes, my lord.'

'You are a most surprising man, for a former routier, monsieur.' There it was – the sting in the tail, as if he could not help but remind me of my low origins. He went on, 'And they say Peter of Cyprus is coming, as well.'

'Why is the Emperor coming?' I asked.

The count nodded. 'Why indeed? To bring a spark to the tinderbox, I assume. I fear that my timing is wrong. I bring the Greeks to make peace just as the Pope intends to make war against Milan, and Outremer is forgotten. You know that I have already heard here that men think we *lost* at Alexandria? That my crusade accomplished nothing and took no towns?'

I said nothing.

The page poured more wine. The count had a slight flush.

'I need to reach the Pope,' the count said. 'Messire, I have come to depend on you in the last month. But these attacks – I assume they have come from my cousin's useless son, the Prince of Achaea, but I cannot make that accusation known. And this is not a form of warfare that I understand. You have foiled three attacks now, messire. Tell me, then – can I make it to Viterbo? Because if Italy is a tinderbox, then so is my own county, and I cannot leave my lady to face a war without me. If I die here, it will trigger the avalanche, and Savoy will be buried.'

'May I send for my notes?' I asked. 'Before I advise you?'

I sent Stefanos for my itineraries. We spent perhaps an hour discussing each of the parties who were manoeuvring towards war.

'If Prince Lionel of England is really to wed Violante of Milan,' the count said, 'we are looking at a new world in the north. Milan has been aligned against the Pope for a generation; they are Ghibellines and Imperial officers from far back when the Visconti came to power a hundred years ago and more. Milan and England? Against the Pope and France?'

Musard swirled the wine in his cup. 'Milan and Venice and England,' he said. 'Against the bankrupt French and the Pope and the Kingdom of Naples and perhaps Genoa.'

'Throw in the Turks and the Mamluks and the whole world is at war,' I said.

The count sat back and threw an arm over the back of his chair. 'And my Savoy is astride the main road between them. Right in the middle. I am a neighbour of the French and the Milanese; I am a friend of the King of England and of the Pope.'

Stefanos returned and made a good bow; he was in the great man's presence, after all. I took my itineraries and laid them out on the table.

'You say nothing, monsieur,' the count accused me.

I shrugged.

'Speak your mind, monsieur. You have earned the right,' the count said.

Have I, though? I asked myself.

Carefully, I went in the direction of my thoughts. 'I mislike being at odds with my Richard,' I said. 'But I do not see alliances of these powers. I see them like men in a mêlée at a great tournament; they band together for a temporary advantage, but they are not really allies.'

The count smiled. 'You are a thinker,' he said. He meant *you are a thinker for a mere brute*, but he didn't say it, quite. 'Go on.'

'Edward of England is a great lord who plans carefully,' I said. 'I'm not sure I can accord the same ... respect ... to the Pope or the King of France. If the Visconti are all like Antonio, they are mercurial, insecure in their power, quick to take offence ...'

The count held up his hand. 'No more,' he said. 'Your wit is as sharp as your sword, but you make me fear for what you see in my own rulership.'

'I only mean, my lord, that the Visconti do not make grand plans. I'll wager that they merely poke the hornets' nest from time to time to see what happens. Their only long-term play is to take Bologna, for which I assume they'd sell their own mothers. Or sisters.'

The count turned and looked at me. 'Never repeat that thought,' he said. Musard wiped the smile off his face.

The count stood.

'I apologise ...' I began.

The count waved me off. 'No. You are correct, but this marriage between Milan and England is a chancy thing and I cannot have anyone suggest that I was against it, or that any of my people spoke against it, perhaps representing me. Trading his sister for Bologna is exactly the worst thing anyone could say right now. In the right ears, that might be the flame to light the bonfire.'

I had seldom seen him so agreeable, and he had another cup of wine while I went over the routes to Siena and then south from there, either on the Via Francigena or the main Roman road.

'There are a dozen places here for an ambush,' I said. 'All the way south to Rome – places that could be held against us.' I had made notes of what pilgrims said; red dots and black crosses.

'We have too few men,' Musard said.

'My lord, if we went south and moved fast, we could make it impossible for an ambush to be set against us,' I said. 'No one has the money to pay enough *brigandi* to cover all the routes south, day after day. But these long delays ...'

'You offer me a criticism, I think,' he said.

I drew myself up. 'My lord, I am not your commander. I am merely attempting to protect you. It would be easier to protect you if you were to keep moving.'

The count pursed his lips, at the edge of saying something.

Richard stood and bowed. 'My lord, we should withdraw, unless you would like to be entertained – a game of cards, perhaps?'

'Nay, I am not such an ogre, and I will not bite Monsieur d'Oro just because he says that I take too much time.' He glanced at me. 'I have to gather … consensus. To the Union of Churches. It is more vital than you know.'

'The Prince of Lesvos said the same,' I offered.

The count nodded.

He looked at my itineraries, laid out in geographical order, west to east.

'The risk is too high,' he said. 'The war is about to start, and I am unprepared, because of a *fucking* fever in Dalmatia.' He shook his head. 'I suppose it is God's will, but *par dieu, gentilhommes,* I have given my fortune and my blood for this.'

'Sleep on it, my lord,' Richard suggested. It was the nicest way of telling your lord that he was drunk.

I returned to Messire di Lippo's house and went to bed late, assuming that my adventures with the count were at an end and we'd be riding soon for Savoy.

We rose in the morning to find that the weather had closed in again. There was rain in the air and the city smelled a little worse. Demetrios dressed me, and I left my sword by my bed and went out into the morning fog with a short cloak and a dagger. I had travelled fewer than a dozen steps before a shape loomed out of the fog: a mounted man, a dozen mounted men.

'Guglielmo d'Oro?' said a voice that was deadened by the fog.

I knew that voice.

'Fiore?' I asked.

A moment later the supposedly unemotional bastard was hugging me like a long-lost brother, which, in many ways, I was.

Nor was it just Fiore. It was l'Angars and Peter Albin, riding with a woman, and another man, silent and withdrawn – my Marc-Antonio.

And with them were Gospel Mark and Pierre Lapot and all the rest of my cut-throats who had survived the march from Jerusalem.

In that moment I knew I could take my count to Rome. In fact, I didn't think there was a force on earth that could stop me ... us.

'I have missed you,' I said to Fiore. 'I have missed all of you,' I said to the shapes in the fog. I walked in among them, and men dismounted, and it was a merry meeting.

Peter Albin seemed a little embarrassed. He dismounted, and I embraced him, and then he blushed – he a grown man – and gestured to his companion. I found that I was looking into the face of the pretty young whore from the Lazzaretto.

She smiled. 'Eh, messer? You know me, I think?'

I laughed. I turned to Albin. 'You fed her and she followed you home?'

She laughed. That was good.

'I love her,' Peter said. 'I think she saved my life.'

I shrugged. 'Fine,' I said. Listen, out there in the polite world, perhaps men do not marry whores, although in my own lifetime not one but two aldermen of London have done so. But among the men of the Companies, many a knight's lady started out with a little financial fornication, as an old friend of mine used to call it. Judge not, lest ye be judged.

Peter flushed again, this time with pleasure. I took them all to the count. With all of them and their grooms, pages, and squires, and all the additional horses, we had almost a hundred men, and one woman. I took Fiore and l'Angars and Albin with me to the count's lodging and Musard carried us straight in, as delighted as I was myself.

'My lord,' I said, 'this is the good Sir l'Angars, with the rest of my lances. And this is Fiore dei Liberi of Udine, the finest lance I have ever met. With these men, I believe that Monsieur Musard and I can promise you an uneventful trip from here to the very side of the Holy Father.'

The count looked like a man who'd drunk a little too deeply the night before, but he raised his head gingerly. 'Now God be with you, monsieur; this is the best news I have heard since my ship turned out of the Dardanelles for home. But I must beg your indulgence – I cannot leave until tomorrow.'

I probably grinned like a loon. 'My lord, with these men, I would take you to Rome even if Lucifer and the legions of Hell barred the way.'

I introduced the rest of them to the count, and then set out to find them lodgings in a city scarcely less expensive than Venice. I spent a happy hour wandering the streets hearing them all explain how they came to be at Florence, and how right Peter Albin had been about their route, and a dozen more tales besides.

I settled them, four at a time, in inns and private houses recommended by the podestà's officers, and then I was left with Fiore and Marc-Antonio.

'You will stay with me?' I asked Fiore.

He shrugged, as if it was of no matter.

'And you, Marc-Antonio?' I asked.

He didn't meet my eye.

'You wish to stay with me, and be my squire?' I asked again.

He was silent for a long time. I was tempted to speak; I didn't want him to baulk at this gate, but he had something to say.

'My father used to hit me,' he said. It was as if I'd torn it from him. Fiore, who could be a difficult man at times, raised an eyebrow and walked out of the room.

Marc-Antonio and I stared at each other for a while.

'You confess that you were wrong in your treatment of the lady?' I asked.

'Yes,' he said.

'And you will state that you will never, ever, use force on a woman again?' I asked.

'Yes,' he said, like a man facing fire.

'Then I am happy to admit I was a fool to strike you. I have always had contempt for men who beat their squires. Fiore once called such a man a school for bullies and cowards, and I agreed. Will you accept my apology?'

Marc-Antonio burst into tears.

I may have shed a few myself.

We rode south through the finest autumn anyone could remember since the plague. It was as if, after an early burst of rain, the old gods had remembered to be kinder to man, and the sun smiled on the fields of Tuscany. Is there anywhere more beautiful?

Siena gave us a fairly chilly welcome, not least because we had just come from Florence, and Florence was Siena's inveterate enemy. However, there I could use my own name and contacts; I had won a small but famous victory for the Sienese, and I was remembered fondly enough, for a mercenary. I rode ahead and signed a contract agreeing to allow only six men-at-arms a day to enter the gates, in exchange for which, for their 'love' of me, the town fathers offered to feed my men and my horses.

I ordered my people to pay. I put Pierre Lapot in charge of overseeing the market and making sure all was done fairly – setting a wolf to guard sheep, you might say, but I knew he'd do a careful job. He was one of the most changed men I'd ever known, and I suspected, correctly, that he was considering swapping the life of arms for a more contemplative one.

We stayed two days in Siena, and had a scare when the count vanished from his lodging. Richard found him; he'd engaged a laundress for something other than laundry. I suppose he found all the close protection stifling to his courtly ways, but Camus and the Prince of Achaea could have killed him, helpless as a trussed pig, if they'd known, and all our efforts and all our soldiers would have been for nothing.

We had words. That is, the count and I had words. Richard stood silent.

'My private life is not your business,' the count snapped.

'Keeping you alive is my business. You made it my business. If you would like, I can ride away now . . .' I said.

'Don't be foolish,' the count said.

'*Foolish?* I asked. Richard was shaking his head at me like mad, but I ignored him. 'Who's foolish? I didn't wander off in the night at the sight of a pretty face . . .'

The count's face turned bright red. 'You may go,' he said.

'I don't care who you diddle, my lord, but I need to be able to watch over you—'

'Go! Now!' The count turned his back on me. Richard came and grabbed my shoulder.

I couldn't think of anything really cutting to say, so I allowed

Richard to push me out the door. We went down the steps to the main floor, where Mayot was lounging at a table.

Richard threw himself down on a wooden stool that was not built to take his weight. It groaned ominously.

He put his head on the table and tapped it three times against the hard wood.

'How do you stand it?' I asked, still incensed.

Richard was laughing softly. 'I stand it easily enough. I like him.'

'He's acting like a guilty boy, not like a great lord. If he wants a girl, someone can find him one, surely.' I shrugged.

Mayot shook his head. 'My lord would not find that suitable. He does not tumble a lass for money. Only for what he calls love.'

I probably tugged my beard. 'I imagine ...'

Richard was shaking his head. 'He could have been killed. By God, William, I don't think he really believes he is mortal.'

'But you like him!'

Richard shrugged. 'You saw him at Gallipoli and the Dardanelles,' he said.

I agreed. 'Yes, when he is on an *empris*, he is a great man. Less so, perhaps, in Siena.'

Richard shrugged again. 'We are not all as moral as you've become, William,' he said.

'Whoa!' I narrowed my eyes. 'This is a change of tack, friend. I was too much a routier, now I am too moral?'

Richard made a face. 'I'm just tired and cranky, brother. I'd like a lass too.'

'And me, if you're finding them,' Mayot said.

'Not in my contract,' I said. It was a weak enough joke, but they laughed, and another day of crisis was averted.

The next morning, early, we rode south, and the count didn't mention the dispute. We rode together until we left Siena by the Porta Romana, a new brick construction in the best Italian style. We rode to Isola d'Arbia on the Via Francigena, and then cut cross-country for a while, re-merging onto the road at Monteroni d'Arbia, where we ate sausage and cheese and drank wine. While I had planned to make more stages, we stayed in the excellent inn at Ponte d'Arbia because the count was unwell. But he bounced up in the morning, and we continued south, having eaten all the oats in the Arbia valley, or so the innkeeper assured me.

I was running out of money, and so was Richard. After the explosion in Siena, I was not anxious to confront my patron, but my fancy new purse from Florence had nothing left in it. Searching through it was fruitful, though; I found the beautiful gloves that I had purchased for Fiore, and I handed them over, and he was … emotional. At least, for Fiore.

'What will I do, without Nerio to spoil them for me?' he asked.

That day I asked him to take half a dozen archers and clear the roads ahead of us, and I didn't see him again until evening. We had developed a system in Outremer, and although the Kipchaks and Sir Giannis's *stradiotes* tended to do our scouting, all of us had had turns, so that it had become habit. We would move along steadily with the column, and the scouts would leave us a guide, both to show the way and to indicate that the area was safe, and in this way we could jog along at a fast walk all day without pausing to worry about our road or our next stop. We took rests, and because we were extraordinarily well provided with horseflesh, we changed horses whenever we halted, so that we arrived at San Quirico d'Orcia atop its magnificent ridge almost before we were tired of riding across the magnificent wheat fields of autumn. The fields were full of folk, and the riches of Italy shone to any northerner. Lines of men and women cut the wheat, scythes flashing, and girls and young boys bundled up the sheaves, but there were no gleaners – that is, no poor folk, so very poor that they followed the harvesters picking kernels of wheat out of the dirt. Father Angelo told me that, since the plague, wages had risen to the point that farm labour was well-paid.

The night we spent in San Quirico d'Orcia was as difficult as I might have anticipated. We heard Mass at the new church of Saint Francis, and then the count went to the fortress to guest there and I dispersed my people and his throughout the pilgrim hostels.

I'll explain briefly for those who have never made the pilgrimage to Rome. From Canterbury to Rome there is a road – the old Roman road, I think, that the legions built – and all along the route there are hostels, like monasteries but maintained by monks and nuns for men and women travelling for the good of their souls. The Knights of Saint John, my own Order, maintained a great many hostels and I tended to prefer them, inasmuch as they had better services for men-at-arms. Because I trusted the knights, I could send ahead and negotiate through them for fodder for two hundred horses, lodging for the count's Greek monks, and so on. Every town required a different negotiation; remember that the Greek monks were as much heretics and schismatics to a small-town Italian curate as if we'd been travelling with Saracens or Cathars. We also had as many horses as a small army, and most of the men in the count's train were hard, dangerous individuals with lifetimes of violence behind them, and that the peasants of the Emilia-Romagna and southern Tuscany had every reason to fear and loathe them.

The Knights of Saint John were my link to these communities and, through Father Angelo, the Franciscans, who were very popular in Tuscany and had many houses and hostels. Just as we had found Franciscans at Jerusalem, so they seemed to line the route to Rome. Between the two, the Order and the brotherhood, we had lodging and fodder, and the communities, podestàs and peasants too, were reassured that we were not going to steal their cattle.

My hostel was like a good inn; the wine was good, the fare plain but delicious, and I was sitting down to eat with two old knights of my Order and most of my men-at-arms when the count summoned me to attend him. I left my wine and walked up the hill to the castle, and made my *reverentia* to the local lord, the captain of his fortress and the count.

Count Amadeus was in a fine fettle, and offered me part of his dinner, which, as I have said before, is reckoned a great honour. So I ate a roast pheasant for perhaps the third time in my life, drank some good wine, and reported to my lord on his Greek monks, who were comfortably entertained by the Franciscans. A Franciscan may have terrifying spiritual visions, he may threaten to overthrow the whole established order in a search for the Kingdom of God on Earth, and he may trouble your theology with searching questions, but all of them are good hosts.

I drank some more wine while the local lord explained that he had two nephews who needed employment somewhere else – indeed, as far from home as could be arranged. I was slow to understand, possibly just tired, but eventually I realised that I had been summoned in hopes that I would take them on: two young Italian knights with no experience of war or anything but life in Tuscany, two men who thought themselves both dangerous and very clever.

Even now, I can recall my lack of enthusiasm, but in the end I took them. The Birigucci brothers, Benghi and Clario, were two young scapegraces who would, as it proved, be valuable men – eventually. They were sent for, and they appeared, brushed and combed and a little too neat, and they failed to hide how very impressed with themselves they were.

'Ready to ride after Prime,' I said.

'Of course, *capitano*,' Benghi said in his beautiful Tuscan Italian.

'We will simply ride away,' I said. 'If you are not there …'

Both boys bowed.

'You have squires? Archers? Pages?' I asked.

Both boys admitted to having grooms. I explained about pages; 'armed and capable', I think I said.

'Beppo is a rascal,' Clario said. 'But I'm sure he will suit.'

'Mind that he does,' I said. 'Your uncle has asked specially for you. I do not really need two more inexperienced lances, gentlemen.'

They withdrew, still arrogant.

The lord of the town made a face. 'I was wondering if you might advance them … some pay,' he said, as if discussing money caused him physical pain.

I shook my head. I am usually eager to oblige any man, but I was almost out of money, and I had not asked for two hot-headed young Italians to join my little company. 'No, my lord. We pay by the month – only experienced men are advanced money.'

The count smiled his lordly smile. 'Perhaps, captain, you can make an exception this time.'

I shook my head. 'My lord, I cannot.'

'I insist,' the count said. He was affable, and he didn't think it was possible that I would refuse. Richard might have saved the situation, but he was already asleep.

I knew that I had to surrender gracefully; my social position demanded it. 'I could perhaps advance them—'

'A full month's pay,' the count said. 'I am paying your lances twenty florins a month, am I not?'

'Eighteen,' I said.

'Exactly,' the count said to the Baron Birigucci.

'Except, my lord, we have never been paid.' I shrugged. I was at the end of my patience; perhaps I was just tired from a hard day of playing captain.

Amadeus turned on me a sort of basilisk stare that was, I think, meant to freeze me to my marrow, but he'd never met Sister Marie. His glare was nothing on hers.

'Further, my lord, Monsieur Musard and I have covered the food and fodder since Venice,' I said.

'Silence,' the count said.

I shrugged with deliberate insolence. 'Of course I will be silent, my lord, only, you need to know these things, if you intend to order me to pay for two lances I do not need while my veterans remain unpaid.'

'You are dismissed,' he barked.

'Forever?' I asked. I was too angry to hold my tongue. 'Or just for the evening?'

Baron Birigucci saved my military career by rising too quickly and overturning an iron candle stand, so that the crash of the last judgement startled us all. I'm sure he did it on purpose, and I bless him for it.

I managed to bow my way out without being dismissed forever. It's odd to think of how a lord must behave, but he was trapped. Once he said forever, he had to mean it, but then I'd ride away with his escort and leave him with two knights and twenty servants in the middle of Tuscany. No one wanted that.

I do not mean to paint him so black. He was merely a product of his class and *ordo*, and no worse than others I have known in England, France, Germany and Italy. Much better, in fact, than most. But I was perhaps too much my own man, and too used to having my own way; or perhaps it was just that with the Order, I had men like Fra Peter to obey, and not so many fools.

In the morning, there were clouds and a light rain. I told Richard of the evening's foolishness.

'Christ, William, never, *ever*, talk to him about money. Everyone knows that. I told you we will pay you. Of course we will!'

I shrugged. 'If he wants to order me to advance money to his friends, he has to pay up,' I said. 'I'm not rich enough to support the Count of Savoy.'

Richard looked annoyed. 'William, are you dense? Listen to me.

He's cut off from Savoy. We're lucky if we can get a message through. He's mortgaged to the hilt from the crusade.'

'I'm not Nerio,' I said. 'I'm not made of money.'

Then I thought about it. Nerio's family were in Florence. They were accounted the richest men in Italy, the richest country in the world. I could probably write one letter and borrow any sum I named.

'Jesu, Diccon,' I said, using the name I'd always called him when we were young. 'I didn't understand. You mean you and he are counting on me footing the bill ...'

'He didn't expect to be this poor,' Richard said. He managed a smile. 'No one's called me Diccon in five years.'

'Make it right with him. I'll try and borrow some money.'

'See it from his place, William,' Musard said. 'He is one the greatest lords there is; he has led *and paid for* a crusade for the Church, and suddenly one of his vassals is in revolt and he is cut off. Hunted. And the Pope is not responding to us ...'

Now I felt like a fool. 'Yes,' I said. 'Monsieur Musard, will you do me the great favour of conveying my apologies to my lord, for my intemperate language, and beg him to disregard anything said, as said in fatigue and perhaps in wine?'

'Get us some money,' Richard said. 'He won't even remember.'

That was a touch too sanguine. The count did not ride with me all day, and we moved fast, passing the usual pilgrim stage on the slopes of Radicofani and pushing on to Acquapendente, or Aquipendium, as our churchman called it – a dramatic modern castle on a high hill, towering over the plain. The castello has five towers and is all new work. The fortification is so strong because this is the Tuscan March, the very border between Siena and the papacy, and they are not always friends. It was a hard, wet day and we were all glad to come to the end of it.

I took it as my turn to ride ahead and make arrangements for our little army, so I went to the castello with Marc-Antonio and Father Angelo and my two pages, with Ewan the Scot as my archer and with Clario Birigucci as my guide. In fact, the guide turned out to be his demonic page Beppo, who appeared to be a thousand years old in evil and reminded me a little of all the bad men I'd ever known. Where the Birigucci boys were tall and handsome and might have passed for military angels with their blond hair and aristocratic noses, Beppo was stoop-shouldered, walked with something of the rolling gait of a sailor, rode like a sack of corn, and had a nose as big as the beak of a puffin. He had two moles on his face that spouted hair and might have had their own teeth if allowed, and he had a cast in one eye, and was, in almost every way, ready to be cast as a villain.

On the other hand, he knew the way to Acquapendente, and he knew the men at the gate and almost everyone else. Granted, women hid their children as he rode down the high street, but he had a fund of stories almost as good as Sior' di Lippo in Florence, and his terrible looks belied both a lively interest in people and a cunning mind.

And he could mock himself and others, which is a fine turn in any man, I find – self-mockery, that is.

My first sign of his humour was at a turn in the road. We could see the magnificent castello rising above the plain, and yet our road kept turning away from it, and finally Beppo led us in a little canter across a set of wheat fields.

'The road was taking too fucking long,' Beppo grumbled. 'Too much sun is bad for my skin.'

This from a man with pockmarks the size of silver pennies and burned as brown as a nut. It took me several such comments to understand the dryness of his humour, and then my tolerance for him began to sprout wings, so to speak.

At any rate, we came to Acquapendente early in the afternoon, and we hadn't had so much as a scent of trouble from the Prince of Achaea in days. Despite that, perhaps because of Outremer, we were very much on our guard. The lord of the town, Baron Farnese, was away; his castellan was as suspicious of us as we of him, and the town itself lacked both a hostel of my Order and a hostel of the Franciscans, so we had no particular advantage.

Beppo snorted in disgust and spoke loudly to the castellan. My Italian – which was, I thought, very good – was not good enough to follow the speed of his imprecations, but Father Angelo laughed aloud, and finally the castellan came down to the gate tower to meet us. It was a small town, he said, and very cramped before market day, and he offered us some fields to the west of the town for a camp.

We didn't have tents or pavilions, so I suggested that as my lord was the famous Green Count, he would have to find lodging for him.

Beppo said, very quietly, 'Something is wrong.'

I considered. I didn't know Beppo very well, nor did he seem like someone on whom any captain would rely. On the other hand, these were his people.

'How far to Bolsena?' I asked him.

'Three hours,' he said. 'A fine town with a good lord.'

I looked up at the castellan. Distrust aside, it was very odd that he wasn't allowing me into his town, and that the gate was shut.

'I must consult with my lord,' I called.

'I will see to it that lodging is found,' he said, but his voice carried more fear than it should have.

'Davide Fermio is no coward,' Beppo said aloud, as soon as we rode down to the plain. 'He is the castellan there. He is afraid of something, and afraid to tell us what the fuck it is.'

Camus, I thought. The sun was in the sky; God was in his heaven. But Camus was here.

I hadn't seen a cloud in our military sky, and yet I was chilled. Perhaps that's too poetic. What I mean is, Camus was more an idea than a reality, and yet I had to act as if he was right there. Holding a hostage in Acquapendente? Out in the country with an ambush?

Should I ride to Bolsena, scouting the last six miles, and find us lodging? Or ride back to the count?

Let me seize this opportunity to bemoan the day-to-day life of the *capitano*. It's not about battles. It's about decisions. They wear you down, they tire you and erode your confidence. Listen, gentles: I am graced with a fair degree of both *preux* and confidence. But as afternoon shadows grew on that road, I looked south towards Bolsena and north towards Radicofani and I couldn't decide.

'Beppo,' I said.

'Boss?' he muttered, in Tuscan.

'Can you get back to the count? With your young lord? Alive?'

He leered. 'Course I can,' he said.

'I need you to get through. You have to assume that there's an armed band in the countryside we just crossed, watching you.' I didn't point. I felt watched.

He shrugged. 'Sure, boss. No one is going to hunt *me* in these hills.' He smiled like Satan come to earth. 'Not more'n fuckin' once, no way.'

Well. No man looking as wicked as Beppo could possibly have lived to be forty years of age without some serious skills. Perhaps it sounds mad to you, but his ill-looks recommended him to me. He had to be one tough bastard.

'I need you to guide the count around Acquapendente,' I said.

He pursed his lips; an awful sight. 'Aye,' he said. 'Hmm. And on to Bolsena?'

'Yes,' I said.

'What's in it for me, boss?' he asked quietly.

I thought of various answers. 'Twenty gold florins and a good horse,' I said.

He spit on his hand and held it out. 'Thief's honour, then, eh, boss?'

I spat in my hand and clasped his. 'Go with God,' I said.

He laughed. 'Hey, lordling?' he called to Clario. He turned his horse, and in a moment the two were riding back along the road. I almost went after them. They were going at a sedate pace, down the middle of the Via Roma.

Ewan grinned at me. 'The de'il no doubt takes a long spoon to sup wi' yon,' he said.

He had a point. I let them go, and rode for Bolsena.

We'd gone about half a mile when we met a dog. The dog was someone's dog – nice manners, a good collar of leather with a fine steel buckle. A courser, not high-bred but not a mongrel, and she wanted to be friends. We were wary of her at first, as she sniffed around our horses, darted between their legs as if we were all hunting together, and made the deep bow dogs make when they want to play, forelegs extended. Then she would dash off ahead, run like lightning a few dozen paces, and wait for us to catch up.

After three or four of these dashes, I dismounted and looked at her collar, and we became friends. I had a little sausage in my purse, and she licked my hand, and that was that. After that, she trotted ahead as if looking for game; once she ran off to the side aways, but she was soon back.

About two miles along, in a deep defile, she began to bark. Until then she'd been perfectly silent, but now she looked at the defile and the brush on the hillside above it and gave tongue at some length.

I don't need to be told twice. I didn't see anything obvious – no twinkle of metal on the hillside, no sound of horses. But I didn't like it, and we were too few to make a fight of it, and Father Angelo was already flagging.

The dog barked and barked.

And then the dog turned and looked at me and ran off into the woods south of the road.

I sat on Juniper, tired, worried, and looking at that hillside. Camus was there; I'd swear to it.

The dog came trotting back. She had that look dogs get – amazed that people could be so stupid. She paused, trotted a few steps back the way she'd gone before, and looked back.

'Woof,' she mentioned.

'She means us tae follow her, ye ken,' Ewan said.

The dog was going south and west, away from the darkening hillside and the defile.

I looked at Father Angelo.

He shrugged. 'God walks in many guises,' he said. 'And this sign is pretty clear.'

Five men trusting their lives to a dog.

And a fool of a *capitano.*

'Follow the dog,' I said. I was the last man off the road. I brought up the rear in case we were attacked, and we crossed a gully, which was bad, and then we climbed a low ridge, and tailed along an empty stream bed. The dog would trot ahead, as she had in the beginning, and come back; several times she stood waiting for us, panting, tongue lolling.

We passed down a long valley where the fields were empty, and the houses we passed were shuttered in broad daylight, with wheat standing in the sun unharvested, and that was a bad sign. There were no peasants. We were on a track, little more than a path.

The dog trotted on.

The first view of Lake Bolsena is staggering: you are high up in the hills, among green woods of beech, and you pass a field of wheat here, rye there, and oats – little chequerboards of gold and brown. And then you turn, and suddenly the sun is shining on a pure blue lake like something in the remotest parts of the Alps, except that you can smell the dinner cooking in the town almost at your feet. The lake is so big that there are fishing boats out on it and their white sails fleck the water.

We were moving fast. We went down the ridge, the steepest on the whole of the Via Francigena. The dog barked once and sprang forward into the town, where the suburbs were unwalled. The old town had high walls and a fine castle, which was virtually impregnable and certainly out of our reach, as the gates were shut.

But there were Franciscans, and we passed our *bona fides* with them, and were pronounced not routiers. Then, and only then, it all came out: there was a group of *banditti*, or mercenaries, in the hills north of the town, preying on pilgrims; one had been robbed, killed, and *crucified*.

Then I knew. Until then I had feared that it was Camus, who fancied himself Satan's child. But to crucify a pilgrim on pilgrimage ...

However, the Franciscans got the gates opened to the inner town, and got me an entrée to the lord. He was affable, a handsome man past military age but still, I thought, capable of defending his own walls with vigour.

He had a beautiful woman with him. He did not introduce her, and she effaced herself, yet listened to us with interest. I watched her, too. She had a full face and a fine figure and she moved with a spirit usually found in horsewomen and huntresses. Like Emile.

'Green Count?' he said with a slow smile. 'I have never heard of such. Does that make you the Red Knight?' He laughed at his own joke, which was not so bad, as I had a red surcoat of my Order and my own red and black arms in one quarter of Christ's shield, so I was surely as red as my lord was green.

At any rate, the Lord of Bolsena shrugged. 'Someone will need to be paid to feed two hundred horses,' he said. 'But I will happily give you house room. I wonder if I could interest you and your lord in helping me rid the valley of this sudden plague of bandits?'

I suspect that I grinned. 'I think we'd be delighted to help you,' I said.

'Splendid,' the lord said. 'In that case, I'll find your fodder and food.'

'I need to go back and fetch my lord,' I said. 'I wonder if you would spare me half a dozen of your men-at-arms.'

He frowned. 'The Count of Savoy, you say?' he asked. He looked at the attractive woman, who smiled and whispered in his ear.

He turned to me. 'I will lead my men myself,' he said, as if he'd only just thought of it.

I took the time to introduce my men, and in the course of my introductions that dog came up. She gave one low whine, and the Lord of Bolsena rubbed her head and then gave her quite a hug, and my estimation of him went up.

'Ah, Beatrice!' he said. 'Where have you been, my love?'

It proved that she was one of his hounds, lost, he claimed, in pursuit of a white stag, or perhaps a unicorn. By then I was quite fond of her.

'She saved us, my lord. Led us on a secret path ...'

'Aye,' the Lord of Bolsena said. 'I have never known a dog so intelligent. Or so like a woman.' He smiled at his lady, who gave him a look of arch indifference, more like a mother than a mistress.

He began to arm. The woman helped him, as did a pair of pages. His captain came in while he was dressing: a tall middle-aged wolf with grey hair, who proved, on acquaintance, to be part of the endless della Scala clan.

I did not want to sound like a madman, but I told them that this bandit had made threats against my lord. To describe Camus seemed impossible, although I suspect I referred to him as a spawn of Satan.

The della Scala captain chewed his moustache. 'Really, he has to be put down,' he said. 'Crucifixion? Grotesque. Is the man unhinged?'

I left my two boys with Father Angelo, mounted Gabriel, who was fresh from a day of being led, and we set out.

We rode back up the ridge and the light improved as we went out of the valley and up to the heights. It was early evening, and I had to hope that the count was alive and moving. He shouldn't have been far behind us, but anything could have happened, and I feared my decisions were all bad. I should have sent Beppo and his lord ahead and gone back myself ...

From the heights, I could see a pair of big eagles or vultures out over the plains.

It had started to rain by the time we went over the ridge, through the woods, and down into the patchwork of fields in the valley north of the lake. We rode fast, alternating trotting and cantering, through the long rays of the evening sun, casting enormous shadows. We crested a low ridge perhaps two Roman miles north of Bolsena and I could see something on the road, and birds of prey above it. In the fading light, it looked like a monster, and it screamed like one, too.

The lord and his captain reined in their horses and crossed themselves. It was a strange moment, with the blood-red light falling on the hilltops while the little valleys were almost totally dark. I caught the dazzle of light on distant metal two hills away, and pointed.

The thing on the road emitted a growling bark.

'What is it?' asked della Scala.

I gave Gabriel his head, and we went down the hill, probably too fast, but I wanted to get this over with. Marc-Antonio and Ewan were right at my back. We came down swiftly into the darkened dell, and there was our monster, bent over in the middle of the road.

It was a man.

He was impaled.

On a stake.

For the love of God, and praying for mercy, what kind of man would do such a thing to another man? A stake driven through him, emerging from his mouth. The poor thing was alive. He was a tinker or a pedlar, and he …

Blessed Virgin Mary, I have trouble telling this. His mouth was working but he couldn't scream any more, because his lungs were slowly filling with blood. I sat there, frozen. I had never seen such a thing, and it was too horrible to comprehend, even for me, who had seen Alexandria, who had been a routier in France. His eyes … God, they are with me yet.

Ewan called, 'Ware!' and saved my life. He slapped Gabriel on the rear quarter and my horse sprang forward past the poor tinker, and the crossbow bolt meant for me whickered along the road for quite a distance, kicking up gravel. Ewan put his dagger into the poor soul, up close, his arm around the man's head.

I was watching the hills. And praying, I own it. It was unsettling, the whole incident. A bolt hit Marc-Antonio's horse, and then another.

But Camus hadn't reckoned with a dozen Bolsena men-at-arms. They came down the hill behind me somewhat cautiously, but they made a great deal of noise, and someone in the ambush lost his nerve.

Let me add two things: first, for those of you who've never set an ambush, it is hard to wait, and then hard to endure the onset of the survivors. And, by God's grace, we had all survived. Camus's *banditti* had left it too late; they couldn't really see in the darkness of the dale, overshadowed on both sides by tall trees and steep slopes.

But the second thing is spirit. Those bastards had sat in that dell watching the tinker *they had impaled.* I'll wager they were there for an hour or two, watching him die. You have to be hard as stone to endure another man's agony like that and not be affected – spooked, haunted, terrified. Every man jack of them knew he was going to Hell. It is one thing to follow a fiend like Camus; it's another to watch the fruits of your own evil while waiting for a fight.

It saps the spirit. I've seen it. Bastards like Camus can deny God all they want. Men like to imagine they fight in a cause – and a good one. No one can watch an impaled man slide down, the inside of his bowels gradually ripping open as the man's weight drags him down the stave. No man can watch that and think himself in the right. I've fought Saracens and Turks and Lithuanians, and the only men I ever knew to impale a man alive were Camus's. I hear the Romans did it – but then, they crucified Christ, too, so God's curse on them.

I put my spurs to Gabriel and he responded. We splashed over a little ford and a man broke from cover to my right in the open, muddy ground around an ancient oak. I saw him as movement, and I leaned and Gabriel turned along a narrow trail, sure-footed in the darkness. I won our little race and sent his unshriven soul to Hell. Then the wood was full of horns, and I saw shapes flitting here and there against the sky – that is, there was a steep slope up, and the sky was still light, so that men running higher on the hill were backlit. Ewan shot one stupid bastard standing in the middle of the road.

Marc-Antonio rode a man down and shouted for help. I had my visor open, enjoying the protection of my new helmet, and I heard him and turned Gabriel. We made heavy work of climbing the hill.

Marc-Antonio was fighting three men. Why three brigands stood to fight a mounted gentleman still mystifies me. He had been taught by Fiore, and his horse was good, albeit wounded, so he turned, and turned. If he'd had a little space, he'd no doubt have finished them.

I had to break into their little circle. Gabriel responded beautifully, put his head down and struck one villain full on. Only then did the other two run. I got neither; I spared a moment for my squire, and discovered that he'd lost his sword.

'In a tree,' he said shamefacedly.

I gave him my arming sword and then had the presence of mind to dismount and secure the bandit Gabriel had beaten to the ground. He was our first prisoner.

There was still fighting by the little ford. We'd broken out of the ambush, but the back half apparently hadn't broken. I suspected that was where Camus was.

'Ewan!' I roared.

'Here!' he called. He was dismounted, bow in hand, and he ran to me, crashing through branches in the undergrowth. One of the best things about heavy harness? Branches mean nothing to you.

'Get mounted and go for the count,' I said. 'Go!'

Ewan looked … doubtful. I was asking him to ride through the remnants of the ambush.

I didn't have time to explain. 'Go!' I ordered and he went like an unhappy dog.

I got a foot in my stirrup and found that I was tired, despite the spirit of combat. It took me two heaves and some of Gabriel's patience before I was back in my high-back saddle.

I was rewarded with the reassuring sound of Ewan's rouncey trotting on the road. It was growing darker in the dell, and there were still calls and screams and horns.

'On me,' I called to Marc-Antonio, and we went back across the stream.

There was no one on the road – no one at all, barring the grotesque figure of the impaled man. The fighting was further up the hill.

I went off to my left, into the brush. I had no reason to do so, bar my feeling, based on the sounds, of what was happening. It sounded to me as if Camus was fighting the Baron's men-at-arms, and perhaps winning. They had never made it to the ford, so that the defection of the back half of the ambush had not affected the fight one way or another.

For Aemilie, here, and the others who have never been in a fight, let me add that a man in armour on horseback in deep woods can be very quiet indeed. Ah, you doubt me, lass? But all the *gentilhommes* here will support me, I think. Horses make very little noise, and armour, which can rattle or clank when a man moves on foot, is relatively silent when a horse walks through leaves.

Regardless, we moved silently, gliding along the flat by the little stream, flush with recent rains, and then I turned up the hill. I heard the della Scala captain's war cry, the war cry of all the Scaligeri.

'Shoot them down!' called Camus. I knew that voice, and I knew where he was, to a few dozen paces. 'Take that one!'

I heard a man beg for mercy, and the sound of a crossbow snapping.

I went forward, Marc-Antonio right behind me.

I got up the steep slope. I'm sure I made noise then, but none of the *banditti* were listening; they were intent on their prey. The Lord of Bolsena was dismounted, and several of his men-at-arms were down, dead or wounded. They were trapped in a little huddle, silhouetted against the darkening sky, where the brigands could shoot them down with impunity.

I could *see* Camus, in outline.

They were about to shoot the Lord of Bolsena.

Conscience is an odd thing, and so is the way we make decisions. I wanted Camus dead – but there were two crossbows I could see pointed at the Lord of Bolsena, who lay pinned under his dead horse.

I'd led the Lord of Bolsena to this.

'Savoy!' I bellowed. 'Saint Maurice and Savoy!'

I crashed in on the bowmen I could see, and my longsword cut right and left. One raised his crossbow, but he was a fool if he thought he could parry a blow from a mounted knight, and I broke his head open. Then I turned my horse and went for Camus.

Marc-Antonio, thanks to God, went for the brigands, and the surviving men-at-arms, released from whatever spell of horror had bound them, burst forward out of their huddle.

'Savoy!' I roared. I cut, one-handed, at Camus. Our blades met, edge to edge. He was turning his horse, and his second blow was down almost the same line as the first, and I got my blade back over my shoulder. It was one of the few times Gabriel has ever misstepped in a fight, but he turned the wrong way, and I had my back to Camus for a critical moment. My desperate over-the-shoulder cut got a piece of his blow. The rest fell on my much-abused left shoulder and left hand, but I had spaulders and maille on, and the blow did me little damage beyond my pride. Little damage, but one terrible effect – I lost my reins.

There's a question knights ask each other: which is more important in a fight, your spurs or your sword? I always vote spurs. I lost my reins, but I didn't waste a beat of my heart looking for them. I had spurs and I had Gabriel, the best horse I knew.

I got my left hand on the pommel of the Emperor's sword and cut up from my left side, the blade rising past Gabriel's ears. Camus missed it in the dark, and I got him, a strong blow under his left arm, but his horse was turning, its head out, teeth reaching for Gabriel's neck. Then Camus rocked forward and his horse sprang away.

We were with him, stride for stride. Gabriel was in the flower of his strength, and he got in a vicious bite at the other horse's hindquarters, and then we were going down the hill, neck and neck in near-perfect darkness, hammering away at each other with our swords, no technique, no finesse, just blow after blow. Some blows were lost in the branches, some missing, some covered by the other man's sword, some going home. I have heard men say 'blind with hate' before, but this is the closest I have come to such blindness. I wanted him dead, and I was not really in control – of my horse or myself.

We came to the stream and both horses leaped. I remember the moment. I remember floating free, trying to put my sword in the bastard, and then we landed, a great shock that drove my knees almost to my shoulders – big horses can jump a long way.

My balance was going. It was a little of everything – trying to reach too far with my cuts, trying to get Gabriel under me ... I began to fall. And as I fought for my balance, my left shoulder caught a tree in the dark, and I was off in a heartbeat, lying flat on my back. I was stunned, the world circling me, and I knew I had only a moment to get on my feet.

I couldn't do it. Camus's opening blow to the left side had done something, and I couldn't get onto my knees. It took me three tries. I was starting to panic when I finally got onto my front, got my knees under me, and began to get to my feet. I could hear hooves.

I stood, swaying, and used the tree that had felled me for support. I could just see the horse coming at me. It took far too long for me to realise that the horse was riderless, the stirrups flapping. It was Gabriel.

He stopped by me and turned, as if expecting me to mount.

The hero of the hour was Marc-Antonio. He had flushed the brigands and rescued the lord's captain, and he received an hour's worth of congratulations and thanks from all of the local men-at-arms. Praise which he richly deserved, and which didn't turn his head.

By the time we'd all found each other in the darkness and caught various riderless horses, Ewan was back with Fiore. I had managed to get myself mounted and greet my lord with some pretence of competence, and we rode back into Bolsena before the moon was fully up.

His lady was waiting in the moonlight outside her gate. She had torches lit and fifty townspeople ready to take horses; I could tell from their clothes they were not grooms, but citizens. The Lord of Bolsena was well-loved, and his lady had a head on her shoulders. Shoulder or no shoulder, I made her a deep *reverentia* when I dismounted.

She shook her head. 'I am no great lady,' she said.

'You are to all of us,' I said, and she smiled.

Later, she served us wine with her own hands, and I watched her, wondering whether she was indeed a servant or a mistress, or something complicated and Italian in between.

Peter Albin was looking at my shoulder. We were all in Bolsena's very comfortable upper hall; I had wine, and I was beginning to come down from the rush of spirit that is combat.

'I don't know your lady's name,' I said.

'Caterina,' he said. 'You know her, I think.'

I smiled. 'I do. But she's helping the lady of the castle serve all the men – I think she has a fine heart.'

Albin nodded. 'Your support means a good deal to me. I intend to marry her and take her home to England.'

'Not too soon, I hope.'

And after we'd all been bandaged, and when the Lord of Bolsena's hall was ankle-deep in cast-off armour, a pair of troubadours came and sang for us: wonderful Italian stuff I hadn't heard much of, and some that was new to me. Landini and some Machaut.

The count rose and thanked us all, pledging all of us, men-at-arms and retainers too.

'But we must finish these routiers in the morning,' he said. 'The Lord of Bolsena and I have agreed it, so I must beg you, my companions, to go to your beds.'

He bowed and kissed the hand of the lady of the hall.

I escorted him to his room.

He was still in his leg harnesses, and I took them off him as if I was a page.

We had a candle, and not much else. Perhaps the darkness inclined him to a confidence.

'The lady ...' he began.

'Yes?' I said, or something equally noncommittal.

'Not the lord's wife, I think,' he said. He drank some more wine.

'Beppo says he is a widower, and she is his ... housekeeper.' I could still hear Beppo's voice, telling stories – bawdy, deeply funny. He was keeping my archers awake.

There was a pause; I got his greaves off.

'Yet a fine woman for all that. She thought ahead, had grain for horses ...' He looked at me.

'I think her a fine woman,' I agreed.

'When I bowed to her ...' he said. 'What is rank? I am the Count of Savoy. But that's nothing but an accident of birth.'

And then he handed me his goblet, as if we were old friends.

I drank some and handed it back.

As soon as it was light, the Lord of Bolsena took all of us back out into the countryside, with twenty men-at-arms, fifty huntsmen, and dogs, including Beatrice. He was angry, and losing a prized warhorse had not sweetened him – neither had the death of one of his vassals. He told the count that he also feared to appear weak to his neighbours, which sounded like France. We had our prisoner from the night before, his hands bound and a halter round his neck. He directed us to a camp, empty, and then to another, where two wounded men lay in a cloud of flies, abandoned by their mates. The Lord of Bolsena's men-at-arms strung them up and let them kick out their souls from old willow trees, and left them there as a warning to others.

There were footprints and hoofprints, and the dogs had the scent. Before Nones we had come up with two of the men and taken them; they made no attempt to fight. At dusk, Fiore and I caught three more. They had bad horses, and no remounts, and they could not keep up a chase in open country. We were halfway back to Florence when we caught them, on a broad plain of wheat fields. I was on Juniper, and she ate the miles. We watched them getting closer and closer, and their hearts must have died within them.

But they didn't even stand by each other. One man's horse foamed at the mouth and fell over, dying, legs thrashing, and the other two rode on, leaving him for us. And then another horse foundered, ridden to death. The last man might have got away. His mount was better, I was sickening of the game, and Fiore and I were the only men-at-arms in sight. We'd outdistanced dogs and men. But his horse cast a shoe and then stopped in the road and would not budge a foot. I rode up one side and Fiore on the other, and we took the man, still screaming imprecations at the dumb animal between his legs.

We made them walk, and it took us another day, a rough, tiring day, to get them to Bolsena. But we'd missed Camus.

The Lord of Bolsena had his notary take the statements of all of our prisoners, and we attested them, affixing seals or signing, or both. None of the five men knew the Prince of Achaea, but all of them knew Camus, by various names, and they were all afraid of him – afraid even to accuse him. But I took copies, in case my lord the count needed them later, and then the Lord of Bolsena hanged all six of them from his gatehouse, including the man who'd guided us. He talked about impaling them all, but it was just talk, and Fiore, who feared no man, pointed out that if we impaled them, we were no better than they.

The man who'd guided us was the first. The Lord of Bolsena asked him how he wanted to die.

'Shriven,' he said. He didn't weep. He didn't beg. He talked for a long time to Father Angelo, and then he walked to the scaffold. The other five yelled at him, begged for mercy, and called him traitor.

He bowed to Bolsena. 'I was once a gentleman,' he said. 'I beg you forgive me, my lord. I followed Satan. I repent of it.'

'I forgive you,' Bolsena said. 'Would you rather die by the sword?'

The man nodded. 'Yes,' he said. 'And not with these dogs.'

Bolsena did it himself, which I admired. The man knelt, without restraints; his hands shook, but by God, I hope I go to my death as well.

The rest of them died like criminals – screaming and fouling themselves.

The next day, we rode for Viterbo. It was only a day's ride south of us – a magnificent ride along the high ridge above the lake. I remember little of it. I was so tired that I might have fallen off my horse several times, and the walk up the last of the slope on the pilgrim road, where you climb a mountain in a hundred steps, or so it seems, was almost the end of me. But the bloom was off our rose; the attack and the executions had left us low. Even the sun on the fields could not cheer me.

Viterbo is a fine town – older and plainer than, say, Verona, but full of Roman antiquities and Etruscan decorations. It is pretty and rich, with a fine market, a huge square just inside the walls and a fine citadel. The Pope had been there for weeks, waiting for his triumphal entry into Rome; no Pope, remember, had resided in Rome for forty years or more. The town was crowded with people: monks, priests, nuns, the great and the small, abbots and abbesses, moneylenders, nobles, ambassadors and soldiers.

Fiore saved me from failure. I was so tired I sat on Juniper, virtually witless, but Fiore moved us briskly through the gates, showed all of our passports, and used the count's name relentlessly until a young knight, a family friend of the Birigucci, offered to see if his sister's nunnery inside the walls might take us all. He proved as good as his word, and we were given cells. I collapsed into a bed and slept the clock round, rising only the next day for Vespers. I had probably been ill, in addition to sheer muscle fatigue and some wounds. Certainly, a full day asleep healed me more than any leech might have done, although my right side was stiff and my left hand was very sore. I think now, having had more than my share of wounds, that Camus's first blow broke a bone in my left hand, right through the gauntlet. At the time, I just tucked the hand in my belt and got on with my business, most of which, to be honest, was being done by Fiore and Marc-Antonio. They found lodgings for the Greek monks, and they arranged an audience for the count at the Papal court, Fiore shamelessly parading his donat's coat up and down until Papal courtiers took notice. So finally, on the tenth day of October, we were presented to the Pope.

It was curiously like a reunion. The last time I'd seen Urban V, he had given the rank of Papal Legate for the Holy Land to Father Pierre Thomas, and Lord Grey had unfurled the Papal standard. I had stood with Peter Mortimer, no longer a routier, but a knight serving the Order of St John.

Three years had passed, and the Pope had aged a great deal. His hair was white, his face thin, and he had the kind of troubled look you see mostly on statesmen with strong ethics and on mothers of large families.

Nonetheless, he received the Count of Savoy in state, in the great hall of the palazzo, and we all wore our best. Marc-Antonio, who was working every minute to be reinstated in my good graces, had polished my harness until it appeared to be made of quicksilver. I wore over it my red donat's coat, which the nuns were kind enough to clean and repair for me, as a fight in the woods and a fall from Gabriel had not increased its lustre by any measure.

The Green Count handed the Pope two banners – one, his banner of the Virgin. The other, to my stunned surprise, was the cross we'd drawn hastily in blood on bed sheets in the taking of Gallipoli, to show the count that we held the castle. The count told the story well, as it gave him an opportunity to play the great lord, to laud his own people, who now included me. It was a good piece of politics and, when he was done, the Papal court was as silent as a tomb.

Urban raised a hand in benediction. He blessed the banner, and the count, and declared him again to be the very 'Athlete of Christ', as he had called him when the crusade had been declared.

After a great deal of formality, we were dismissed, but only to go to our lodgings, take off our stiff satins and jewels – not in my case, you understand, but the count's – and return to the palazzo for a more intimate meeting with the Holy Father.

You may imagine that I watched the crowds like a hawk. The last time I had left the Pope's presence, I had been attacked by the Bishop of Geneva's men-at-arms, led by Camus. I understood that the bishop was still in Avignon, manoeuvring to make himself Pope at the next election, along with that part of the faction of French prelates who were adamantly against the Pope moving the office of the papacy back to Rome.

So many factions. And most of them packed into Viterbo.

Back we went to a private audience with the Pope. He received us seated on a low throne, with a dozen cardinals and some other bishops, and he asked the count to tell him the history of his campaigns in the east. The count was kind enough to mention me several times, as well as Richard and Georges Mayot and others. He told the whole story of the campaigns, first against the Turks, and then the Bulgars, but it was almost unrecognisable, couched in the language of chivalric romance, as if dysentery and foot soldiers had been absent from the whole thing.

And then we came to the delicate matter of the Emperor – that is, the eastern emperor. The count lauded his own success in the east, and described the Emperor's conversion in glowing terms, even going so far as to mention the Emperor's financial guarantees about his conversion, a matter which Nerio had told me was absolutely secret. The Greek monks were then led forward and presented. After the count's fine speech, the Pope must have expected that our dozen Greek monks were theological representatives who had come to make their obeisance to the head of the western Church.

The Greek monks were theologians, all right. No sooner were they introduced than they began to toss questions at the Pope, as if he was on trial. Three of them spoke Italian, and all of them had fair Latin, and they were not a bit hesitant to ask the Pope difficult questions. It was all completely unexpected.

Let me add to this moment of disaster by saying that Urban V was perhaps the finest Pope I have ever known and that, had he been prepared, the meeting might have borne better fruit. But he was not prepared, and he was, I think, mortified. It had appeared that the Union of Churches was actually in his grasp, and then a dozen monks were haranguing him as if he was a scholar accused of heresy.

Amadeus was not a Latinist, or not much of one, and he had no Greek at all, but he knew the tone in the questions, and hastened to silence the monks, but by then the damage was done.

One monk, Brother Michalis, I believe, spoke into near complete silence.

'We will never submit to what you call "your authority",' he said in Latin. 'You have no authority over true Christians, except as the Bishop of Rome, and even that is debatable, as you hold many unorthodox beliefs.'

Men like Brother Michalis are very dangerous. They think that their beliefs entitle them to say shocking things – to break agreements and to start wars. I will confess that, as a man who has read some of the texts, as a soldier, and as a Christian, I cannot pretend to fully understand the controversy that separates the Greek and Roman Churches. But I will say that there is nothing I have ever heard in any of the arguments from Greeks or Latins that would justify a war, or even a coldness. It still seems to me, now that any chance of union is dead and buried, that the Pope's position rested on his insistence that the Greek Church accept his authority unconditionally, which was never a position calculated to win him any friends in the east.

It scarcely matters now. But listen, all of you: in the autumn of the year of Our Lord 1367, it seemed that we had it in our grasp: victory over the Saracens; the liberation of Jerusalem; the Union of Churches. We were going to turn back the clock, rebuild the alliance of east and west, and change the world. What had the Green Count fought for, if not that? What had we all fought for?

Urban rose from his throne, raised his hand, and denounced the monks as heretics.

I was there.

When he was done, they were marched from the Pope's presence and held in a side chapel awaiting his pleasure. I could see and even hear them from where I was – an allegory, if you like, of the role of the Greeks in Europe. The Pope turned on the count, although not with any anger.

'We cannot fully express our disappointment,' the Pope said. 'We had thought that you were bringing us representatives of an Emperor contrite in his reflections, and instead you have brought us a dozen heretics burning with the righteousness of their own error.'

'Holy Father, I beg your indulgence, but I promise you that the Emperor of Constantinople has given me his word—'

'Whatever he promised you, he sent these argumentative schismatics . . .'

'Holy Father, I beg your forbearance.' Now, I had never heard the count use the word 'beg' in any context whatsoever, and I could scarce believe my ears. 'Holy Father, the Emperor himself will present himself here, before your eminence, to protest his conversion—'

'We will believe this when we see it,' the Pope said heavily. 'We have prayed, aye, and fought – against the Visconti, against the Lords of the Marches, against the English and the routiers, and against the Saracens. The last thing we need is further division within the Church of Christ.'

'Holy Father . . .'

'No more today,' the Pope said. He made a dismissive gesture.

'Holy Father,' Amadeus said, stepping forward. I could hear the unaccustomed desperation in his voice, and despite our difference, in this I was very much on his side.

The Papal camerlingo and a number of other officers froze. The Pope's acting gonfalonier stepped between the throne and Amadeus. Hands went to sword hilts.

That's how it was, in October of 1367.

Amadeus, Count of Savoy, was not to be silenced by some glares. He leaned around the gonfalonier. 'Holy Father, these men may speak their minds, but they have been sent by the Emperor to arrange for the union of the Churches.'

'Let them submit!' Urban barked.

I had never seen him like this. Not for the first time or the last, I wished for Pierre Thomas, risen from the grave. He knew both Churches intimately. And he knew the Pope.

Amadeus also knew the Pope. He'd had several audiences, and he had, in addition, contributed directly, or so I have heard, to this Pope's election. Despite which, the Pope turned his head away from the Count of Savoy. His eyes wandered, and then ...

The Pope's pale blue gaze rested briefly on me. I could see the recognition in his eyes; I was wearing the surcoat of the Order. I have red hair, and I'm four fingers taller than most tall men – I tend to stick out.

I could not let the hope of the East die without a word in its defence, even if the advocates of the Greek Church were a pack of fools.

'Holy Father,' I said, with a *reverentia* all the way to my knee. I was thinking furiously. Fiore says I looked like a thunderstruck fool, and he was there. 'Holy Father, I am only a soldier of Christ and not a theologian,' I said. 'But I have read the Bible and I have spoken to these worthy men ...'

'Did we not first meet you as a reclaimed sinner? A routier who had been saved by our legate in the East?' the Pope asked.

'Holy Father, you did.'

'Even now, your brother brigands and robbers, rapists and arsonists, are making war against us in the Kingdom of Naples. Even now, our throne totters, and mercenaries and routiers would bring down the Kingdom of Christ. And you will speak to us about the Union of Churches?'

Well. He was looking at me – in that moment, he reminded me of my sick, angry old uncle. And that is the sin of anger, friends. He was, for the most part, a good man. But he was in the grip of rage. If he had been an archer or a page, I might have slapped him.

Instead, I did my best to marshal my thoughts like a constable reviewing unruly militia. 'Holy Father, I will speak.' Fiore says I barked it.

The hall fell silent. Even the Count of Savoy turned and looked at me.

'Holy Father, Eminences, gentlemen, ladies,' I said. I remember saying all the formal things while I tried to imagine an argument that would get through his anger and his desire for pre-eminence. I could only think of one. 'I cannot speak as a theologian,' I said. 'But I can speak as a soldier.'

Some men laughed.

'Holy Father, I know what it is to have my authority questioned. To have other knights, or perhaps lesser men, ask each other if I am fit to lead them. Even to have a senior knight of my Order tell me that I cannot lead, because I have not enough quartering in my shield, or enough years in the Order. And yet, I know *so* much about the habits of authority, Holy Father, that I know when the proper reply is a blow, and when the proper reply is a joke, a smile, or even a discussion.'

I didn't have him; that is, he was not convinced. But he was listening. My knees and hands were trembling.

'Holy Father, I have fought. I have fought at Alexandria, and at Jerusalem. I have fought throughout Syria and I have fought in Morea and in Bulgaria. I have fought alongside many Greeks, men who worship as these worthy monks worship. I have faced Mamluks and Turks and Arabs with these men at my side. I have heard their piety and their prayers. In the east, where Jerusalem is lost to us, there is a single bulwark to Christendom – decayed, less than it was, but still very great. This is the Christian Empire of the East, at Constantinople. If it falls, what then? And how can it hold without our help?'

'Let them submit to our authority,' the Pope said.

'Holy Father, would you submit? I ask you not as Pope, but as a man. Would you submit, if you were Patriarch of Constantinople? Can we not save the empire first, and discuss *Filioque* later?'

When I said *Filioque*, half of the heads in the hall snapped round.

'What do you know of *Filioque*?' asked one of the monks in his Greek Latin.

The Pope leaned forward. He was *listening.*

'I know that if you weigh all of the arguments ever made about the nature of God in one side of a balance, and put a Turk's arrow on the other side, the arrow, even with a shaft of cane and a head of bone, will tip the balance,' I said.

The Pope looked at one of the cardinals who sat close to him.

'Holy Father,' I said, almost pleading. 'Count Amadeus has lost friends, fortune and blood to bring you these men. I beg you to hear him, and them.'

The Pope rose to his feet. 'This interview is at an end. I have been given much to think about, much over which I will pray. Please, all of you, take counsel with each other, and we will meet again.' He made the sign of the cross, and it appeared to be made directly over the Greek monks. For their part, they all inclined their heads, apparently accepting the blessing.

The Holy Father left the hall, sweeping out in a rustle of long wool robes. The count approached the Papal seneschal, and the two of them stepped aside together, the seneschal's hand on the count's arm.

Brother Michalis stopped in front of me. He planted his feet like a fighter. 'There is only the Truth, and God,' he said in Latin. 'Your wars are but shadows – your kingdoms are not the Kingdom of Heaven. We do not need your soldiers to save our souls.'

I stood in dumb silence.

'Still,' he said with a patronising shrug, 'it is praiseworthy that you spoke for us, and put this man in a better frame of mind. We hear that his little kingdom is threatened with war.' He shrugged.

'I hope that your understanding of truth and God is better than your understanding of the minds and hearts of men,' I said, in Greek. 'Because for the most part, you sound like an arrogant prince, a tyrant of the Word, and not like a man of God.' I struck with the Greek words, like a carpenter pounding in a row of nails, and he flinched, as I had intended.

'I am not arrogant!' he insisted.

My thrust had gone deep, I could tell, and I nodded my head.

I was moving to Fiore's side when one of the many priests intercepted me. At least, I assumed he was a priest, although he wore a sword and a short cote-hardie and might, in fact, have been any soldier or knight I knew.

'Messire Guglielmo le Coq?' he asked, with a civil bow.

'*Si, Excellenza. E le?*' I asked, at my most cautiously polite.

He introduced himself, one of the many soldier-priests that surrounded this Pope. He turned his back on the Greek monks. 'I have come at the behest of a prominent man,' he said carefully.

Just like Avignon, that mare's nest of intrigue.

'Yes?' I asked. The count was leaving, with Georges Mayot and Richard at his shoulders. He glanced my way and nodded coolly. I was the captain of his escort, damn it; I didn't want to waste my time playing spies and courtiers.

'Are you currently in the service of Giovanni Acudo?' he asked, giving John Hawkwood his Italian name.

I looked at him carefully. 'No,' I said. 'But I may be next spring. So please, no insults.'

He bowed. 'There are no insults intended. It is a delicate matter.' He looked around.

The count was being bowed into the courtyard. I had perhaps a minute before our horses were brought. I did not intend to leave my lord standing, not while Camus's assassins were still a danger.

'I must go,' I said.

'My lord would speak to you,' my priest said with a bow.

'Send to the convent of Saint Mary Magdalene,' I said, turning.

The priest frowned. 'Can you not—'

'Not right now,' I insisted, and I bowed, turning, and all but ran for the doors.

I left it a little late. Half the College of Cardinals was in the courtyard, and the famous Count of Savoy was already mounted. Even our dozen Greek monks were on their donkeys, and Fiore was slapping the beautiful white gloves I'd bought him against his armoured thigh in impatience.

They had Gabriel by the bridle – a pair of Papal pages, probably nobly born boys from Orvieto families. Gabriel was just at the base of the steps.

It was irresistible.

I trotted down the steps like a man-at-arms in a hurry. But I didn't pause for Marc-Antonio or the mounting stool.

I leaped.

I got one hand on the saddle-bow and vaulted onto Gabriel's back, with scarcely a groan. I was in full harness, and while I've done it before and since, I've never done it with a thousand men watching.

Make that a thousand and one. I turned Gabriel, and I saw that the Pope was standing at the grand windows in the central apartments overlooking the yard. I had a devil in me; I made Gabriel rear, and I touched my visor to the Pope.

He laughed aloud.

I turned Gabriel and trotted to the head of the column, where the count sat in emerald splendour.

'You do like to draw attention, do you not, Monsieur Guillaume?' he said. He gave a slight shake of his head, and we rode out of the Papal palace.

I was just getting all my armour off, with Marc-Antonio untying my laces and points, and Stefanos stacking the larger pieces on an oiled linen sheet while Demetrios got a start on wiping it all down with an oily rag, when a blond boy appeared with an old nun. The nun was more than a little scandalised to find me in a shirt and braes and an aging arming-vest and hose – fairly naked, by convent standards. But she stood her ground.

'I am the doorkeeper,' she said in good Latin. 'This young man will not state his errand but says he has a note for you, my lord.'

I bowed to her and snapped my fingers at the boy. He bowed to the floor and gave me a parchment, folded tight and sealed with a violet wax seal.

As I expected, it was from the Pope, signing under his own name, Guillaume de Grimoard.

I turned to Marc-Antonio. 'I need clothes – simple, brown. Also, I need an audience with the count, as soon as he can spare me the time.'

Stefanos began laying out my simplest travelling clothes: a brown cote-hardie with pale yellow hose, and a clean shirt. For quality, they were new and Venetian-made and fine enough. On the other hand, without my sword belt, I'd pass for any apprentice or under-master in Viterbo – if a little more fashionable.

The real advantage of good servants is that they are fast, they do not argue, and they behave, in a social crisis, like good soldiers in a military crisis. The Greek boys had been with me long enough to know how I wanted things. Marc-Antonio, leaving aside his lechery, was growing into the kind of squire men dream of, which meant, to me, that it was probably time to make him a knight.

I was dressed, just putting my magnificent sword belt over my plain clothes, when Marc-Antonio returned from the count's apartments.

'Any time, my lord. Immediately, if it suits you.' He bowed.

I nodded.

'Purse?' Stefanos asked. I didn't usually wear a purse on my sword belt. In Italy and France, gentlemen usually have people carry their purses, sometimes even their swords. They don't wear them themselves. It is different in England, I know.

Regardless, I reached for a plain purse and slipped it on my fancy belt. I didn't know how long I would be gone or whether I might need money. A visit to the Pope, especially when he represents himself as a private person, is a little like an *empris* or a deed of arms: you have to be ready for anything.

I walked down the short hall that separated my cell and the second cell that Marc-Antonio and I shared for two suits of armour, and found Monsieur Mayot on duty, fully armed. After the various attacks, we were alert at all times: one of us was always on guard in full harness, and everything the count ate was tasted, first by a little hunting dog named Alice, and then by Richard Musard.

Regardless, Mayot passed me into the little hall. The count was standing at the window, reading a letter. He raised a pair of parchment envelopes.

'Two for you,' he said, with a casual smile that told me I was in favour.

I knelt anyway. He nodded and beckoned me to my feet with a twitch of his hand.

He nodded again, clearly dissatisfied with something. 'Speak,' he said.

'My lord, I have been summoned by the Pope,' I said.

He raised an eyebrow. '*You* know the Pope?' he asked.

'I served Pierre Thomas,' I said. 'I have had two audiences with the Pope.'

'And you just speak up whenever the mood takes you?' the count asked. Then he shrugged. 'Never mind my temper, monsieur. You did us no harm, and you may have done us some good, by speaking.'

'As to that, my lord,' I said, 'may I speak freely?'

He made a face. 'Not too freely,' he said with an odd smile. 'I think I would fear it, were you to speak too freely.'

I bowed.

'Say your piece. I won't bite,' the count said.

I nodded. 'My lord, you are the Count of Savoy – a relative and an old ally of Bernabò Visconti of Milan.'

The count glanced at Richard, and then back at me. 'I am to be lectured on diplomacy by an Englishman, I find.' He sighed. 'And yet, you are no doubt correct. He thinks I am some manoeuvre of Bernabò's. Sweet Christ, for an hour of honesty and straight talk in all this ...'

'My lord, the Greek monks say he feels at threat ...'

'And yet, of the two of us, I'm the one who the Prince of Achaea is trying to kill,' the count said. He shook his head. 'Why do you think the Pope summoned you?'

'My lord, the Pope cannot be seen to debate with any man, much less with Bernabò's brother-in-law. He sends for me precisely because he cannot debate with you.'

Savoy fingered his beard. 'We can only hope,' he said. 'Go, with my blessings.'

Richard walked me to the door. 'What possessed you?' he asked.

I shrugged. 'Richard, could you bear to see those monks dismissed without a hearing? After all the crap—'

'Oh, not that. You spoke brilliantly – I admired that,' Richard said. 'I mean when you vaulted into the saddle and stole the show like a mountebank at a fair. My lord the count goes to a great deal of trouble to be at the centre of things ...'

I shrugged again. 'It was foolish,' I said.

Richard smiled. 'Yes, it was,' he said. 'Now go and see the Pope.'

I didn't go alone. I took Fiore. When there's a great deal on the line, Fiore is the man.

We followed the blond boy through the streets. We walked around the palazzo and entered into the working yard, where food and wine was delivered. That day, though, no delivery wagon could enter, because a dozen girls were hanging linen. We went into the stables, and then through the laundry: tubs of water, dozens of women washing, and hundreds of shirts and albs and other vestments in white linen, some embroidered, some with cutwork – a fortune in men's clothing. The smell of strong soap was everywhere.

My little blond angel took me up two flights of inner stairs, and then we were above the kitchens. The smell of food – rich, savoury food – replaced the smell of soap. Someone was having roast pork; a fat capon, well-laced with herbs, was visible as we passed the long tables of the kitchen. The Papal meal was about to be laid.

My little cherub led me up another flight of steps and we passed a working room – just some tables and benches, and two clerks copying. Then we entered a small *studiolo*, panelled in intarsia to hide a set of book cupboards and scroll cupboards, each panel covered in patterns – inlaid squares, triangles, and circles predominated, a riot of shapes that was almost uncomfortable to the eye.

And there was the Pope – or rather, there was Messire Guillaume de Grimoard. He was dressed in a wine-coloured gown that would not have been out of place on a Venetian aristocrat or a Florentine merchant: good wool, English wool, with gilt-silver buttons, about a hundred of them. He had hose on under the gown, and his buttons went to the floor.

I thought he was asleep. His eyes were closed, and I stood silent for a moment

His eyes opened.

'I am not asleep,' he said. 'I am only resting my eyes.'

'Certainly, Holy Father,' I said.

'We need you to perform a task for us, Messire Guglielmo,' he said. 'We had not been aware, until now, that we share this name.'

'Yes, Holy Father,' I said.

'You know Giovanni Acudo?' the Pope said.

'Yes, Holy Father,' I said.

'And you know Ambrogio di Visconti, too, we have little doubt?'

'Yes, Holy Father,' I said.

'Do you know Gòmez Albornoz?' he asked.

'No, Holy Father,' I said, bludgeoning my tired head for an idea of where this was going.

The Pope folded his hands in his lap. 'Messire Guillaume, we need someone to tell us why there is no news from the south.' He shrugged. 'Are you aware that all Italy is close to war?' he said.

'Yes, Holy Father,' I said.

'That Milan is under interdict? And that they persist in sending soldiers against us?' he asked.

'Yes, Holy Father.' If you are waiting to hear me make some smart remark to the Pope, I have to decline. Sometimes the point of obedience is to obey.

'Our servant, Cardinal Albornoz, lies dying, but his nephew, Messire Gòmez, is in the field, facing your Hawkwood and this Visconti bastard.' He glanced at me. 'We need you to go and find out what is happening, and tell us. We need you to go quickly. We don't have Juan di Heredia. You see? I remember you quite well, Messire Guillaume. You rode to the Holy Roman Emperor and then to Venice for us, looking for Peter of Cyprus. And as you have yourself said, you have fought everywhere. Soldiers respect you. This is not a mission for a priest.'

'I will do my best, Holy Father,' I said. I wanted to protest that I was in service to the count, but he was imperious in a way that few men I have known could be; he really was 'the Pope', and in his own eyes, he was the incarnate power of the Church of Jesus Christ, above all earthly authorities.

I was taken out the same way I went in, and I went straight back to the count.

He was eating. He gestured and a chair was brought, and I was given a cut of good beef and some chicken – perhaps the same sort of chicken the Pope was having. The spices smelled the same.

'The Pope wishes to send me on a mission to the south,' I said. 'If you permit me to go, I will be gone ten days – perhaps more.'

The count frowned. But then he nodded. 'Where are you going?'

'Naples,' I said.

I never got anywhere near Naples.

Where I was bound was the *Kingdom* of Naples. The kingdom ran far into the north: almost as far as Urbino, where, if you recall, my sometime friend and debtor, Antonio Visconti – last seen at the Lazzaretto, borrowing money and horses from me – had headed to meet his half-brother Ambrogio. I knew all that; I had already had my suspicions that Hawkwood was serving with the Visconti. I had never heard of the Spanish captain, Albornoz, but he didn't sound like much. The best intelligence I could get in Viterbo was that Albornoz had marched east, over the mountains and into the Kingdom of Naples, about the time we were passing through Verona, and nothing had been heard since.

I had lots of time to consider what Hawkwood might have been trying to tell me as I rode east myself, with a pair of riding horses and Marc-Antonio. We stayed in convents and abbeys, with a letter from the Pope, and I wore my harness night and day. We changed horses almost every hour, stopping only to drink a cup of wine and pray at the odd roadside shrine.

At Perugia I heard that Albornoz had lifted the siege of Urbino and the Visconti had pressed deeper into the kingdom, passing south of Ancona. I turned south myself and rode to Foligno in near-constant rain. Within a day, I was looking out over the Adriatic. My pretty new steel harness was getting rustier by the day, and I imperilled my immortal soul by cursing the supreme pontiff almost hourly.

On my fourth day out of Viterbo, I was riding south and east, headed for the coast in a steady rain, when a pair of men on tired horses appeared out of the haze of water in front of me. No one had any colours to show on a rainy day; I was swathed in a cloak, and so was Marc-Antonio. The two men came on, flogging their horses unmercifully, and something told me they were trouble.

I had a lance. I checked my sword and flipped my visor down, the enormous advantage of spending all day in harness being that you are very, very difficult to surprise. And let me add that this was my new helmet, the one that had spent half a year in my baggage – you know you are rich when you can forget a new helmet. This was one of the new-style armets, with hinged cheekpieces and a greatly improved visor, a wonderful piece of armour.

Hah. That's not the story, of course.

The two men halted perhaps three horse lengths away.

'Will Gold,' called one, through the rain.

'You have the advantage of me,' I called back.

'I was Andrew Belmont's squire,' he said. 'John Renfrew.'

I nodded, although I didn't remember him.

We were closing, though I still did not trust him, for all he was English.

'You're a little late for the fighting,' he said. 'Nice horse.'

I nodded.

'Want to sell her?' Renfrew asked.

'No,' I said.

'Well, that's fine,' he said, and he reached for his sword. 'I felt I had to ask. You and your friend can just dismount, and we'll be on our way. These horses will be fine in a day.'

I shook my head. 'I'm afraid not.'

'See, Will, it's life or death to me and this friend o' mine,' Renfrew said. 'We got beat bad. Hawkwood's run off, Visconti is taken, and fucking Albornoz is hanging any routier he catches. So, if you don't mind ...'

'Just keep riding,' I said. 'I'll slow up the pursuit. Go.'

Renfrew flashed a tired smile. 'Well,' he said.

Then he struck. He drew his arming sword from the scabbard and thrust, all in one motion. It should have been deadly, except that he lowered his shoulder to get his sword clear of his belt, and that one motion gave the whole thing away, and I dropped my lance into his draw. He and his tired horse were on my shield side, very close. The shaft of my lance hit his horse's head and then his rising sword arm, and I was already going for my sword. Marc-Antonio was three paces behind me and he already had his sword out.

Renfrew cut at me. I was out of distance. He leaned too far, counting on his horse to move under him, but that nag was done, and he leaned out ...

I caught his sword, then the cuff of his gauntlet, and I pulled and dumped him on the road.

Marc-Antonio, on a good horse, with a lance, was a match for any routier ever born, and Renfrew's companion was also dropped like a sack of meat.

Renfrew rose to his knees in the muddy, sandy road. 'Fuck you,' he said ruefully.

'I'd start walking west,' I said.

'I don't suppose we could beg for your horses,' Renfrew said.

'Nope,' I said.

We turned and rode east, at a trot, and we left them there.

*

An hour later, I met with the outposts of the Papal army. I had a letter from the Pope, and after an anxious hour wherein I was accused of being a spy, or a routier, I was taken to Galeotto Malatesta, Lord of Rimini, who was commanding Albornoz the Spaniard's advance guard.

He was a piece of work: a braggart with an endless litany of his own good offices, but he was impressed with my Papal letter. He gave me wine and complained about Albornoz, who was, he said, too young for high command and not a 'real soldier'. His implication was obvious: that he himself should have the command. And he managed to imply that he'd done all the hard fighting.

'You defeated Ambrogio?' I asked.

He nodded. 'We broke both of his flanks and rolled him up. The vaunted Acudo ran like a fox chased by hounds.'

I listened as politely as I could, and then he escorted me to Albornoz. On the way, he pointed out an olive grove. Every tree, and there were hundreds of trees, had a corpse dangling from it.

'That is how our Spaniard makes war,' he said.

I couldn't tell whether his comment was admiring or admonishing.

Albornoz was a slim man in a fine, plain harness. If he was a typical Spaniard, it is no wonder that the Moors are being driven from Spain; he smiled very little, talked little, did not brag like Malatesta, and his eyes seemed to go everywhere. But he was courteous, if a little cold.

'We have fought two battles,' he said. 'Every man counted. I didn't have a man to spare as messenger. Indeed, as the Holy Father has not paid my men, I thought perhaps I'd been forgotten.'

I gave him a note from his uncle's steward. 'Your uncle, Cardinal Albornoz, is dying,' I said. 'I'm sorry.'

He read it, nodding. 'You are English?' he asked.

'Yes,' I said.

He nodded. 'Hawkwood got away,' he said. 'I captured both of the Visconti mongrels.' He met my eyes and his were hard as tempered steel. 'I hate the English. Your people have ruined my country, burning and looting, and they do the same here.'

I suppose I was meant to be terrified. Instead I was tired and angry.

'If you could write a report on your battle,' I said, 'I will take it to the Pope.'

'My uncle is more important than the Pope,' he snapped. 'We will triumph here; we will clean out this nest of vipers the way we will clear Spain of her enemies, and then we will make something.'

I wondered if I was in a camp of madmen.

'You write the report, Englishman. Only, let me show you how we make war.'

He led me out past the cook lines of his camp, where hundreds of men were dangling from trees.

It was … horrible.

'I will kill every one of them,' he said. 'All the routiers.' He looked at me. 'Tell your friends. Tell them to go home.'

I said nothing. But there were men I knew there, hanging like rotten fruit – men in their arming clothes, a few still in leg armour or sabatons. Men who are hanged usually shit themselves; there's no two ways about it. The smell of rotting men, and excrement, and death, was terrible. It was not the death of chivalry, but perhaps the antithesis of chivalry. Those were not good men – not saints. But most of them were not much worse than I.

'They surrendered,' I said.

Albornoz shrugged. 'What of it? They are vermin,' he said. 'Tell the Pope.' He smiled at me, and all his courtesy was gone. 'Tell your friends. Go and find Giovanni Acudo and tell him. Tell him I have halters for all the English. I will make all of you take this last shit. Understand me?'

I shook my head. 'Tell him yourself,' I said. 'I'm off to report your battles to the Pope. Because you couldn't spare a messenger.'

'This is what war is,' he said. 'Do not pretend otherwise. Do not pretend you are so high and mighty.'

I suppose I shrugged. 'May I see the Viscontis?' I asked.

I was taken to a cell in the little tower, where both Visconti brothers were kept, probably in the arming clothes in which they'd been captured. Both had been beaten. Both were more angry than afraid.

Albornoz waited, listening to every word, relishing their discomfort, their fear, their anger. While he stood above the trapdoor, a dozen of his knights came in, with Malatesta and some of his knights. They were muttering about money.

I was reasonably sure that no one in Albornoz's feudal force had been paid for a long time.

I climbed back out of the pit. 'Will you ransom them?' I asked, loudly enough so that Malatesta would hear.

'Maybe the younger,' said the Spaniard. 'Ambrogio will keep a long time, I think. Or perhaps the Pope will want him as a token against his father. Indeed, perhaps both of them . . .'

'Antonio isn't worth a hundred ducats,' I said.

'I know,' said the Spaniard. 'I thought of hanging him.' He smiled.

Malatesta frowned. Unlike Albornoz, Malatesta knew what would happen if one of Bernabò's sons was hanged, even a bastard son.

I took a breath and attacked. 'Did the Pope order you to start the great war? The war with Milan?' I asked. 'It was my understanding, directly from the Holy Father, that we are trying to avoid this war. Did the Pope order this?'

'No, Messire English Knight of Both Sides. No, he did not. Indeed, I think perhaps he wanted . . .' He shrugged. 'My uncle wants them all hanged. The Pope is not here.'

'I will buy Antonio from you,' I said. 'If you hang one of Bernabò's sons, there is no place on Earth you will be able to hide, and the war will come.'

The Spaniard looked at me. 'You are just another routier,' he said.

I was tired, and angry, and sad. 'No,' I said, 'I am a knight. I am a knight volunteer of the Order of Saint John. I have just returned from fighting the Infidel in the Holy Land. Who the *fuck* are you? I came here at the Holy Father's orders and you are giving me a ration of shit. Give me Sir Antonio, or perhaps we will see who exactly is a knight.' I walked straight at him and stood very close. I was a foot taller. Perhaps it was stupid. I don't know where it came from. Perhaps I'd had a year of being mild, pious, and careful. Perhaps too many *my lords.*

The Spaniard glared at me, his eyes afire. 'You think I would fight *you*?'

We were having this spat in front of most of the lords of the east coast – about a third of the knight service of the Kingdom of Naples. And here, too, were men I knew; not many, but a few. Malatesta himself had commanded cavalry for Siena.

And I had a name.

It might have gone either way, but Malatesta of Rimini laughed.

'I want to see you fight, Spaniard,' he said. 'He's calling you out.'

'I have no intention of fighting this Englishman,' the Spaniard spat.

I sneered. 'Oh, that's too bad,' I said, or something equally arrogant.

Malatesta made a face. 'Well,' he said, 'that sort of thing may be acceptable in Spain ...'

The other Italian knights laughed, gently mocking the Spaniard.

Some of the younger knights shouted, 'Fight!'

My small Spaniard turned four shades of red. I thought he might explode.

'I hope you aren't afraid?' asked Malatesta, with amused venom.

He looked at me and I saw him, by force of will, overcome his anger. 'Very well, Englishman,' he said. 'We will run a course together. If I win, you are my prisoner. If you win, you may have Sir Antonio.' He nodded. 'Is this satisfactory?'

I didn't nod.

I bowed. I'd become very adept at bowing, and using bows to reflect my opinions; I was almost a courtier. So I bowed, and turned away. I held myself very straight, and went back to the camp, where Marc-Antonio and I ate a meal in stony silence, drank some wine with our Italian 'hosts', slept a fearful night, and rose at first light.

I had made a fool's bargain with a man who had, as far as I could see, no sense of honour. Albornoz was an oddity; I've known dozens of Spanish knights, and they are the most punctilious gentlemen about fairness and good manners. I assume Albornoz was raised in the Church. Only the backbiting of the cloister could explain him.

I had too much time to lie and think; to wait for dawn, with my shoulders tight and my stomach crawling. I was sure I could take him, but I had made a poor bargain, either way.

The lists were marked in stones along the edge of a ruined farmer's field. My opponent wore his war armour and carried a sharpened lance. When I saw the carthorse he'd provided me, I knew that he intended to kill me. I had put him in a difficult position; if I was dead, I could not tell my story to the Pope.

I went and talked to the horse, a short-legged heavy cob with no redeeming virtues and a tendency to bite. He was just big enough to carry a man in armour. I wasn't sure he'd had any training at all, and in a course run with no barricade, an untrained horse might be worse than no horse at all.

Albornoz rode over to me. 'You like your horse, Englishman?' he asked.

'This is what you account a warhorse, in Spain?' I asked.

He shook his head. 'You can withdraw. Apologise to me in front of Malatesta, and I will let you live.'

'And miss running a course with you, fair sir?' I said in Italian. 'And the pleasure of riding this … animal?' I asked. I did my best to put a good face on it, and to make the Italians laugh. I was scoring in *sprezzatura*, that mysterious quality by which Italian knights define manhood.

Albornoz was not.

Both of us were wearing harnesses rusted almost brown, which perhaps says something about us. I took my time looking him over, looking for weakness. He wore a much older style than I did: a heavy coat of plates over double maille. My armour was lighter and better in every respect. My horse was far worse than his; how I rued having left Gabriel behind in Viterbo. I couldn't ride a joust on Juniper – she was too light – although I considered it.

I was fully armed, and waiting to die. Marc-Antonio had left me at first light, and I had to arm myself, with a little help from a pair of Malatesta's pages – odd lads, but not bad.

I walked out, tried the saddle on my terrible horse, and resorted to prayer.

I prayed. I knelt by that miserable horse, and I prayed a dozen paternosters, until I was master of my shaking legs.

Then I thought of sitting in the rain in Provence, with a halter around my neck. I thought of my choices.

All in all, this was a better way to go. But those olive trees full of dead men-at-arms struck me in my heart. It was as if I couldn't catch my breath. I still think of them.

And in that welter of thoughts, I looked up and I saw him enter the lists mounted and my spirits sank more, if that seems possible. His big gelding was well-trained, and he was going to ride rings around me, even if I survived the first pass.

I sighed and got to my feet. It's funny how you don't run, or save your own life, by a craven apology. Funny, when you think of the reality: had I bowed to him and craved his pardon, I doubt it would have changed my life by the width of a blade of grass, and God knows Emile wouldn't have cared. I was thinking that as I rose from my knees. And I was wishing that my armour was polished.

And then Marc-Antonio appeared. He was on his Arab, and he was leading a big Arab stallion who looked familiar to me; in fact, it was the very horse I'd sold to Antonio Visconti.

That horse was no Gabriel. But compared to the carthorse I was given, Bohemund was the very destrier of legend.

We lined up – no fences, no barricades, and only Malatesta for a marshal. There was no salute from my adversary; for my part, I flicked my lance at him, as much to show the strength of my wrist as to 'salute' him.

I try not to fight angry. War is business, unless something intervenes. So it is with chivalry. A good man-at-arms cannot make war while angry, or he will do dishonourable things.

But Albornoz had made me angry. I mounted my borrowed stallion, and in two turns, I knew we could be a fair team, and then I let the reins go – not on the horse, but on my rage. I pounded Albornoz the way a squire pounds a quintain. Spaniards are often fine jousters, but again, I have to guess the bastard was intended for the Church and his uncle's cardinal's hat. He was small, and fast, but his speed was no help. On our first pass, he tried to slam his lance down on top of mine, but almost hit my horse with it instead. I caught it on my shield and flicked it away. My coronel caught him just a finger's width to the inside of his bridle hand, under the shield, and he was unhorsed. My lance tip didn't penetrate his coat of plates, but it must have hurt – broken ribs, to say the least.

On the second pass, I unhorsed him with a simple strike to his helmet. He was barely able to sit his horse, and he lay for a long time. When he eventually rose, it was to challenge me to fight him on foot.

I was still angry.

I was still angry, and that is not a good way to fight. I suspected that I was helping Malatesta undermine the authority of the Spaniard who'd just led them to victory; there is Italian generalship all over. I dismounted and drew my longsword. When he struck a sword forward *garde*, I laughed. I laughed so loudly that men wondered, but it was a classic, one of the things Fiore would have told him never to do.

In less time than it takes to tell it, I had my blade around his neck and I dropped him face first in the dirt. His ribs were cracked, and I was a foot taller and outweighed him by half the weight of my harness. He may have been a fine commander, but he was not up to facing me in single combat.

I didn't kill him.

But I did step on his back, pressing down harder than necessary, and force him to yield, face down in the field.

Better if I had killed him, perhaps. I certainly didn't make friends with him, the Pope's favoured commander.

On the return trip, they told us at Foligno that the Pope and all his entourage were headed for Rome. The newly liberated Antonio wanted to ride north as soon as we were free of Albornoz's camp, but I was not having any of that; I intended to take him to the Pope, for reasons of my own.

Foligno was full of surprises. I heard that Hawkwood had passed through with just ten lances at his heels, and I saw Andy Belmont and covered his bill for wine and salves. He was wounded, and I sat with him awhile.

And then we rode for Rome.

I had the whole ride to listen to Antonio thank me and berate me by turns. He was curiously untouched by the deaths of three hundred companions, murdered in cold blood. Like Malatesta, I think he saw that as the fortunes of war.

'My father will destroy this Pope, and lay waste to the Marches with fire and sword,' he said. 'Albornoz thinks he is the big man. Wait. He will find out why my father is called "The Beast".'

In short, Antonio did nothing in our ride to make me feel particularly good about having rescued him.

I had too much time to think, and in thinking, I began to see how stupid they all were. Bernabò was about to go to war with the Pope because of his vanity; the Pope refused to make concessions to save the Eastern Church because of *his* pride; the Green Count refused the Prince of Achaea his patrimony because of *his* pride, while the Prince of Achaea, who was as rich and well-born as any man could ask, used his riches to make war on the count for a perceived slight and an inheritance that might, or might not, increase his worldly wealth.

I felt, in my anger, that at least I understood the Karamanids and the Mamluks and the King of Cyprus. Italian diplomacy was ... something else again. And we had yet to see the bottom of the well.

It was also during that week that I began to lose patience with the Pope. Or rather, having seen Malatesta and Albornoz, I had to wonder if the Pope's 'goodness' had any real translation in the field. I confess it: those routiers hanging in the trees made me sick … sick of all of it. Albornoz was the Pope's man, and that sat in my gut like bad food.

We arrived in Rome after two days of hard riding, and we were wet, cold and miserable. To our delight – and delight is not too strong a word – we were ahead of the Holy Father, and the city was virtually empty, with every senator and noble gathering his retainers or fawning on the Pope at Sutri.

We didn't actually enter the city, but came to the Monastery of San Paolo on its outskirts at dusk, a mile and more off the great Via Appia. After passing the dense, ancient villages of the countryside, it seemed remarkable to enter the gates of the monastery and see fields of winter wheat rolling away in the autumn sunshine. Of course, the gates were locked at first. Marc-Antonio had to climb up on his saddle and jump over the wall.

There were clouds over the city, and lightning, but a brilliant sun shone on the tall, yellow stone buildings, and we got our horses under cover and untacked in an empty stable. It was as if we were expected; the mangers were full and there was clean new straw that smelled of summer and sunshine.

Only when all of our horses were rolling in the straw did we meet one of the inhabitants, a pretty nun who looked at us without a shadow of shyness and demanded to know by what right we were using her stables.

'You are late,' she said. 'Who opened the gates?'

'I did,' Marc-Antonio said.

Marc-Antonio bowed to her, and was courtly, and she was completely unimpressed. If I had known Roman women better, I would have known what to expect: she had a brilliant smile, wide, sparkling eyes, and she was not afraid of us or anyone else.

She was hard not to like.

I showed her the Pope's pass, which, unlike Malatesta or Albornoz, she kissed with reverence.

'He will pass down the road tomorrow, or so we are told,' she said.

'We only need to stay here for a night or two,' I said. But then I thought of the count, and lodgings in Rome.

She nodded, and looked at us carefully. I might as easily have been a decent knight as a routier, really, in my rust-stained harness and my red-stained coat of arms. Marc-Antonio had a nice maille haubergeon with a standing collar and a new breastplate; he looked dapper, and his boots were good. Antonio Visconti looked pretty bad, in stained hose, with arming shoes and no armour. She took that all in.

'You have the Pope's letter,' she said carefully.

'Tomorrow I will also have the Count of Savoy, his whole train of fifty men, as well as a dozen Greek monks,' I said.

She put her hands on her hips. 'A moment ago you only needed a day,' she said.

I bowed. 'Demoiselle, a moment ago I was only negotiating for myself, but this is a big place, and close to Rome. And Rome will be packed.'

She smiled. 'You will pay?'

I was out of money; my purse held perhaps ten gold florins, and I wasn't sure how to get more. I was almost sure the count was out of funds.

On the other hand, I wanted a bed and sleep. 'Yes,' I said.

She tossed her head. 'Nobles,' she said. 'Listen, sir knight. Everyone is away. Everyone who ought to be in charge here. Father Corso may throw you out in the morning, or the abbess.'

'I understand,' I said, and she turned her back as if we were harmless novices. I liked her courage, and I liked her better when she took us to three decent cells, furnished only with washbasins, a wooden cross and a bed.

'Can you feed us?' Marc-Antonio asked in his most pitiful voice.

She rolled her eyes. 'Do I look like a cook?' she asked.

However, she led us to a kitchen, and served us all noodles and some sausage and a rich red wine. So the answer was that, yes, she did look like a cook. By then, we were all three besotted. She was small, but held herself very straight, and she never crossed glances with any of us, but she delivered a little mockery, a jibe or a raised eyebrow, as if to keep us in our places. She rattled the pasta plates down, and refused any attempt by any of the three of us to help her.

Sir Antonio's eyes began to follow her everywhere she went.

Marc-Antonio glanced at the Milanese knight and then at me.

'We are going to treat this nun with the most perfect courtesy,' I said.

Marc-Antonio nodded, very serious, as if he'd never flirted with a nun in all his life.

Messire Antonio fingered his scraggly beard. And nodded. 'She's handsome,' he said.

'She has been splendid,' Marc-Antonio said.

The two younger men stared at each other.

I finished my wine. 'Sister, are there prayers?'

She flushed, wiping her hands on a linen towel. 'I will say my prayers on my own, if you please, messire.' She nodded. 'I would recommend the same to you, I think.'

My companions went to their cells; I doubt that they prayed. I eventually found the chapel by wandering around. We were in a magnificent building. It had literally hundreds of cells. And it was one of four such, all built around a single courtyard with a fountain, and around the outside were ancient pine trees, so large and so old that Caesar might have leaned against one.

There were two very old monks in the chapel, and half a dozen ancient nuns, and my hostess. I didn't have my book of hours, so I prayed my rosary while they read psalms. None of them so much as glanced at me.

I felt a little like a knight in an Arthurian romance – mayhap Giron Le Courtois or Lancelot du Lac, my favourites. That is, the ancient anchoress and the pretty nun and the beautiful chapel were all there; if there had come a sweet fragrance and then the Grail, I might not have been so very surprised. And, indeed, the fragrance was not lacking. The pines outside had a remarkable and beautiful smell, and the chapel had the literal odour of sanctity: frankincense, myrrh, and other scents besides.

At any rate, they ended their worship, and I rose. I was in the back, kneeling on the floor. The older people passed me, and I could see one of the nuns was shaken; her hands trembled, and not from age.

She was afraid. Of me.

I bit my lips in vexation. I stopped the young nun and she flinched a little as I stood.

'We will harm no one here,' I said.

She looked at me. 'Good,' she said, with her usual asperity. But I knew that she felt she was protecting them. From us.

Listen, you men. You think it brave to face your foes in armour. I agree – I know your worth. So think of a nun, armoured only in a desirable body, who shields her old people with her courage, no weapon, and nothing but her wits? We might have been routiers.

Who is brave now? Who is loyal?

The next day, I rode to the Pope. I found Fiore first, and then the count and Sir Richard, and so, instead of being a poor captain who abandoned his lord, I was enabled to be a fine captain who found his lord lodging in an impossible situation. The Pope stopped at the Farnese castle on the hill above the monastery, and ambassadors and great lords fought for a pile of straw on the stone floor, and all of my lances, archers and pages included, slept on clean sheets at the Casa des Pins, as I found the locals to call our monastery.

I saw them all situated, and the count was attentive and genuinely thankful, a rare show for him. Then I took Fiore, because I was tired of being alone, and went to see the Pope with Messire Antonio by my side. We weren't waiting long; as soon as the Pope heard that I was there, I was sent for.

The Holy Father was in a small room, panelled in heavy, dark wood. He had one attendant, the blond boy I had seen a week before, and he was still wearing boots and spurs.

'Messire Guglielmo,' he said with satisfaction. 'A week? Less? You must be the fastest horseman in Italy.'

'Not so very fast, Holy Father,' I said, or something similar, and then I knelt and told him my tale. I'd had a hundred miles of Roman roads to decide what to tell; I told no lies. And I included my own distaste at the forest of dead men. I didn't leave that out, although I didn't mention that Albornoz and I had a passage of arms, if you want to call a drubbing by such a high name.

He sat back and steepled his fingers. 'My son, do you know why we waited so long at Viterbo?' he asked.

I shook my head.

He nodded. 'Cardinal Albornoz was my strongest ally here. We sent him to restore order in the See, and he gave his life to that cause. He was in the saddle for twenty years, and although he was not a knight, he defeated most of the best captains you've ever heard of; he took Fra Moriale, he liberated Rome . . .' The Pope glanced at me.

I was still kneeling.

'We waited for him,' the Pope said. 'Our entry into Rome was his triumph, the fruit of his labours, and he is our John the Baptist.'

I nodded.

'He died the day you left. We assumed his nephew had won. We had the numbers, and Malatesta, for all that he hates us, is a fine captain.' He looked at Antonio. 'This is the Visconti captain?'

'Holy Father, this is Messire Antonio Visconti,' I said. 'Sir Ambrogio's brother.'

'And he is our prisoner?' the Pope asked me.

'Holy Father, he happens to be my prisoner. Also my friend.' Actually, this was stretching matters; I wasn't sure if I even liked Antonio. But I had an end in view and I was learning to play the game of Italy.

'You want us to send him to his father as a peace offering?' the Pope asked, with some humour.

'Yes, Holy Father.' I suppose I should not have been shocked to be seen through so readily.

He nodded. 'We will think on it.'

He dismissed me after some praise, which I will not repeat. He did say, 'Knowledge that Albornoz is victorious makes tomorrow all the sweeter.'

And as soon as we were clear of that room, Antonio launched into a torrent of abuse against the Pope and his intentions for Italy.

Fiore shook his head. 'He could have had you taken or killed.'

'He wouldn't dare. My father would have him killed,' Antonio said.

Fiore looked at Antonio with his mild, pale eyes. 'I doubt it,' he said. 'Why do you say such things?'

'I wonder myself,' I said.

The next day, we all rode into Rome. The count was given a place of honour very near the Pope, and Antonio was led before His Holiness like a captive – they had included him, and he was forced to wear a little sign with his name and rank.

It was, I am told, a Roman triumph in the ancient style, mostly designed by Maestro Petrarca. Nor was I the only Englishman; there were English clerics, perhaps half a dozen. I found them by the sound of their voices, which sounded like home.

My twenty lances had spent the night at the monastery making and mending, and the monks and nuns, having returned from Viterbo, had pitched in with a will, the more so when the count produced hard coin to pay for our lodging, so we entered Rome at the count's back with our steel mirror-bright and our clothes brushed. I wore all my best, my enamelled belt and a jewel in my hat. I led my little company, but several times I was summoned to ride by the count, resplendent in emerald silk, with the Pope's golden rose carried before him on a silk cushion carried by two pages, with his lance and his great helm carried on their saddle-bows. He bowed, and waved, and from time to time threw handfuls of copper coins with some silver mixed in for the crowd.

All in all, it was a staggering piece of theatre. There were jousts and a little fighting at barriers, but the count forbade me to participate on the basis that I was required to serve him, which suited me.

In fact, Fiore and Musard and I had an anxious day. Rome is a giant, sprawling ruin of a city; there's always plague there, and the place is filthy, especially in comparison to Venice or Florence. But the old bones are beautiful, and the oddest thing is that the city has space for many times the population she has now. It was worse fifteen years ago, I promise you. Almost as bad as Constantinople. So we would ride for a while on an empty road, well paved by the ancients, between old houses of sagging stone, their stucco coming away or fallen in little piles of ugly white plaster or gone entirely. And then we would turn a corner, or come down a big hill, and enter what were really like little towns, or parishes, within the ancient walls, and suddenly there would be thousands of people, screaming for the Pope or waiting in respectful silence.

And all day, we had to watch the count. He reared his horse, he scattered coins, and we watched for the dagger or the crossbow. Half of Rome is covered in huge old buildings, and I hurt my neck watching balconies and loggias above us.

I might have saved my neck muscles. Or at least taken off my new helmet, now once again well polished. Try craning your neck all day in an armet.

No one attacked us. We overreacted a dozen times; the one I

remember best was the count scattering a particular handful of coins. There happened to be more silver than bronze in the toss, and he did not throw the coins far, and two dozen dirty small boys ran in under the horses. Behind them were two or three big apprentices. Just for a moment they appeared to be armed, and Musard struck one to the ground and I had my arming sword out and pointed at another before we realised they had painted silver wands for one of the demonstrations.

We apologised and rode on.

By the end of the day, I was as hungry as a hunter and as tired as if I had jousted *and* fought on foot, but it was a magnificent event, and I must say that old Petrarca did the Pope proud. He and Boccaccio also acted as ambassadors – Petrarca for Venice and Boccaccio for Florence – and they were treated better than most of the worldly princes by the Holy Father.

I chose to wait on the count at the magnificent dinner after the triumph; that is, Richard Musard and Fiore and I served him as noble pages, so that we could watch over him and his food. This proved far more pleasant than I had expected. The air of festivity extended to the servants, and Richard and I both knew how to serve. We passed dishes, and I think I can say with pride that I saved the Pope's roasted and gilded pheasant from a disastrous fall and even saw it to his high table while still warm. They served sixteen dishes; until then, I had never seen such a magnificent dinner.

All of that is beside the point – except for comparison to what is coming – but they served the dinner in the square of Saint Peter and they had both outdoor and indoor kitchens. The whole dinner was more than a little chaotic, and some of the pages and servants either did no work or simply never found out where to go to fetch a dish. It rained for a little while, and one of the cooks couldn't get her fire started. I went over with the tinder kit from my purse and she gave me a look that effortlessly conveyed that no man in fine clothes could possibly be of any use to her, so it gave me infinite satisfaction to start her fire. She wasn't supposed to be in charge of the kitchen, I'll wager – there were male cooks in fine clothes pontificating for that – but the woman seemed to be the only one who knew where the *verjus* was.

But my point is that the count sat with Masters Boccaccio and Petrarca on either side of him. Both of them had servants, but their lads were lost, or drunk, and Richard and I ended up serving these noble authors alongside our own count. They were both extremely courteous and thankful, and they composed a little rhyming epigram about the nobility of the table service, which I'll trot out if I ever need work in a kitchen again. Now Petrarca I knew rather well; he'd come and read to me more than once, and I had read a few of his pieces with Emile, although I confess that Emile and I preferred Boccaccio's *The Decameron*.

I had never met the Florentine poet, but Petrarca was quick to introduce us all, including Fiore, whom he remembered.

It proved impossible to watch all the food; on the other hand, Musard and I came to the conclusion that no assassin could predict who might get what dish. We did our best, and we helped serve the Pope as well, and I saw to it that both Antonio Visconti and the Greek monks, who made the triumphal entry as captives and were probably not intended to dine, were fed. The Greeks, at least, thought better of the Pope on full bellies, although Antonio still burned as hot as before.

It was at that dinner that I heard again from Boccaccio that Florimont de Lesparre had challenged Peter of Cyprus, an anointed king, to a fight, on foot, with swords. And stranger still that Peter had accepted, and that they were coming to Rome. I heard this from Boccaccio, who, hearing that I had served the King of Cyprus and was one of his barons from Petrarca – who, while a delightful old man, had a tendency to name-drop and exaggerate the importance of all of his acquaintances, myself included – put his hand on my arm and asked me *why* the King of Cyprus would agree to fight de Lesparre.

'He's an arrogant fool,' I said. 'De Lesparre, not King Peter.'

Boccaccio flicked his eyebrows in a knowing way. 'In Florence, I suppose we'd just make the man disappear.'

'That might be commendable,' I said.

'You are not a partisan of this de Lesparre?' Boccaccio asked.

I glanced at the count. I was standing with a towel on my arm, and he was seated, lounging in a camp chair we'd provided, because the Pope's stools were so bad. I smiled at him, more informal than I usually was, but, despite the presence of the Holy Father, it had become a loud and informal evening.

He smiled back. 'I am a little surprised that Messer de Lesparre survived to adulthood,' he said.

Boccaccio laughed aloud. 'That bad?'

'Even for a Gascon ...' the count said.

I poured them both wine and went for the next course.

It was a magnificent dinner, and it was followed by a week of festivities. Everyone in Italy was in Rome, or so it seemed, and we stayed at the Casa des Pins, safe and well fed, riding back and forth to ceremonies. The crowds of people included several of the leading bankers of Italy, and I found a representative of the Bardi, my preferred house, and was able to draw on my own funds without beggaring Emile.

The man laughed. 'You make game of me, eh?' he asked. 'I have here a note on your account that Master Davide of Venice has paid you six hundred gold florins for saffron. Your account is very much to the good.'

I laughed. I had *forgotten* the saffron. Not Master Davide, however, and God's blessing on him. I handed a shocked Marc-Antonio one hundred golden florins for his own.

'Not a courtesan,' I begged him. 'Buy armour, or a sword.'

He laughed.

The count was also able to negotiate a bill, too, so the abbot of our monastery was satisfied with our coins and our care. I put down some hard coin for my archers and pages. I paid them for one month, which almost beggared me, and almost all of them, many fresh from Jerusalem, made the round of the churches. Indeed, we all went to Santa Maria Maggiore together and then ate in a Roman tavern.

The count had another ceremonial interview with the Pope. This time, the whole of his escort accompanied him into the old Lateran, and we bent our knees to the Holy Father and he blessed us one by one, and blessed our company banner.

Afterwards, out on the great Borgo Santo Spirito, Pierre Lapot shook his head. He was walking with Beppo and l'Angars.

'I'm an old sinner,' he said. Missing teeth made him look as sinister as he was, and gave him a dark lisp. 'And now I've been to the Holy Sepulchre and I've been blessed by the Pope as well.'

L'Angars grinned. 'That'll save you a thousand years in Hell, brother,' he said. 'Only ten thousand to go.'

Beppo laughed. 'The men I killed are still dead.' Everyone laughed.

He looked around with a comic turn of his ugly head. 'I mean. *If* I ever killed anyone. Hypothetically speaking.'

But no one laughed at our little banner, with the Virgin in satin, and the nuns at San Paolo added a little to the embroidery when they heard that the Pope had blessed it, so that the Virgin's face took on a look of real kindness that might encourage a poor sinner. We still carry it, although I confess we've repaired her so many times that she looks more like one of the flightier Greek goddesses and less like the patient mother of God, but the Corner girls made her in Chioggia and the good sisters of San Paolo made her beautiful. It took the Pope's armies to put slashes in her, but that story is yet to come.

After a hectic week, the count made his preparations to leave. We left our Greek monks with the Pope, though no promise that they would get a hearing could be extracted. The count paid to get a good horse and arms for Messer Antonio, and he rode north with us. We also had Maestro Boccaccio, as he was going to Florence and had no escort. We had a vague feeling of having failed: the churches remained divided. I almost spoke to the count about it, but the routine duties of commanding the escort kept me away from him. I could see he was sad – mayhap even angry. I asked Richard.

Richard shook his head. 'He worked for three years for the union,' he said. He shrugged.

Let me just add that Richard and I were almost there. We were easy with each other; some mornings we slashed at bucklers together. And as you've no doubt noticed, at some point I'd developed a regard for the count, too.

We took a different line back through the hills than the Papal procession had taken coming to Rome as we headed south. If you have ever travelled with an army or a great lord, you'll know that one night of hosting someone like the Pope and a fine town has no meat and no wine left in it – maybe no grain, either. We took a line to the east to get food and forage, and then went west to the post station at Sutri, and then we went north and east to Viterbo. We hadn't lost a man to the fevers in Rome, and when a man fell sick, we had Maestro Albin, who was as fine a leech as Italy had to offer; just his presence gave our people heart. Our little company was clean and neat, and well-trained in a way that many routiers never achieve; trained at the simple things, like moving and camping, keeping clean, cooking, staying dry, tending to kit and to horseflesh. We'd been together a while; we had no slackers.

We were cautious, though. I wished that I had Sir Giannis and his lighter cavalry, but we made do, as we had fine horses and plenty of them. Archers and pages became our *stradiotes* and they went far ahead of us. Ewan the Scot had a special talent for that kind of mission, and he would sometimes go as far as our next lodging, a day ahead. He said it was just like roving the Borders, which made some of my Northern Englishmen frown. We had a big archer we'd picked up in Greece, Michael Burn. He towered over other men, and he had a wit, but he was from Cumbria, like Hughes, and he never let Ewan forget it. Burn was a good man on a scout, too, but we didn't send them out together.

We didn't have so much as a sniff of an enemy. The weather grew colder, although the rains were not bad. I remember it as a golden week to Orvieto, but I see here that I have written 'rain' three times.

Orvieto is another of the finest towns you'll ever see; Italy abounds in them. Orvieto has a magnificent cathedral, more like a jewel than a building, all red and blue tile on the outside, and inside is the finest statue of the Blessed Virgin I had ever seen. She was so magnificent, under her canopy, that my breath was taken away, and I had to return the next day, take Mass again, and then pray there, so moving did I find her. There is also a Saint George in antique Roman armour, and I purchased a drawing of him for my walls, and to show Maestro Petrarca, if ever I met him again. The dragon at his feet didn't look like much of a threat, to be truthful – rather like a man slaying an otter.

From Orvieto we made our way through the hills to Tuscany, where we were met by a company of Florentine cavalry sent out by the Council of Eight expressly, they told us, to see to Boccaccio's needs, but more, I think, to keep watch over the count and my little band. The Florentines were being cautious: if the whole of Italy had been a tinderbox before the Pope's triumphal entry, it was now a laid fire, the wood shavings and the little scraps of bark ready for a great blaze. There was a rumour that the Emperor – the Holy Roman Emperor, Charles IV himself – was coming with ten thousand lances to support the Pope against Milan.

Our second night in Tuscany we spent in the hilly country south of the city, at a tiny hamlet called La Pietrella. The Florentine gentlemen had prepared barns for us, and the count was to stay in the manor house.

I had taken note of the number of military horses picketed just outside the town – perhaps fifty. We had double their numbers, and the Tuscans more again, so I had no fears of trouble. Indeed, I heard from the corporal of the Florentines that the horses belonged to the famous *condottiere*, Giovanni Acudo.

I grinned.

There was no inn. There was, however, a wine shop. As we had had a sunny day, and had arrived mid-afternoon, Fiore and I elected to have a cup of the excellent local wine after prayers and see if the great Acudo was really on offer.

I was expecting to see Hawkwood there, and there he was, slim, well dressed, and not at all resembling a man who'd recently been defeated in a pitched battle.

He shot to his feet as we entered, and we embraced.

'Will Gold,' he said, with his hands on my shoulders, 'I always forget how big you are, and how red your hair is. Sit and drink with me.'

I introduced Fiore. Hawkwood wouldn't take no for an answer, and Fiore found himself crushed in an embrace.

'How could I forget him?' Hawkwood said. 'The best blade, and the first to tell you of it.'

Fiore had the grace to look rueful.

Hawkwood introduced us to his cousin, Anthony, and most of the rest of the gentlemen I knew. I sent Marc-Antonio to find my erstwhile captive, Antonio Visconti, who arrived a short while later.

That night, many stories were told, and before our third cup of Tuscan wine, Richard came, and l'Angars and half our people. We told of the Holy Land and the fighting in Outremer, and Hawkwood nodded, clearly pleased.

We were all in our cups when the watch changed. I had set a watch, and so had Sir John; Pierre Lapot went out with Ewan and Gospel Mark, and before the bells tolled again, Sam Bibbo was sitting by me, none the worse for wear, if a little greyer atop his head.

Finally we left off telling our stories, and asked Sir John and his people for theirs.

Hawkwood pointed at Messer Antonio. 'If you've come with this scapegrace,' he said, 'you know what befell us.'

He settled back, took a sip of wine, and looked around. 'Ah, well, mayhap you do not know all of it. Bernabò sent Ambrogio south – not in the name of Milan, but as a "Free Company", a sort of kick at the Pope. We didn't expect to find Albornoz and the whole army of the Papal See waiting for us at Urbino. I told Ambrogio to retreat; he would have none of it. I told him to hire more lances, too. He said the Lords of Milan needed to make war on the cheap this autumn, as they were spending all their gold on a wedding.' He looked at me. 'I'm glad you took my hint not to come, lad, but he'd have turned you away. I never saw a man so bent on his own destruction. We went south, burning the country, but Malatesta knew the country better than we did.'

He smiled his fox's smile. 'Every day we were a little more hemmed in. We fought Malatesta, and honours were even. I confess I thought we'd escaped. I had no idea that Albornoz had another army, or the means to pay them.'

'He didn't,' I said.

Hawkwood smiled, as if that proved some point of his. 'If he wants them to fight next year, he'd better pay them,' he said. 'Any road, we retreated, and found the road cut behind us. Ambrogio gave a brave speech about victory or death, and I bought two guides and paid them to get us out through the hills.'

'You left us to die,' Antonio said.

'Yes,' Hawkwood said pleasantly. 'Strictly business, Messer Antonio. I wasn't being paid. I had chosen to ride along with my good companion, Messer Ambrogio, on an *empris*. And desperate last stands are fine for personal quarrels, but they do not pay the bills.'

'How many did you lose?' I asked.

'Six men-at-arms and two archers,' he said. 'Belmont returned wounded but singing your praises. Renfrew returned unwounded and claiming you betrayed him to Albornoz.'

'I don't see him here,' I said. 'And if I *had* betrayed him, he'd be dead.'

'Exactly.' Sir John looked around. 'I'm guessing he's afraid of you. He's said some very uncomplimentary things.'

Just for a moment, I was reminded of what it was like in a mercenary company. I had become so used to the Order – to Sabraham and men like him – or the Venetians, or even the Green Count's professionals. I had forgotten what it was like when the dogs bit each other – the petty animosities, the stupid accusations.

Like Italy. Or Turkey.

'He attacked me,' I said.

Sir John poured me more wine.

'Albornoz massacred all the men-at-arms who surrendered,' I said.

Belmont nodded. 'I told him.'

Hawkwood shrugged. 'It's a dirty business,' he said.

'That's all?' I asked.

He looked at me. 'Ambrogio made a point of telling the Malatesta heralds that we were a Free Company. Brigands and routiers.' He looked around. Bibbo was nodding.

'This is how the Milanese pretend they are not making war on the Pope. But that made us bandits, not knights, and Albornoz, the old one, the famous one, had said that any time he took a routier he would hang the man.'

Perhaps it was thinking about brigandage, and being a routier, but I suddenly realised that Richard was missing. He had been there, listening . . .

'Where's Janet?' I asked.

Hawkwood leaned over. 'That woman is as mad as . . . one of those old women who live on the outskirts of villages. Dresses like a man. Wears armour. Won't go home.' He raised his hand. 'I know, we *are* her home. And she's a good *gens d'armes.* But I told her to keep the books and stay out of sight. She's probably in her tent.'

I looked at Belmont, who had once been her lover, or so I understood.

He wouldn't meet my eye.

'I'll just go see if Musard is doing well,' I said, and I rose.

Bibbo slipped out with me. 'It's not so bad as it looks,' he said. 'Sir John left most of the lads north of Bologna. He said that following Ambrogio would be a shitshow, and no mistake there.'

'I never doubted Sir John,' I said. 'I was more worried that he'd doubt me.'

'Ye're a little more like a great lord than I expected,' Bibbo said. 'It suits ye, tho'.'

Now that I was out of the little wine shop, it was almost pitch-black; little towns have no lights and no watch.

I didn't need a light. I could hear Richard shouting.

It made my stomach flip just listening to the anger and the pain in his voice, but I ran there, with Bibbo at my heels, and we found them shouting like a fishmonger and a fishwife at a watchfire.

I hadn't seen Janet in three years.

It wasn't so much that she was beautiful. She'd always had simple good looks – a straight back, broad shoulders, a good figure. Perhaps it was just that I'd never seen her dressed as a woman. There she stood, dressed like a lady going to church: a long blue kirtle and a matching overgown, dark, heavy silk. Her blonde hair seemed to burn in the firelight, and her face was red with anger.

'We were never married!' she shouted.

'You loved me!' Richard shouted.

'You never even knew who I was!' she shrieked. 'You wanted a great lady, to make you greater. You wanted *what* I was. You didn't want *who* I was.'

'You are my wife,' Richard said.

There are few tasks more thankless than stepping in between two friends having a fight – more so if they are lovers.

'I am not,' Janet said. 'And I never will be.'

I was fairly certain that Richard had another wife in Savoy, and absolutely certain that he had other consolations.

Bibbo grabbed my sleeve. 'They ain't using their fists,' he said. 'Leave 'em be.'

That seemed wise. Bibbo was always wise, and I realised how much I'd missed the man.

Janet looked at me across the fire. Her anger vanished; she was always mercurial.

'Will Gold,' she said. She made a delicate curtsy, and I returned as good a bow as I would have made for the count. She smiled. 'Aren't you a proper lord,' she said in French.

'Damn you,' Richard said to me.

'Me?' I asked.

'Don't interfere,' he snapped.

'Richard, she is my friend too ...'

He turned on his heel and walked off into the darkness.

I was my brother's keeper, and in some way, he *was* my brother. I followed him into the darkness. I found him leaning against a tree, and what we said is nobody's business.

But we … were friends. Not just allies.

That was good.

In the morning, there were many hard heads, and the Count of Savoy was more than a little surprised to find that he was riding north with one of the very routiers he most despised. The two men looked at each other like two terriers over a bone, but in the end neither of them bit, and they were, if not cordial, at least courteous. Hawkwood only came with us as far as Florence.

He rode up to me at the crossroads. 'Well, *Sir William*,' he said. He grinned. 'Listen, lad: in the spring I expect we'll have real war. Good hot, juicy war, with a lot of hard fighting and good pay. You seem well suited here – how long is the contract?'

'Christmas,' I said.

'Well, then, if you want employment in the spring, I'll be raising five hundred lances,' he said.

'Free Company?' I asked.

'Milan,' he said. 'Good money, William.'

'Milan?' I asked. 'Against the Pope?'

'Everyone will be against the Pope, in the spring,' Hawkwood said. 'You'll see.'

We went north from Florence without Hawkwood, but my lances had been paid there, as the count was suddenly in funds. The first day north of Florence, I rode by the count for the first time that trip, and he hawked from time to time and shared his wine with me from a glass flask prettier than anything I owned. Later, we watched Stefanos and Demetrios throwing quoits. Both of them could throw anything with accuracy – a shell, a stone, a dart. I called out my praise in Greek.

'You speak Greek,' he said.

'A little, my lord.' It was tempting to point out that he'd known that for two months, but I could tell he was trying to get to something. The great cannot always, or easily, bridge the gap to the rest of us.

He nodded. 'What do you think of our monks?' he asked.

Again, it was very tempting to ask him why he hadn't asked me that back in Venice. I probably didn't shrug; the count was not the sort of man with whom a shrug was good communication. But I met his eye. 'Arrogant. And far, far too sure of themselves.'

He nodded. 'I suppose I saw them as monks …' he said.

I couldn't think of anything witty to say. So we chatted about his little sparrowhawk, and about the weather, and he smiled.

'Your *compagnia* has been a revelation to me, as if one of the saints appeared at my side and whispered to me.' He looked back over our column, with his two banners prominently displayed and our own small Virgin back in the centre, carried that day by l'Angars.

'I hope that we gave satisfactory service,' I said.

He nodded. 'Better than satisfactory, Messer Guillaume.' He glanced at me, and just for a moment his eyes kindled with what appeared to be delight. 'You are not wearing your surcoat,' he noted.

I had taken it off at Florence. I can't tell you exactly why. I suppose that I felt that our mission was over. No one had ever challenged my wearing it, but I had taken the monks and the count to Rome, seen the Pope in his eternal city, and now I felt … secular. Perhaps it was meeting John Hawkwood; perhaps it was seeing Sam Bibbo.

Perhaps I was done with the Pope.

Bibbo had come with us, and Messer Antonio Visconti had gone with Hawkwood – we called it a trade.

'I am getting the worst of this deal,' Hawkwood said. 'Take care of Bibbo. He's one of my best.'

'It's only until spring,' I said.

We'd pulled off our gauntlets and clasped hands. 'In the spring,' I said.

Any road, I wasn't wearing any surcoat – just my sword belt over my polished breastplate. I didn't feel naked. If anything, I felt free.

'I wore it to serve you,' I said, with more than a grain of truth. 'Now it would be no service. And, my lord, if I may be blunt, I am happy to be done with the Pope.' That was as far as I was willing to go.

He nodded.

It took us a week to ride to Pavia. The count was in no hurry to get there, I could tell, and he made diversions, but for the most part we were on the Via Francigena, and the count stopped and prayed at many shrines, and distributed alms. I gathered from titbits, and from Musard, who was glum and silent since he'd seen Janet, that the Pope had refused to accept or pay any share of the count's expenses, even though he'd promised to do so at Avignon two years before. I knew that the count had paid Nerio almost thirty thousand ducats in the spring, and even a man as rich as the Green Count of Savoy had to be challenged to find such sums on a regular basis.

But I was allowed further into the count's thoughts and, as we rode, I came to understand, even through his carefully guarded conversation, that he, too, was done with the Pope: we were going to Pavia to negotiate his part in the coming conflict. In alliance with Milan.

We were almost at the magnificent gates of that city. I had taken to riding with the count; it would be me and Richard, Fiore and Mayot, most days. We'd ride ahead to a shrine, or watch the count hawk. One day we raced our horses like boys – Juniper won easily. I was quite conscious that we'd replaced his usual circle, but Fiore was undemanding and Mayot was usually quiet and sometimes actually morose, so Richard and I bore the brunt of conversation.

Perhaps I spend too much time trying to explain the count; but most people have never lived with a great noble, and they do not understand how complicated such men and women can be.

He turned to me, apropos of nothing.

'I will be in Pavia a week,' he said. 'I wish to assure you that I can pay your company.'

Odd. Out of character. But I'd already seen that he was deeply unhappy and that he dreaded Pavia.

I smiled. 'We are here for you,' I said, or something like that.

'This is not a friendly city,' he said carefully, looking at Musard, who winced.

'Count Galeazzo and I have been allies and enemies,' the count said, 'and I do not know where he stands on the matter of the Prince of Achaea. But let me say that, careful as you have been of my person, now we need more care and perhaps actual protection. If there's a perfect place for a murder, it is Milan or Pavia. If the Visconti want me dead, it will be difficult for me to stay alive.'

I reined in, forcing him to do the same. 'My lord, if it is so dangerous, then do not go.'

He smiled ruefully. 'Any brave knight knows he must go where he durst,' Savoy said. He shook his head, looking at the towers of Pavia. 'I am conscious that all of you watch over me. Help me get through Pavia alive, and we will, I promise you, be avenged for all this inconvenience and fear. Yes, gentlemen, I say fear.'

He was moved, I could tell. And yet, he was not wrong. I had some loyalty to him by then. He was no longer merely the *patron*, the employer. He had become 'my lord' as Francesco Gatelussi had. It is one thing to serve, for money or habit. It is another to serve from genuine love, and regard.

We entered Pavia by the great southern gates, and we were escorted through the pretty streets to the old palace, which was more like a fortress than was quite right. But they had plenty of stables and barracks space, and as we were visiting officially, and for a week, I needed to put our horses out for good, cheap fodder. I lost most of a day seeing our horses cared for and put out to pasture – no need to spend sunny days in a stinking stall.

And November had sun. The warm Lombard sun poured down, disdaining the coming winter and giving us balmy air and loving breezes.

A few evenings later, young Francesco told me most of the court news over dinner, with Richard and Fiore interrupting.

'It was a lesson in diplomacy,' Gatelussi said. 'I saw it happen, and I wish I might have recorded it. My father would have been impressed.' He took a drink.

Musard frowned. 'My lord is pursuing his own sovereign policy . . .'

'He's changing sides,' Gatelussi said quietly. 'They're all lining up all over Europe for the big fight, and Savoy has just left the Pope and come over to the Visconti.'

'Who have, themselves, just left the French for the English,' Fiore said.

'That's too simple,' Musard said. 'My lord is following his own policies for the good of Savoy. Savoy needs good neighbours . . .'

'Gentlemen,' I said, 'might I understand what has happened?'

Gatelussi looked around and spread his hands, and Fiore nodded, indicating that the younger man could hold forth.

'The first day, Galeazzo Visconti met with us and made a great show of offering to "mediate the dispute" between the count and his cousin, the Prince of Achaea. The message was, "Watch yourself, or I will back Achaea and you will have a war on your hands."'

'Jesu!' I said.

'Exactly,' Francesco said, sounding more than a little like Nerio. 'But let me say that our count was clearly expecting such . . .'

Musard leaned back. 'He was.'

'Just so,' Francesco said. 'And he suggested, fairly graciously, that he didn't need "mediation" in a discussion internal to the House of Savoy between a lord and his vassal. Anyway – and here I put words in the count's mouth – with the Pope and the Holy Roman Emperor descending on Milan in the spring, the count didn't imagine that the Visconti needed another outlet for their glorious knighthood. Or rather, that between the wedding with Prince Lionel of England and the armies already in the field, Milan lacked the money to fight Savoy.'

'You're like a diplomatic jester or jongleur,' Musard said. 'I wouldn't have put it that way, but the summation was accurate, if impertinent.'

'Impertinent should have been my middle name,' Francesco said. 'The second day opened with the count telling tales of his adventures in the east. My father, and Messer Musard, and even Messer d'Oro here, were singled out for praise, and the count dwelt at length on the Union of Churches.'

'Oh,' I said, or something equally witty.

'Exactly. As the Visconti have many investments in Greece and are neither Genoese nor Venetian, they would be happy to see the Churches unified. In fact, the Visconti might be happier if the Western Church joined the Eastern and the titular head of the world Church sat in Constantinople and not in Rome.'

I could see it. The Visconti and their allies had a fair number of cardinals and power in the Church. The first Visconti to take power in Milan had been an archbishop, or so I'd been told. 'The Visconti would support Union.'

'Exactly. And the Visconti, despite Violante's dowry, Bernabò's mistresses, and the war over Bologna, have more money than anyone else. Galeazzo even offered to help defray some of the expenses of the Green Count's crusade.'

'He paid for Antonio and all his lances to go with the count,' Musard said. 'But then, Antonio is Bernabò's bastard.'

Gatelussi nodded. 'I believe that he offered the count fifteen thousand florins.'

Musard looked away, Mayot pulled on his beard, and Fiore laughed aloud.

'That's it, then,' Fiore said. 'So I assume that Galeazzo offered the count a free hand with the Prince of Achaea …'

Richard growled.

Francesco smiled. 'My pater would have been impressed, Messer Musard. He did no such thing. Instead, he simply allowed himself to boil over in his indignation at the young Prince of Achaea's impertinence and incautious behaviour, and the count was allowed to see the diplomatic letter being sent by the Count of Pavia and the archbishop, declining to be involved in a purely internal Savoyard matter.'

'Masterful,' I said.

We all ate our *cervit* of hare and noodles and drank wine and thought of what was to come.

In the morning, I was the count's attendant. We went into the audience hall, which was larger than the Pope's and hung in tapestries of real magnificence, every one of which depicted scenes from *Lancelot du Lac*. The Count of Pavia's court were dressed elaborately, in tight cotes, buttoned from neck to crotch or lower, with great hanging sleeves and tall collars that made them look like tulips. It was not the Venetian style, and it used a lot of fabric, most of which was silk brocade of the most expensive kind. Galeazzo had his in cloth of gold, with vipers embroidered all over it. He was the most richly dressed man I'd ever seen, and I thought of the Pope in his old English gown and his riding boots and tried not to make a face. Even Galeazzo's *poulaines* appeared to be gold. The toes, which were long, were stiffened to rise slightly, which, to me, made him look a little antic, or even ridiculous, but he was not in any way a silly man, for all his love of the dramatic.

We bowed; the Count of Savoy bowed as to an equal, and then we were seated with effusions of praise and congratulation. Count Amadeus introduced me, and the Count of Pavia asked flattering questions, made me draw my sword, and then, when he'd toyed with me, dismissed me with a look, as if to say that soldiers were easy enough to buy.

'You must run a few courses with my son,' he said. 'Gian Galeazzo is at the age where any man might want to be a knight, or a soldier, eh?' His comment implied that, on mature thought, most men found better things to do, like running city states. He beckoned, and we all stood silent, even Count Amadeus, while a messenger was sent for Gian Galeazzo.

Instead, a train of noble ladies appeared. They were led by a woman of such excellent carriage that I knew she must be the countess. Her facial resemblance to Count Amadeus, and their instant regard for each other, showed me that this was indeed Galeazzo's wife, Bianca. She appeared to me to be no more than twenty-five or so – Emile's age, or close to it. She had blonde hair and clear blue eyes and a very serious face. She had the reputation of being a pious lady. At that first meeting, I could only mark her down as an extremely well-dressed woman, in a rose and gold silk kirtle with a matching pink silk overgown trimmed in fur and a high headdress in a style I had never seen before. We had another round of introductions. Because I was standing with a sword in my hand, I drew the countess's eye and she asked after me, and her brother bade me put my sword away and I gave her my best bow.

'Messer d'Oro might even be said to have saved my life,' he said, the first I'd heard so much praise from him. 'I reckon that he's kept me alive and in humour for two months.'

Lady Bianca had care written on her face, but for a moment the lines around her mouth were erased, and she smiled. 'Come, brother,' she said. 'So much praise must tire you.'

Count Amadeus laughed. To me, he said, 'She has always mocked me.'

'Someone has to,' Bianca said. But, quite spontaneously, I thought, she put a hand on my arm. 'Please protect my brother,' she said. She glanced at her husband. He smiled.

That was . . . chilling.

'I imagine a lord so bold and debonair might be difficult to guard,' Galeazzo said.

'He is a pleasure to serve, my lord,' I said. Really, if you think about it, there was no other possible answer. I could tell that Galeazzo was either enjoying a grim joke, or issuing a threat, or both – I didn't want to seem threatened, or even aware. I have often found this the best way to respond to a threat; the pretence that you never understood a threat to have been made can defeat the project entirely.

'Guard him nonetheless,' Bianca said clearly. 'I would be devastated if anything were to happen to him.' She looked at her husband, who smiled and inclined his head.

'And this is my daughter,' she said. Her ladies parted – they were all beautiful, as beautiful as any women I'd ever met, except perhaps the Emperor's court in Krakow – and in the midst of them was Lady Violante.

Sometime you gentlemen must tell me your first impressions of that lady. I saw her at thirteen – she was still far more girl than woman. But the beauty of face was already there, and the curious eyes. Too open, and too demanding, and too ... too much. I have seen those eyes on archers after the sack of a town, but never on a thirteen-year-old girl.

I bowed. She said something conventional.

Lady Bianca took my hand. 'But you must be the Countess d'Herblay's husband!' she said. Then her hand went to her neck – a gesture that betrayed unease. 'Of course, I am sorry. D'Herblay was her first husband, and he is dead.'

What could I do?

Count Amadeus said, quietly, 'I am well satisfied that Messer d'Oro had nothing to do with d'Herblay's death.' I had never loved him more than that moment. He didn't need to say it. But silence would have been damning and I happened to see the look on Galeazzo's face.

I knew in one flicker of his heavily lidded eyes that the viper had spoken to Turenne and perhaps to Florimont de Lesparre as well. I *knew*. And I knew that some part of this had been stage-managed, either to discomfit me or to humiliate the Count of Savoy.

'D'Herblay died at Alexandria,' I said.

'You were there?' Lady Bianca asked.

'I was,' I said. 'I was there with the Order of Saint John.'

That was not in their little play; and Lady Bianca had already warmed to me, so she put her arm through mine in an affectionate way. 'Emile grew up with me,' she said. 'At least, during the summers. We used to ride together. I hope you will take her a letter, and perhaps some silks.'

Everyone breathed out. Perhaps nothing had ever been intended, or perhaps Galeazzo, who was a great one for what he called 'testing', merely wanted to see what I was made of.

Young Gian Galeazzo came, at last. He wanted to see my sword.

'How many men have you killed?' he asked.

'Enough to go to Hell for it,' I said.

He turned quickly.

'If I am not careful,' I added.

He wasn't listening. He asked some questions about Alexandria, and frowned. He was a slight youth, but handsome enough, in a heavy-lipped, northern Italian way. His sister had certainly got the lion's share of the good looks, but he had his mother's upright carriage and his father's burning eyes. He was dressed well, but plain enough, in a good red wool doublet and silk hose.

'Once you held the city, could you not have killed all the Saracens there?' he asked.

It seemed to me a terrible question from a sixteen-year-old.

I shook my head. 'The sack was bad enough, my lord,' I said. 'And an army, no matter how large, cannot really massacre a city the size of Alexandria. And men – even soldiers – may hesitate to kill …'

Galeazzo snapped his fingers. 'I have not really asked the count here so that you could instruct my son in ethics,' he said.

'Not my uncle Bernabò's soldiers,' Gian Galeazzo said. He smiled. 'Or my father's, or mine. If we order it done, it is done. Perhaps *we* should have marched on Jerusalem, Pater.'

'Let us secure Bologna first, my son,' Galeazzo said. 'Then Jerusalem.'

'Can we come to an agreement, cousin?' he said, turning to Count Amadeus. 'I believe we have found that our roads lie together. And besides, it would so please my lady wife, were you to come with us to the wedding.'

'And other things,' Count Amadeus said.

Galeazzo glanced at me. I was the only man in the room who was not one of his family or retainers.

'Perhaps you would allow your man to take my son for a sword lesson,' he said.

'I do not need a sword lesson from a foreigner,' Gian Galeazzo said.

'Perhaps,' the Count of Pavia said carefully, 'you would go and have a sword lesson with this worthy knight. I would hate,' he said gently, 'to have to say this again.'

I knelt by Count Amadeus.

He nodded. 'Of course, I would be delighted to see your son so instructed,' he said. 'Messer, be so good as to take this young man and teach him a little of your prowess.'

'You are sure?' I asked. 'I could send for Fiore.'

He smiled. 'That might be a trifle severe for so young a man, don't you think?' he said. His eyes were calm.

I felt the tension, but I was willing to wager that the count did not feel under threat.

'Go, messer,' he said.

I rose. I bowed to Lady Bianca, and then turned to bow to Lady Violante.

It was a small thing, but it jarred me.

Gian Galeazzo had moved to his sister while I addressed the count. He had his hand on her neck – his fingers wrapped her white neck from behind. It was … wrong.

He didn't hurry to take them away. His eyes met mine.

'What will you teach me, I wonder?' he asked.

Violante hissed. Like the very viper. It was a surprising sound from a small woman.

'Hush, good sister,' Gian Galeazzo said. 'Come, English knight.'

We walked out together. He did not want to match swords, I could tell.

'What will you teach me?' he asked again.

I shrugged. 'Do you have a master-at-arms?' I asked.

'Three,' he said with some derision. 'One for jousting, one for riding, one for the sword.'

'You do not enjoy the exercise of arms?' I asked him. 'My lord?'

He smiled with apparent warmth. 'Why spread your own legs when you can hire a strumpet to do it all for you?' he asked sweetly.

I might have bridled, but I had met sixteen-year-old boys before. 'Perhaps,' I said. 'Although if you have a philosophy tutor, you know that reasoning by analogy has its dangers.'

'Oh,' he said. 'I had no idea you knew words like "philosophy" and "analogy".'

'I even know words like "tutor" and "strap",' I said.

'You wouldn't dare,' he said.

I shrugged. 'Not for a casual insult. But try me, my lord, and we'll see. And since you disdain the art of arms, I assume I can throw you to the ground and humiliate you pretty thoroughly and you can't do anything to defend yourself.'

'I'm not so bad,' he said.

'Let's find out. Where is your *salle d'armes*?' I asked, and in three minutes we were at the magnificent stables. There were three other young men following us, and they were clearly his friends. When we climbed the steps to the *salle*, they joined us.

I saw Demetrios in the stables, working on our horses, and I sent him for Francesco and Fiore, if they could be found. And then I asked my young lord to take up a sword.

'Let me show you by how much I am your master,' he said instead. He pointed to one of the young men. 'Attack him, Alonzo.'

Alonzo drew his sword and his dagger. He was perhaps a year older than the young lord, and he had seen some fighting. His sword and baselard were sharp. I had to assume he was some lordling's son.

He was more than a little hesitant in the way he held the sword.

I picked up a wooden waster off the rack. 'Don't be foolish,' I said in my *capitano* voice. 'Sheath your sword.'

'Kill him,' the count's son said. 'I'll make it good.'

The young man stepped into my range, and I broke his sword with one blow.

Hard wood isn't like steel.

He looked at his broken sword for a moment, and in that moment my point went past his shoulder, my 'blade' went across his shoulders, and I threw him, hard, into the wall. He bounced.

The same throw I used on Albornoz. It's a good throw.

I picked up his baselard and jammed it between the floorboards, which had finger-width gaps because it was, after all, a stable. Then I used the heel of my boot to kick the hilt until it broke. It was a pretty weapon – a match for the sword.

'That was foolish,' I said.

I expected the count's son to go to pieces, or perhaps to order his other friends to attack me, but instead, he nodded.

'My, my,' he said. 'I am impressed.' He sketched a little bow.

'I'll fucking kill him,' the young man on the floor said.

'No, you won't, and if you go for him again he'll probably kill you,' the young lord said. He nodded to me. 'I have never seen that done. Teach me that.'

So I did. It is one of Fiore's standard motions, taken to its logical extreme, at least the way Fiore taught it to me; the throw is just a turn of the hips.

The change in the young man was so drastic that it was as if I was dealing with another young lord entirely – an attentive, polite young man. And the one I'd tossed into the wall muttered a lot, pouted, and went down the steps just in time for Fiore and Gatelussi to come up them.

Is there anything more embarrassing than trying to teach a complicated pattern in front of the man who taught you?

'And this is?' Gian Galeazzo asked.

'My sword teacher,' I said. 'Messer Fiore dei Liberi. A knight of Udine.'

Gian Galeazzo nodded. 'And this other man?'

'You have heard of the Prince of Lesvos?' I asked.

'My grandmother is a Doria and Genoa is close enough to throw a stone at,' the boy said.

'This is his oldest son. Francesco Gatelussi.'

Francesco bowed.

Gian Galeazzo bowed. He looked at me. 'I was misinformed about you,' he said. Then he turned to Fiore. 'You teach me,' he said.

Fiore spread his hands. 'Sir William is adequate,' he said.

Gian Galeazzo shook his head. 'Why learn from the student when I can have a lesson from his master?'

It was a good point, but no one likes to be commanded by a stripling, especially an arrogant stripling. However, Fiore took over. And in the end, that was a pleasure, because Fiore was insensitive and even brutal, and had no care for the boy's rank, if he even fully understood it. And Gian Galeazzo was one of those annoying students who try to ask you why they have to do this, and isn't this other thing better, and can't they turn your sword like this …

Fiore took the sword out of his hand by turning the pommel and then threw him to the floor, almost casually.

'No,' he said. 'That would be stupid.'

Now, Fiore has told me I am stupid not less than one thousand times, from the day we met to the last time we played together. I was hardened to it, but the Count of Pavia's rich son probably had little experience of it, and he was ashamed and that made him angry.

He tried several little ways to get back at Fiore and after the third, I stepped in.

'My lord,' I said.

He glared.

'Messer Fiore is not a patient man, and he is not a sword tutor to princes,' I said. 'Believe me when I say that if you annoy him, he will break your hands.'

The young man paused.

I bowed. 'Listen: we have misunderstood each other. I think your father … meant something by this lesson. But we mean nothing more than to give you good instruction. You cannot fight Fiore. Believe me, young lord – I can barely fight him, and I am pretty good. So please, accept the lesson, stop playing, and let's return to your father.'

He said nothing – not even an inclination of the head. But later when, soaked in sweat, he accompanied the three of us back to the great hall across the perfectly manicured lawn, he suddenly turned to me.

'You give good advice,' he said. 'And you are correct. I mistook you for a bravo. I see now you are the real thing. How much for you to serve me?'

That was all. That was my introduction to Gian Galeazzo and, indeed, to the Visconti.

We went back into the hall. Count Amadeus and Count Galeazzo were signing some papers. Lady Bianca was gone.

Count Galeazzo rose and looked at his son in surprise. 'Well?' he asked.

'I learned a great deal, Pater,' Gian Galeazzo said. 'Indeed, I learned more than you might have intended.'

'You have a tendency to do so,' Galeazzo said, and his displeasure was obvious. He looked at me, and then at his son. I bowed.

'Your son was an excellent pupil,' Fiore said. That was the problem with Fiore: he didn't really do social convention well, and he had forgotten that, as he hadn't been introduced, he couldn't speak.

Perhaps the Count of Pavia was above such concerns. He looked at Fiore. 'My son was an excellent pupil?' he asked. 'I am …'

Fiore shrugged. 'Boys are all fools,' he said. 'He is less foolish than most.'

Count Amadeus worked hard to cover a smile at his cousin's discomfiture. And Gian Galeazzo shocked me by grinning – the most natural expression I had seen from him, and the first that was not somehow planned or practised.

'Well, well,' Count Galeazzo said. He felt he'd lost a point somewhere, but I didn't know what it was.

'Sir William is the best blade I have ever seen,' Gian Galeazzo said.

Well. That little piece of adolescent praise was to haunt me a long time.

'Is he?' Count Galeazzo said. He looked at me. 'I will remember that.'

And he did.

November kept a sting in her tail, and although we rode into Lombardy in weather that might have suited a late summer in Tuscany, we rode into the Alps in winter.

Travel in winter is very difficult, but it is not impossible, unless there's heavy snow or an avalanche, and again, our long string of spare horses made the very difficult merely hard. There was no question of making camps as we crossed the mountains, and we stayed on the major roads and went through the Mont Cenis pass, still on what most pilgrims considered the main route of the Via Francigena.

Most days we were up at first light, stumbling into the stable yard of an inn that made us pay in hard *specie* for minute quantities of straw and oats for our warhorses. We slept in our clothes and were lucky if we got our boots off. In the mornings we'd be out of our blankets with no hope of bathing and rarely hot water to shave, let alone time to strop a razor or hone it. The servants scrambled to fend for themselves early enough that they could serve us food. We knights scrambled to get into our harnesses and see to our horses, all so we could ride out of the inn gate into a brilliant day, or a shower of stinging snow or, worst of all, a little burst of freezing rain. Then seven or eight hours of sodden progress, occasionally passing other parties, or making way for a heavy wagon, on a road never more than three horses wide and sometimes reduced to a single trail the width of a horse's rump, with a four-hundred-foot fall on one side and a wall of sheer rock on the other. The weather wasn't yet cold enough to fill the paths and passes with snow so that they became untenable, but twice we passed long sections where we had to go single file. The lead men were breaking trail through knee-deep snow, and the horses had to guess where to put their feet, despite all of which, we didn't lose a man or beast – switching horses often seemed to be the key to managing everyone's good spirits and fatigue. But from Susa to Barberaz above Chambéry, we were in the mountains on the border of the principality of Savoy. Even when we climbed all day, the great peaks like Cenis herself towered above us to right and left, and when we had a snowfall, the world was white and the sunlight could hurt your eyes and make it hard to see.

We were a large party, and merchants wanted to travel with us. We ended up with a convoy of almost thirty carts and various mules, horses, and single pedlars on foot. After two days of dealing with their various lethargies and quarrels, I had Sam Bibbo put them under discipline, and I told all the merchants that if they didn't obey me, I'd make sure they didn't get to France. Then I moved them into our column and put l'Angars in command of half the lances, in the rearguard. I kept Fiore to be the principal bodyguard for the count, along with Richard, so that I could command the column. Richard was a fine man-at-arms and a deadly fighter, but Fiore could handle anyone I'd ever met.

We sent Ewan or Mike Burns forward every day, sometimes with three archers, sometimes more. They would ride as far as our next inn, make arrangements, find beds or at least warm floors, and ride back, examining the travellers en route and asking hard questions in the taverns about bandits and strangers. In stories, the mountains sound trackless and bandits attack suddenly. In real life, the Alps are well travelled and you just can't hide twenty horsemen. They leave a lot of hoofprints, they chew up a ford, all sorts of marks betray their presence, and when they stop, they need a lot of straw and oats. That's why a party as large as ours was so safe.

Despite all that, we took every precaution. The count's food was tasted twice: Albin's lady friend, Caterina, who had become a company regular by then, was at home in a kitchen, and we sent her into the kitchens as soon as we stopped, and she'd get to know the cooks and watch the food prepared. No one minds a pretty girl in the kitchen. Caterina was an excellent spy. Her loyalty was not in doubt. She was an agreeable woman with an air about her that made men want to talk, and her Venetian-Italian was pleasantly foreign.

Every night, one man-at-arms and a handful or archers and pages would ride out at last light and make a long loop up and down the roads, looking for anything or anyone unusual. Every morning, Francesco Gatelussi would do the same – he was an early riser. He'd get out of the inn gate and check the area around the inn, so we couldn't be surprised at the outset.

It was all for naught, but that's how precautions work. And we did it rain or snow or moonlight or pitch-dark, and it was all routine.

As we got closer to Chambéry, the count grew increasingly tense.

'He is bound to attack me soon,' the count said. 'Once I am at Chambéry with my feudal host, he has no chance.'

'He may think that we have you too well defended,' I said.

He shook his head.

Musard frowned. 'William, you don't know these mountains. An avalanche could clear all of us off the road.'

'An avalanche has to be set by men,' I said. 'The men have to be up on the hillside, and to get there they'll leave prints in the snow, and the local villagers will know they are there.'

The count nodded. 'He will attack,' the count said.

Musard nodded. 'Camus,' he said.

Well, in that much, I knew they were right. But I thought that Camus would give himself away – some elaborate demonstration of the extremity of his evil – instead of just making a cut for the throat. He scared me; yet he was not an opponent I would fear as much as, say, one of the Armenian princes, or a Karamanid chief. What they lacked in evil they made up in sheer experience.

We stayed at the monastery of Saint François-Longchamp, hard by the defile at La Chambre. We only passed the defile after seizing both ends. That took work, but everyone agreed that it was the most dangerous point on the whole march. L'Angars took ten men and climbed past it and then came down above.

No ambush.

We were two days from Chambéry. It was December; my company needed rest, our tack was worn and the horses needed good barns with deep mangers and heaps of oats. Gabriel looked bony.

We rose very early the next morning, as the days were short and we had to pass what Richard called the 'Switchback', a long section of road over which we'd have to pass in single file.

Gatelussi went out before first light, into a light snowfall. He came back without incident and I sent our scouts out. It was Ewan's day, and he had two archers and Beppo, the Tuscan gargoyle, who tipped his hat and hunched his shoulders against the cold. The four men rode off into the snow. They would ride to Saint-Pierre-d'Albigny, or perhaps all the way to Chambéry itself, depending on the weather – about ten miles, and some of the hardest terrain of the whole pass.

As the monks began to sing Prime, we rode to the gate. The count was interested in hearing the service, as he was in his own demesne and the monks were his vassals, and his family had endowed the place. The abbot pressed us to stay and said it was a poor day for travel.

I rode out into the blowing snow. It was worsening since I'd sent the scouts, and I can remember trying to get the wool of my outer hood to cover my mouth. Gabriel was unhappy with the weather and with being ridden every day, too; he was fretful.

I rode back to the count. The abbot stood at his stirrup. He was from a local noble family – the two of them obviously knew one another well.

Count Amadeus spoke to Richard, and Richard stiffened, and then walked his charger over to me.

'The count wishes to stay and hear Prime,' he said. 'We will spend the day here.'

I might have bridled, but I had no need. The weather was blowing worse by the moment. I felt for Ewan and Beppo, but otherwise, most of the lads would be better for a day by a fire, or so I thought. In half an hour we had our beasts back in the stables, with blankets on them and warmed mush – a horse feast. I got out of my wet things – wet almost through from half an hour in the snow – and I put on my Venetian clothes, a little the worse for wear, and went to Prime late. The monks sang very well – surprisingly well for being isolated in the mountains.

We spent a comfortable day. We didn't play cards or talk bawdy; the monastery was not like some I've seen in Italy, but a place for serious and mature contemplation. Mostly we discussed the possibility of the war between the Pope and Milan heating up. There were merchants at the monastery from as far away as Bohemia. They thought their King Charles, who was Holy Roman Emperor, would crush Milan like a nut.

Later, some of our merchants put together a deputation to the count, and they found me after we left the chapel, intending to protest the lost day.

The bearded Italian merchant who presented their protest was unknown to me: well dressed, and, by his accent, a Florentine.

'Will you take this to the count?' he asked.

'No,' I said. I smiled. 'That would be foolish. Tell your friends that the count is paying for an escort of men-at-arms to take him at his own convenience to his castle at Chambéry. Your convenience has never been consulted because you are not paying. Despite this, my people have organised your forage and your bedding every night for almost a month. You have had a smooth journey, for men travelling in winter. Don't be ungracious.'

He nodded. 'I've already told them that,' he said. He shrugged. 'I drew the short straw. Some of 'em are right bastards.'

That piqued my interest. 'Really?' I said. 'Perhaps I should explain to them myself. Take me.'

So my Florentine, Niccolò something or other, led me down to the hostel by the stables. There were a considerable number of merchants – almost thirty, as I say – and a dozen of them were men without horses or wagons.

I told them pretty much what I'd said to the Florentine.

One of the pedlars looked odd. 'We need to go today,' he said.

'No one is stopping you,' I said. 'You can go, although, given the time, your chances of making it to Saint-Pierre-d'Albigny are not very good.'

The man looked as if he might catch fire; he was flushed, and his hands were shaking.

I ignored him, giving instructions for the next morning. When I was done, he came and took my hand.

'My lord,' he said, like a dog fawning on his master. 'My lord, is there anything I could do for you – anything – that would make you leave today?'

I locked his hand against me, wrapped his arm, and pinned him, face down, against the floor.

'Marc-Antonio?' I called out, and my squire appeared.

'Hold this man. Hold him until I'm ready to question him.' I looked at the tinker. 'I'll send you a friar to shrive you.'

His eyes were wide. 'I have done nothing,' he said.

'Why are you so eager for me to leave today?' I asked.

'I am eager to arrive,' he said, but his eyes gave him away. He couldn't reach mine. He flinched visibly.

'My lord . . .'

I shook my head. 'Take him away.'

Marc-Antonio took him and pushed his right arm behind his back and then frogmarched him away.

I got a dozen men-at-arms together and rode out into the snow. It was unpleasant out there, but the tinker had convinced me that Camus was waiting to ambush me, and I was damned if I was going to lose Ewan.

The further I rode, the more odd it all seemed. The snow was blowing so hard that any idea of ambush seemed insane. I couldn't imagine crossbowmen hitting anything in the wind and snow.

I couldn't really track Ewan either. A couple of times I saw tracks that might have been his – a big, shod horse – but we were scarcely the only military party on the road, and some of the local merchants used big horses.

It was very cold.

The Birigucci boys were as good as gold, a pair of warrior angels in armour with heavy wool cloaks. They knew mountains, and they were patient, and because they were so young, older men like l'Angars and Lapot were not going to whine in front of them. We kept moving. Sometimes the lead men had to break a trail through a wind-blown drift.

We were coming up on the 'Switchback'. I could see the loom of trees ahead and we were climbing steadily.

A squall hit us. For as long as it takes a priest to say the Eucharist prayer, we were all but blind. I kept Gabriel going – he was deeply unhappy, and trying to tell me so – and the blowing snow was so harsh on my face that I thought of closing my visor for relief.

Armour has an odd effect in a high wind. It is a windbreak. Even though it can get cold, it stops a high wind as well as it will stop a lance, and that's something. A few layers of padded arming garments underneath and you're fairly warm. Until you raise your arm. Then, by God, you are frozen to the skin. Under my arms I have eyelets in my arming doublet – marvellous in Outremer in high heat, but deadly in a Swiss pass in a blast of snow.

The squall began to taper off, and it was growing dark – it wasn't just my imagination.

And then lightning flashed.

I had, until then, never seen a thunderstorm of snow. Lightning flashed. A crack of thunder roared very close – that bolt probably struck in the trees fifty paces above us.

Gabriel let out a noise, very un-horse-like – more like a lion's roar. It was a challenge. There was another horse, very close.

Armour. The lightning flash had reflected on armour.

I was already drawing. Instinct took over. My right hand went to the hilt, and I drew, back-handed, thumb up. No idea why I made that choice, but it meant that my great war sword emerged from the scabbard like an enormous dagger.

The man-at-arms was to my left, and he only saw me when Gabriel let out his battle-roar, but he had his sword in his hand and he cut at me.

I had enough sword clear of the scabbard to cover his blow, and I stabbed, overhand, and my blow went under his guard and down into the top of his thigh, where he had no faulds, just maille. Blood spurted, incredibly red against the white snow in the now almost continuous lightning.

I got my sword in both hands – both hands on the blade. I cut at him with the hilt. In fact, I used the quillons like the spikes on a poleaxe, and one went in through his cheek. He spat teeth and fell as the downturn in my quillon caught on his jaw, and he was pulled from his saddle like a salmon from a river.

I looked around. The man bleeding out at my feet had a red and blue surcoat and a good horse.

There was nowhere to go but forward. I put spurs to poor Gabriel and he surged with his back legs and we went up the ridge. The road got steeper. There was ice underfoot, and Gabriel's shoes didn't grip, and we slid, and I had time to wonder if I was going to die in an ice fall.

Then he gave a mighty spring and we were moving, up and up. At some point I'd put my visor down – no idea when. Later, Clario Birigucci told me that crossbow bolts were flying about me like a cloud of swallows when a barn door is opened, but the wind spoiled any attempt to aim, and I didn't even see the bolts. I just went up.

And then I was at the top. The view was so staggering that I lost a moment, despite my fear. I could see for miles, all the way down the valley, and there were thunderheads *below* me, and flashes of lightning, almost constantly.

I couldn't see anyone to fight.

I turned Gabriel, left and then right.

There *was* no one to fight.

I turned Gabriel all the way around. And there, behind me, were our ambushers. The Biriguccis and l'Angars and I had ridden through their ambush in the squall. The squall was dying away and I could see them below me. Far below me.

Pierre Lapot was down, his horse bleeding out in the snow. Gerlain, one of my Bretons, was covering him, trying to pull him up behind and fighting by turns.

I looked down at the mêlée. There were more men coming out of the woods to my right, but they, too, were below me, and they were focused on Lapot.

I was looking for Camus. I didn't see him, and time was passing.

Lapot was holding his own.

Rob Stone was just dismounting. I didn't think his arrows would be any more effective than the crossbow bolts.

I pointed with my sword, now held more prosaically by the grip. 'We clear the slope in one charge,' I said.

With Marc-Antonio, there were five of us, and we had perhaps fifty years of fighting experience among us. We formed close instinctively as if we were a mêlée team.

'Charge,' I called out, and we started down the hill like an avalanche of horseflesh. I don't remember fighting anyone. We had the hill behind us, our horses were better, and we had surprise and luck – a formidable phalanx against which some armoured brigands had no chance. We unhorsed a couple and turned, raising a great spray of snow.

Gerlain had Lapot up behind him, and he followed us. The archers hadn't loosed a shaft, just unsheathed their swords.

We hadn't lost a man. Lapot's horse was the only casualty.

But now I was truly afraid for Ewan and Beppo, and I knew we had to push on, cold and wet and tired as we all were. I led the way, knowing that there were crossbowmen in the wood line.

We got over the top. I had another moment to admire the view, and I could see four tiny dots moving against the pink-white light on the snow below us in the far valley. Way off to the west, I could see Chambéry, or perhaps just the monastery above the town.

I had to hope that the four dots in the valley were Ewan and Beppo and the archers.

I sat, looking down into the Chambéry valley, and it all came to me. I needed to think of this like a battle, not like a road. I had the high ground, and it was very valuable.

I waved to Rob Stone. 'I need you and all the archers to clear the wood line,' I said. 'And then hold the hill.'

He looked at the woods. 'Don't know how many they are.'

I pointed to the Birigucci. 'Help the archers clear the woods.'

Clario grinned. 'Watch me!' he said, and without another word, pivoted his horse and charged, at a gallop, towards the wood line.

What a fool.

But a glorious fool.

Bolts sparkled in the grey light.

'Damn,' Stone said, and led the archers across the ridge-top field. Benghi let out a war cry and dashed off after his brother.

I was stunned. I couldn't believe the stupid young man had just ridden off across a snowfield in the face of an unknown number of crossbowmen, and it was a lesson I've never forgotten. Never, ever, underestimate the stupidity of brave young men.

Clario was down before his horse was halfway across the snowfield. He took two shafts.

It is terrible to give orders and watch them obeyed. It is terrible, I think, to command men whom you like – with whom you have lived, and perhaps prayed, and grown. It seemed absurd to be fighting Camus inside Savoy, a well-ordered principality, a rich place.

I looked back over the snowfield. Rob Stone was down too, but Benghi Birigucci was carving a red path through the crossbowmen. I was watching. I had to keep a reserve; I had no idea how many men I was facing.

I was pretty sure that Camus was out of crossbowmen. Wherever he'd hired them, and my suspicion is that they were out-of-work Genoese oarsmen, he'd used them up. The men looked thin and tired.

And where was the bastard? I kept turning my horse, looking at every stand of trees, every snow pile, every bend in the road. I could see the tracks where half a dozen of his men-at-arms had fled our charge. Only three of the enemy crossbows had stood their ground. The rest had fled, and my Englishmen were butchering them in the open trees. The action wasn't hard to follow, even at twilight.

None of it made much sense, but then, in war, nothing ever makes much sense. The four dots coming up the valley grew larger. I was sure it was Ewan and Beppo. By then, Beppo was riding oddly, and his horse was labouring.

I wanted to go and look after Clario and Rob Stone. Stone was moving, two hundred paces away, but I couldn't give up my position – the top of the ridge, the perfect view – and five uncommitted men-at-arms. But it was killing me, watching Clario, watching Stone, and doing nothing – listening to the massacre of the crossbows, doing nothing.

Finally, I sent Lapot, on foot, across the snow, and he went right willingly, jogging along.

I was busy watching him, when I realised I hadn't looked at the four dots for a while, and I whirled. They were closer, but they had dismounted. They were on a switchback below me, perhaps four hundred paces down and a thousand paces of road between us. Ewan was loosing an arrow.

I couldn't make out any adversary, but the steep ridge could hide an army. The light was failing. If I went to Ewan, I was potentially leaving Rob Stone and Clario to die in the snow, or all of them to be swept up in Camus's as yet undeveloped counter-attack.

If I did nothing …

It was, literally, two sides of a ridge, and me balanced on a knife's edge between.

I looked back. Lapot was with Clario.

He waved.

Beppo raised a latchet, a light crossbow, and shot it. I didn't see the bolt at that range, but I saw how fast he pulled the prod.

'On me,' I called, and slammed my visor down.

I cantered down the steep road with Marc-Antonio right at my heels and l'Angars not far behind. We flew like the wild hunt, on the very edge of darkness, and the hooves of our war steeds raised sparks off the rock of the road. Gabriel was blowing great gouts of steam like an equine dragon. Perhaps our wild careen down the ridge took us two minutes. I have no idea, but it seemed to take forever.

We turned a corner and there was Pennyweather, one of Ewan's archers, face down on the road, his blood black against the moonlit white of the road. I knew him from the hood he wore over his armour. His bow was unstrung in his hand, and his rouncey was standing over him.

I shot by, and realised too late that there was a man by the rocks at the turn. More than one man …

An axe hit my helmet. I suppose I had a flash to move my head – perhaps Gabriel's speed baffled my opponent – but the blow was hard enough to rock me forward, thankfully not hard enough to unhorse me or dash my brains out in the snow.

I flashed around the hairpin turn, close to the outside, still trying to regain my seat. Gabriel skidded on all four feet like a cat, and sat almost all the way down on his haunches, so that I nearly went over my crupper.

A man with a lance materialised out of the gloom. He was at a trot. The lance was coming for my eyes, and I had a two-thousand-foot drop behind my horse's back legs.

I have no idea what I did. Perhaps nothing – perhaps it was all Gabriel. He went forward, swarming along like a dog, low to the ground, rather than like a high-spirited horse, and as his front legs pulled us forward, his back legs pushed off and we turned on Gabriel's forefeet. I got some of my sword on the lance. The tip tore the spaulder from my left shoulder, popping the straps and the lace point and causing a lightning flash of pain. I swung my sword. It wasn't elegant, but my blow came in on the charging rider as his horse turned to follow mine – a solid blow to the helmet. Pointless, in most circumstances, but in this turn, my opponent was trying to handle his lance. His weight was forward, and my blow turned him in the saddle. His horse sidestepped like a good warhorse, striving to get its weight under it …

… and vanished over the edge into the darkness.

They were already breaking past us, half a dozen men on tired horses. I turned Gabriel and gave chase, trying to find Camus. Now we were riding uphill. Luck, or good fortune, or my battle-brilliance, had caught Camus's second ambush between two bodies. They had feared to rush Ewan, and the result was disastrous for them. The road was like an archery range – difficult in moonlight at moving targets – but men on horseback are big.

Ewan's arrows were telling. Marc-Antonio unhorsed one. L'Angars took a staggering blow to his helmet and went down, and then I was pushing Gabriel up the steep slope, trading heavy blows with a mad-faced blond man. He looked familiar, but his face was frozen in a snarl of hate – his mouth was open, and he kept bellowing, but not a war cry. My Gabriel matched his roan stride for stride, and I was playing for his unguarded face. He was just pounding at me, hoping for luck.

Fiore doesn't believe in luck.

After three strokes, I began to parry his hammer-like blows with some science. Then Gabriel surged ahead and I had to fight behind me. I reined in, Gabriel slowed, the other horse shot by, and deceived my opponent's blade at the cross and my cut went into his face, cutting his mouth and both cheeks so that his face seemed to open in four parts, and he screamed. His scale-gauntleted hands went to his face, sword abandoned, and I put the point of my sword in under his arm.

My left shoulder felt as if I'd wrenched it, or taken a sword thrust. If I had had an astrologer, he might have had something to say about my shoulder, although Fiore said that I was a weak offside parry and that was why I kept getting hit there.

I prefer Fiore to an astrologer.

Rob Stone was dead. Clario Birigucci had a bolt in his groin, and we stood around him, waiting, to be honest, for him to die. But when he didn't die right away, I realised how precarious our position was. More than half of our enemies had escaped, and we were cold, exhausted and had wounds.

I got Clario up on his brother's horse and put Lapot on the horse of one of the dead enemy men-at-arms. Believe me that we stripped their dead and took their horses – the routier lives in every man. Clario didn't die when we mounted him. He had blood coming from his nose, and I assumed he'd die in his brother's arms, but at the base of the ridge he was still alive.

Benghi wanted me to leave the two of them at the first farmhouse, but I demurred. I could see awakening to find them both crucified on the road. I shouted him down; it was an ugly scene. I was prepared to use force to make him obey, and he was prepared to do the same.

'You are killing my brother, you fuck!' he shouted.

'I am doing my best to *save* your brother. If you ever want to serve me again, keep riding.' I had to say it. I rode up close, daring him to try to punch me. Daring him, although he had his arms around his brother, a cloak around them both.

'Your brother's only hope is Peter Albin,' I said. 'Let's get him there.'

'He needs to be warm! He needs to lie down—'

'No,' I said. I was trying to keep from anger, trying to make this strictly business – trying to be Hawkwood, with his immense authority, or the Earl of Oxford, or Peter Mortimer. But then I thought instead of Pierre Thomas, who had had an endless reserve of goodness and an incredible ability to turn the other cheek.

'I will save your brother if I can,' I said, as kindly as I could manage.

'You sent us to die,' he spat. 'You just watched.'

I took a deep breath. 'Move,' I said. I wasn't sure what to do with that accusation. I felt badly; indeed ...

But not badly enough, even on the edge of collapse, to rise to a nineteen-year-old's taunt.

He was wavering.

'Move. And your brother will live. Go, now.' It was, in the end, Fra Peter's tone of absolute certainty that I managed, and Benghi obeyed. He turned his horse; the rest of my people didn't look at me or him, and we rode as rapidly as tired horses would allow. I knew that men needed water and the horses were too cold, but it was dark, and I wasn't allowing man or horse a break until we reached the monastery.

But I had found Ewan the Scot.

'How far did you get?' I asked.

'All the way to the gates of Chambéry,' Ewan said. 'I raised the alarm, told them where their count was, and turned back. We saw armour on the hillsides. I knew they were out here, and we rode through their first attempt – they was late getting up, I'll warrant.'

Beppo nodded. 'A *brigan* must rise pretty early to deceive Beppo,' he said.

'And Pennyweather?' I asked.

Beppo shrugged. He glanced at Ewan, who rode on stony-faced.

'I told him to halt and dismount, and he kept riding.'

My memory of Pennyweather was that he had been a little deaf. In a helmet, while riding? The poor man would have had no idea what hit him.

The monks were saying Vespers when we rode up to the gate. But they got it open in no time, and Clario Birigucci was still alive. Under Albin's direction, we got him off the horse and onto a stretcher, and then onto a bed.

I went and made a report to Richard, who sent me to bed.

We didn't leave the next day, but everything changed. Messer Ogier came from Chambéry with twenty Savoyard knights. There had been an avalanche on the road. They'd brought peasants to clear it, and Ogier thought that the avalanche had been forced. But twenty men-at-arms and their armed squires put murder beyond the Prince of Achaea's means. Much as it hurt me to rise, I managed to get my companions to Chambéry, where a small crowd gathered to greet their long-absent count with very genuine cheers. We went straight into the cathedral, where the countess had prepared a *Te Deum* for the count's return.

I was still in harness, and my shoulder felt as if I'd been kicked by a mule. My whole left arm was bad, I was unshaven, and so tired that almost everything seemed to hurt, as if I'd been drunk for days. But I managed to swing down from Gabriel's back. I straightened my sword and walked with Fiore in the rank behind Ogier and Musard into the cathedral through an aisle of merchants and Savoyard bourgeois who were cheering their lungs out. The countess was waiting on the steps, and they exchanged a frank kiss. Bonne clearly had some fire in her; the count's eyes widened, and the crowd cheered again.

'Messer d'Oro?' A page, a very young page, was actually tugging at my fauld. 'Are you Messer d'Oro?'

'I am,' I said.

The page bowed. 'My lord, the Lady Countess asked me to say that your wife is here, and wishes …'

I glanced at the count. He didn't need me. I followed the page.

Emile was lying on a bed. She didn't look pale and wan – she looked wonderful.

'You took your time,' she said, and raised the bundle from her breast. 'But you're in time to name him. Even though you missed all the work.'

Christmas at Chambéry was one of the best of my life. The count had money. He paid me, and I paid my people, and Emile found them all lodgings in the town. Fiore had intended to go home, but then he made mysterious comments about some other trip.

'He wants to go to Genoa,' Emile said, after church. 'How do you not know that?'

We proceeded to have one of those conversations – the kind married people have – wherein each thinks that the other is more than a little foolish. Emile couldn't imagine that I'd ridden from Florence to Rome and back to Chambéry without asking my closest friend about his love life. I tried to explain that it was so difficult to imagine Fiore as a devotee at the shrine of courtly love that I preferred just to ask him hard questions about fighting.

'He never said a thing,' I mumbled.

'Interesting that he mentioned her as soon as we were together,' Emile said. 'Of course, I did travel home with her. I have invited her for Christmas.'

Emile didn't seem exhausted by childbirth; if anything, she seemed enlivened by it. Two children in two years is a heavy load for any woman, but Emile just laughed.

'I'm built for babies,' she said.

There's really only one response to make to that.

The week before Christmas court, we made a circuit of her nearby estates. I had never seen any but the townhouse in Geneva; I had no idea, really, of how rich she was. But it was pleasant, if cold, to ride abroad, with l'Angars and Fiore and Gatelussi as company and protection. Everyone was on edge about the Prince of Achaea. I heard a fair amount of speculation about what courses were open to him, now that Milan had apparently spurned him.

And even then, the Prince of Achaea was yesterday's news. All the talk at court was about Prince Lionel of England, who was already on his way to Paris – or perhaps he wasn't – who was coming to be wed to Siora Violante of Milan, and who would be the count's neighbour. His marriage to the Visconti was rewriting the map of northern Italy – even as the Holy Roman Emperor threatened war alongside the Pope. The web of alliances was crystallising, forming like icicles on a mountain cottage: stronger with every thaw and refreeze.

Against the coming wonder of a prince of England, the Prince of Achaea could not compete, and his name faded away. I was still cautious, and Richard Musard kept very close watch over the count.

The other interesting discovery at the court of Chambéry was that Richard Musard was a very important man indeed in Savoy. I knew this already, but when the count was in his own lands, Musard was all but paramount. Yet he did it with grace. None of the native Savoyards seemed to begrudge him his position as favourite and, best of all, our fragile new friendship was not ruined by his sudden accession to power. Instead, I met his wife, and we danced, and went on a hunt together. We hunted chamois, with crossbows, across the snow. I never saw a chamois, but we did see some other mountain goats. I shot one of those, assuming it was a chamois, and there was some laughter.

It was good-natured laughter.

Bonne, the count's lady, smiled at me. 'I have done the same,' she said. 'And they are just as cruel to me.'

Musard bowed. 'And I. It's almost a requirement of coming to Savoy, shooting the wrong goat.'

I also got to see how close my lady wife was to the countess. Of course, Emile was a countess in her own right – her relationship with Bonne de Bourbon was a good deal closer than mine with the count – and, of course, Amadeus of Savoy knew her very well from their childhood.

I had found the count easier to like when he was in danger. Now, in the bosom of his court, he was at his aristocratic best, or worst. He noticed me from time to time, mocked my lack of hunting skills, and wondered aloud that I was such a fine dancer, as if that obvious slight to my birth and training could be construed as a compliment.

In fact, as soon as Emile was out of her accouchement, she had me dancing – with an Italian instructor, and with her.

'Christmas is all about dancing,' she said.

'I thought it was about the birth of the Christ child?' I asked.

'My love, is he not "lord of the dance"?' she shot back, as good an answer as I've ever heard. But, thanks to her and Maestro Senis's tutelage, I was a tolerable dancer, and I could leap and turn with the rest of them.

Two days before Christmas, a convoy came over the Alps from the coast, and with it was Davide Doria of Monaco and his niece, Bianca: a lively girl, with a narrow face, features so fine as to be elfin, and long brown hair. I was there when she slipped from her horse; she waited to be caught by Fiore, who put her on the ground. They looked at each other and both blushed. I was afraid for a moment they'd kiss in public and we'd all end covered in blood.

I had not met Davide Lornier Doria, one of the coast's merchant lords, before. He owned six ships, and he had fought at Crécy – against us, of course. He was perhaps forty-five. He seemed to have a sense of humour about his niece.

'My brother's willing for them to wed,' he said to me, before the bells had rung for Nones. 'And all of us are deeply conscious of the value of a connection with this court.'

It's a funny world. I can make a decision in the snow about which way to lead my reserve – who to kill, who to let die. But put me at a court and ask me to manage my closest friend's attempts at matrimony . . .

Luckily I had Emile. She had the whole situation in hand, the same way she knew the balances due to her on every estate she owned, and the names of every new child born in any of her houses or villages. She knew Fiore's prospects to the soldo, and the Dorias, even though they were in banking and shipping, were worth twenty times as much. Emile made sure Fiore appeared with the count; she paid for him to have several fine suits of clothes, which I'll warrant he still owns. And when, on Christmas Day, he showed signs of irritable mooning after the young lady, I took him over the mountain to the monastery to fetch young Clario and his brother. Clario had failed to die. He'd had three weeks, and, after the count rode away, Albin had grown bold, cut the bolt and drawn it. Birigucci had begun to heal.

Albin met us in the yard of the monastery. 'Don't praise me,' he said. 'Praise God, because taking a bolt in the groin without losing your balls or your life is a miracle from God, not a healing by the hand of man.'

Clario didn't share the view and had become Albin's devoted admirer, and Caterina's too.

He couldn't ride, and so we put him on a litter between two mules. We had about seven miles to go, back to Chambéry, and I was still conscious of the Prince of Achaea and Camus, although they seemed less a threat in bright, snowy sunshine. Nonetheless, I had Sam Bibbo and Gatelussi and a dozen men behind us, and I had Fiore. I was willing to fight all the legions of Hell, let alone the Bourc Camus.

We didn't see an adversary, and we rode along, listening to the Christmas bells ring in valley after valley, and the road, while snow-covered, was passable. We got Birigucci to Chambéry and installed him in Emile's townhouse with his brother. It became clear during the ride that Benghi couldn't find a way to apologise for his words to me when his brother was dying, so when we were dismounting, I made the time to help him with his brother's stretcher.

'You can stay here as long as you like,' I said, or something to that line. He had to smile back.

'I'm sorry ...' he began.

I smiled. 'No matter. I don't have a brother, but I imagine losing one would be terrible.' I offered my hand. 'I have a sister; I almost lost her to plague.'

'So sorry,' Birigucci said.

'Never mind,' I said. It's odd, how hot you get, and how quickly an apology lances the boil.

'We have done everything together ...' the boy said. And he did seem like a boy, although he was fewer than ten years younger than I.

No matter, while we'd spent Christmas Day in the saddle, my lady had bargained with Messer Davide of Monaco, and made the best part of a marriage agreement.

After church we dined, and then we danced. The music was not, I fear, as good as that at the French court, or in Venice or Florence, and some of that, I'm told, is the mountain air. But we managed somehow, and Countess Bonne showed that she could dance as well as my wife. The two of them led a dozen dances, and I was much thrown together with the count, who fingered his gold cup and raised an eyebrow at me a couple of times.

'I need to talk to you,' he said. He waved his cup at me. 'Later.'

Whatever that was supposed to mean.

It didn't take me long, at Chambéry, to find that, however much I loved Emile, this life was not for me. Out on the road, leading the count's escort, I had begun to imagine a career with Savoy as one of his captains. But the reality of Chambéry was different. He didn't need me at all. And it was not as if Emile needed me to 'manage her estates'. She was the best estate manager I've ever met; she knew her business better than I knew my company.

But I'm not altogether a fool. I didn't announce my intention to go fight alongside Hawkwood in the spring. I merely used the thought of Hawkwood to soothe my own ruffled feathers. Instead of hating the count, who seemed to have forgotten that I had served him for almost a year without pay, I began to think of how I might expand my little company before I went south in the spring. I wrote to Sir Giannis, offering them employment if they chose to remain in Italy. I wrote to Hawkwood asking how many lances I might bring, as a sort of subcontractor, and I wrote to Nerio with news of the north and of the Prince of Achaea.

But that is all by the way. Christmas night, I danced, and smiled at the Green Count without rancour, knowing that all too soon I would be gone.

After we'd all danced, there was a second supper, and the seneschal clapped his hands for silence, and announced that the count would speak.

The count announced the decisions in two lawsuits. He knighted the elder of his squires, and gave a farm to the master of his bowmen, who had gone all the way to Constantinople and back. Then he gave an estate to Richard Musard, and another to Ogier, working his way through the whole of the Savoyard crusading party, awarding lands and titles. He gave away a fortune, but he demonstrated that he knew what good lordship was, and both his men and his wife nodded in appreciation.

Some time after Ogier, he called me forward. I admit I had hopes by then: the seneschal had given me a significant look, and Emile had summoned a page, who brushed my best wool hose. But I didn't expect the Order of the Black Swan. Richard had it, and Ogier, and Mayot; but Ogier and Mayot were the count's childhood friends, old companions, and, to be frank, well-born.

Richard was grinning from ear to ear.

I knelt, and the count put the collar around my neck. He leaned forward. 'Ah, Sir William,' he said, in tolerable Anglo-French. 'You are not always best pleased with us, I think. And we have our faults, the House of Savoy, but we are not frugal or ungenerous. We reward good service, and your service has been exemplary.'

People cheered me when I had my Order. You may say 'a bauble, worth perhaps a hundred ducats', but the Order of the Black Swan was known everywhere – still is – and never again would anyone enquire after my birth before allowing me into the lists.

Two days later, I was summoned from my lady's solar, where I was reading to her from Boccaccio while she sorted wool colours.

The count was trying cote-hardies for yet another function. As usual, the one he was trying was emerald silk, this one cut in the French style, with padding almost as impenetrable as armour.

There were a dozen tailors and sempsters attending him, but I had grown used to the ways of the truly rich, and I ignored them as he did.

'Are you available in the spring?' he asked. No preamble.

'My lord, I have an understanding with Sir John Hawkwood . . .'

The count looked at me. His arms were spread; there was a man kneeling on his left side, marking the hem of his cote-hardie, and another measuring the arm skye, and he had to look back at me like a dancer.

'You can join Sir John when I'm done with you,' he said. 'I need your company to escort me to Paris in the spring. Then we'll all go to Milan and so will Sir John. You'll be with him before active campaigning opens.'

The next day, the count stood godfather to my son, named Richard for my father. He told me that he would stand for Fiore's wedding, and then he showed himself surprisingly well informed.

'Master Albin,' he said. 'I owe him as well. Perhaps if I were to stand for his wedding?'

The Count of Savoy, standing forth at the wedding of a penniless doctor to a poor Venetian woman? It was the kind of social gesture that could make a man's career, that could shout flat any attempt to blacken a woman's name.

'We would all be in your debt,' I said.

I wrote to Sir John.

Perhaps ten days after Christmas, the count summoned the Prince of Achaea to attend him at court. The prince declined, and instead sent the count a formal challenge. We were warned of the challenge by a real herald this time. After some consideration, the count chose to take the situation seriously and sent me, and Richard, and Sir Ogier – all members of the Order of the Black Swan – with a herald of our own.

The challenge was brought by a party of armed men in the prince's red and blue livery, led by Camus.

We met in the snow, perhaps five leagues from Chambéry where the valley widens by the little church.

Camus had ten men-at-arms with him. He seemed unconcerned to be deep in the count's homeland.

'Your count is in hiding?' he asked.

'Give me your cartel and go,' Ogier said. 'Your master is a rebel and a fool and all of you would do better to find someone else to serve.'

Camus looked back at his own men, who were stony-faced.

'It might have been better if they'd all run away years ago,' he said. 'But it's far too late for that.' He reached into a bag at his saddle-bow and produced a scroll in an ivory tube. 'I assume that your count is too much of a coward to actually fight, but here it is anyway.' He looked at Richard. 'You and Gold are fuck-buddies again?' he asked.

Ogier stiffened and Richard reached for his sword.

I laughed. 'Ah, monsieur,' I said. 'Once your gibes were so shocking, and now they have lost most of their effect.'

His face worked. 'I will have you, Gold. Dead at my feet, your guts in a heap beside you. I'll kill you, and your little boys, and your little girls. I'll wipe you from the Earth and laugh.'

I shook my head. 'No you won't,' I said. 'Laughter takes joy, and you have none, even at victory. And anyway, monsieur, I believe I've now bested you the last three times our swords have crossed.' Even though my hands were shaking, my voice was good. 'Now scurry on back to the Prince of Achaea, and tell him whatever you like, so the grown-ups can go back to their party.'

'I'll show you Hell,' Camus promised.

'I've already seen Hell,' I said. I shook my head. 'I looked around, and I didn't see you.' I nodded. 'But I did see d'Herblay. He said to tell you hello.'

'Fuck you, you sanctimonious hypocrite,' Camus spat.

I had never bested him so completely. I laughed. It was a little forced, but not bad. 'Ride away now,' I said. 'Before we all mock you.'

'I do not fear your mockery,' he said. 'I—'

Fiore spoke up. 'You know,' he said across Camus, 'if I killed you now, no one would avenge you. The count might chide me a little, but there would be very few repercussions. Your master is an outlaw and you yourself are friendless.'

Camus paused as if considering the point.

'I will kill you all,' he said again.

'Unlikely,' Fiore said.

The Prince of Achaea's case, as a vassal exceeding his inheritance, began to go through the count's courts. Now, I have no reason to love the Prince of Achaea: he hired Camus, and he was a nasty piece of work. But he never had a chance with the law. To say that the Savoyard courts were corrupt would be unfair; they were, simply, the count's courts, and the men in them were his appointments. By arranging for Achaea's abandonment by his international allies, the count had guaranteed the result.

He couldn't keep himself from announcing each step in the case, as his cousin was summoned, formally declared outlaw, and as charges were levied against him. The count seemed to relish his cousin's legal extermination a little too much.

Otherwise, it was a very pleasant winter. We hunted chamois, and I gradually learned to get above them and not try to stalk from below. We lay in soft feather beds, or danced, or went on short rides that were rewarded with steaming cups of hot wine. If it wasn't as blissful as Lesvos, neither was it bad; I proved adept at being a drone, and Fiore kept me fit.

We had a fine wedding for Albin and his Catrina. It was an affair of my company, and I mean no disrespect when I say that never was an unfrocked priest (which Albin was, in secret) and a whore married with more friends about them: the Count of Savoy and his countess, my wife and her ladies, Sir Ogier and Musard and his Bonne. We packed the little church in the valley and all the ladies combined to sew the Venetian girl her trousseau, and she, to tell the truth, wept for a day, unbelieving of her good fortune. My wife was teaching her to read and write; that was her wedding gift to her doctor. I gave him three books, with some help from the archers, who rode over the mountains in winter to fetch them.

And we gave them a fine *charivari* ... a loud party that lasted past dawn.

*

Winter was jolly, but spring didn't ever seem to come to Chambéry. We were still racing sleds down the streets in March to the cacophony of the count's marvellous bells. But, in the dying days of March, I rallied my company.

I appointed one of the squares for my muster and inspection, and ordered that every man should appear with his horses and arms. Sam Bibbo had entered, without apparent effort, into the place of master archer. Gospel Mark made no attempt to contest his pre-eminence, and I didn't know how that had been managed, but there they sat at the head of twenty-four archers, mostly English, but with two Picards and half a dozen Flemings among them, as well as a Greek. They had the best horses of any group of archers I'd ever known – a year of campaigning and some losses still hadn't depleted our stock of Arabs.

To their right were my men-at-arms. L'Angars was their corporal, for all that Gatelussi did a good deal of the work. Young Gatelussi had spent a good winter at court; he was going home after Paris, but now with contacts at the courts of Burgundy and Savoy that would probably help him when he was Prince of Lesvos, just as his father intended. Our men-at-arms were a mixed lot – the Birigucci brothers were from an ancient noble family, and Pierre Lapot was merely a dangerous Gascon – but two years of prosperity and employment had provided every man with good harness and decent clothes, and the muster was, for the most part, a pleasure. There's always an awkward sod. In our case, we had Witkin, and never was a man more aptly named. He was Gospel Mark's inseparable companion, even though he was never clean and had, on the last day of March in 1368, palpably and obviously sold his helmet, bow and maille to a pawnbroker and had nothing but the most ridiculous excuses to offer.

But Witkin was our only failure. The pages were mostly Savoyard boys, with a sprinkling of Greeks and Italians and one runaway English servant named Tom whom I took for myself after Bibbo recruited him. My two Greek boys were still too young to bear arms beyond daggers; Tom, despite being a skinny lout, was strong.

'Had any weapons training?' I asked him. I was sitting behind my table with Sam Bibbo and l'Angars and Fiore, and each man had to come forward, be inspected and draw his spring bonus.

'Nay, lord,' he said, not meeting my eye.

'Ever killed anyone, young Tom?' Bibbo asked.

'Maybe,' Tom said.

'What'd you kill him with, then?' Bibbo asked.

'His mouth,' l'Angars said, and men laughed. And it's true, Tom's breath was offensive fifty feet away; he needed to have some rotten teeth pulled.

'Ma fist,' Tom said.

'Christ,' l'Angars said.

'Do you want to come wi' us, Tom?' Bibbo asked.

'Oh, aye,' the young man said. 'If'n you'll take me, and if'n you pay.'

Bibbo also raked Witkin over red-hot coals for selling his kit. It proved, though, that he had it under the table, already redeemed from the pawnbroker, so even as Witkin made his mumbling, impossible excuses – dogs ate his maille, a boy stole his helmet when he was asleep, his sword broke when he was sleeping from the frost – even as he spoke, his gear was piled up before him and finally Bibbo put the pawnbroker's ticket into his hand.

Bibbo looked at me.

I looked at Witkin, who had stood his ground against Turks and Saracens and Frenchmen. 'Do it again and you can find other employment,' I said in my newly learned *capitano* voice. I guess I did it well – the good-natured catcalls and ungentle mockery ceased. Men looked away.

'You're not a child,' I said. 'You're better than this, Witkin. You drink, and you lie. Do better, or don't march with us.'

'Everyone drinks!' Witkin spat.

There was a hush, as if they all expected that the *capitano* might make him vanish in a puff of smoke, or perhaps turn him into a frog.

'Exactly *because* everyone drinks,' I said, 'is why you're an arse for lying and selling your kit. You were the only one of all of them to do it. Last chance.'

Witkin was considering further protest, but Gospel Mark shoved him away from the table and growled, 'Shut the fuck up, you useless bastard.'

When they were all mounted, Fiore and I rode through the ranks and looked at them all. We had almost seventy men, and they were excellent. It was enough to raise the heart of any soldier, and the next day, when the count looked them over, he nodded.

'I will have the finest escort,' he said with his usual smug satisfaction. And it was the count himself who pointed at Marc-Antonio, in a new white harness. 'Time for that one to be a knight,' he said.

On the second day of April, we set off for Paris.

I hadn't been to Paris since the summer of the year of Our Lord 1358, at the height of the Jacquerie, when the King of France was still a prisoner in England, and when the Dauphin, the Mayor of Paris, the Jacques, Charles of Navarre and the English were all on different sides. It had only been ten years. But those ten years …

We rode from winter into spring as we rode down from the mountains. The countess, Bonne, came with us, as did my Emile, and then it was rather as I had imagined the year before. I was an acceptable courtier and a good escort commander, and Emile danced attendance – often literally – on the Countess of Savoy, and flowers blossomed as they passed, or so it seemed. It was a remarkable spring; there were flowers on every hillside and in every village. France was rich again, and if there were bones on the roadsides and villages with more roofless huts – they always look like rotten teeth in an old mouth to me – than there were newly thatched roofs, still the place looked better than it had on my last visit. We had a dozen Savoyard courtiers, every one of them a veteran of a couple of major actions. There was no practical way in which the Prince of Achaea could hope to ambush us, but Fiore and Gatelussi and l'Angars and I kept up the good habits of the season before, scouting with archers, keeping a watch at night, even in good towns like Lyon, whose suburbs I had once burned with a party of brigands and routiers. I remember riding through Chalon-sur-Saône to the sound of Emile, my Emile, teaching Fiore one of Machaut's love songs so that he could try it on his lady. She'd long since gone back to Monaco, but marriage was in the air and Fiore, so single-minded about everything, was determined to be a courtly lover and was willing to put his not inconsiderable skills to the task: dancing, poetry, singing … I half expected him to produce a lute at any moment.

We had days of rain, and because the count was in a hurry we pressed through them, so that we arrived at the castle of Nemours soaked to our various skins, the gentle with the common, and we were greeted with hot hippocras and enough wool to preserve us all. We were well fed, and there, I remember, I overslept. Me, the *capitano*, and I had to scramble into the courtyard a few steps ahead of the count.

'It is odd to be in France,' I said to Musard.

He shook his head. 'I'm always afraid I'll wake up and find it was all a dream and I'm a routier,' he admitted. It was the third or fourth time he'd said that; I knew him now to be a more haunted man than I'd thought at first.

On the sixteenth of April, we arrived at Paris. The count had an enthusiastic greeting from the royal court: he was a near neighbour and a good ally. We were all housed in the Louvre, which for Fiore meant a palliasse of not-very-clean straw right under the slate of the roof, with a drip, while for me and Emile, a countess in her own right, it meant a tiny room with a bed we brought ourselves, possibly because most of the time our room was someone's closet. Our window leaked when the spring winds blew from the south. But despite all that, we had more than most and, after I had inspected the archers' quarters, I had a word with the count and moved them all to an inn out in the Faubourg Saint-Germain.

That same day, Prince Lionel of Clarence arrived. Eh, Master Chaucer?

I met Master Chaucer, there, almost as soon as I returned to the Louvre – wandering the halls with a bundle of straw, looking for a place to sleep. Oh, my friend, am I unfair? Well, my memory says that I gave you the space my archers had tried to live in, and you were happy for it, and then you took me to the English prince.

Well, you have all seen how joyful Monsieur Chaucer and I are with each other, so you can imagine. Bells tolled, and dogs barked. Ha ha!

I introduced Emile to Chaucer, and Chaucer introduced me to you, Monsieur Froissart, and through you, to the good Duke of Burgundy and the Hainaulter lords in his train. I really only mention this to say that, although we were but three days in Paris – and most of that spent attending the Count of Savoy at court and law court as he pursued an old debt of nine thousand gold ecus owed him by the king – and some land contingent on that—

Chaucer, you frown. Do I misremember? Tell your own version, then. This is mine.

Any road, even as we attended our various lords, talk turned to arms and deeds of arms, and I brought Fiore along so that the good duke, the Countess Bonne's brother, as well as some of the other Hainaulters and English lords, could meet him. I was always eager to show him off; he shone in any company that wanted to discuss fighting.

And so there we were, a dozen of us, English and French, Hainault and Italian and Savoyard. We were waiting outside the antechamber where the count and the King of France were discussing finance, or just possibly the Prince of Achaea, when I looked up and there was Boucicault.

I was standing with my shoulders wedged comfortably into the panelling, with a pewter cup of good wine in my hand, between Musard and Fiore, who was holding forth on the best way to use a spear in a foot combat.

I looked up and saw Boucicault, and saw, too, his shock.

'William Gold,' he said.

I bowed. 'My lord,' I said.

He just stood there, shaking his head. He was beautifully dressed, but then, so was I; I had a fine white wool cote-hardie from Venice, with some fripperies and the Order of the Sword from Cyprus on my shoulder, and the Order of the Black Swan, a gold collar, round my neck.

Boucicault grinned. It took time, but it came. 'Of course, I've heard of you from time to time,' he said. 'You was at Alexandria.'

'I was.'

Boucicault nodded. '*Par Dieu*, William, you have certainly made something of yourself. What brings you here?'

'I am leading the Count of Savoy's military escort,' I said.

'Still with Musard, I see,' Boucicault said. Of course, this had to have seemed odd to him; he'd been part of the plan to take me, and Musard had, to all intents, sold me. To Boucicault, and Camus.

'Yes,' I said.

Musard nodded. Boucicault had a strange relationship with the two of us – if you've been listening, you know that we wandered between enmity and friendship and rivalry in arms all our youth. But now Boucicault was filled out, taller and stronger even than I remembered him, and older – a few years older than me. Mature, perhaps. The best jouster I ever faced, except Fiore.

I introduced them.

'You are a Knight of the Sword,' Boucicault said.

I bowed. 'I have that honour.'

'You know that King Peter of Cyprus is in Rome?' he asked.

I shook my head.

'He has agreed to fight some Gascon adventurer. To the death. In the lists.' Boucicault shrugged.

'Florimont de Lesparre?' I asked.

'The very man,' he said.

Then Boucicault joined our banter about fighting with spears, and we all moved on, but the subject was not dead. We went on to discuss the possibilities of war: the French knights were eager to have du Guesclin lead them against us, by which I mean the English, and there was some obvious ill feeling. I was sorry to miss du Guesclin, as I held him in high regard; he was in the north, laying siege to a castle, or so I was told. From war between England and France, we turned to war in Italy. Almost every man present thought that the Holy Roman Emperor, with the Pope, would take Milan in the spring, and that the English were fools to tie their chariot to that of the Count of Milan.

Two Germans present, quiet, dignified men, maintained that the Holy Roman Emperor was so embroiled in Bavaria that he would never cross the Alps. And Boucicault, who seemed to know whereof he spoke, said that the Pope was having trouble paying his captains. The consensus by the end of the evening was that the 'Great War', as we had all come to think of it, was not going to happen – that despite the web of alliances surrounding both the Pope and Milan, events like Prince Lionel's reception in Paris showed that the peace was sound and the world was not going to war.

That evening, at a very formal dinner with the King of France, the Duke of Burgundy, the Count of Savoy and Prince Lionel, the subject of the King of Cyprus surfaced again. This time it was the English prince.

'I remember the King of Cyprus,' Lionel said. 'I found him very … impressive. *Preux.*'

'Still,' the King of France said. 'Why would a king agree to fight a commoner?'

'Sir William Gold there is a Baron of Cyprus,' Boucicault said. He was apparently very close to the King of France.

I was well below the king, although not as far away as I might have been were I not married to Emile. He looked at me. 'Sir Guillaume?' he asked. 'You serve the Count of Savoy?'

'I have that pleasure, Your Grace,' I said.

'And yet you have a look of some familiarity,' he said.

I rose and bowed. I might have described the circumstances under which I met him in fifty-eight, but it would not have seemed flattering. 'Yes, Your Grace,' I said.

He nodded, as if he had just remembered where he had seen me.

'You are English,' he said.

'Yes, Your Grace.'

'But you have served Cyprus.' He glanced at Machaut, who was quite close to him. Machaut had been chattering with Emile; really, we all knew each other, at some remove.

'Yes, Your Grace,' I said.

'How, my lord?' the king asked.

I glanced down, and then at Emile.

Count Amadeus laughed. 'Sir Guillaume is too gentle to say so, but he saved Cyprus's life at Alexandria.'

'With a dozen other knights,' I said.

The King of France's gaze locked with mine.

'You are the man who stormed Corinth,' the king said.

'With Fiore, here, and some gallant gentlemen,' I said.

The king smiled.

Machaut said, 'And Sir Guillaume held the lists at Didymoteichon, in Outremer, against a team of Saracens.'

What the hell do you say? I was trying to think of something. Fiore says my mouth was open like a fish out of water, gulping air.

Then the King of France rose from his seat.

He bowed to me.

Well, there you have it. The summit of all my ambition, in a sentence. At the court of France, the King of France bowed *to me*.

Bah, none of you have any sense of what an honour that is.

Never mind. That's not the point. And see, Chaucer will confirm it happened – it's not all my vainglory.

'So you know the King of Cyprus well,' said the King of France, when he had seated himself, and people had stopped applauding.

Chaucer, I appeal to you … they applauded, did they not? Thank you, Master Chaucer.

'Not so very well, Your Grace,' I said.

'Nevertheless,' the king said, 'tell me why he would fight this other knight.'

'De Lesparre called him a coward,' I said. 'In public, before hundreds of witnesses.'

King Charles – this is Charles, fourth of that name, by the way, who had been Dauphin during the Jacquerie – nodded. 'Such a man could be arrested,' he said.

The French nobles looked pained.

'Your Grace, King Peter depends on his … *preux* to preserve his ability to lead.' I decided that a shrug was not appropriate when dealing with the King of France, especially the same King of France who'd dedicated his reign to destroying the routiers. He had to know I'd been one.

The king tilted his head slightly. 'So he will fight?' he said.

'I would expect it, Your Grace,' I said.

The king turned away, finished with me.

'If the King of Cyprus can fight a commoner,' a voice drawled, 'perhaps the mighty Duke of Savoy might condescend to face the lowly Prince of Achaea in the lists.'

I turned.

The man wasn't sitting at our pair of tables, but off to the right, with the churchmen.

He was the Bishop of Geneva. Bishop Robert – Camus's usual employer, the Count of Savoy's cousin, and Emile's cousin as well. A man who liked to pull the legs off insects.

'Unthinkable,' the King of France said.

'Oh, but my lord, surely it is unthinkable that you should seat not one but two *tard-venus* at your royal table, but there they sit like toads in a pond.' The bishop still had the same odd eyes, the same impression of viewing the world with an intense and childlike curiosity.

Of course, a great many people looked at me, and others looked at Musard. Heads craned round.

Count Amadeus yawned. 'My cousin is young, Robert,' he said. 'I do not wish to kill him, as I most certainly would if we met in the lists.'

Robert of Geneva smiled, as if he was beneficent. 'Whatever the outcome, it would save this kingdom and its courts a great deal of time and money,' he said.

Amadeus still wore his smile. 'I don't think it is a business of this kingdom,' he said.

Robert of Geneva nodded. 'Well, you should,' he said, and every one of hundreds of people listened with the greatest attention. 'Because the Prince of Achaea has presented his case to the King of France, along with his offer to do homage as the king's vassal.'

Amadeus looked at King Charles.

Charles smiled. 'A mere formality,' he said.

'Neither his holdings in Savoy nor his holdings in Morea are subject to France,' Amadeus said coldly.

'They are now,' Bishop Robert said. 'There is precedent.'

'A mere formality,' the King of France said, his smile unbroken. 'I will look into the matter, and the courts will examine the status of the prince. And Savoy.'

There it was. I didn't need it explained, and neither should you, but in a word, Savoy was an independent country – a county in rank, but a place with no overlord. The Counts of Savoy swore fealty to the Kings of France for certain towns and cities, but not for Savoy itself, just as the Prince of Wales does fealty to the King of France for Gascony but not for, say, England or Wales.

But in his bid to change his inheritance, the Prince of Achaea was willing to go to the King of France and abandon his independence. And the King of France was well known for his acquisitive ways. He would add Savoy to his kingdom.

Prince Lionel was no fool. He looked up and down the table, looked at Bohun, his principal advisor, and then cleared his throat. 'I did not think that Savoy was ever subject to France?' he asked.

King Charles smiled pleasantly. 'Let the courts decide.'

'French courts?' Amadeus of Savoy said.

'You want my cousin to be tried in your courts,' Geneva said. He smiled. 'I thought perhaps you would praise the principle. We have only done what you did.'

Amadeus sat back. 'We will see,' he said.

Geneva looked at me, and his smug superiority was like a blow.

*

On the nineteenth of April, we left Paris for Chambéry. This time, we had forty English knights, twenty French knights, almost a hundred ladies, and minstrels and servants, as well as a dozen wagons and Prince Lionel himself. We had Chaucer and Machaut and Froissart there, and a mule train of gifts.

We were the bridegroom, and we were riding through spring, to a wedding.

Count Amadeus was as cold as ice. But when we were five miles outside Paris, he rode aside from Prince Lionel and summoned me to his side with a wave.

'I will fight this Prince of Achaea,' he said.

I probably looked shocked.

He shrugged without petulance. 'It is now the best option,' he said. 'There's little use in fretting. I prayed on it last night and I have spoken with my brother-in-law, the Duke of Burgundy, and with Bonne. We all agree.'

'I understand,' I said.

'You do?' he asked.

'Your Grace, if you fight him, you will beat him, barring some evil miracle or some deception.'

'Nonetheless, your friend Fiore has the name of the best sword in Italy. Is this true?' the count asked.

I revelled in the moment at which I could make Fiore's fortune. 'Yes, my lord,' I said.

He nodded seriously. 'The prince will be at the wedding,' he said. 'Cambrai will be there as well – we're fortunate he didn't travel with us.'

'Cambrai?' I asked, wracking my brains.

'Ah. My cousin Robert, formerly Bishop of Geneva, is now Archbishop of Cambrai,' the count said. 'And will soon have a cardinal's hat.'

I sent a prayer to Heaven.

The count was looking at the distant mountains, as if very eager to be there. 'We will exchange cartels at the wedding,' he said.

I nodded.

'I will train with Monsieur Fiore. You will attend to the precautions, with Monsieur Musard.'

'Yes, Your Grace.' What else could I say?

'Musard says that you have a personal ... feud ...with this Bourc.' Amadeus of Savoy glanced at me.

'Yes, my lord,' I said.

'Hmm,' he said. 'Please tell me the basis of this feud.' He glanced at me. 'The legal basis.'

He made a business of raping nuns and turning boys into animals. That didn't seem to answer.

'My lord, among other things, he attacked the Papal Legate in Avignon,' I said. 'And he has led attacks on you, at least twice.'

'He is a routier?' the count asked.

'He serves the Archbishop of Cambrai, who has some hold over him. He has threatened me and my wife ...'

Amadeus nodded. 'Leave this to me,' he said.

We rode on. We had superb music; we ate dinners in flowering orchards and listened to Machaut's latest compositions played by his own minstrels. Lady Bonne and my Emile led all the women in the party, clad rather daringly in just their kirtles with garlands of flowers, to dance, and I was never more thankful that I had spent the winter learning, as I did my lady no disgrace and was agile enough. And Emile and I began to teach Fiore to dance; he learned very quickly, and became instantly enthusiastic on the benefits of dancing. When Fiore was engaged, he was ever an enthusiast. He actually took to lecturing me on the benefits of dance.

And here we come to the glorious first of May. We were at Ceneserey, or close to it, and the count and his lady had arranged for the local seigneurs to meet us. I didn't know them, and perhaps I was not conscious enough of where I was. Later, I realised how often I had fought over these very ridges – in fact, I had ambushed Camus here, in this very valley, when he tried to take Cardinal Talleyrand. I should have been more alert. Even as it was, though, we had vedettes out in the fields and we watched the local villeins dig us earth ovens so that the count's servants could cook us dinner. We had precautions in place.

There was also a display. The area had known ten years of peace and the local lords were inclined to show their wealth. There were tables spread in the fields, and the sun was bright and the evening long. The grass was rich and green and newly cropped, and while the count, Prince Lionel, Lord Bohun and their ladies dined at tables, the rest of us lay on the grass or ate sitting up. A dozen of us dug a table: an old routier trick where you dig two short trenches in the loam and put your feet in them; the space between with a cloth on it is a table. It was a glorious meal of game and the first fruits of spring. I particularly remember asparagus, which I do not believe I had eaten before. And then we listened to a poem by Machaut, some songs by the ladies, and even the birds sang. The sun set so slowly that it seemed that the golden twilight would never end.

And later we danced, and all of us sang together. Emile was as beautiful as I had ever seen her, and we danced until she had a sheen on her flesh and I felt drenched in sweat. Dancing is almost as much work as fighting, and there I was on a warm May night in English broadcloth and silk, with wool hose … Afterwards, she wanted a cup of wine, and I had left my little pilgrim bottle by a tree, and so we walked off into the apple trees. I put a hand on her side …

'You have converted the count,' she said, looking back. Count Amadeus was sitting with Prince Lionel as if they were old companions; Prince Lionel was telling a story, and Richard Musard was already laughing. 'Soon, he will cease to talk to me at all, and conduct all his business with you.'

'Are you angry?' I asked. I had other plans entirely, and was not expecting her tension.

She shrugged. 'No. But everyone always likes you, which I confess, my love, can be a trifle wearing.' She smiled, a little bit of the woman I had once known, with a colourful past and no great opinion of herself.

'I am only here on your sufferance,' I said.

She looked away. Then she looked back. 'If he really fights the Prince of Achaea,' she said, 'you know that Cambrai will cheat. And you know how much will hang on that fight.' She shook herself. 'I knew I should never have left Lesvos. My love, I do not enjoy being a great lady as much as I enjoyed our lemon tree. I barely see my babies – I file documents and deal with lawsuits …'

'And dance on spring evenings …' I insisted, taking her in my arms.

'Well, there is that,' she admitted.

'And flirt with your friend, the King of France,' I said.

'Hardly friends. But I have known him since … well, since about the time I met you.' She flashed a smile.

'Don't you think …?' I began. I was at a loss for words; unusual for me, I grant. 'Don't you think, as a man who began his career of arms as a cook to the archers, that it is I who might have every reason to make people like me? And that perhaps it is not so easy for me?'

She smiled, kissed me, just a brush of the lips, and then away. 'I admit that you do have some compensations,' she agreed. I realised that she had led me by the hand far from the circle of fires and the dancing, and that we were on the broad lawn of grass beyond the trees – grass deep as leaf mould and soft as a carpet.

'Red hair?' I asked. I was kissing her.

'Not the one I was thinking of,' she said.

I kissed her again.

'Do you know what the principal advantage is of wearing a green kirtle?' she asked.

'Yes,' I said. We both laughed a little, but I did know the advantage of a green kirtle, too. I began to make love to my wife; we weren't hurried, and it was the perfect spring evening …

I heard a distant voice calling '*Capitano!*'

After the third call, Emile turned her head away from my lips. 'They really want you.'

'I want *you,*' I said.

'Don't be silly,' she said, and sat up suddenly. Maybe a woman's sense of these things is better, but Marc-Antonio came running up through the woods, his sense of my location frustratingly unerring, which justified Emile's straight arm pushing me away. By then we were both standing, and she appeared slightly flushed, but otherwise almost prim. I had on a long cote-hardie as befitted my status, and it hid … well. It hid me.

'My lord!' Marc-Antonio called, beckoning to me and turning to run back towards the fires.

I gave up, turned, and sprinted after him.

By the time I reached the huddle of people in the open-air kitchen, Demetrios was dead. I was told later that he'd puked his guts out, breathed hard for a while, and then rolled on the ground, clutching his stomach in agony. His brother Stefanos sat nearby, weeping.

When I came up, he had only stopped rolling in agony by a moment; I may even have seen his last paroxysm.

The ovens were still burning. Most of the staff were either sitting around them, or standing looking at the corpse of my Greek servant, clinging to each other.

Fiore came from the other direction, running. Beside him came Peter Albin. He'd been with the count and Prince Lionel; he was increasingly welcome in the count's inner circle.

I knelt by Demetrios, felt his forehead, and felt the elasticity of him, the coolness. He was dead. He smelled foul and looked worse.

Albin sniffed once and said, 'Poison.'

I had already formed the thought. 'What did he eat?' I asked. But I didn't really have to look far. The count's silver cup that I had seen over and over since we were in Bulgaria lay on the ground, bespattered with blood and vomit.

All the wine was in pitchers; it had been brought by the local lords and provided straight into our provisions.

Fiore seemed to know what he was about. He sniffed the pitchers one by one and at the third, jerked his head back. '*Arsenico*,' he said, in Italian. Albin nodded sharply.

I heard him, but I was already running for the count.

He was lying on the ground.

I called his name, '*Amadeus!*'

He rolled over and looked at me. Sane, healthy. Later, I discovered that he was playing a jape with the prince.

He sat up.

I knelt by him. 'My lord,' I said, breathing hard, 'do not drink any wine.'

'You called me by my baptismal name,' he said, gently chiding.

'I thought ...' I paused.

He gave me an enigmatic half-smile. 'What?'

'My lord, one of the pages is dead from poison.'

He stood up, his enigmatic smile banished. 'Sweet mother of God,' he said.

He came back to Demetrios's body. Emile was there, too. We tried to hide the death from the English. Fiore was looking at the barrels.

No one knew exactly where any of the wine had come from. That is, the senior cook, who was shaking at how close his lord had come to death, thought perhaps some of the wine had come in pottery flagons, and perhaps a few pitchers had come already filled.

Fiore shook his head. 'This is too bad,' he said, a strong expression for him.

'Demetrios is dead.'

'Yes, you will find that inconvenient,' Fiore said.

In fact I'd quite liked the boy; he had promise, and he'd worked hard. And in one filched sip of wine, he was dead. Stefanos admitted, days later, that he had dared his brother to drink from the count's cup.

'I killed my brother,' Stefanos wailed.

He did, too. But he saved the count.

You didn't know that part, did you, Master Chaucer?

It says here we didn't reach Bourg-en-Bresse until the eighth of May, and Chaucer is nodding, which means that our progress was slower than that of an army of snails. I don't remember that, but then, I was in a dark place because of the boy's death and it was made darker by Sam Bibbo's quarrels with Bohun's archer captain, a big man called Hobhouse. Their quarrel was pure foolishness – or rather, was merely the usual sort of thing, men and experience and reputation.

I tried to stand aloof – Bibbo could fight his own battles. I paid no attention when I knew my horses were late coming up from a picket line; the Bohun party had moved them … I ignored the morning when the count questioned why his precedence had been changed in the line of march – I knew that Hobhouse had taken his archers to the head of the column without orders. But our fourth or fifth night on the road after Demetrios died, Hobhouse tried to take over two of our campfires under some absurd pretence of seniority. I was at one of those fires, in a nasty old wool gown, helping Marc-Antonio with our harnesses. Hobhouse came up, striding like a man of vast importance.

'Build your fires closer to your own camp,' he said. 'Get gone now – these are our fire pits.'

Marc-Antonio glanced at me.

So did Gospel Mark. None of our corporals were there, and I no doubt looked like a servant.

'No,' I said. I suspect that, despite my attempts to be chivalrous, I told him to fuck off.

He put a hand on his dagger.

'Draw that and you are a dead man,' I said. 'I am Sir William Gold, and I will, without a qualm, put your own dagger in you.'

Hobhouse narrowed his eyes. 'You ain't wearing no belt nor spurs,' he said.

I shrugged.

'I'm camp master,' he persisted.

'No,' I said, 'you are not.'

'Damn your eyes,' he said. 'I am that, made so by the earl.'

I nodded. 'I'll just visit the earl and fix that, then,' I said. I didn't change my clothes, or my level of anger, which was foolish. I did send Marc-Antonio ahead, and he darted into the earl's pavilion and a steward came out.

'The earl will see you,' he said.

I ducked through the flaps of Bohun's pavilion. The great man, for so he saw himself, was seated in a chair, reading from a book of hours. He looked up.

'William Gold,' he said. 'I remember you when you were a cook's boy.'

It wasn't said in a friendly manner. It was meant to take me down a peg.

I was too angry to care. 'Your archer,' I said.

'Hobhouse?' Bohun said. 'My captain of archers.'

As the earl had fewer archers in his train than I had in mine, I thought the title a little grandiose. 'Very well, my lord. Your captain of archers is attempting to give my men orders.'

'He is the senior archer,' Bohun said. 'I don't know your man.'

'He is not part of my retinue and, begging my lord's pardon, I command the escort of this column.'

'You are delusional,' Bohun said. 'You are some hedge knight. I am the Earl of Hereford.'

'My lord, I may be a hedge knight to you, but I am bid by the Count of Savoy, my liege lord, to protect the column. *I* have that duty, my lord, and it is specific. You are protecting the prince. We can co-operate, but I choose the camps, and your archer, my lord, has no place whatsoever in these decisions, much less waiting for my men ...'

Bohun raised his hand to silence me. 'I'm telling you—' he began.

I'm quite loud – I bore down on him. 'Waiting for my men to

build fires before he orders them away? No, lord, I will not be silent.'

Bohun was quite red in the face.

'I do not expect my arrangements to be interfered with again,' I said. 'Thanks for your courtesy, my lord.' I bowed, and left his tent.

Later that night, I was summoned by the count. He was looking at a pair of gloves, but he glanced at me.

'Tell me of your quarrel with Bohun,' he said.

I bowed. 'No quarrel, my lord. I merely explained how the column was to be commanded and directed.'

Savoy smiled. 'The prince spoke to me,' he said.

I bowed.

The count nodded. 'Well,' he said, 'I will assume this is why you Englishmen kill your kings so often. Take care, William – you have made no friend with the earl.'

I was not enjoying myself and, indeed, I spent a fair time in prayer since we buried the boy back in the orchard. Some of the younger knights would ride ahead and wait at fords and streams and pretend to be knights-errant from the romances. I had to keep my archers busy, scouting widely, as if we were on a *chevauchée*, which the local seigneurs might have resented, if the count had allowed them. I knew Camus was out there, and the easiest way for the Prince of Achaea to triumph was still to arrange the count's death. We were tasting all of his food again; we watched over him to an almost embarrassing degree. I won't even mention Lady Bonne's fury on one occasion when our watching him grew too close.

We had an enormous, and valuable, baggage train, and we were crossing some of the very country that the routiers had held, and taxed, in the fifties. I was careful to use my French knights to talk to the peasants. I had to practise all the arts of diplomacy to avoid offending Lord Bohun, now described as the 'Commander of the Prince's Escort', who imagined that I was some paid captain, often ignored me, and yet, because he had never served in the east, had not the slightest notion of the kind of care we exercised about securing our march route or our camps. And equally, as Emile was very much in looks, I began to note that a dozen or so of the English knights and squires were increasingly devoted to her. One morning, as she emerged from our pavilion to greet the day, there were five of them waiting. One had flowers, and another a pretty little hawk as a gift.

I've never been a particularly jealous man, and Emile enjoyed a little admiration. And it was a damn good hawk.

The last morning before Bourg-en-Bresse, I found a cat, its entrails pulled out and its poor body crucified carefully on a little cross of sticks stuck in the roadside. I looked at the hillsides above us.

I knew his eyes were on me that moment, so I dismounted and pissed on the ground. I knew the bastard was out there, watching us, and I knew that Bohun could have no concept of the danger.

At any rate, once we arrived in Bourg-en-Bresse we had a fine dinner in the hall of the lord, and then it proved that our preparations were inadequate and we didn't have sufficient space for people to sleep. Emile gave our room to Lord Bohun, the Earl of Hereford, because he had, somehow, been forgotten. My remaining Greek page, Stefanos, then served us well by finding us space in the loft over the stable. After some wandering back and forth, we ended up with quite a little party, with some of the best lances in France lying on hay, drinking good wine and flirting – mostly with my wife. She and her ladies were the only ones bold enough to adventure the loft, although, as Emile said in the morning, it was more spacious and comfortable than any of the rooms, and Lady Bonne, I was told, was bitten badly by bedbugs.

Every day, after we halted, the count would have a lesson with Fiore. I was privileged to see a few of them. More than once I was called upon to be the count's companion, which could be a little like being his whipping boy in a harsh school. Despite that, the service raised me in his esteem, and there were some signs of informality in his regard. He stopped calling me by my title, and he began to mention me in the kind of tone he used about Richard – part serious, part mocking.

Let me add, here, the thing Froissart wants me to say: he was an excellent man with his hands. He was a near-perfect jouster, and as good a blade as I ever hope to have to face. Fiore had his measure quickly enough, but the count was quite able.

'Do you enjoy teaching him?' I asked Fiore. It was in the stable at Bourg, I think.

'For the count, I am more of a guide than a teacher,' he said. 'He is a fully formed knight – he has some profound thoughts and practices. Indeed, I have to work to defeat him.'

As usual, Fiore's manner suggested that he didn't have to work very hard to defeat the rest of us, which was, for the most part, true. But it's never really pleasant to hear.

The count was pleased with Fiore too. I enjoyed watching the two of them practise, and it was on these spring evenings that I saw what I still think is the full evolution of Fiore's theory. If theologians can have theories, so can swordsmen. He taught the count a system to make use of crossings, reducing a complex jumble of half-instinctive judgements on close fighting to a game.

By close play, I mean those times when you and your opponent are close enough to touch each other with a bare or gauntleted hand. In armour, it is often essential to play for a grapple or a throw, rarer in battle than in the lists, but such techniques can be the difference between life and death, and Fiore was a fine wrestler and applied many of his wrestling lessons to the sword and even to jousting.

Finally, three days later, we reached Chambéry. The town was hung with banners; the cathedral church had a magnificent High Mass, and we had a feast on the evening of our arrival that was only barely exceeded by the still more lavish entertainment the next day.

But before the feast, there was jousting. The count formed a team from his own knights, and for the first time I was invited to serve with him. He led his team in person, and his jousts were open to all comers. He had a purse and a fine prize for the winner.

Boucicault captained the *venans*, or the visiting team. Humphrey de Bohun, the Earl of Hereford, who had been at Alexandria (although I'd seen him but twice) and who had served both with and against Hawkwood and the White Company, was pleased to joust, and he had a dozen English men-at-arms. They did not want to join with Boucicault's team, and so a second team of *venans* was formed in defiance of the custom. Both Boucicault and Bohun made it clear that they wished to break a lance with the count.

The heralds and marshals had it all in hand, and there, as I remember, Master Chaucer came into his own, organising the pairings for the jousts and accepting no dissent.

My first opponent was one of Bohun's knights: a very young man with a firm seat and an expensive horse. We ran three fairly unexceptional courses. He played very conservatively, and he was too good a rider to be unhorsed, although we both broke our lances into showers of splinters each pass.

Count Amadeus didn't quite unhorse Bohun, but he did lay him back over his crupper, and I know that he hit the earl so stoutly that he didn't choose to come back into the lists for the rest of the day. Boucicault ran three passes with my lord count, and both of them looked like heroes from the Grail tales, but only the lances were injured.

It was not my best day. I was not unhorsed, but I lost a stirrup on one pass, and Gabriel and I were almost knocked down by a French knight on an elephantine horse. Still, at the end of the day, Boucicault put an armoured arm around me.

'I remember when you could scarcely get the lance into the rest under your arm,' he said. 'Now you are deadly.'

I probably blushed like a maiden – praise from such as Boucicault is praise indeed. This was a man who trained every day, and climbed ladders in armour for exercise. I wondered what he might be like running a few courses with Fiore.

My curiosity was not to be fulfilled. One of the English squires took a lance in the throat – he wasn't killed, but he was badly injured, and the count declared the day's sport at an end. A parade of pages in emerald green appeared, including my young Greek, drafted for the duty. Each boy had a goblet of solid silver, and every jouster received his goblet, full to the brim with red wine.

The count was just drinking his, toasting Prince Lionel, when a messenger, covered in mud to the waist, pressed his horse into the lists. Men cursed him; some were there in velvet-covered brigandines and corazinas, and they didn't need to be spattered in spring mud.

I was still basking in Boucicault's praise when I realised that the messenger under all the mud was de la Motte, one of my own men-at-arms from the old days, who was serving with Sir John Hawkwood.

He bowed to the count.

'My lord,' he said. Everyone fell silent.

'My lord, Count Bernabò has sent me to beg you to come with all your strength.' De la Motte glanced at me.

'What has happened?' Amadeus asked.

'My lord, the Pope has marched by way of Mantua, and the Holy Roman Emperor has crossed the Alps and bid defiance to Verona and Milan. Count Bernabò has taken the army into the field. Sir John

Hawkwood has been at the gates of Mantua since the first of May.' De la Motte was well-born; he knew how to speak to a nobleman, and he was clear and distinct.

The count glanced around, but his eye fell on me.

'I will send an advance guard immediately,' he said.

PART III

MILAN

May 1368 – July 1368

We had a hasty council that evening. Stacked like cut firewood, the problems confronting us appeared too thick for any axe: assassins hunting the count; the possibility of war, open or hidden, with the Prince of Achaea; and now, the reality of the war we all thought had been avoided – open war between the Holy Roman Emperor and the Pope on one hand, and the Milanese and the Green Count on the other.

But the count was a good lord and a good captain, and his plan was reasonable. He kept Richard Musard to direct his own protection, and sent me east with all the knights he could spare, and my own company, to join Bernabò and Sir John under the walls of Mantua.

He gave me only young knights with good squires: twenty lances of Savoyards, without archers, but good young men, most of whom had been to Bulgaria and the east, and their squires, who were often older men with more experience of war. He ordered them to muster the next morning, which would have been the morning of the thirteenth of May, and they surprised me by being attentive to their duty. They all had warhorses and riding horses, with mules for fodder and oats.

I kissed Emile in the courtyard of the count's palace, in front of Prince Lionel and the count and the earl, and she leaned over and kissed my ear. 'I'm pregnant again, sir knight,' she said. 'Try not to be away this time.'

I laughed.

'Come home,' she said. 'My feet get cold without you, and I'm too old to find another lover.' She smiled, and I loved her – oh, God, how I remember that parting – and my lances formed, and the count …

Bah. Never mind. It was a good day: the promise of a great adventure, and the honour of leading such a brave little force, almost two hundred men.

The great war had come. I was as eager as an old warhorse at the smell of wood smoke and warm wool. I'd had a long winter of comfort. I'd been a courtier and, to be fair, I had very much enjoyed some of it – the dancing, the time with Emile.

But this was war – a great war fought by the greatest captains. The count was raising his whole host. It was his plan to demand the service of the Prince of Achaea, so that he could keep the man where he could see him. And it was in his head that if Achaea came and served, they'd patch it up. I think he was wrong; Richard and I knew how constant the attempts had been, and I still do not think that the count believed in Achaea's willingness to kill him.

I didn't have to worry about any of that. I merely had to cross Lombardy as fast as I could. The count would come with a feudal host, and a bridegroom, and Emile; he would be weeks behind me.

I bowed, vaulted into my saddle, waved to my wife, and we rode forth in a column of four men abreast, led by Sam Bibbo, who was proud as Pontius Pilate. The moment we were clear of the gates, I had archers out in front and on my flanks, and a rearguard of picked knights led by Francesco Gatelussi. Our baggage was on mules, between the two bodies of men-at-arms, with Fiore in command. Every man, from knight to page, had three horses. We had a letter from the count for fodder and oats across Savoy, and we went like the west wind. We didn't stop at the monastery the first day, and indeed, our winter march seemed like a snail's pace against our spring ride – forty Roman miles a day or more.

The count had warned me that his cousin, the Lord of Montferrat, might try to oppose us – ironic, as he had been my first employer in Italy, when I was with the White Company. I was careful to pay for everything as we crossed his lands, and he, in turn, ignored us, or perhaps our passage was so rapid that he didn't have time to react. We spent a night in Turin, but I had the men in their saddles at dawn the next day, regardless of whatever pleasures Turin might have offered, and we were away along the Via Francigena towards Pavia. We rode from Turin to Pavia in a single day, across the endless sunny expanse of Lombardy on a good, if dusty, road – twelve hours in the saddle. But the Visconti, however strange their family, took good care of their soldiers, and they had been forewarned of our coming, and there were beds in inns for the men, a room at the castle for me and Fiore, and stables for jaded horses.

I rested my people a day at Pavia. It was an odd day, as I was nearly exhausted and had endless work to do, gathering supplies and replacing anything that could be replaced – every broken sword blade and lost buckle. Galeazzo Visconti sent for me himself and stressed to me the desperation of his brother Bernabò's position: he and Hawkwood, with the Veronese, had attacked Mantua, trying to take the Gonzaga city off the board before the Pope's army could come up. At the same time, the Holy Roman Emperor's army was coming down from the north – fifty thousand horses by some reports.

Let's consider this a moment, friends. Here's Mantua, or Mantova, as the Italians say. Here's the Emperor, above it, with fifty thousand men; here's the Pope in the south, with at least fifteen thousand; here's Bernabò and Hawkwood at Mantua, just south of the gates, with perhaps eight thousand men. Bernabò's closest ally is on the wrong side of the Alps.

At odds of seventy thousand to ten thousand, near enough, my two hundred might not seem very important, and indeed, they might not have been. But Milan was raising its excellent city militias, and they were just starting to march east. Thousands of men with crossbows and handgonnes, or great pavises and heavy spears. All of them had good armour; Brescia, Pavia and Milan were the centre of the armour industry across all the Latin lands. The Moors and the Turks prized Milanese armour. And every Milanese pavisier had a coat of plates, a kettle helmet and a good shirt of maille on his back; iron gauntlets on his hands, too.

Be all that as it may, it was a sobering interview with Galeazzo. I had not previously seen the counts of the Visconti as vulnerable men, with normal emotions, but now I saw Galeazzo rub his hands together far too often, and stare off into space before answering.

As I rose to leave, he waved me back. 'Give my son a sword lesson,' he said.

As I say, an odd day. I went to find Fiore, and then we went looking for his son, Gian Galeazzo, and found him in a window bower in the huge, old stone fortress. It's gone now, replaced by the glorious brick castle that the Visconti built after the war, but that stone pile was gloomy and had an air of tragedy about it at the best of times.

Perhaps the building made the men, because that air of desperation, of torment … The Visconti device said it all, the viper with a man in his mouth …

Perhaps I don't want to say it. Chaucer knows, and Froissart.

I found Gian Galeazzo with his sister, Violante. She was flushed, but her eyes were empty, like many a man I've known who's seen too much horror and too much war. They were odd, sad eyes on a thirteen-year-old girl. Her hair was unwashed, and lank, and she would not meet my eye.

Gian Galeazzo smiled at me. 'Swordplay, messer?' he asked, as if I had not found him tormenting his sister.

I indicated Fiore, who led him away to the room over the vast stables. I turned to Violante, bowed, and made a *reverentia*.

'My lady,' I said, 'may I be of service?'

She shook her head silently.

'My lady?' I asked.

She wouldn't look at me – shrunk away as if I had offered to strike her.

'Let me help you,' I said.

She smiled. It was a terrible smile – purposeful and bleak together.

'You could kill me,' she said. Then she ran.

Blessed Virgin Mary, that's what she said. And then, while Gian Galeazzo swaggered swords with me an hour later, I slipped in my fatigue, and my wooden waster clipped him on the thumb, a sloppy blow at a sloppy cover, as too often happens. I didn't break his thumb, but it swelled up like an apple.

He didn't cry or whine. He was no simple villain; he was, in fact, very brave. But after Fiore had looked at it he said, turning to me, 'You could do me a great favour, my lord.'

I bowed. 'I am not a lord,' I said.

'You hold a barony on Cyprus, and Prince Francesco has granted you another,' he said. 'My father told me this, that I would judge you by your worth. Tell me, messer – what can I do to stop this English lordling from coming to marry my sister?'

It was, in its own way, as shocking as Violante's request. 'My lord?' I asked.

'Come,' he said, 'I do not want this marriage. My father will not listen to me. How can I keep this Englishman away?'

'My lord, he is mere days behind me on the road,' I said.

He tried to flex his thumb. 'It is her fault,' he said. 'She is so beautiful.'

Later, I lay on a fine bed, with Fiore on the next one. I had drunk off three cups of wine. Fiore was staring at his bed hangings, which were, as I remember, Arthurian.

'What did he mean, *it is her fault*?' Fiore asked quietly, as darkness came down across the fields of Lombardy.

I remember thinking about Fiore – about how he was. 'I do not wish to discuss it,' I said, after careful consideration.

'Ah,' he said, into the darkness. After a while, when the tumble of my thoughts had almost calmed, he spoke again.

'Do you not think it odd,' he said, 'that, for the most part, we like the Pope, and that the Visconti are so obviously loathsome, and that the Emperor made us knights, and the count has, let us be honest, barely noticed our existence – yet here we are, about to ride to war for the Visconti and the count, against the Holy Roman Emperor and the Pope?'

I lay there, wishing I had Emile to deal with the Visconti girl. Emile had had a darkness in her; she had overcome it, but I knew that girls could have as much darkness as men, perhaps more. Emile would know how to talk to Violante – I was sure of it.

I thought of Fiore's question.

'Listen, my friend,' I said.

'I am listening,' he said. 'It's too dark to see.'

I probably sighed. 'Listen, then. When you go to fight in a tournament, what is the purpose of the tournament?'

'Practice?' Fiore asked.

I should have expected that would be Fiore's answer. 'What would the purpose of a tournament be to a Ramon Llull, or de Charny?' I asked.

Fiore's bed creaked as his weight shifted. 'Practice?' he asked.

'No, no. It is honour. A tournament is a fountain of honour. It is an honour merely to be allowed to fight, an honour to participate, and more honour to fight well, to be seen to be skilled and brave. Yes?'

I could hear him breathing. 'Honour in winning,' he said.

'Honour in just going and fighting,' I insisted. 'You risk your life and your fortune, and you gain honour.'

'I suppose,' he admitted. And after a pause, the new, thoughtful Fiore said, 'Yes, I admit it. I agree.'

'So it does not matter what team you are on in the mêlée or who you joust against, does it?' I asked.

Fiore laughed. 'Of course it matters. I may be on a team of fools, or may have to joust against Nerio or you or …' He made his bed creak again. 'That's not what you mean, is it?'

'No,' I said.

'So you are suggesting that we needn't enquire into the justice of a war, or the character of the captains – war is a great tournament, and it is an honour to participate?'

I lay there a while.

'Are you asleep?' Fiore asked.

'No,' I said. 'I'm thinking that I'm a witless fool, and you have the right of it.'

I could hear him laughing. 'I do?'

'Of course we should enquire into the justice of a war …' I said. 'But we are also mercenaries.'

'Oh!' Fiore said. 'Of course. That makes it all right.'

'You spent too much time arguing with Nerio,' I said.

'Why?' Fiore asked.

'Because you sound just like him,' I said.

The sun was not three fingers clear of the flat plain of Lombardy when we rode out of Pavia. A day's rest had done wonders for our horses, but I didn't press them. We couldn't hope to make the new fortified camp south of Mantua in one day, even a twelve-hour day, and I disliked entering enemy country so precipitously. So instead we halted just after noon at Cremona, still inside Milanese territory, and I went the rounds of all my men, sending them to bed early with a minimum of wine and a good meal. I inspected the horses with Sam Bibbo.

'I could ha' handled that blowhard, Hobhouse,' he said suddenly.

I nodded. 'No doubt,' I said.

'Bernabò's a right bastard,' he said, glancing at me to see how I'd take this.

I remember laughing in the anonymous darkness of the stable. 'Sam, his nickname is "The Beast".'

Bibbo laughed too. 'Aye. Well. He comes by it honestly, is all.' He pointed out some spur-galls on one of the Savoyard horses, and then said, 'I like serving the count. He's a decent eno' soul.'

That was true, too. It had taken me a year to think of him warmly, and it had come by stages, but ...

'I like him fine,' I said.

'No one likes Bernabò,' Bibbo said. 'They're afraid of him. He's Camus, but with more power.'

'Jesu,' I said. I crossed myself, and then said, 'But we'll be with Sir John.'

Sam Bibbo looked troubled. 'Aye,' he said.

The next day was damp; the sun rose red in the east and the rain began while the shadows should still have been long. We were already a-horse, moving along a broad, sandy road that ran almost due east towards the distant impression of mountains or low clouds in the distance. I had Milanese guides – four wealthy peasants on ponies – and I gave each of them two gold Venetian ducats and promised as many more when we met up with Bernabò, a name which made every one of them cross themselves.

We had thirty miles to go. We were away early, moving through country that was ostensibly friendly with almost fifty lances – about two hundred men, and let me say what a terrible number that is. Not enough men to fight a stand-up battle or even to face a real army, but too many to slip by unnoticed or take cover, for example, in a barn or set of outbuildings.

So I sent all of our archers and pages – at least, the boys who spoke Italian – away on a broad front, just as we would have on a *chevauchée* against the French. The archers formed a sort of wide bow in front of us, bent in an arc, and we came up behind in a tight column, moving along the Mantua road. I stayed back with the baggage and with Fiore – the centre of the column is where a commander ought to be. I didn't need Vegetius to tell me that. We had one of the guides with us, and there was another with Bibbo, and the last two were kept apart, one with the advance guard, which was with l'Angars, and one with the rearguard, under Gatelussi. This was Hawkwood's system:

to keep the guides separate so they couldn't conspire. I also had my pilgrim itinerary – here's the page I used that day. See how it has been wet? We got a rain shower mid-morning, just as Bibbo rode in to show me the lie of the land. The next village was San Giovanni in Croce – see here? With the little cross for a church?

I climbed that church steeple while we watered our horses and everyone changed. We were fifteen miles from Mantua, and we hadn't seen an enemy. But we were north of the River Po, and Bernabò and Sir John were, at least nominally, south of it.

The plain in front of us rolled on like the plain of Heaven: fertile agriculture and rich villages as far as the eye could see, hills to the north, and the valley of the Po to the south. Mid-May: everything was green, and the clouds were breaking after the morning's rain.

I questioned three of my guides. All of them agreed that there was a bridge at Casalmaggiore, and that Bernabò had the castle, or had a week before.

I've mentioned before what command is really about. It sounds simple, taking two hundred men from Chambéry to Mantua in spring. Two hundred men, six hundred horses and mules, three tons of supplies; crossing the Alps, crossing the plains of Lombardy, and picking the right route to meet up with our allies. A spiderweb of paths and roads, some wide, some narrow; bridges out from spring floods, or places where no bridge had ever been built and the banks were collapsing; bedbugs and surly villagers; men-at-arms with a taste for felony, or merely a desire to quarrel with each other or some girl's father; cooks who have forgotten their olive oil; permissions for our men-at-arms or our slatterns to go to local churches; archers who steal chickens or chalices; and lost horses. Found horses! One day I noted that our horse herd had grown by a noticeable amount and, upon questioning, Gospel Mark revealed that he and Ewan had 'found' a dozen fine riding horses, all bearing the marks of the Visconti.

I won't make a chronicle of it, but when I stood in the steeple of San Giovanni in Croce, the whole burden of my next move was on me. I was not a great captain; I was a man with fifty lances, half of which were not even his own. The responsibility weighed on me. Not to mention the concerns about my pregnant wife, Camus, the murder of Demetrios, the possibilities of assassination . . .

'I want to go south, to the river,' I said.

Fiore, who was with me, was trying not to look down. Somehow, I had known him for years and not realised that he was averse to heights. It was comic; Fiore had so few flaws that it was, in a way, good to know he had this one.

'Good,' he said. 'I think I will go down and see to my horses.'

'You think south is the way to go?' I asked. I admit it – I was keeping him in the steeple.

'*Certo*,' he muttered. Then he realised that he had to go *down* the ladder and he baulked.

Bibbo was looking under his hand. 'I don't know,' he said with real hesitation. 'I was here in '65, but I don't remember, right enough.'

No one was going to help me. I looked at my pilgrim itinerary, and it was no help at all – it didn't name any village after San Giovanni until Mantua.

'South,' I said.

Then, somewhat cruelly, I said to Fiore, 'Shall I go first?'

He was taking off his sabatons.

Heh.

We got down out of the tower well enough, and let me tell you that climbing a church tower in plate legs and sabatons is more exercise than a man facing battle needs to have.

I came down, drank watered wine with Gatelussi, gave the orders, and my column turned south. I left Gatelussi in San Giovanni for as long as it took Lapot to say three *Credos*, so that if someone came at us suddenly from the east, we were prepared.

No one came at us. It was hot, and the sun was suddenly brilliant, and men were winding turbans around their heads.

Bibbo appeared a little before midday. 'Men across the river,' he said. 'Trying to stay hidden.'

There was no way we could stay hidden. 'Try crossing at the ford. Send a pair of scouts – send Ewan ...'

'Aye, Sir William,' he said with a half-smile, to indicate that he had been directing scouts, foragers and village-burners longer than I'd been alive.

I heard his horn ten minutes later, while picking sausage gristle out of my teeth with my pricker, and I ordered the column forward. I assumed, correctly, that any men on the south bank of the Po were our own – but imagine the pleasure of my surprise when I realised it was Sir Giannis and his dozen *stradiotes*.

We shared a well-armoured embrace.

'You, here?' I said, or words to that extent.

He gave a minute, Greek shrug. 'Eh,' he said, expressively. 'De Mézzières has no use for us, and the Emperor is still in Constantinople. A man must eat. I had your letter last autumn . . .' He shrugged.

'Tell me the lie of the land,' I said.

He raised an arm. 'Our main camp is at Guastalla, just a few miles. We have an earthwork fortress a few more miles to the east – Borgoforte, they call it. Hawkwood crossed to the river at dawn, intending to raid into the suburbs of Mantua. But some militia said they saw armour in the west, and Lord Bernabò sent me.'

'We are not expected?' I asked, thinking of Galeazzo's messengers.

Giannis shook his head. 'Not for weeks,' he said.

'And the Emperor?' I asked.

'Close. But north of the Po.' Giannis smiled. 'To me, you understand, there is only one Emperor, the Emperor of Constantinople. Not this *Holy Roman* one.'

We turned east on yellow dirt roads south of the Po. We passed Guastalla, where we watered our horses. The camp was large, for ten thousand men, and more Milanese militia were expected every day. But Lord Bernabò was at Borgoforte. Lord Cangrande of Verona – one of the endless della Scala family – exchanged gossip with Father Angelo for a few minutes and then begged us to ride east in haste.

'There is fighting,' Lord Cangrande said.

We changed horses again, and before Nones we were at Borgoforte, a fine position with a huge, round earthwork *bastide* and a swarm of peasants digging to add outworks to the north while forty men put stakes into the top of the ramparts. It was a formidable work, dominating the north shore of the ford across from the sand flats on the south bank. Bernabò, never a man for half measures, had put a bridge of boats across at his ford. Altogether, it was very like Roman works I had heard described by Petrarca.

We rode up to the riverbank and Giannis gave the password for the bridge, and just as I was thinking of Petrarca, there he was – the most remarkable example of that kind of premonition I have ever experienced. He was in a boat, a long riverboat, which was being held by the officer in charge of the bridge. L'Angars was just taking the advance guard across. I rode down the bank to the edge of the water.

'Maestro!' I called out, and Petrarca looked up from the book he was reading.

'Messer Guglielmo!' he called. I dismounted and walked out on the plank laid to his riverboat, and we exchanged pleasantries, and I had the delight of showing him how closely the bridge and *bastide* resembled the description he himself had read aloud to me from Vitruvius the Architect, years before in Venice when I lay, half-dead, recovering from d'Herblay's assault.

The maestro laughed. 'I was sitting here reading,' he said. 'And I never noticed this at all. And perhaps, to me, the reality is disappointing. So dirty – so many animals and sweating men.'

'Ah, but *illustrio*, those Romans must have sweated like pigs to build the Pantheon, or a marching camp.' I made him laugh. 'What are you doing here, in the middle of a war?'

'I am on my way to decorate the illustrious wedding of the Princess Violante and your English Duke of Clarence,' he said, and I laughed aloud.

'My wife will be there by now,' I said. 'Send her my regards.'

We parted with goodwill, and later I sent him two good bottles of wine from the camp.

My next meeting was not so pleasant. I'd seen the bustle of men across the river. I was surprised to see so few soldiers, and almost no men-at-arms. But as I crossed the bridge, I saw a clump of armoured men on big horses near the bridge, and I rode up to find Gatelussi nose to nose with Lord Bernabò.

Fiore caught me before I joined the group. 'There's fighting to the north. They want us to go.'

Forewarned is forearmed.

I had never met Bernabò, but he had every reason to be called 'The Beast'. He was huge – a hand taller than six feet, as tall as King Edward but wider and thicker – and the warhorse he bestrode was the size of a small elephant. He had thick black hair that grew even from his nose and ears, and a double-forked black beard that made him look more than a little like Satan.

'You are the English knight who gave Gian Galeazzo a sword

lesson?' he asked. 'See? I know you. Now I need you to ride north. There is fighting – I have no men.'

In fact, he was surrounded by men. He had almost two thousand men-at-arms for the garrison of the great round earthwork, and another eighteen hundred militia, mostly working as labourers.

'Do you doubt me, Englishman?' the giant belted out. Every word he said, he shouted. And the men around him were lickspittles.

It wasn't worth debating; Sir John was in trouble, and we were to hand. Something was wrong, but I wasn't going to sort it out there and then.

'Let's go,' I said. I turned to Giannis. 'Will you stay with me?'

He gave that enigmatic little smile he often used. I never really learned what it meant, since I've seen him do the same in moments of great emotion. '*Certo.*'

I rode along the column and ordered Sam to wheel them from column into line, and I pulled my first and last divisions across the road so that we were a three-sided box with me in the middle.

'Our old friend Sir John Hawkwood is in trouble,' I said. 'And we're just in time to take care of that. Listen to orders and don't get carried away. The Mantuans won't have anything the Turks didn't have.'

Most of them laughed.

'Double pay?' Lapot asked.

'If we win, I expect there will be double pay,' I called out, and men nodded, pulling at gauntlets and checking the hang of their swords and the length of their stirrups.

This was where high training counted, and our superb horse herd, the product of campaigning in the Holy Land almost two years before. Every man changed horses. The knights and men-at-arms mounted *fresh* chargers, and the archers and pages mounted fresh rounceys, although the old veteran archers like Ewan had Arabs – better horses than many a knight.

Giannis went off immediately, probing north from the lines beyond the earthwork fortress. His dozen Greeks spread out.

It was a little less than ten Roman miles to Mantua. We could move fast, and we did; our horses were fresh, and we had practised moving behind the screen of our light horse.

We found the first corpses an hour after Nones – a dozen dead men who seemed to be Mantuan militia – and Richard Grice with three archers, watching some prisoners. I knew Grice; he'd been one of my lances in my first *condotta*, and he was as pleased to see me as I him, and de la Motte as well – the two of them had been virtually inseparable.

'I'm worried,' Grice said. 'We hit the Hungarians at midday and blew through them. But Sir John followed them north, and he ain't been back.' He looked at de la Motte. 'Did Bernabò get my messages?'

I shook my head. Grice had a bad sword cut on his left wrist – not severed, but angry and red and still bleeding through the woman's shift wrapped around it like a bandage.

'Fetch me Master Albin,' I said. The Mantuan militiamen were sullen. The two captured Hungarians were staring blankly into space, and there was little to be got by interrogating them.

I looked north. The shadows were getting long; Mantua was still three or four miles away.

I hated to lose a man, but Grice was in too precarious a position to be left. Any city patrol would snap him up, retake his prisoners and take all of Sir John's wounded.

For that matter, most of the Savoyard pages, while they had crossbows, were too young for field service, and had no armour and little training. But they'd look like a decent body of horse at a distance.

'Messer Albin,' I called. He had just rewrapped Grice's bandage after applying some pressure and a hasty stitch – not something you want to watch every day.

'Sir William,' he said, correctly. In the face of the enemy, a little courtesy is very useful.

'Peter, I would like you to take command of the wounded and our Savoyard pages, and retreat to Borgoforte. I can give you twenty young men and forty horses. But I need to move.'

Albin, who was dismounted, bowed. 'I deem it an honour,' he said.

I nodded, and called the pages out of the ranks. Then we went forward. Indeed, Giannis had never stopped moving, and we went a mile, and then we could see Mantua, the way you can see London when you come in from the east, across the Lea.

We crested a very shallow ridge, and there was John Hawkwood.

Probably easiest if I explain what had happened to him. He'd gone north at dawn to raid the suburbs. It was not his first attempt on

Mantua, and the Mantuans had laid an ambush with almost their full army, four thousand men, in a wide, shallow 'V', with the Hungarians as the bait. But the Hungarians got too far away, as men will do, and thought they'd lay their own ambush, making everything too complicated. William Boson, one of Hawkwood's corporals that I didn't know, caught the Hungarians, or caught sight of them, and Hawkwood, the fox, manoeuvred out onto the plain and came along the fields, keeping the woods between him and the Hungarians. His surprise was complete, which sounds impossible, and no body of Turks would ever have been taken so. He took twenty captives and as many Mantuan militiamen, who had no business there anyway, and he went off after the rest, hoping to deprive Gonzaga of the whole of the Hungarian *banda*.

Then he had the luck of the devil. He went right into the ambush – and galloped straight out the back. It had been set too shallow, and the Hungarians could not rally. Hawkwood's men-at-arms, formed very close, rode through the ambush without losing a man.

So far so good, but now Sir John and his hundred lances had four thousand men behind them. Sir John turned east, hoping to simply ride around the wing of the ambush, but four thousand men take up a great deal of space, and Hawkwood had taken losses clawing his way free from the suburbs. Men told me later that the fighting was house to house, yard to yard, and never a chance to rally, with the flanks crumbling all the time.

As the sun began to set, Sir John began to lose his rearguard. He was clear of the suburbs, in the fields north and east of Mantua, around Parenza, south of the Mincio river. He was losing horses to an endless shower of crossbow shafts. He had the whole army of Mantua chasing him, and he'd lost almost a quarter of his *compagnia.* Just south of Parenza, the fox made his stand. He found two woods, like a good Englishman, and dismounted his men-at-arms between them and put his archers behind them, with some pages and squires off on one flank to keep the Mantuans from going around the woods.

I knew none of this at the time, but I didn't need to know. I came over the shallow ridge, with Giannis up ahead, pointing with his sabre, so I knew something was up. I could see Mantua, and Pietole, a big suburb, off to the east. Just in front of me were the two woods, so that I was coming up behind Hawkwood.

I was also coming up behind the body of Mantuan men-at-arms closing on Hawkwood's rear.

Here's why training matters. We were in the right place, at the right time, but we were only there because we'd crossed three hundred Roman miles in a matter of days. As the sun set on our seventh day from Savoy, we were well closed up, on fresh horses, and every head was turned towards me, ready for orders.

'Bibbo!' I called. 'Archers on you, follow Sir Giannis! Giannis, off to the left now, and cover us.'

Half a smile, and a twitch of the sabre; his eyes were already on the ground to his left, which was almost black with Mantuan infantry. There appeared to be thousands of them ... because there were. But they were in no order at all. I could see clumps of banners all across the plain, and indeed, later I heard that many of the better armoured men had already walked home to eat their suppers.

Militia.

'Knights!' I called. The Savoyards looked like avenging angels; the men who had been to Jerusalem looked bored. But very proficient.

We had forty lances, and I made two lines from the column of march. I put the best lances around me, and put l'Angars in charge of the second line.

I turned to Lapot, who had our banner of the Virgin. 'Let's see her,' I said, and he unfurled our flag.

I didn't order them to cheer. But our little Virgin had been across the world, and the Virgin is the patroness of the Savoyards, too, and they let forth a shout like the crack of a trebuchet.

Fiore was next to me, naturally. Who else would I want on my right?

He looked at me and grinned. 'At times like this, I miss Nerio,' he said.

'And Miles,' I agreed.

'This will be very good,' Fiore said.

The battle was laid out before us, and we were eager for it. We manoeuvred at a trot, where our opponents, with their backs to us, could at best manoeuvre at a walk. I suppose that for the first two hundred paces they might have imagined that we were Imperial knights come to aid them, or some such – men believe what they want to believe. But even after we went from the trot to a heavy gallop, they didn't turn.

I unhorsed two men without breaking my lance, and used it on my third opponent somewhat unchivalrously, sweeping it like an oar across the backs of two squires. One fell, and my sharp point caught the withers of the second horse and it tossed its rider in the air.

The Mantuans burst away in all directions. They had been forming, cautiously, and laboriously, for a finishing blow at Hawkwood, but we'd won the race. And now we were in a different contest: there were fortunes to be made, because we were unhorsing the very cream of the Mantuan nobility. We were only forty horses, but the surprise was complete, and our archers and pages and Greeks made us look like twice our numbers, moving to cut the men-at-arms off from the Mantua road.

The whole line broke.

At my back, Marc-Antonio, bless him, scooped up both of my dismounted opponents, and while I was cantering across the open ground into the rear of Sir John's position, he was making himself wealthy by knocking down fleeing Mantuan knights. I will admit that I lost my company in the next half an hour. If a new force had threatened us, we'd all have been taken, and not a man was going to obey me – even l'Angars.

Sir John was sitting in the setting sun, his armour brilliantly polished. He was calm, if a little grim-looking, but he managed a smile as I came up.

'Will Gold,' he said, 'as I live and breathe.'

We watched the Mantuans race for their walls together. William Boson, who had a bad cut across his nose because he had no visor, gave orders, and Hawkwood's weary archers got on jaded rounceys.

'A bad day's work,' Hawkwood said bitterly.

'We'll share our ransoms,' I said.

Hawkwood nodded slowly. 'You're a good lad,' he said.

Three days of prisoner exchanges followed. We were paid our ransoms on the spot, for knights taken within sight of their city walls, and we traded all of our Mantuan infantry for Sir John's men lost in the fighting in the suburbs. It was all very civilised.

I went north and east twice – once with twenty of our men and Giannis, and again with Sir John.

We jogged along over empty country north of the Mincio, moving fast so that we wouldn't be caught out by enemy patrols. We saw nothing.

'Where the fuck is the Emperor?' Sir John said. He was angry, tense and very tired.

I had never seen him like this. He was dispirited. Finally, after we recrossed the river, I offered him my flask. 'What's wrong, John?' I asked quietly.

He looked at me. 'I don't know, exactly,' he said. 'Thanks again for the rescue, by the way. Don't think I'm too fucking proud to admit I was rescued.' He spat.

I could tell it rankled. The whole army was talking of our daring rescue. Bernabò sent me a purse of money; Cangrande sent me a pretty arming sword in a velvet scabbard.

Hawkwood fumed.

Men are men. He was the best soldier I have ever known, and he was used to having the acclaim. He probably took it for granted. I saw him considering, but I'd like to think his friendship for me won out over any injury he fancied I'd done his reputation.

'Listen, Will,' he said. 'A week ago we had a riot – English against Germans. Some of the Milanese sided with the Germans. Men were killed.' He shrugged. 'I sent Antonio Visconti to Bernabò to plead our case; he hasn't spoken to me since. And he sent me on that raid ...'

'And abandoned you,' I said.

Sir John reached down and half-drew his sword. He plucked a scrap of parchment from the blade, where it had been cunningly hidden.

It wasn't much bigger than a dagger blade, that scrap of parchment, and on it, written in scribal Latin, was a description of Hawkwood's company, their march order, and the route from Borgoforte to Mantua.

'Jesu,' I said.

'We had it off one of the Mantuan militia,' Hawkwood said. 'But a dozen of the prisoners knew that they had a spy—'

'You were sold out!' I said.

Hawkwood nodded. 'Occupational hazard,' he said. 'But I'll tell you, young William, I am tired of untrustworthy employers and foolish antagonism. And Germans. I think most of the German men-at-arms in service to Milan are still loyal to their Holy Roman Emperor. The Pope has excommunicated all the Visconti – men are deserting.'

'They say the Emperor has fifty thousand men,' I said.

'Yes,' Hawkwood agreed. 'Yes, they say that, but where in Hell are they?'

It was Giannis who found the Holy Roman Emperor. He had moved much further south than we expected – still on the north bank of the Po, he was actually south and east of us, at Ficarolo, forty miles away. It was there, not in the north, that the Papal army met the Emperor's. And it was there that a skirmish happened that helped determine the course of the whole war.

It was unplanned. Hawkwood went east, on the south bank of the Po, with my whole company and with most of his, and Sir Giannis and his stradiotes. We made a camp in the fields south of Carbonara, and ate noodles, and drank wine. The weather was beautiful, and we kept outposts all night – I checked them myself. The solution to any tension between me and Sir John was simply to accept his orders. My little company joined his, and in the process I learned that one of his many points of bitterness was that Bernabò had only hired him with forty lances, as if he was a captain of little account, whereas some of the German captains had five hundred lances, and yet would not risk leaving the *bastide*.

But with the addition of my people, and the Savoyards, and Giannis, he had more than a hundred lances, enough power to risk activity in the open ground, especially on our side of the river. And let me add that while our lord Bernabò was very clever at finding pretty peasant girls and forcing their fathers to put them in his bed, he wasn't much as a general. The man's sexual appetite was incredible, and the day after I brought back Sir John's people from Mantua, he interrupted a meeting of his officers to entertain himself with a girl – nor did he trouble to hide his activities from us. I'm no prude, but this is not the behaviour of a captain in the field. I've said before that whatever Sir John's preferences, I never saw a woman in his tent, nor anyone else but his squires.

I've left my road, as is so often true – in this case to say that Sir John led us east on his own account, as much to prove his worth like some young bachelor knight as for any great military matter. We made camp, as I have said – small fires, and pickets out all night. And before it was light enough to see, we were tacked up and moving east.

We left all the older men, and anyone with a bad horse, at Carbonara, with Sam Bibbo in charge of the camp. He rounded up peasants and pressed them to build a little *bastide.* With our retreat secure, we raced down the south bank of the Po. I rode with William Boson, who in two days had changed from resentment to friendship. For my part, it was a joy to speak French like a good Englishman.

Ah, you laugh, but in the summer of 1368, the *lingua franca* of the English Company was Norman French. Probably still is.

Carbonara to Ficarolo is just six miles. We covered those miles in an hour or less; the sun hadn't risen, and there were miasmas and mists rising off the river, and we couldn't see the other side.

Giannis swept the ground ahead of us, and Sir John sent a dozen of his archers to occupy a stand of woods. We were close to Ficarolo, and we hadn't seen a banner, or even a pennon.

I could smell wood smoke, though. And as I rode along the river, I realised that while there was river mist, there was also smoke – the smoke of a thousand cook fires, the mightiest army I had ever seen. It was so large that it took me a moment to accept the scale of the camp I was seeing. I had literally failed to see the forest for the trees.

Our whole column slowed, and then stopped.

Fifty thousand men take up a great deal of space. And don't imagine tents. Rich knights may have a pavilion, but militia build huts, or force local peasants to build them, so that the pavilions of the knights were like flowers in a manure heap, and the huddle of richer, silk pavilions half a mile away, mere points of scarlet and green, were no doubt the Emperor and his household.

We spread along the riverbank, looking for crossings, but there were none to be found and, after a few minutes, we retreated under Sir John's orders to the wood that had already been cleared and declared safe by his archers. There we dismounted and ate our sausage. I was already enjoying being a corporal – no longer in command, and now merely making interesting decisions and routine orders. You might think that I missed command; you would be wrong.

The mist was just starting to clear, and the birds were loud, especially the doves, when suddenly one of Giannis's stradiotes came in. He talked to Sir John, who beckoned to me.

'Cavalry crossing the river,' he said.

I took Gatelussi and l'Angars and all my men-at-arms and went south, staying well back from the bank. I made a dash for the next stand of poplars. We went into it, expecting an outpost, and found it empty, although there was a little fire pit and a whole loaf of bread. We ate the bread and watched the river.

Five hundred men were crossing. They looked like more, as most of them had two horses, and they were swimming across. The river wasn't too high – some men never had to swim – and they made good time, but the river was three hundred paces wide, and we had time to eat our chunks of bread and drink a little watered wine …

The first line of swimmers made it across. They clambered up our bank, the horses shaking themselves, the droplets of water flying like jewels in the bright, sun-laced air, and then the first flight of arrows struck them.

I doubt three men were hit in that volley, but some horses were hit. The men swimming were *Turks.*

You'll never credit it, but the Pope and the Holy Roman Emperor had hired Turks. Why not? They were superb light cavalry. It was a scandal at the time, of course – the Pontiff hiring Turks to fight Christians.

I was there. I think the Turks were cocky; they didn't think the Italians were much of a threat, and they were overbold. Certainly, in Outremer, no one would have sent his whole command across a river without sending scouts. On the other hand, from one end of the Holy Land to the other, I never saw a river that you needed to swim.

Most of the Turks turned south, away from the archery. That sent them right into our arms, and they didn't flinch. We came at them from close. I'd fought Turks, and had no interest in trying their bows to see if their strings were dry. We came around our little woods and into them, and then it was a fight.

My first opponent was a grinning villain on a big horse. He had his sabre out, and there was little art to our fight. We swaggered swords, and raced along, and he thought his stallion would outrun Gabriel. He was wrong. My fifth or sixth cut went into his turbaned steel cap; the peak held my edge, but the blow stunned him and he fell. His back-blow caught my arm – just the sort of thing Fiore tells you to guard against. We all do stupid things in a fight, but my vambrace held, although I had an almighty welt.

We took a dozen of them, and Gatelussi got two more. Our archers stopped the men coming over the river, and Boson charged down the Turks who turned north. Most of them got away, but we had twenty prisoners, and they were doubly surprised: first, that we didn't massacre them, as they had been told by the Pope; and second, that I spoke some Turkish, and told them to be at their ease. Mehmet Ali, their officer, was untroubled by capture. Turks are easy to like, and we chatted in my halting Turkish and his execrable Italian as we raced back to our camp.

But it was Hawkwood who proposed that we offer them double their wages to change sides, and we sent Mehmet Ali back, ostensibly to arrange an exchange. Then we retreated, leaving a picket at Carbonara, which we convinced Bernabò to reinforce that night.

Two nights later, the whole of the Turkish company came across the river, and joined us. Bernabò loved them; and suddenly he loved us. Hawkwood's prestige soared, and I have heard that the Emperor's confidence in his Papal ally plummeted. Listen: the enemy had ten times our numbers, but they hated each other – Pope and Emperor, Guelph and Ghibelline, an unholy 'Holy Alliance'. And when we stung them right in front of their camp, we apparently gave them an utterly false idea of our numbers. They imagined us bold; they thought we were flooding the south bank, and the Emperor abandoned his notion of forcing the line of the Po at his camp, and elected instead to march along the north bank of the Po, all the way to Mantua, and try his luck against the *bastide* at Borgoforte. He may even have imagined that he was outmanoeuvring Bernabò, who had not, in fact, moved any further than to ride back and forth between Guastalla and Borgoforte, hunting animals and maidens. It took him a week to move thirty miles, and during that week we watched his every move. Gatelussi won the praise of the whole army by crossing to the north bank, riding alone – without my permission – to the front of the Emperor's army, and *jousting* with a dozen Germans, unhorsing four of them, and then riding back. It had no military value – it was a piece of youthful folly, but he was knighted by Bernabò for it, and God save us if this tale is only about me. He was a brilliant knight, as good in an ambush or a sortie as in a joust, and he will be a great lord.

Aside from little follies, we did nothing to impede the Emperor's progress. And so, on the last day of May, he had his camp set east of Mantua, taking up the whole plain, and eating every ounce of agricultural produce Mantua could provide. Bernabò was not entirely a fool; we were feeding our army off Mantua's fields and granaries, and so was the Emperor, and this was a form of warfare with which we English are fully conversant.

I had had a week, by then, of sitting in Bernabò's pavilion, listening to his lickspittles laugh at his japes, and watching Antonio, his bastard son, alternate fawning civility and brusque revolt. Like Hawkwood, I very quickly developed a devotion to patrolling; it was preferable to watching his heavy-handed courting of men and women. To be fair, Bernabò's lights-o-love were always provided for, which made him, if not good, at least less bad than some of the other lechers I knew. And compared to his tyranny, his lechery was not likely to be the sin that sent him to Hell, but it was nonetheless ugly to watch, and the worst of it was that he thought that it was some form of prowess.

Regardless, the day that the Emperor decided to make his attempt on our *bastide* – which was, incidentally, two weeks higher and stronger than when I'd first pointed it out to Maestro Petrarca – that sunny morning, I was a mile east of the bastion, wearing a frowsy wool pull-over gown and a pair of boots so old that they hung together only by willpower. I was lying at the edge of an irrigation ditch, watching the Emperor's knights and officers attempt to form his army. I'd already sent Gatelussi back with a message for Sir John; I was fascinated by the process. The Imperial army was not a whole: it was one hundred companies of five hundred men, some of whom were themselves merely accumulations of other groups. The enemy army spoke more languages than the Tower of Babel, and there seemed a definite stress between the German-speaking and Italian-speaking portions of the army.

They had about forty thousand men, having left garrisons at various crossing points, and we had about fifteen thousand, and the mighty walls of the *bastide.* And the enemy had a better command structure: the Emperor was a hardened veteran, a knight with campaigns behind him, and his officers were used to him; the Pope's captains were also trained men with vast experience.

But that's where the advantages ended – numbers, and command. Both vital, but not everything. Our army had good spirits; since the fighting between the English and Germans, the Visconti had made every effort to patch the quarrel, mostly with gold, which is usually a good patch. And we had all the English. That was not nothing; often, in those days, each side had an English Company. They'd sit opposite each other, doing little. But on the banks of the Po, because King Edward had asked us, in a public letter, to abjure the Pope and fight for Milan, we had perhaps two thousand Englishmen, knights, men-at-arms, archers and cooks.

And then we had all the armour.

Venice was neutral, although the Emperor Charles had, arguably, marched across Venetian lands. But Venice as a neutral party was very much inclined to favour Milan, and Venice had vast stores of munitions. And Milan was the centre of Europe's arms and armour industry – so much so that every militiaman had more armour than Sir John required of a new man-at-arms. We had artillery, in the form of a vast trebuchet mounted in the middle of the *bastide*, which Bernabò, or possibly Petrarca, had nicknamed 'Troy'. And the Milanese had gonnes: big ones that threw a ten-pound ball, and small ones that two militiamen could move and fire as a team. Hundreds, if not thousands, of their militia were armed with handgonnes. I'd never seen them in such numbers; I had my doubts.

I knew Bernabò mistrusted his Germans, but since the company of Turks changed sides, the Germans had been much quieter. It's odd, but in my life as a mercenary, I have seen this many times. Men desert to armies they think will treat them better; after a while, the desertions go only one way.

At any rate, I lay at the edge of my ditch, chewed grass like a yokel, and listened to the officers attempt, in broad Southern German, to get Italians and Bretons and the Pope's raw Romagnol levies to co-operate. I could see Malatesta; he was not in command of anything bigger than his own company, and I could see from his body language how angry he was. I watched him bicker with an Imperial officer – and, of course, the Guelph against Ghibelline divide was so old in Northern Italy that there was too much blood on the balance for the two armies to love each other.

All things together, I didn't think the odds were too bad.

The Imperial army wasn't formed until almost midday, by which time I'd slipped back to my horse, taken my scouts, and ridden all the way back to our camp, where I changed into my best. As Fiore said,

'If I'm to die here, it will be in my best.' This was, without a doubt, the largest battle any of us had ever seen.

I had my new helmet and a mostly new harness; over it I wore a short silk cloak, just to keep the sun off. My helmet had a red and black silk turban, and I had a lance pennon to match, and an embroidered cover on my helmet's aventail with my arms.

And I had a shield. I loved that shield; I had carried it across half the world. It didn't have my full arms, because the maker, in Cyprus, hadn't really shared a language with me, but it did have my spur rondels in bars of sable and scarlet, each half against the contrasting colour. It was scarred, and knocked about, but the paintwork was radiant. The day before, a travelling illuminator had touched it up for me, and I'd given him dinner in return. He was a very learned man, much above shield painting – he decorated manuscripts and painted for churches – and he, too, was making his way through the war to Milan for the wedding. He worked for Cangrande, and his name was Altichiero. He and Fiore discussed drawing – have I not mentioned that Fiore could draw, beautifully? Sometimes, when you had a bad habit, he would draw you, and show the way your hip stuck out, or your hand turned. Anyway, he put my new Savoyard arms on my shield, with my distinctions from the count and the Order. Sword of Justice. Order of the Swan. Nothing for *Spatharios*, more's the pity.

Altichiero was even better at drawing men, and he made a drawing, just a few pen strokes, of Fiore thrusting at me with a longsword and me stretching to make my cover. I carried it for years but lost it retreating from the Paduans last summer, I'm sorry to say, because it was very fine. But I still have the shield.

At any rate, I was very fine, and so was Fiore, and so, in fact, were all our men-at-arms and most of our archers and squires. The count was a good patron, and the Milanese had made every effort to perfect our equipment at Pavia. I rode to Sir John, who was in white armour without any decoration, but had a white wand in his hand like the captain he was, and a big hat. We English had a joke that we tried not to make among Italians, that the size of a man's floppy hat showed how important he was – a joke that was also a truth. Bernabò's hat was as big as Milan itself. Sir John's was not small, and yet he didn't appear ridiculous.

Between our two contingents, we had about one hundred lances.

We had more archers than men-at-arms, though not by much. Some of our squires were also men-at-arms, and a few pages. But English archers were thick on the ground that summer, as the Prince of Wales had closed his campaign in Spain and many good lads were out of work. Hundreds came to Italy, and at least two hundred signed on with Milan, or directly with Sir John or me, in the last week before the fight.

And we had the Turks, or rather, I did. It wasn't that they wouldn't obey anyone else; merely that Giannis and I spoke more Turkish than anyone else in our army. That had some irony to it, but Mehmet Ali seemed happy enough with us and, in the end, that proved a deciding factor in Bernabò's battle plan. He put us on the right – the place, in most arrays, of most honour – and in this case, well outside the safety of the *bastide*. On the other hand, we were well-mounted, and we would have open ground in front of us, and a nice wide ditch on our flank, or so we discovered when we deployed.

The Imperial army had deployed too far away, a common enough mistake, and one I have made myself. Because we deployed from our camp, much closer, we had our array settled long before the Imperials were ready to try us. Our line, from the ditch to the camp of Borgoforte, was more than a mile long and, against all the advice of every war leader since Vegetius, we had gaps in it, left for the guns to fire through. The Imperials had a much longer line, but they had not reconnoitred well; the ditch that secured our flank went off to the north and east, wider where they were deploying and much narrower by our position, so that their army would have to narrow their frontage as they came forward. Our Turks slipped down the bank of the river and then popped up beyond the drainage ditch, with wide open fields in front of them, and then they hid themselves in the woods by the river.

Looking off to my left, I could see the Veronese with their ladder banners, deployed in close order: pavisiers in full armour and carrying big shields and heavy spears and, behind them, crossbowmen. They had gaps in their array for wedges of Veronese knights, who were reckoned among the best in Italy. Beyond them was the German horse – about two thousand barbutes. And then …

And then the earth walls of the *bastide*, upon which were the ranks of gonnes and gonne carts, and the massed handgonners. I was in full agreement with Bernabò that the place for militia was behind walls. I couldn't imagine that the Emperor would attempt to storm them.

Opposite us was the enemy left – in this case, the Papal army and, in particular, Romagnol levies and some of the Papal professionals. As they came forward, their line writhing like a snake, Hawkwood smiled.

'It is Albornoz,' he said.

All around me, Hawkwood's veterans stirred themselves.

I could see the Spaniard. He was well-mounted, and by him was the Papal gonfalonier with the same flag that I had followed at Alexandria.

'Sometimes, it is a strange world,' I said to Hawkwood.

He smiled. 'You are a good knight, William. Sometimes, I think that you are far more a knight than you ought to be.'

The Papal army halted six hundred paces away. By then, morning was gone. The pleasant spring air had turned hot, and everything smelled like campfires and horse sweat.

The Imperial army to our left went forward towards the walls of the *bastide*.

Off at the end of my line, where my archers were just cutting stakes from the trees, I saw movement, and a flash of bright silk, and there was Gatelussi, cantering across the plain. He had a scarf on his helmet – a beaked basinet – and he rode along our ranks and my archers cheered him, and indeed, he looked like Galahad.

'Order him back,' Hawkwood snapped. 'I don't want to provoke Albornoz. If he doesn't mean to fight, let him stay over there.'

I shouted twice, and then, at the edge of sending Marc-Antonio, I had a thought. I might have smiled.

I changed horses, off Juniper and on to Gabriel, and cantered easily across the young green wheat and the hard-packed earth. I was aiming to intercept Gatelussi.

But before he even saw me, a knight emerged from the Papal lines. He trotted towards Gatelussi, and the two put their lances in rests and went at each other, with eighty thousand spectators cheering themselves hoarse.

Gatelussi was perfect; it was his moment, and he thrust very slightly at the moment of contact, just as Fiore taught, and his man went down.

By then, there was a man riding for me. I knew it was Malatesta.

He knew me. In an odd way, it was almost a relief. I knew I wanted to play the game of chivalry, and Malatesta was, if not a friend, also not an enemy like Albornoz. War is not simple; chivalric war is the least simple of all.

But there was no friendship in the way he came on, and I met him in the same spirit, and we both shattered our lances. He was rocked. I had Gabriel, and I turned first, sword in hand, and the cheering almost stunned me. Even through my visor the sound was incredible.

Now he was turning towards me, but Gabriel was faster at that, too, and I struck, a single hard blow, right to the side of his great-helm, *mezzano*, and I snapped his head over, and reached for him.

Almost.

I couldn't quite get his neck. By a finger's breadth, I missed capturing Malatesta. He drew his dagger and tried for my horse's neck, and I shot my shield forward and covered Gabriel, slamming the edge into his outstretched forearm. His vambrace held my edge, and only then did I realise that two turns had brought us very close to the Papal army. But Malatesta was a proud man and a fine knight. He didn't run for it, but turned his horse again, this time inside my reach, and he delivered a brilliant cut, a feint that led to a strike with his pommel. Instead of reins, he had a dagger in his free hand; he stabbed, and I cut. The pommel strike just clipped me. The dagger missed, because I thrust with my shield edge, pushing his head back. My sword went into the open space above his elbow on his bridle hand – pure luck, as I was mostly parrying.

He raised his hand.

I saluted. He meant I'd hit him, and we were done. I let him go. I think that's what friendship is, in war.

He saluted with his sword, to show he was unbeaten; both armies roared, and I turned Gabriel away. I was quite close to the Papal lines, and Albornoz, clear as day, shouted, 'Get him! Get him!' at his crossbowmen.

Malatesta began to bellow, in Italian, that they should do no such cowardly thing.

A dozen obeyed Albornoz. Their bolts flew; none hit me, because crossing targets are difficult. Gabriel got into his stride, and I raced for the drainage ditch. I stayed as close to the Papal infantry as I dared, because that made the aiming harder. No young sprig took a hack at me, and I reached the ditch untouched. It was the narrowest point. I had no choice, no time to deal with my fear. I just sat down hard and let Gabriel jump.

And he did.

I swear we were going so fast that it took me half a mile to turn him, a huge arc raising dust in the empty field beyond the ditch. I had to ride all the way back to the riverbank, and along the sand, threading past the Turks. Gatelussi was already back, and the English cheered me, too.

I rode up to Sir John, and I expected censure.

He laughed. 'Not exactly what I meant,' he said.

I nodded. 'Malatesta came for me …'

'Never you mind,' Hawkwood said.

'Shall I lead the Turks …?'

'No!' Hawkwood said, a little too ferociously. His eyes all but burned at me.

I bowed.

A little later, he turned. 'Listen, William,' he said. 'I have been beaten twice in the last two years. I spent last winter a prisoner, and the ransom almost broke me. Bernabò almost didn't hire me – he says I'm an old woman who will bear no more sons.'

For a man who seldom revealed strong emotion, I could feel his anger, his frustration.

I bowed.

He shrugged. 'So let me choose my moment with the Turks. Let me tell you and Andy how I see this.' Andy was Andrew Belmont, and I knew him of old. In fact, it was as if no time had passed; Andy and I had been Hawkwood's right and left hands before.

Andrew Belmont was one of the handsomest men I ever saw, like Nerio, and he was like Mars that day, in blue and brass. He was handsome in more than looks; he saluted me. 'Wish I'd ridden out with you, William!' he said.

We trotted clear of our lines. The Papal troops were in a little confusion; I think they'd just received orders to move forward. Off to my left, the Emperor had thrown his knights, dismounted, right against the *bastide*. They had armoured handgonners with them – the first time I'd ever seen them, I think. That is, men with a handgonne and heavy armour too.

'He's an idiot,' Andy Belmont said, but he said it in a tone of wonder. 'He'll never break into the fort.'

The trebuchet arm began to move, and before I could comment, a load of stones and gravel flew through the air. I couldn't see any result, but I heard the screams, and then I heard the gonnes fire.

Hawkwood pursed his lips. 'Not our fight,' he said. Then he looked at the Papal troops. 'That's our battle,' he said.

'If the *bastide* falls ...'

The handgonners began to fire, and so did the Milanese militia. Long rolls of popping, like distant drums, and a hellish, sulphurous stench drifted towards us on the wind.

'If Bernabò loses the crossing, we're all prisoners, and I'm going back to England,' Hawkwood said. 'The *bastide* will not fall. Bernabò is not a fool. He's just a buffoon, but a buffoon with a brain and some good soldiers. Look! Albornoz is starting forward.'

It was true. The whole Papal line was moving.

'Andy, stay with me. William, take your own lances and twenty of mine, and go to the end of the line, right against the ditch. Dismount and wait. When you hear from me, attack.'

I left Andy getting his own orders to stiffen the line of archers. My men-at-arms were already on the right, and I sent my archers forward. Bibbo had them dismount, and I told off the horse holders. Look, ordinarily, one page holds his lance's horses – one archer's, one knight's, one squire's. Yes? But because we were stiffening the end of the line, I had to have pages for every three men-at-arms. And in the centre, we needed pages for every three archers. I didn't have an order to arrange it all and Bibbo was already busy being a master archer. So I did it myself, pushing boys left and right until all the horses were taken care of. That takes time.

Then I cleared the archers off my front. The rest of the line needed them, whereas I had eighty men-at-arms, most of them in something like full harness. Nothing was going to threaten us, more particularly, not an endless horde of untrained infantry pavisiers. They were coming forward carefully, and they were being compacted by the drainage ditch, as if they were coming down a funnel, if you can see that. They got deeper and tighter, deeper and tighter. I could see Sir John's plan now, and why he didn't want to send the Turks early.

Bibbo held the war bows until the pavisiers were less than a hundred paces away. He'd more experience of war in Italy than I – I left it to him. The reason was that no arrow will penetrate a pavis – not even a big war arrow from a big Englishman. Bibbo had the men shoot obliquely, and had some men loft their arrows high, for a plunging fire.

They scored hits. Not many, but some. Infantry are a more difficult target than horses, and Italian infantry are better armoured than most, and the big shields are tough nuts to crack. But the English archers had seen it all. They lofted arrows, and they shot flat, and all of them loosed fast, and the effect was not immediate, but it was palpable. The Papal line became uneven, and the advance slowed, and the result, combined with the funnel effect of the ditch, was to make their line into a mob.

Marc-Antonio appeared and dismounted. 'Sir John says attack – pin them out there. He's sent for the Turks.'

Another thing I have always loved about Sir John: clarity. He wanted me to go forward along the ditch, to hit the mob of pavisiers before they reached the archers. Our archers could fight – few better. But, in light armour and without heavy shields, they would be at risk, and despite the influx of men coming from Spain, archers were not so easy to come by. Besides, they were our people.

'Get ready,' I called. Everyone knew what I meant. In a big company, you develop orders – special words, like a code. But in a small company, there was always time to pass the word. Everyone knew we were going forward. The fully armoured men were in front; I was cap-à-pie, shiny steel from the crown of my head to my pointy steel toes. I had maille under my plate, and I was, in every way, a living shield for Marc-Antonio behind me.

'*En avant!*' I called.

We went forward at a gentle walk. I held my spear, twelve feet long, at the mid-haft with my left hand. Marc-Antonio held it at the butt.

We could move fast that way, the files as neat as Roman legionaries, because the spears welded us together. All I had to do was stay even with Fiore. I looked right and l'Angars, on my left, looked at me, and we went forward in the new wheat, our sabatons swishing along.

Off to my left, a company of Papal crossbowmen raised their weapons. I had my shield on my arm; I kept it up to protect my face.

'For what we are about to receive ...' Lapot said. He always said it when arrows were inbound.

The bolts clattered around, and a squire took a ricochet off one of the Savoyards in the throat and went down. No one in the armoured front rank got much more than a dent.

We had about fifty paces to go.

'Close up!' I called.

The pavisiers had stopped advancing. They were huddled together. An officer or a *Contadini* knight was shouting at them to get their spears down. Half the poor bastards had their spearheads in the air so they wouldn't stab their friends.

There were only eighty of us, in a battle of seventy thousand. Really, it sounds absurd. I couldn't see a thing – my visor was down. I knew that Fiore was there because I could feel him with my right hand, and I knew that l'Angars was there.

Forty paces.

No one that I could see through my visor wanted to fight. The pavisiers were shuffling, and their spears shook like young ash trees in a wind.

Thirty paces. I looked left. As far as I could see, the Papal line had halted. I could hear Albornoz roaring, his odd, Spanish-accented voice calling for the line to form.

Twenty paces. 'Close up!' I yelled. '*En avant!*'

Fiore and l'Angars couldn't get any closer. I could feel their hips against mine as we rolled forward.

Ten paces.

'Swords!' I called. We've all done this; we all let go of the spear in our right hands, leaving it to the squire, and we draw our longswords. Most of the veterans already had their swords in their left hands or pinned by the blade against the spear haft. It takes time and training to trust your scabbard and your draw. The squires take control of the long spear, put it right over your shoulder. I dropped my shield. Someone would pick it up, and I needed both hands.

I drew. The Emperor's sword, the one he'd given me, came into my hand like a living thing. A longsword. Long, but not too long.

I took mine in both hands. Right hand on the hilt, left hand on the blade, about halfway to the point. *Mezza spada.*

Five paces. We stayed at five paces for what seemed an eternity, because the pavisiers were backing away as fast as they could drag their big shields. Their formation, which had rippled and compacted because the drainage ditch narrowed their frontage, was now compacted from the other direction as the men in front tried to back up.

They had to stop, and we were on them.

Fiore said later that there was another volley of bolts from the *ballestrieri.* I do not remember it. What I remember is the horror on the face of the young Italian in front of me, as I pulled at his pavis with my left hand and stabbed him over it with my right. I was a monster of steel, from the depths of Hell, loose in their ranks with eighty other demons, and they screamed.

Well.

They wanted to break. But they were so deep and so packed together that they couldn't break, which may have been Albornoz's plan. He was a canny bastard.

But so was John Hawkwood.

Our Turks raced out from their cover. They had about five hundred paces to cross in the time we covered a hundred. As we were wearing leg armour and they were on horseback, it was almost a tie. In fact, we struck home slightly earlier, and then they appeared on the other side of the ditch, perfectly safe except from the *ballestrieri.* They rode *past* the pavisiers and then began to shoot from *behind* the Papal flank. They had horn bows, as powerful as an English yew bow; they were fifty feet from their targets, shooting into exposed backs. They rolled the shafts off their fingers and the pavisiers, many of whom were in padded jacks or arming coats with no other armour but a kettle helm, began to die, not by the ones and twos, but by the dozens.

Suddenly, like a dam giving way in spring, I was free. I had no one to fight, and in fact my blade cut mightily through empty air – when you cannot see, you can get panicked when you can't feel friend or enemy.

I turned. Fiore was with me, almost back to back. I could see Lapot, with the Virgin, and I ran to him – ran, trundled, jogged. Crept, perhaps.

The pavisiers gave way from the ditch, and flinched back, and back again.

They were trying to form at right angles, to get the big shields up against the Turkish arrows. At the same time, because they'd never closed on the main line of the White Company, the English archers now had the flank of the new line as a target. For perhaps one terrible minute, the Turks and the English both enfiladed one arm of the angled line. Later, I saw the ground, and there were more than a hundred corpses there – more likely three times as many.

I turned, got my visor up as much by luck as by skill, and shouted at Marc-Antonio. 'Horses!' I called.

Marc-Antonio turned and ran for the pages. They were only a hundred paces away, and Marc-Antonio didn't have leg armour or sabatons. He ran, and no bolt felled him.

Again, training told. The pages trusted the order; they came forward eagerly.

Arrows flew from the left and right, driving the corner of the enemy line back and back. It was no longer a corner. The militia were no longer attempting to reform. They were like sheep huddled against a storm, and I hadn't lost a man.

I saw Andy Belmont off to my left, and beyond him, Boson. Boson had the White Company banner, and it dipped and rose.

Behind me, unnoticed by me, eight of Giannis's stradiotes threw two great oak boards across the narrowest part of the ditch, where it was just fifteen feet wide, and began to lead their horses across. But the Turks didn't wait for that.

They rode down into the ditch, and then they rode straight up the other bank. I'm told a dozen of them didn't make it, but hundreds did.

The first Turk came up the bank and gave a long scream, like a tortured soul.

Stefanos ran up, and I took Gabriel from him, and Marc-Antonio was into his charger's saddle. As fast as I mounted, Lapot was already there, and brave Stefanos mounted and began to blow short notes on his horn. One of the pages handed me my shield.

I felt none of the usual fatigue. Oh, there was icy sweat running down my back under my arming cote, for sure. But I felt like a knight of romance – the field open before me, and the enemy breaking.

Forty knights, forty squires, forty pages, give or take, and three hundred Turks.

Loose in the back of the Papal army.

We weren't all, though. Hawkwood kept his men on foot, but there he was, unarmed except his white baton, which pointed like an arrow at Albornoz, and the Papal army was already beaten. To Hawkwood's left, the Veronese came on, their pavisiers better armoured and much better trained, and their knights all mounted.

The Papal militias began to throw down their shields.

The Turks rode past them. They needed no orders – they simply swept along the rear of the unravelling line, loosing arrows into helpless men.

Albornoz was no fool. He knew the day was lost, and he knew what he had to do, and he did it. He gathered his household knights around him, and Malatesta's Romagnols, and he aimed them at the Turks and charged, scattering the Turks like chaff on a windy day. The Turks could no more stand the charge of mailled knights than the pavisiers could fight us on foot. The Turks raced away, shooting backwards over their saddles. They had done their damage, and in fact, as soon as they were gone, the Papal army broke up faster, because they had a clear route to safety.

I wanted Albornoz, but it was not to be. He charged after the Turks, and then he rode clear. I saw him. He was two hundred paces distant, and the gap was widening. I would have had to wheel my whole line to go after him – virtually impossible, and to no purpose.

Remember, I had my visor up. So I could see.

I could see all the way to the *bastide.*

I could see the Imperial banner, which was huge. It was *on the face of the* bastide. The Imperial knights and their heavy handgonners were storming the fort. In fact, even as I watched, the banner went forward.

And I could see the Emperor.

I pointed him out to Fiore, and he laughed and threw his sword in the air and caught it.

'Of course!' he said.

It was ... impossible. But then if we could take the Emperor, in battle, we would be the richest and most famous knights in the world.

I led my men across the back of the Papal army. They were broken. The Veronese and the White Company were, for the most part, merely following them, making sure they kept running. One of the wedges of Veronese knights crashed into the fleeing Papal infantry, killing hundreds of men. Off to my left, another wedge of Italian knights slammed into the Emperor's reserve of Bavarians.

The Imperial army was not breaking up. But they also couldn't tell what was happening at our end of the line – dust, and the Turks, gave the impression of a bigger force than was actually pursuing Albornoz.

Cangrande della Scala was sword to sword with the best knights in Germany. He could not break them, and they could not break the Veronese. It was, and I think will remain, one of the most famous fights of the century. I rode past it.

I had a hundred men, and I kept going. I was riding down the back of the enemy army, a chivalric thief in the night, so to speak, and then …

Maybe two hundred paces away, Emperor Charles IV pointed with his sword, and his household began to retire. His household knights were among the best in the world, trained like his tournament team – probably the equivalent of Petrarca's beloved Praetorians. They wheeled by squadrons, something that I had never seen done at that time.

There was smoke everywhere. Thousands of gonnes had fired. Hawkwood says it was the thickest powder smoke he'd ever seen, and the Germans had set fire to the *bastide*'s wall of stakes.

By then I was a hundred paces away. I was also close enough to see the fighting on the *bastide*, where the Imperial handgonners had some sort of explosive bombs that they threw over the palisade; a secret weapon that was making chaos out of Bernabò's impregnable fortress, and adding to the smoke and flame.

But I was a hundred paces from the Emperor. Thanks to the rout, the Turks, the swirl of dust and the powder smoke, we were unseen. Just one hundred paces.

On a battlefield, that's an inch.

One of the Imperial knights glanced our way, and in one glance, Lucius van Landau knew my harness and my arms and my shield.

So close.

The third squadron of Imperial knights wheeled back, but they didn't retire. They wheeled until they aligned with our front.

Well. As soon as I saw them wheel I knew our game was up.

So damned close.

And, as Fortuna, or Tyche, or God, would have it, the Imperial knights on the walls of the fortress saw us, and ordered the handgonners to retire. The men on the slopes of the grassy walls turned and ran. Their pages held their horses, and suddenly we were in a maelstrom of enemies.

I only saw one of the Landau brothers who I'd known from '64. I ended up opposite a man in black armour, with a white rose on his shield. My war lance shivered under my arm, broken all the way to the butt, and his lance broke cleanly in the middle, but our horses crashed in, breast to breast, and we raced to draw our swords. We tied. Our swords crossed rising – something I have never known before – and crossed with both points down, but before I could think of anything, I was past. His blow, faster than my cover, hammered into my armet, and it left a dent, but not in my head. I tried to turn, but in that time Marc-Antonio had plucked the black knight from his saddle as if he was in the tilt yard against a straw-filled dummy, and he carried on, passing me.

I cut in behind him, Gabriel dancing clear of a falling horse, and then I had three, or perhaps four, fleeting engagements – a crossed sword, a pommel strike, a man I think I dismounted with a sweep of my arm – and then I was behind Fiore, and it was like the tournament at Krakow. He knocked a man sprawling with a blow to the man's helmet, and I scooped a foot and tossed the man over his saddle and got the reins.

And then Fiore burst out the back of the mêlée. I was right behind him, and there was Lapot, waving our banner, and Stefanos, of all people, who had threaded the whole fight, and to whom I gave the German knight's horse.

I could see the Imperial banner, but it was further away, and a second squadron of lifeguards waited. They were watching us.

I turned and plunged back through the knights we'd charged. There was no other choice – the Emperor was too far away, too well-guarded.

A trumpet was blowing behind me, and the German knights began to fall back on their trumpeter, rallying back to the first squadron.

Stefanos blew his horn – perhaps in emulation, or mockery. But our people came together, and we had not done too badly – a dozen empty saddles. We closed.

Gabriel was tired. I could tell.

I looked back. Cangrande della Scala was still locked up against the Bavarians. But the Imperial banner was retiring. The lifeguards, if that's who we fought, were going with the banner.

We turned our jaded horses, and trotted heavily towards the flank of the Bavarians. The shieldless flank. But we were just too slow, and before our weary horses could trot across the dusty ground, the Veronese broke out the back of the mêlée. In seconds, the Bavarians were gone, flowing away like water from a broken bowl. We swept in, but we only caught a few. I took a single prisoner, a young knight who, braver, or more foolish, thought he'd go sword to sword with an Englishman. He seemed to know all my tricks, and I could neither put my pommel into his teeth, nor get it behind his neck for a throw; likewise, I baffled his thrusts and cuts. We went round and round, our tired horses flagging, Gabriel's proud tail drooping. The lad was good.

No one interrupted us. I didn't know it, but we were probably the last men fighting.

At last, perhaps because I was bigger and had worn him down, he attempted to make two cuts in one time. It's a common error – I've done it myself. He cut *fendente*, and then he tried to cut *reverso* in the next tempo. But he was tired and, by then, slow. I covered the first over my head, and had all the time in the world to countercut, a heavy blow, right onto his sword hand. I didn't penetrate his iron gauntlet, but I broke all his fingers, and his sword fell away.

'*Je se rendre*,' he said.

I led him back to camp to the cheers of the Veronese. They had prisoners of their own, and Cangrande, who was as chivalrous as a tyrant could be, had had the fight he wanted, with good German knights. Indeed, everyone in our camp was in high spirits; we'd faced the Imperial army and driven them off. Our casualties were absurdly light and, indeed, so were the Imperial casualties. The Papal army took all the losses, and even there, fewer than a thousand men fell – nine hundred of them, I'd guess, to English and Turkish arrows. It was an archers' battle. In the centre, the Imperial rush at the *bastide* had met with the volleys of the Milanese handgonners, and the stench of sulphur covered the battlefield, but few enough of the imperials had fallen.

What I didn't know until I was back at my pavilion, sending an exhausted Stefanos to find bedding for my prisoner, was that the Imperial army had, in fact, breached the walls of the *bastide*. They had broken a body of Milanese guildsmen standing in front of the palisade, and then, using swords and axes, they had cut their way into the fort. Only a dozen got in, but it was close. Hawkwood said later that it sounded as if, had we not cracked the Papal troops, the Emperor might, in fact, have taken the *bastide*.

Well. He didn't. It wasn't really a battle – not the 'good, fat war' that Antonio had predicted. It was bloody and hellish for a few minutes, but it was the first meeting of the two great antagonists, and neither was willing to risk the throw. The Milanese still hadn't committed their resources, and the Emperor wasn't sure what he was willing to risk.

Still, it was the 'great war' that everyone had predicted. The Pope, the Emperor, Florence, England, and even France were committed. Milan had won the first skirmish, and while the Emperor had not suffered, the Pope had certainly lost.

The war was hot. Or so we all thought.

And so, that night, in Bernabò's great pavilion, a dozen of us sat around, looking at the little clay pots that the German handgonners had thrown. Several of them were taken intact, because the fuses burned down and didn't ignite the black powder inside. I had seen similar devilish devices in Outremer. The Mamluks and Greeks both had them full of Greek fire, but I had never seen them explode, and Andy Belmont led us all outside and set one off.

Then we went back to meet with Bernabò, expecting an exhortation; Hawkwood hoped to be ordered to raise five hundred lances. We feasted our prisoners, and drank deep, and Bernabò did praise Sir John. Then he dismissed us, but when the pavilion was cleared of the captains, Bernabò's pages came and begged us – that is, Sir John, and Andy Belmont, and me – to stay.

Bernabò went out, into his double-belled private pavilion, like a silk and canvas palace. He came back with a woman whose beauty, by the light of his silver hanging lamps, was almost absurd: blonde hair, of course, and pouting lips, and eyes so bright that nightshade might have been involved. Her waist was tiny – her figure resembled that which limners often give to Mary Magdalene and seldom give the Virgin. I felt for a moment I knew her from somewhere; her face was familiar.

He had his hand on her back, and his caresses were too intimate for public company, but he was Bernabò Visconti, and such concerns meant nothing to him. It was, somehow, all the more difficult because instead of fondling his leman in front of forty men, as he had done before, there were just the three of us: Andy Belmont and John Hawkwood and me.

She made a little sound, somewhere between a sigh and a moan, as his hand went down her back. It was obvious that she wore nothing under her silken kirtle.

'The Duke of Clarence will want all the English,' Bernabò said, without preamble.

The girl's eyes rolled a little. Bernabò had one of her hands, and he caressed the wrist, and a spot of colour appeared on her throat.

Hawkwood cleared his throat. 'What are your orders for tomorrow?' he asked.

Bernabò leaned down and whispered something to the girl, and then kissed her ear.

'Tomorrow we ride to the wedding,' he said. His deep voice was even rougher than usual. It seemed possible that he was going to take the woman right in front of us. I could not look at her. My embarrassment was acute; under the embarrassment was anger. He was doing this deliberately, and I couldn't imagine why, and I could only think of Father Pierre Thomas, and Fra Peter Mortimer, and even the Green Count.

'Wedding?' Belmont asked. I looked at him, and he was watching the girl.

Our eyes met, and Andy winked, and somehow, I felt a little more steady. Andy's amusement was the proper response, and I was acting like a nun meeting a *fille publique*.

I admit my first thought was that 'wedding' was some code, or an allusion. It took me ten heartbeats to remember that the Green Count, Prince Lionel, my wife, and most of the literati of Europe, were making their way to Milan for the wedding of the century.

I suppose I had imagined that war was important – special, somehow. That once the 'good, fat war' was launched, we would be hotly engaged in 'important' campaigns.

'I want all your Englishmen,' he said. His hand passed across one of her breasts, and the woman was less than perfectly pleased. Her body stiffened, and she turned slightly.

The spell was broken.

'You want my whole company?' Hawkwood asked.

'Of course,' Bernabò said, bored with his game. 'The prince will only have a dozen knights with him – he will need an escort, and jousters for the tournaments, and he may need protection ...'

I leaned forward. 'Protection, my lord?' I said.

Bernabò's burning eyes turned on me, and his bony brow glowed with sweat. 'Perhaps I misspoke,' he said, with a smile. 'You have met my nephew? Gian Galeazzo?'

Hawkwood frowned. 'What possible threat could there be to the Duke of Clarence at his own wedding?'

Bernabò laughed. 'Ask Antonio,' he said. 'But be ready to ride in the morning. Don't worry about clothes. Galeazzo will have everything for you.'

We rode into Pavia as victors from the field of battle, leading the whole of what had, at various times, been the White Company, the Company of Saint George, and a few other names. Our armour was polished, and most men's surcoats were still bright, and the horse tack was not bad.

We made a brave show. And we had a fine day. The sun shone down on us, and made our spears and armour glitter like the stars of Heaven, or so I heard Maestro Villani describe it.

But the sullen population didn't cheer us. They had all been mustered at the other gate, the Turin gate, to cheer the English prince and the Count of Savoy.

As it was, our parties met in the middle of the city, under the grim walls of the old stone fortress, and our company enfolded theirs in a steel embrace. The last five leagues to Pavia I had been in a ferment of worry. No sooner did I let go of the war behind me than I returned, in my head, to worries about the count, about Camus, about Robert of Geneva.

And truth to tell, gentles, I am not usually much given to such worries. That is, I am not a man for revenge. Oh, perhaps, if some man fouls me in a mêlée, I will return the favour, especially in the heat of anger. I am no better than the next knight at turning the other cheek, and I read portions of the Gospel with some shame.

But without the hot blood, I can rarely rouse myself to anger when cold. Even with d'Herblay, who did me as much harm, I think, as any man could, I did not plot against him, and when he was under my sword, or rather, my poleaxe, I still didn't kill him.

But the killing of young Demetrios was a terrible thing. It is difficult to describe; it makes my skin crawl even now. It is like the crucifixion of the old pilgrim on the Bolsena road – an act outside of the bounds of violence. To use poison ... it is cowardly, base, and also, to my mind, far worse than a sword thrust. A sword thrust will only injure the intended target, but a cup of poison may strike at anyone, including a twelve-year-old boy. I had known Camus was capable of anything – the mad criminal attacked the Pope's legate on the very steps of the Papal palace in Avignon, for goodness' sake – but the crucifixion of the pilgrim told me that Camus was like the inmates at Bedlam: he had not done this terrible, blasphemous thing to frighten us. In fact, it might very well have been that we'd miss his work altogether. He did it because he *enjoyed* it. Likewise the attempted poisoning of the count.

So, for the first time, I considered something like murder. Revenge – pure and simple. Knowing that he would be at Milan, I began to prepare myself: to meet him, to listen to Robert of Geneva, to deal with the Prince of Achaea. I'm glad I was thinking of these things because, although I had no idea how bad the wedding would be, I was, in my head at least, a little prepared.

Pavia was almost pleasant. We enveloped the wedding party, and there was Emile, dressed in blue, on a pale gold horse that matched her hair, and she was not ashamed to embrace me in front of all the noblemen and women of her party. And I was next embraced by Richard Musard.

'Damn, I am glad to see you, brother,' he said, as his horse and mine tried to chew affectionately on each other's bits.

'Bad?' I asked.

His eyes said *not here*.

I bowed in the saddle to the count and he smiled, a broad, natural smile.

'Covered in laurels, eh, messer?' he called out, and waved his hand vaguely, in the way of great noblemen everywhere.

Heralds in the Visconti arms began to call out for 'the Companions' – meaning 'the English' – to follow them to their billets.

We brought the whole of the company: almost a hundred lances, both of the Birigucci brothers, as well as Francesco Gatelussi, Antonio Visconti and a dozen other Italian men-at-arms who followed John Hawkwood. We had Picard archers and Flemish archers and

Breton knights and Norman men-at-arms; we had a dozen Gascons, a smattering of Germans left over from the days when Albert Sterz commanded the company. We had four Hungarians, we'd picked up two Turks from Mehmet Ali's company, and we had a dozen Greeks and a single Egyptian who had followed Lapot all the way from Alexandria to Pavia. And Janet – you'll remember Janet. She entered Pavia on horseback, in her armour. A woman, and a French woman at that.

But we were, nonetheless, 'the English'. Everyone called us English – even Salim, the Egyptian boy, was openly called English by Bernabò. And years of fighting together, men and women, of whatever actual nation, had welded us into a single body. We gave orders in French; we argued about food in Italian; we sang songs in English.

I mention this here because, despite our apparent polyglot nature, we were impenetrable, and the wedding showed us just how essential that impenetrability was. Every man and women, from captain to slattern, knew each other. It was impossible for a stranger to penetrate our ranks, or our camp, or our kitchens.

Any road, l'Angars and Boson led the company away to prearranged billets, guided by the heralds. When the Visconti organise, they do so brilliantly, and every man and woman arrived at his billet to find clean straw and a cup of wine at the expense of his hosts.

I kept a handful of knights back. I put Fiore at the count's side and Pierre Lapot at his back, and I kept Gatelussi by me, as his birth entitled him to join the wedding party, and I saw the count nod a very small agreement.

Musard was seen to breathe a sigh of relief as we rode through the old castle's gates and into the deep shadow of the tunnel to the courtyard, where a phalanx of pages waited to take our horses, and Galeazzo Visconti waited with his lady, the count's sister, Bianca. I could see them, framed by the mouth of the tunnel up ahead, if I peered past Fiore's armoured shoulder and the prince's. I could see murder holes over our heads. Anyone foolish enough to rush the gate would be trapped here while boiling oil or red-hot sand was poured on their heads. I'd seen a man die that way at Alexandria, and it still makes me shudder.

My wife reached out and took my hand. Bless her, she knew I was having one of those moments – all of you who fight for a living know them. It was dark in the tunnel and darkness and enclosure hits me somewhat. The murder holes …

Bah, never mind. Emile took my hand, and I pulled off my gauntlet, the better to feel her smooth palm. She turned to me, and I felt, or heard, movement.

One of the murder holes was open.

'Ware!' I shouted.

Fiore touched his mount with spurs, and his horse, outraged, exploded into the count's horse. The count was thrust against the wall of the tunnel, his left leg scraping against the rough stone, but he kept his seat because he was an expert horseman, and he burst from the tunnel, past the prince.

A crossbow bolt flashed from the roof of the tunnel and went into the rump of Fiore's charger. It went in up to the fletchings, and the horse screamed and fell.

The Earl of Hereford and I were on either side of the prince by then and, whatever differences we'd had before, we covered him together. Which was as well.

The count was trying to dismount; his horse was rolling its eyes. A dozen men with partisans went charging up the interior steps to the wall. Men were running in every direction, and I happened to see Gian Galeazzo. He wore an expression of intent interest that, in that moment, reminded me strangely of Robert of Geneva.

He smiled.

A knot of grooms came out of the stable block to my left. They were closer to the earl, who had his sword out, but he ignored them, his eyes on the tunnel and the murder holes.

'That was meant for the count,' I said.

Bohun turned. 'The count?' he asked, incredulous.

Richard Musard was shaking his head furiously.

More guards ran by, and then two men in full armour appeared on the walls.

Two pages took the count's horse's bridle.

Fiore hovered over him, and Bonne was alone. I saw her, and in that moment I saw one of the grooms stumble. He was … drunk, perhaps, which seemed impossible.

He looked at the count. He looked at Fiore, who was like a protecting archangel in steel, and then he looked at Bonne.

I knew. I don't know how I knew he was an assassin, but I knew, and I touched Juniper with my spurs. I went past the astonished prince, without apology, just as the groom raised the knife he had under his apron.

Fiore was turning, also alerted. But too damn far away.

But Lady Bonne was no blushing maid. She was a huntress, and she knew her horse. She backed, see-sawing the reins, even as the man went for her, his eyes glittering, not with malice, I think, but terror. His motions were jerky and unreal, like one of the walking dead that terrified me as a child when my nurse told me terrible stories.

He lunged madly, and stabbed her palfrey. The horse reared, hurt and terrified.

I had on the arming sword that the della Scala family had given me, and my draw was late, but the sword was short. Just the tip of my sword caught his wrist.

He turned.

Lady Bonne fell off her palfrey. It was a slow fall – her saddle had no high back, like a knight's – and she couldn't keep her seat as the horse rose higher and higher.

She rolled to her feet.

The dagger came down again, driving at her back, and my sword came down after it, following his wrist. He turned away, blood fountaining from his severed arm. Lady Bonne was on the ground. The dagger was lying by her side, the groom's hand still gripping it.

One of the Visconti guards shot the dagger man with a crossbow. The bolt went in one side of his head and out the other, taking most of his face with it; the bones of his skull were shattered.

He was dead instantly, of course.

I turned, my light sword threatening the whole arc of my vision. I put my back to Lady Bonne and looked for Emile, who was under her horse, having dismounted – a princess who could always rescue herself.

Fiore had his longsword in both hands. Count Amadeus was behind him. Prince Lionel was sandwiched between l'Angars and the Earl of Hereford.

No one in the courtyard moved, and then we heard a scream, a loud crash, and the snap of several heavy crossbows.

I looked up at John Hawkwood, who had a sword in his hand, for once.

He wore a look of deep cynicism. 'Someone was just shot trying to escape,' he said.

Neither assassin was taken alive, so Sir John's comment was correct. The Visconti were outraged, and before the day was much older, the man who had posed as a groom was identified, and his house searched. A hundred gold florins were found, and his terrified wife implicated his brother, who was seized and executed. Without interrogation.

The other man, the man who'd shot at us from the murder hole, was an enigma. He was small and dark. One of the Visconti men-at-arms said he'd seen the man before, in the kitchens – a southerner, or a Moor.

Fiore and I, with a little help from Peter Albin, walked through the tunnel in the evening. We walked up and down, measured the sight lines, and then I went up into the rooms over the arch, lay full length on the floor, and peered at Fiore standing below me.

Half an hour later, when all the food had been tasted and all our people were settled, I met with Sir John. I couldn't think who else to tell. I found him sitting on the camp bed in his small room, Andy Belmont leaning against the wall, spinning dice in a cup.

Hawkwood looked up and smiled. 'William,' he said, with a nod.

'Sir John,' I said.

'The crossbow bolt wasn't intended for Amadeus,' I said. 'It was intended for Prince Lionel.'

Hawkwood sighed. His nostrils pinched; he put his right hand to his head. 'Of course,' he said.

'What does Antonio know that we need to know about protecting the prince?' I asked.

Sir John looked at me. And shook his head, pointing at the ceiling. 'Nothing,' he said loudly.

We put watches on Count Amadeus and on the Duke of Clarence. Bonne was uninjured and unbowed, a tough lady indeed. Countess Blanche, the Green Count's sister, was more distraught than anyone that this should have happened in her own home. Galeazzo clearly felt that killing a few people solved the problem, and Gian Galeazzo, his son, was nowhere to be found.

*

Some time later I got into bed next to my wife, who curled around me despite the warmth.

'The lemon tree looks better and better,' she said. 'Before God, William – I saw you move in that tunnel, and I thought, sweet Christ, he's going to die in front of my eyes. Why did we ever leave Lesvos? I miss my children. I am not ready to be parted from Edouard any longer. And my little Richard – it is cruel to leave a child at his age.'

'We can send for him,' I said.

'We can just go back,' she shot back. 'I am not sure I can let you have the life of arms, William. Sooner or later, you won't come back. And then who will I be?' She lay beside me, and I thought she might cry, but instead she said, 'Turenne will be at the wedding in Milan. And perhaps de Lesparre.'

I lay there, thinking of them.

'I could just deed my estates to my son,' she said. 'And you and I could go to Lesvos and never come back to this cesspit.'

In the morning, we took every precaution. Musard and Fiore and I worked with Lord Bohun and John Hawkwood, and between us, we arranged as perfect a cordon around our principals as we could manage. We held something very like a *mostre* in the courtyard, and we let every man-at-arms and every archer see every servant of the count, or the prince, and vice versa. We introduced Master Chaucer and Master Froissart here to the archers, and walked them around. I enlisted Chaucer to help.

He had some experience, after all.

We isolated table service to six people for each notable. We arranged for Froissart and Chaucer to be served at table with the prince, so that they could help cover him. Every morsel of food was tasted, first by mongrels, and then by people – Musard and me, mostly. I couldn't bear to force some child, someone's son or daughter, to take on such a hazard.

The pressure was relentless. Far worse than war. And we were in Italy.

Two hours after Prime, we rode out into the sunny plains of Lombardy. Now we had the whole of the Visconti clan and their escort, as well as Violante and Gian Galeazzo. Bernabò was gone to prepare the extravagance of our entry into Milan.

It was a twenty-mile ride and it was, in itself, an extravagance. I thought we'd do it in a day, but that was not what the Visconti had in mind for us. Instead we rode only as far as Cascinetta, a town so small it was not on my itinerary, but there was a castle and a hunting lodge – one of Bernabò's.

When we were in sight of our destination, I left Fiore and rode back along the column to Messer Antonio, who was riding with the Visconti men-at-arms.

'Race you,' I said, without preamble, and I gave my riding horse her head.

Of course, Antonio could not resist a challenge, and we galloped out over the wheat fields, earning the curses of a dozen peasants, and then leaped a ditch and raced along the next parallel road. My Arab was fleeter than his Italian nag. When we were close to the *castello*, I turned my mare in a broad circle and brought Antonio to a stop in an oak wood of perhaps a hundred trees.

'Why does Bernabò feel that the prince needs protecting?' I said.

Antonio looked around. He flushed bright red.

Then he swore for a while – a rich, blasphemous stream that suggested a lifetime of practice.

I waited him out.

'Antonio,' I said softly.

He looked at me. He couldn't meet my eye, or rather, he met my eye like a young girl just learning to flirt. Touch and away.

'Antonio,' I said again.

'Christ,' he said. 'I can't.'

I walked my horse over to him, and pressed in so close I could have kissed him. I pitied him, but at some remove; I couldn't let him go. 'Antonio,' I said for the third time. 'In the last year, I think I've saved your life three times.'

It's a rotten thing to say. My advice? Never remind a man you saved his life. But there's a time and place for everything.

'I fucking know,' he spat.

I shook my head. 'What is the threat to Prince Lionel?' I asked.

Antonio looked at the ground. 'A lot of people want him dead. And his death would ... unravel ... Galeazzo's position on a great many things.'

I reached over and lifted his chin. A pretty insulting gesture, between men. I needed to see his eyes. 'Does Gian Galeazzo hate his father?' I asked.

'No,' Antonio said, struggling to look away. 'No, fuck your mother. No. He just loves his fucking sister.'

It's one thing to think it, and another to hear it said. 'Gian Galeazzo is trying to kill Prince Lionel?' I asked.

'No!' Antonio said. He looked away. 'No. But. Maybe, when someone *else* is trying to kill the Prince, some guards . . . look the other way. Listen, we are all very close. Galeazzo does not like to hurt his son, but this is a thing that must happen. Bernabò says it must happen. Bernabò says . . .' He looked away. 'My father makes the decisions, and he says the little couple must part, yes?'

'Gian Galeazzo hates *your* father,' I said.

'Eh. Maybe. Everyone hates my father.' Antonio looked at me. 'Please . . .'

I shook my head. 'Antonio, I will just tell you, because I am mild – pious, even. If my wife dies, if my count dies, I will make it as ugly as possible. You understand? I make no threats.'

Antonio shook his head vehemently. 'No one would touch the count. His sister made us promise . . .'

He turned white.

I nodded. 'So all this has been discussed. We are caught in a family quarrel. In the middle of a war with the Pope and the Emperor.' I looked at him. 'Man to man, now. The Prince of Achaea and his people will stop at nothing to kill the count. And my wife. And me. I'm sorry to make this personal, Antonio. But *you owe me*.'

Antonio shrugged. 'Family comes first,' he said.

I had the words in my mouth – the same words Camus said. I almost said them. *I will kill everyone you love.* I could taste the words, because, in truth, I knew that I could. If the Visconti killed my Emile . . . my count, even.

He saw it in my eyes. He flinched. 'I will see to it,' he said. 'My word of honour.'

I chose to accept this. Anything else would have meant a dagger fight right there.

*

We rode into Cascinetta together. We were the last to arrive, and what we found looked more like a market than a fortress or a hunting lodge.

Bernabò had said the company would 'have everything new'. He wasn't jesting. Even as the count's household and the men told off as the day's guards separated the count and Prince Lionel and took them to their rooms, Sam Bibbo and William Boson and I were briefed by a dozen senior servants. There were tailors sitting in rows on clean rugs in the bright sun. There were saddlers and armourers and even, God save us, a glover.

It was a little like soldier's heaven. Every man walked forward when his horse was unsaddled, brushed and hobbled. He received a neat pile of cloth, wool and linen and silk, and then walked from station to station, where cloth was measured and cut, quickly marked with a cross-stitch tailor's mark, and then on. Every man got two new shirts, two pairs of braes, two pairs of hose, and a handsome doublet in the Italian style, with a long row of brass buttons down the front – every one of which bore the Viper. A pair of shoemakers repaired, or offered from ready stock, both shoes and boots, for every man, knight, man-at-arms, page or archer. A trio of cutlers sharpened swords; armourers repaired, restrapped, or replaced. A waterwheel and three sweating Bohemian archers polished helmets to a mirror shine.

The steward approached me with a bow and escorted me around. I didn't receive a pile of cloth, more's the pity, but I was measured several times.

'My lord will be expected to dine with the prince at the wedding table,' the steward said. 'What is my lord's best colour?'

'Scarlet,' I said. 'The brightest red that can be found.'

The steward looked at me carefully. 'We will see,' he said.

I was happy to have my arming sword sharpened. I'd come to like it, despite its short length, and I was surprised when I drew it to find that it didn't have as much as a single nick. But the cutler found marks with his thumbnail, and he ground it smooth in seconds.

More than a hundred soldiers, and they were all served in two hours. And then the sempsters and seamstresses sat around under awnings, on the ground, and sewed. It was remarkable; I'd never seen so many people sew all at once. I gathered that Bernabò had hired most of the mature women of the village to sew for him.

'My mother is from this town,' Antonio said. 'My father takes good care of these people. They would give their lives for him.'

'He is spending a fortune on our company,' I said.

'Wait until you see the wedding,' he said.

We had a pleasant evening – at least, until one of the green-clad huntsmen started screaming. I was lying with Emile, wondering whether I had waited long enough after pregnancy, and how she might receive my advances. She was chatting about household matters. At the first scream she produced a dagger – that's how on edge we were.

I rolled to my feet, drew my arming sword and ran to the little portico of my cabin, which was the company guardroom. Hawkwood was emerging with a baton in his hand.

The man screaming was Bernabò's chief huntsman. A dozen of his hounds were dead – poison. Only three dogs were left, and their mournful howls proved that dogs know when death has come. The huntsman was beside himself. He loved those dogs more than most people, I expect.

No poisoner was found. I combed the woods with a small band of men and torches, but we found nothing.

In the morning, we rode out of the gates. I had taken a shift guarding the prince and the count; we had them on one corridor. I managed to get another hour of sleep with my wife, and awoke to find an entire suit of clothes in scarlet velvet and salmon pink silk laid out for me. I enjoyed Emile's teasing admiration. I had enough spirit to chase her round the solar in her dishabille, and then enough sense to praise her taste in clothes: blue and buff and red, in magnificent Milanese brocades.

I was proud to find that Marc-Antonio and Stefanos had my armour polished like a set of interlocked mirrors, and as clean inside as out, allowing me to wear my new velvet finery under my breastplate. I was not the only one looking splendid – the company looked like a prince's bodyguard. In one night, a set of craftspeople had transformed them from some well-trained English routiers to characters from a chivalric romance. They closed in around the prince and the count and countess, leaving the army of Visconti men-at-arms to cover their own lords. And we sent them first, and the Devil take the laws of courtly precedence.

*

When we arrived at Milan, the whole of the Visconti heritage was there to wait for us: six hundred men-at-arms, whole legions of guild militia, and thousands of Viper banners. And the women: there was Bianca, Bernabò's formidable wife, on a palfrey large enough to carry a knight; there was Bonne, the count's wife, and her ladies. But otherwise, it was a very masculine turnout. It looked as if we were approaching an army – so much so, that Sam Bibbo turned to me and muttered, 'If they want a fight, we can take 'em.'

The reason for the array was plain as soon as we approached, because in the exact centre of the Visconti army stood Galeazzo, and with him was his daughter, Violante. She did not look blank today; her eyes did not look bruised. Her hair blazed like white fire, and her eyes were wide, and so was her smile. She looked at Lionel, and he looked at her with joy.

I watched Gian Galeazzo, who was twenty horses away, with the knights of the household, the Casa.

He had his visor down.

As we rode into the city, the people shouted for 'joy', or at least earned their pay, shouting for England and the Visconti. It is not my favourite city, but it would have raised your heart – bright new crosses of Saint George everywhere, as if it was London itself. I was just behind Lady Violante, as she waved at people on balconies above her, and raised her head, and smiled.

Then I knew why Bernabò's mistress looked familiar to me. She was an older version of Violante. The thought sickened me. It is the sort of thought you might be ashamed to confess to a priest. I spent the rest of the entry trying to rid myself of it, even as I watched the crowd for paid killers or madmen.

It was not until we reached the great palace in the centre of the city that we joined up with the rest of the notables. They were all waiting: hundreds of the most powerful men in Italy and, in some cases, the world. There were ambassadors from Venice, and Genoa, and even from the Holy Roman Emperor; an ambassador from Constantinople, and another from Florence, far more magnificently dressed. There was the Count de Turenne, and there, Robert of Geneva, the Archbishop of Cambrai. And with them, Florimont de Lesparre. In front of them stood the Bourc Camus and, towering over them all, the Prince of Achaea.

All together, in one place.

I looked at Emile, and she smiled.

'I've lived my whole life with them,' she said. 'It's best to keep them where you can see them.'

I have never loved Emile more than in that moment. Her courage was always magnificent; in that moment, facing a wall of enemies, she tossed out a jest.

I turned, allowing the column to pass me, and cut in between l'Angars and Bibbo.

'You see them?' I asked.

L'Angars smiled. 'All of our friends,' he said.

Ewan laughed, a rank back. 'Fuckin' miracle no one's put an arrow in de Lesparre.'

I looked at Bibbo. I didn't say anything – Froissart, you may not like this part. But Bibbo and I knew each other. He nodded. That's all.

I made the rounds of my archers, and then went back to the head of the column during Bernabò's speech of welcome. Archbishop Robert made a point of staring at me all through the speech. I ignored him.

At a signal from the count, I followed two Visconti men-at-arms into the vast palace. I had Richard Musard with me, and William Boson from Hawkwood's company. The Earl of Hereford couldn't leave the ceremony – too obvious.

'These are the count's rooms,' the taller man-at-arms said. He showed me into a pair of rooms, really a full apartment, with a solar and two fireplaces and a sort of library, or office.

'And the prince?' I asked.

'In the north tower,' the second man-at-arms said.

'Show us,' I said, and we walked across two courtyards. I remained polite, even cheerful. Richard looked ready to commit violence.

We went through the kitchens.

'I'd like to meet the head chamberlain,' I said.

The younger man-at-arms shrugged. 'I wouldn't know anything about that,' he said.

'Find someone who can arrange it,' Musard said.

Both Visconti men-at-arms stopped. 'What did you say, Moor?' asked the younger one.

I stepped between them. 'Sir Richard Musard is a Knight of the

Sword,' I said. 'And our lords will not be coming into this castle until we have met with the chamberlain.'

They both looked at me. 'That's impossible,' one said.

The other said something like, 'Who the fuck are you?'

Richard leaned against the wall, took out a dagger, and began to clean his nails. 'I'll tell you who I am,' he said in flawless Italian. 'I'm a man who is going to walk back out to the Count of Savoy and tell him that, no, the rooms assigned are not acceptable.'

'I'll get somebody,' said the younger man, and he walked off.

The older man shrugged. 'These are the rooms assigned.' He shook his head. 'Just take them.'

He turned and led the way, obviously impatient, and we came to the north tower. It was almost completely separate from the rest of the yard, had its own entrance, and four floors. One of the floors was storage.

I walked up to the roof, from which I could see all the way to the Alps. When I came down, there was a tall man in a nice, dark blue brocade with a gold chain. His lips were pursed so tightly that I thought his cheeks might split.

'Just tried to bribe me,' Musard said.

Boson nodded.

'We'll take the tower,' I said. 'May I have your name and style, sir?'

Blue brocade bowed, not very deeply. 'Manfredo Orgulaffi,' he said.

'Messer Orgulaffi, this tower will suit us nicely. Please have all the rooms cleared – the prince will have the upper two floors, and the count the lower two floors.'

Musard glanced at me.

Orgulaffi frowned. 'That is impossible.'

'Immediately, please, and then nothing further will be said.'

'No,' he said.

I shrugged. 'You were told that they needed to be lodged where we could guard both of them at the same time. My men-at-arms will not be split up. You were told this.'

Orgulaffi was outraged. I think his outrage was genuine – no one had told him any such thing.

'You are making work for my people,' Orgulaffi said. 'That is a storeroom.'

Musard shrugged. 'Not our problem,' he said. 'Best get to it.'

I watched them clear the rooms. I looked in chests, raised an eyebrow over a pile of linseed-soaked rags, and watched their embarrassment as they found a rat's nest. By the time they were almost through, the bells had rung for Nones, there were a hundred men and women working on the tower, and I was seeing something like the whole turnout of servants. By then, Gospel Mark and Ewan and Witkin came in, sent by Bibbo.

'Watch them all. Get to know their faces,' I said.

'I want t'know that lass better, any road,' Gospel Mark said, watching a slim girl stand on her toes to reach a shelf. 'Let me help ye, love,' he called.

Before Nones was done, the count's belongings came in, and then the prince's, and there were jams on the stairs. Richard created a sort of office, or guardroom, on the ground floor, and we installed Messer Ogier as soon as he was free from church.

I took Orgulaffi aside. 'I do not wish to offend you, messire. But the Count of Savoy and the Prince of England are only going to eat what I see made for them and taste myself, and they will only drink what I see prepared and taste, or Messer Ricardo over there. This I promise you. And they will only be served by our own people and, by God, from this moment, no one but our own comes into this tower. We will empty our own chamber pots and sweep the floors and make the beds.'

He held his head high. 'I have sent for the chamberlain,' he said.

The chamberlain proved to be Antonio Pallavicino, a man of rank; I had heard his name mentioned with respect by Nerio. I bowed, and repeated my injunctions.

'This is disrespectful to my lord,' he said.

I shrugged. 'We mean no disrespect. Surely you were told that assassins attempted to kill the prince and the count and his lady, at Pavia.'

'This is not Pavia,' Pallavicino said.

I just smiled, as one would with an erring child.

'I will summon Lord Bernabò,' he said.

I nodded. 'If you must.'

Ogier made his rounds and reported that all was well. We had a string of men-at-arms and archers from the courtyard, through the kitchens, to the tower, handing coffers and boxes and leather travelling cases, hand to hand, so that we knew that no one had touched them. One of Boson's Hungarian archers reported that a tall man with light eyes had offered him money to put something in a box. Gatelussi went to see if he could catch him.

I was still in my armour, and my pretty red velvet was soaked with sweat.

Bernabò appeared, in person. Despite the heat, he wore a man's white gown to the floor, lined in ermine – a thousand ducats or more of fur. He strode up to me as if he might bowl me over, and I'm not a small man.

'You've seized a whole tower?' he asked me. 'Fucking English, you'll take anything not tied down.'

'My lord, you ordered me, yourself, to defend the prince.' I nodded at a passing leather case with the Royal Arms of England on it.

Bernabò nodded. 'So I did. Orgulaffi, whatever this man or that black man tells you, that is my law, you understand me?'

Orgulaffi bowed.

'Lord Bernabò, Messer Orgulaffi has made every attempt to co-operate with us,' I said.

Bernabò smiled, and showed his many white teeth. 'Good,' he said.

I looked at Orgulaffi. He shrugged. 'Why didn't you tell me you were following Bernabò's orders?' he asked.

I shrugged back and won a smile.

'*Bene*,' he said. 'Let us see how we can prepare food your people will eat.'

In the end, Emile went and slept with the Countess of Savoy, and I had a single camp bed in the 'office' that Musard had arranged. You two will remember where they put you. First in another wing, and then Chaucer moved you in with Petrarca – a divine inspiration, since even Robert of Geneva worshipped Petrarca.

Most of our men-at-arms were billeted in the town. We assigned rotations and changed our guard in the courtyard, and then marched through the kitchens, a deliberate show of force. The Visconti men-at-arms didn't like us, and they followed us, but at least we knew where we stood.

That night, Orgulaffi came around with a schedule of chapels and churches. That is, there were so many noble guests in Milan that the Visconti had prepared a list of churches and assigned guests to each of them. Sir John was asleep on my bed. He was forty-six that year, and I had already seen that he tended to hoard his strength. But he rolled off the bed, combed out his beard, and dressed neatly.

'Church?' I asked. We were assigned to Sant'Eustorgio, a fine, if old, brick church. The count and the prince both intended to attend Compline, which was supposed to be especially magnificent. I hadn't been before, and it was a major pilgrimage site – the burial place of the Magi, the three kings of the Nativity.

Sir John smiled wryly. 'I'm not after saving my soul, young William. By Saint George, the number of parts of a man that can ache after a nap.' He stood there, rubbing away at his thighs; then he stretched his legs like a dancer. 'If you are lucky enough to live so long, all this will come to you,' he said. 'Aches, pains, bad eyes, grey hair ... what joy.' He shrugged. 'I assume there will be another attempt on our charges. I want to see it all.'

Before we departed, in close order, he walked through the tower and reviewed our watch list. He and I and Richard Musard and Count Amadeus had a complex set of ties. The count cordially detested Sir John, whom he viewed as a false knight and a traitor; Sir John saw the count as a pompous arse; Richard and I were in between these two poles.

But, that evening, all was cautious amity. The count came down to the guardroom and he and Sir John bowed to each other. But they didn't address each other directly – rather, Richard and I spoke to the count. I spoke to Sir John. It wasn't the best arrangement to protect the prince, and when you added in the Earl of Hereford, and his apparent jealousy of me, you have a rich wedding soup of bad feeling and envy.

Or it might have been. But Sir John viewed the protection of the two lords as business, and in the pursuit of his business, Sir John was very thorough. And his reputation, a little marred by two defeats and recently enhanced by a victory at Borgoforte, was sufficient to render the prince and Lord Bohun, Earl of Hereford, pliant, and even friendly. Sir John passed his orders, and they were orders, via me, to the count, and via Bohun to the prince. And he was obeyed.

'You know what goes into wedding soup, in Italy?' he asked.

I shrugged.

'Anything you have to hand,' Sir John said. 'Don't fret, lad. Geneva is just another rich bastard. Drunk on power. Willing to do something dark to get what he wants.' Hawkwood's face was impassive.

He looked at me. 'Don't make it personal, William. I know you and Musard hate Camus. Don't make it personal.'

I took a deep breath and did my best.

Prayer always helps me, and off we went, a column of armed men, to pray at Compline.

I believe that I have said that I often meditate on the Nativity – it was the first meditation that Fra Peter taught me, long ago when I was his squire. So the church housing the relics of the three wise men at the Nativity was likely to have special meaning for me. And I loved that church. I was fascinated by the beauty of the side chapels. I was busy looking for the tombs of the Magi when I realised that the 'other' Savoyard party had been assigned to the same church. I saw the Archbishop of Cambrai coming down the nave. He was dressed in all his vestments, and carried the staff of his office. At his shoulder was the Prince of Achaea.

I was between them and our party. Prince Lionel was praying at the main altar, and the count and countess were arranging cushions in preparation for the *Benedictus*. I should note that Italian churches can be both more and less formal than English churches – people sometimes come and go, men chat, women gossip.

Geneva stopped, perhaps an arm's length from me. Monks were singing the first psalm behind me. I had my little book of hours in my hand, and my paternoster wrapped around my fist, as I had just been praying.

'Out of my way,' Robert of Geneva said.

I am not sure I had ever been so close to him. Usually we were farther apart – last time, he'd had Camus between us.

Trying to keep Sir John's strictures in mind, I bowed, correctly.

'Perhaps it would be best, my lord, if you and your party stayed here, or went to one of the side chapels.' I was glad that I got it out.

'Out of my way,' he snapped.

'No,' I said. They had perhaps twenty men-at-arms with them, all armed. Not as many as we had, but enough. But, for whatever reason, Geneva was in front, with the Prince of Achaea just behind. Camus and de Lesparre were well back.

The archbishop raised the shepherd's crook so that the iron-shod base was at my chest. 'Move,' he said. 'You are impeding your betters.'

And then Sir John appeared at my shoulder. He must have been watching. He stepped up, and he wasn't in armour. He looked, in fact, like a prosperous burgher in a small English town. He didn't radiate menace; he didn't suggest violence.

'My lord Archbishop,' he said. 'Is there a problem?'

He might have been a notary or a lawyer.

Geneva glanced at him. 'Move! Out of the way. The front of this church is ours. Sit at the back.'

Hawkwood nodded. 'Of course, Eminence. Only – no. *You* may sit at the back, or in the side chapels. You are late, and we have the front. And, my lord, with great respect, you are merely an archbishop; everyone here outranks you.'

Geneva's eyes widened. 'You dare? Do you know who I am?'

Hawkwood smiled. 'All too well.'

I can only admire, even now, Hawkwood's imperturbability. I was shaking – Geneva always had that effect on me. He was not human. If an angel of God came and told me that Geneva was possessed by a demon, I would have not a whit of surprise in me.

The gangly Prince of Achaea flushed. 'I am the best born here,' he said, but there was more whine than force to him.

Turenne's men-at-arms were pushing forward, spreading on either side of us. But not for long. Musard slammed a spear haft against the floor, and our men-at-arms came out from pillars, and formed up. They were forty feet away. They were in armour, and carried spears and swords.

Geneva's eyes narrowed. 'Send me the Count of Savoy,' he said. 'I do not speak with servants, except to chide them.'

Hawkwood nodded, as if the request were reasonable. 'Alas,' he said, 'the Count of Savoy is at prayer.' He stepped up, very close to the archbishop. I had never seen anyone, not even Camus, get so close. 'Perhaps I should make my position clear, my lord.' He smiled. 'For my own part, I am here to protect the count and the prince. From ... anyone. And if anything, anything at all, should happen to either of my employers ...'

'Don't threaten me,' snapped the archbishop.

But he stepped back.

Sir John looked at his hands. 'No threat, my lord. I have three hundred Englishmen under my hand. I promise that you, and these worthy gentlemen, and all your servants, would die. In a bloodbath. And that nothing – not the Visconti, and not your little band of criminals, and certainly not this amateur,' he indicated Camus casually, 'would stop me.'

'You dare—' the archbishop said.

'Do you understand?' Hawkwood asked.

'I will have you—'

Hawkwood glided forward. The Prince of Achaea flinched. Camus drew, pushing forward. I drew.

Hawkwood merely placed a hand on the archbishop's great pectoral cross.

'Tell me. Say, "I understand."'

I had never seen Hawkwood like this. Suddenly he was Satan, or the Archangel Michael; he burned. He was …

Terrifying.

The archbishop stepped back, almost into Camus's sword.

Hawkwood's smile was steady.

'No. You are not capable …' The archbishop knew he'd flinched, and his usually well-modulated voice was shaken.

Hawkwood bowed. 'I see that you understand,' he said. He didn't back away. He turned away, showing his back to a forest of drawn swords.

I was grinning.

The archbishop looked at me as Sir John walked away. His composure was already restored; two men at-arms pushed past him to cover him.

'I have a little surprise for you,' he said.

I bowed. I wasn't John Hawkwood. I backed away, as I would have from a wolf baring its fangs.

That was Compline.

The next day was the day before the wedding. We cooked the count and the prince breakfast on a pair of ancient iron braziers we had in the company gear, and we heard Prince Lionel exclaim at the quality of the hot sausage. Sam Bibbo himself made the mustard.

After Prime, we had the whole day before us, and neither the count nor the prince was minded to cower in our rooms. So we traipsed about the city on foot, with a dozen men-at-arms and a lot of shuffling. At one point I posted Ewan in a church tower to watch the streets below. Most of the lads were keen for the game, and it was then that we had the first fruits of all our practice. Ewan spotted two men behaving oddly and signalled Gospel Mark. Mark followed them aways, and watched them watch us.

Interviewed an hour later, Witkin said he knew the men from the night before. He had been walking along an alley behind the main boulevard of elegant shops, pacing the two men, who wore long gowns to cover their jupons.

Now, Witkin was in many ways a strange man. He kept to himself, he was nobody's comrade, and he was often in hot water with Rob Stone. But for all his strange ways, he was quick-witted.

And violent.

So while the two men-at-arms – Camus's men, young, hard-eyed thugs – watched the count and the prince, Witkin walked up behind them with his five-foot oak staff in his hands like a bishop's crook. He bellowed, 'Stop, thief!' once, and laid one of the men-at-arms flat with a swing of his staff.

The other man turned and got the butt of the staff in his throat-bole.

'Stop!' Witkin apparently cried again. 'Thief!'

Then he kicked each of them a few times, and the Milanese joined him. A crowd is an ugly thing, especially when it thinks it is dealing with thieves.

An hour later, when he joined us, Witkin was his usual unrepentant self. 'They meant you harm,' he said. 'Sir John, the count, the prince. Makes no mind which.'

I looked at him. Sam Bibbo, standing at my shoulder, was clearly not, for once, on my side.

'You killed them,' I said.

Witkin shook his head. 'Nah, Sir William. Milanese killed 'em. I just fucked 'em up, like.'

In fact, they had been kicked to death. An ugly way to die.

Of course, *someone* had helped crucify the pilgrim back at Bolsena. *Someone* helped poison the wine that killed Demetrios.

Bibbo gave me a sketchy bow. 'Word wi' you, sir.'

We walked off under the portico of San Maurizio al Monastero

Maggiore. Nuns scurried to get out of our way as if we were two demons from Hell, which may, sadly, not have been far from the mark.

Bibbo jerked a thumb at Witkin. 'He did us a favour,' he said. 'Witkin is always in trouble. This should get a bone, eh, sir?'

'He murdered ...' I began.

Then I simply changed my mind. 'Right,' I said.

Bibbo smiled. 'Good. Thought you'd see it that way.'

We strolled back.

'Well done, Witkin.' I handed him the usual reward in my company for good service: a gold florin. 'Don't drink it all in one place.'

Witkin gave a pretty good bow. 'I ...' He couldn't think of anything to say. 'Thankee.'

'At your service, Witkin.'

'And yours, my lord.' He turned away and looked in wonder at his florin.

'Thanks, Sam,' I said to Bibbo.

He gave me a wry smile. 'Glad I have somewhat left to teach,' he said.

The count's chamberlain met with Orgulaffi, and they arranged lunch for us at one of the city's mercantile taverns, which, like this fine place, master innkeeper, was able to serve the highest nobility, and had no problem with allowing Ewan and Gospel Mark and William Boson into their kitchen. Stefanos served us at table, in a closed room. I glanced into the kitchen and saw Caterina sitting on a table, swinging her legs, and Peter Albin, in apprentice clothes, cutting meat.

Neither the prince nor the count had any idea how well covered they were.

After a light meal and some fine wine, we heard Mass, and I had a moment, as the prince and count were well taken care of, to browse the stalls outside Sant'Eugenios. That's where I purchased this pin, engraved with the names of all three wise men. A nice token of a pilgrimage that made up in violence what it lacked in grace. I still wear it, as you see. It's to remind me.

While I was chaffering for the brooch, Bernabò approached with a dozen courtiers and was entered into our party. Our men-at-arms had already come to understand the process – who could approach and who could not. Bernabò embraced Prince Lionel and then Count

Amadeus and finally Sir John, waved his arms about, and strode off, like any lord.

I was just making my purchase when Count Amadeus came up, with Musard and Ogier and Fiore all around him.

'A moment, gentlemen,' the count said with a smile.

All three knights turned their backs. That's all the privacy you can have when you are Count of Savoy and men are hunting you.

'Messer Guillaume,' he said. 'I have been asked if you would fight tomorrow.'

'Fight?' I asked. 'At a wedding?'

'Galeazzo has planned a dozen entertainments for the wedding dinner, and he wishes to include a joust and a foot combat. Gian Galeazzo asked for Fiore for the joust, but I will send Ogier. Your Sir John agrees.'

I nodded.

'But Galeazzo expressly asked for you to fight on foot. He was most pressing, as was his son.' The count glanced at me sidelong. 'So says Lord Bernabò.'

'You know I am at your service,' I said. 'Fiore will be jealous.'

'Fiore will be well rewarded,' the count said. 'Three things I feel you should know.' He looked around. 'First, my courts have attainted the Prince of Achaea for failing in his feudal duties. And further found him to have no case in the matter of his inheritance.'

Emile had already told me, but I wasn't going to blab.

'Second, your opponent during the dinner will be Camus.' The count's mild green eyes went to mine. 'They mean to kill you. I do not know how.'

I nodded. Fiore was six feet away and hearing every word.

'Third, I have written out for you a deed. It gives you the privilege of conducting a private war against my contumacious sub-vassal, the Bourc Camus. It is the best I can do to protect you.' His eyes remained on mine. 'Do you want to fight?'

My heart beat like a drum sounding the alarm. But I knew I could beat Camus.

'Yes,' I said. 'What weapon?'

'The weapons of war, on foot,' the count said. That meant a spear or axe, with a sword on one hip and a dagger on the other.

I nodded and began, with trembling hands, to pin on my brooch.

*

Some time later we were all at the practice for the great ceremony, which was to be held in the square in front of the shabby old cathedral. We were all to process to the square in front of the new palace at Porta Giovia. It was all brick – that's all I knew about it then. It grows more magnificent every year, or so I hear.

So we practised. We saw the Archbishop of Milan, and the Archbishop of Cambrai close beside him. I had a difficult time imagining that God's grace would touch a wedding performed by Geneva. Then we processed to the new castle, about fifteen minutes for one man, but we had hundreds of guests, each with a claim to precedence, and hundreds more men-at-arms.

The entire route was lined with soldiers – every militia from every guild, all the men who were not at Borgoforte.

I was walking along with my wife when I saw the lists. They were set up in a square halfway along the processional route and Gian Galeazzo, who was, apparently, the master of ceremonies for the next day, explained in his high-pitched, commanding voice that two knights would run three courses each, beginning as the wedding party approached, and then two knights would fight with weapons of war, on foot. He showed us where the married couple would sit, and how the movable barriers would create the space for the foot lists.

I thought that the foot lists were ridiculously small, with the royal box behind them and a well head on the opposite side.

'At least we'll have cool water,' Fiore quipped.

And we would be right on top of the wedding party, who would be seated within weapons' reach. I wondered if Camus was mad enough to throw himself on the count or the prince.

I was leaning on the solid oak barriers when Janet, of all people, came through the crowd. She was dressed as a woman, and she moved with the sort of regal grace you see mostly in great ladies, despite a plain woollen gown with very little decoration. Her only nod to her 'other life' was a plaque belt, a knight's belt, worn low on her hips.

I introduced her to Emile. As we were all walking in apparent informality, Emile had taken the opportunity to buttonhole Violante, the bride. Her brother, Gian Galeazzo, was close by. My understanding was that he was not just master of ceremonies, but also master of the lists. He was talking to Boucicault.

Suddenly I knew which French knight would cross lances with Fiore. And there was Fiore himself, just making his bow to Janet, for whom he had an old passion.

She didn't return the passion, but she seemed happy to see us all. She and Emile embraced on being introduced, and Janet said something unusual.

'Your husband and Richard Musard saved my life,' she said.

I'd never heard her say it.

I was testing the strength of the list boundaries. The corners were set deep in the square, and the cross-supports were as solid as the stone underfoot.

Janet was speaking low to Emile, and Violante looked shocked. Her hand went to her throat; her beautiful face was suddenly splotchy with colour, as if she'd failed to blush.

Emile just nodded and put her hand on Janet's hand. Violante burst into tears. Emile hugged her close.

'What are they talking about?' Fiore asked. I looked past him to see Musard looking at Janet with unconcealed longing.

'I assume you are running your courses with Boucicault,' I said to Fiore.

He looked at the famous French knight. 'Ah,' he said. 'Good. No, it will be me.'

Boucicault came our way, ducking under the crossbars of the foot lists. He was magnificently dressed, but there was something about him that always made me feel inferior – his grace, his clothes, his riches. Despite which, as you know if you've been listening, I like him – always have.

We bowed to each other. He was introduced to Fiore; there were more bows.

He took my arm. 'Excuse us, gentles?' he said. I glanced across a dozen heads at Sir John, who, with Ogier, had the escorts.

He nodded. The nod merely meant that everything was working.

I nodded back, and stepped aside with Boucicault.

'I just heard from Turenne that you are fighting Achaea's champion for his rights in his inheritance case. Is that true?' He looked both ways.

I won't say I was stunned, because it was so typical of Geneva's usual methods . . .

I shrugged. 'No,' I said. 'I am fighting a demonstration bout to entertain the visitors. Gian Galeazzo asked for me, but it might just as well have been Ogier or Musard or William Boson or Andy Belmont.'

Boucicault nodded, pulling at his beard. 'I knew something was rotten.'

'Surely he can't just make it so by saying it,' I asked, pointing at Achaea, who was visible due to his height.

Boucicault shook his head. 'You know the poison de Lesparre has spread about the King of Cyprus. And now he's saying that you and the Count of Savoy have called him a coward.'

It was my turn to pull my beard. 'He's a fool and a blowhard,' I said. 'But he's no coward.'

Boucicault leaned close. 'My point is that someone is going around saying these things, and they will gain currency. Who is this Fiore? He is your friend?'

'Imperial knight, fought in all the actions in the Holy Land, has served on Peter of Cyprus's tourney team. The best lance I ever saw, save mayhap you.'

Boucicault was a true knight. He broke into a broad smile. 'Ah!' he said. 'This I will enjoy very much, then. We will make friends after.' He bowed to me. 'Watch yourself. A great many people here mean you harm, and there are … people … in my own embassy …' He looked around. 'I disapprove of them.'

I nodded. And bowed. 'Thank you, my friend.'

He nodded. 'I like to see who you have become.' He put a hand on my shoulder, the man who had once tried to hang me, and walked away.

I burrowed back through the crowd, mindful of pickpockets and assassins. Violante was smiling at Emile, and the two were quite animated. Gian Galeazzo was surrounded by his own courtiers – all young men. I pushed in, as gently as I could, but Gian Galeazzo parted them for me.

'Ah, my famous English knight,' he said. Seventeen-year-olds are not that good at dissimulation. Even when brilliant and ruthless. I could tell he was up to something, but, complicated boy that he was, I could also tell that his admiration for me was genuine. He showed me off to his friends like a prize horse or an art object.

I asked him for the rules of the contest and he rattled them off in a fair way. They were very Italian – that is, more was left unsaid than was said. We would bear our own weapons, we were to fight in war harness, and each of us would be allowed six blows. There would be small pavilions at either end of the square where we could change for the grand dinner.

'You and this Bourc, you hate each other very much, yes?' he asked, a little too excitedly.

I shrugged. 'No, my lord.'

'We hope to see some blood,' one of the young men said.

'Perhaps you should come and fight yourself,' I snapped. I was not best pleased with the proceeding, which seemed framed, as far as I could see, to allow someone to cheat.

Why? Because axes and spears can be long or short, heavy or light, can have spring catches, hidden blades – all sorts of tricks. A dagger can be poisoned. 'Weapons of war' didn't 'allow' such things, but it made them almost impossible to detect.

'You are the best fighting knight I have ever seen,' Gian Galeazzo said to me. 'I look forward to seeing you defend us.'

'Defend?' I asked.

It turned out, that, according to the luck of the draw, I was the *tenans*, the defender. I would be in the Visconti corner, with the new bride and groom at my back. My opponent, Camus, would represent the 'visitors' or *venans*. He would, in effect, represent the French and the Pope and all those who opposed Violante's marriage.

Including Gian Galeazzo himself, I suspected. And he was up to something. He had that excess of energy that betrays a man who is plotting.

Not much I could do. I exchanged glances with Sir John. Violante had rejoined her father, and we were all moving again. I slipped under the edge of the lists, and there, of course, was Geneva, watching me with his voyeur's eyes.

'I look forward to tomorrow,' Geneva said. He nodded. 'Many of my debts will be paid off.'

Janet, of all people, came up to me. She was the only woman in the whole crowd to wear a rondel dagger, which she wore rather provocatively. She smiled at Robert of Geneva. 'Are you a friend of William's?' she asked.

'This is the Archbishop of Cambrai,' I said.

She took that in. 'Oh,' she said. 'In that case, fuck off.'

The shock of being spoken to in such a way, by a woman, was worth any inner torments I was suffering. Geneva's face went paper-white, and then red.

One of his attendants, mistaking Janet for a woman, so to speak, stepped up threateningly. He only meant to tower over her. She stamped on his instep and drew his sword as he fell.

People screamed.

Janet tossed her hair. 'William?' she asked.

I shook my head. 'No, Janet.'

'*Ah bien. Au revoir, monseigneur*,' she said to Geneva. 'Like I said: fuck off.'

He retreated faster from Janet than he had from Sir John. In fact, he scuttled, and he was hurried on his way by a dozen of our people mocking him.

Someone, probably Stefanos, threw a clod of horse dung. It was accurate.

In the shoving that followed, Janet turned to me. 'They are saying that your wife is accused of adultery and murder, and you are defending her in the lists tomorrow. Do you know that?'

'Who is saying that?' I asked.

'I heard it from Violante Visconti,' she said. 'Who, for my money, has the same experience of men I have.' She nodded.

I will not go into details, but Janet has been attacked, and survived. I knew what she meant.

'I love your wife,' Janet said. 'Can you get Richard to stop staring at me?'

'Probably not,' I admitted. I was thinking myriad thoughts, as one does: Gian Galeazzo and his sister and Bernabò and his thousands of women and Antonio and his views on 'family'; but also that I had missed Janet far more than I allowed; that I was delighted that she and Emile took to each other; that Geneva had now been humiliated twice and we were provoking him; that Boucicault had as much as told me that the French embassy was plotting against the wedding. And through this tapestry of conspiracy shot personal threads: Boucicault and me; Richard and Janet; even Witkin's desire to be valued.

It made my head spin. I wanted to just get through the next twenty-four hours. But I knew, somehow, that I had to do better than that.

I had to work to get through, intact, with my friends and my lords intact and un-dishonoured.

Clearly Geneva and Turenne were spreading rumours about my fight, but why?

An hour later, safe in our tower, John Hawkwood put his finger on it.

'Geneva is like a mountebank at a fair,' he said. 'He wants us all to be looking the other way. The attack, if there is an attack, will come during your fight, William. And he wants us keyed up, on edge, and looking at the wrong thing.'

'What the hell can he be planning?' Musard asked.

Sir John raised an eyebrow. 'We can count that it will be over-complicated, and more guided by malice than by tactics,' he said, as crushing a denunciation of Robert of Geneva as I've ever heard.

Sir John told Bibbo to keep the pressure on the French and the archbishop's people.

That took the form of half a dozen of Camus's men, and two French men-at-arms, being caught outside a brothel and beaten. Badly.

It's an ugly business. Nor did I always approve, any more than Boucicault. But in this case, we felt that we had the upper hand, and that this was much like a siege. It was vital to keep the initiative, and put the pressure on our opponents all the time.

We went to Compline, the night before the wedding, and none of the archbishop's party attended. Then we trooped home. I settled all of our people, and then made up my bed in the guardroom.

We swept the tower, causing Lady Bonne to make some awkward comments, but her complaints stopped when Musard found an infernal device – a clay pot with a smouldering fire inside, tipped to drop and smash above a doorway.

'Score one to them,' Hawkwood said.

'How the hell did they get that in here?' we all asked, and that, sadly, was not answerable.

Count Amadeus took charge, and ordered everyone to bed. 'We have a watch. We have found their device, and in truth, *mes amis*, these coals would no more light this old oak afire than light my horse. This is a provocation – most effective if it keeps us all awake.'

'The count is correct,' Hawkwood said. 'The attack will be to-morrow.'

*

The bells were ringing for Vespers and, outside the tower, a handful of monks were making their way to the chapel to say the hours. I woke up to the bells. I lay there for a few minutes, looking around the guardroom. I had a lot to worry about, and I rose, slipped into some old shoes, and padded about, checking the posts, inside and out. All of our people were alert: Savoyards, White Company, and my own people – no one was asleep. That raised my spirits a little, but I was as spiritless as I have ever been. My heart beat too hard; I seemed to start at anything. I had had poor dreams when I had managed sleep.

I came back to the guardroom, kicked off my shoes, and found my wife on my very narrow camp bed.

She put her arms around me. 'Some one of the ancients contends that women rob men of their strength,' she said. 'I see it differently.'

I protested.

She leaned over me. 'Our friends are at both doors,' she said. 'Give me a little of your time, soldier.'

After we disported, she lay beside me a while, and then she rose.

'Sleep,' she said, and it was like a spell. I slept.

I awoke late. People tiptoed around me, even the great Count of Savoy, but when Prince Lionel rose, I did too. He had comported himself with great élan – though if Chaucer tells the story himself, I'm sure we'd hear more about the Duke of Clarence, eh?

My harness was laid out in the courtyard. I borrowed l'Angars's beautiful, Milanese-made *ghiavarina*, and played with it a little – lighter than my spear, and much prettier. You may laugh, but anyone who has ever fought in a public list knows that what you look like matters.

I saw the Duke of Clarence dressed; he looked magnificent. I saw Marc-Antonio and Emile take my magnificent suit of clothes off to where I would dress, if I lived that long.

I knew a great deal of fear, and I spent a fair amount of time doubting myself. Nay, brothers – I tell you this to be an honest man. There was something in that hour that almost unmanned me, and I owe a great deal to my wife's ready humour and her refusal to accept my fears. She didn't mock me; she merely held me up, as if her hand was under my arm, crossing a stream. And, as the morning wore on, I mastered myself, and Fiore and I began to arm. Then we settled, and shared a cup of watered wine.

Before Terce, the prince and the count left the tower, with Sir John commanding an army of attendants and men-at-arms. Janet and Sister Marie were included, dressed as women, but with concealed weapons. Janet was attached to Lady Bonne, and Marie, as ever, to Emile. Let me add, for those of you who cannot imagine a woman in the life of arms, that a few armed women hidden away can be a great advantage against a hidden enemy. No one expects armed women.

Regardless, Fiore and I heard the shouts of the crowd as the bridal party and the groom's party approached the square, and then time seemed to suddenly contract, the way it does on the eve of battle, and our contests went from immovable objects far distant on time's great wheel to immediate monsters rearing up before us.

Before me, I should say. Fiore was so calm as to seem inhuman. He was a perfect foil for me, and as I strode around the castle yard, he came and put me in a chair.

'Don't waste your spirit,' he said.

I talked too much, and he put water in my hands. 'Drink water,' he said.

About half an hour before we were due to go to the lists, he turned. I was chattering to cover my flurry of spirits.

'What will you do when you enter the lists?' he asked.

I probably looked at him like a dumb animal.

'The wand falls. What do you do with Camus? Do not tell me that it depends on what he does. You are twice the fighter he is. What game will you play?'

I took a deep breath. 'I want to play close and throw him,' I said. 'It will get the fastest end.'

Fiore nodded sharply. 'Good,' he said.

'Is it the right choice?' I asked.

'How would I know?' Fiore asked me. He shrugged. 'You've fought him five or ten times. I haven't. But it is the right *kind* of plan, and I agree that you don't want the play to go on long. If Sir John is right, and I fear he is, you want this over as quickly as possible. Before, perhaps, they can act.'

Then we practised two close plays. My *ghiavarina* was a spear, a heavy spear, which could also be used for some sweeping cuts. My opponent had declared that he would use a pole-hammer with a spike – in effect, the opposite weapon, capable of heavy cuts, with a sort of back-up thrust.

Fiore modelled the pole-hammer with Witkin's staff. I found that my best tactic, even against the master, was a domination of the initiative with rapid thrusts.

I worked up quite a sweat, but I felt better. And then I apologised to Fiore.

'I'm costing you spirit, when you should be thinking of your own engagement,' I said.

Fiore shrugged, dismissive. 'No need,' he said. 'I know exactly what I will do.'

An hour later we were still standing at the edge of the lists. That is, Fiore was sitting on his big half-Arab charger, and Boucicault was already up on his, forty paces away. There was already a fine crowd – the biggest I had ever seen to watch any chivalric sport. But the procession was delayed. We had messengers every ten minutes. The wedding ceremony had started late – something about the consecrated Host.

An hour later, and my hard-won calm was fraying like a rope under too much tension. My opponent wasn't even there. I wondered if I was to be left without a fight, or whether, in fact, the fight had always been the distraction, and the attempt was coming in the procession, and here I was, useless. Against that, Fiore and I agreed, we had an army of competent friends protecting our principals. We were where we were supposed to be, and there is comfort in merely doing the task assigned. The count and Sir John had chosen us.

When the procession was an hour and a half late, Boucicault rode over to Fiore, and they clasped hands, and took turns curvetting and displaying their horsemanship around the ring, so that the good burghers of Milan cheered them. Finally, young Gian Galeazzo rode up, splendid in gilt armour, with twenty beautifully kitted knights at his back, all costumed as heroes of the Trojan War. He was well organised; he saluted all of us, enquired into my opponent and sent a missive to Turenne and Achaea, asking where he was. Then he donned a magnificent tabard in the Visconti arms, and four Viper flags were raised at the corners of the jousting lists. Fiore went to one end and Boucicault to the other.

The wedding party approached, led by a regiment of guild militia, trumpeters and drummers.

Prince Lionel looked like a young King Arthur. He was magnificent in red and blue and gold, his hair shone on his shoulders, and he wore the garter on his leg. But he was fully eclipsed by his Guinevere. Lady Violante, whatever hardships she had endured, smiled like the Lombard sun showering us with splendour. She wore cloth of gold, and even it was not brighter than the smile on her face.

Hundreds of children strewed rose petals in their path as they approached, and they wandered like lovers, the prince's eyes seldom straying from the beauty of his lady.

Gian Galeazzo, if he was against the match, gave no sign, except that, as I watched him, I felt he was over-controlling the horse he was on. His emotion communicated itself to the horse's feet, as the horse kept moving, stamping, and moving again. By contrast, Fiore's horse was as immobile as the rider, and so was Boucicault's.

The bridal party entered the lists, and was roundly cheered, and then took their seats in the box. Gian Galeazzo sent a herald to me. He said that, as they were running so late, he intended to start the joust before the whole procession had come up.

I thought it irregular, and I wondered where my opponent was.

Fiore looked over the crowd. 'William,' he said, 'none of our people are here.'

He had a point.

I had Marc-Antonio, and Stefanos. I sent Stefanos, with a dagger in his sleeve, running for some blades. 'Get me five archers,' I said. 'Anyone.'

I looked across the lists, and saw Turenne. He was smiling broadly. Boucicault said something and Turenne shook his head. Boucicault reacted angrily.

Whatever it was, I knew it was on.

'The Lord of Pavia wishes to proceed,' the herald said again.

'I would like to await Count Amadeus,' I said.

The herald rode away across the lists. Then he was back. 'Lord Gian Galeazzo insists that we cannot wait any longer. The crowd is restless. The bride and groom need food and rest.'

You need to understand this. I held out as long as I could, but I was not then, and am not now, a great lord. The *social* pressure was too much – the third request came from Boucicault. I could not very well tell him that the French ambassador was plotting a murder and he was a tool; I had no evidence.

'Jean,' I said, 'there is some plot, and they want to begin early.'

Boucicault nodded. 'I fear there is something,' he said. 'But … my horse is tiring, and these people press so close.'

I stood on a chair, and I could not see Savoy's banners.

Then I saw Emile and, beyond her, Janet. They were close by Violante – in fact, Emile was chatting with the new Duchess of Clarence. And spreading out to the right was William Boson and, behind him, Sam Bibbo.

'Let's do it,' Fiore said. 'I'll take my time.'

I waved to Gian Galeazzo.

The first pass was excellent. Both men placed their lances neatly. Both struck high and inside on the other's shield, and their lances shivered like trees struck by lightning, and both rode on, their bodies erect as if they were riding for pleasure. Boucicault's horse got a splinter of oak in its chest, and that caused delay. I heard drums in the distance.

Turenne was demanding that Boucicault get back in the saddle. I kept looking for Geneva and not finding him.

The second pass was very different. Both men attempted more difficult targets. Boucicault went for Fiore's helmet, and Fiore went to parry Boucicault's lance. Only a jouster could judge the sheer complexity of what followed: Fiore's lance crossed Boucicault's, the French knight changed his point of aim and his seat in the last heartbeat – a magnificent feat of jousting. Fiore gave a deft wriggle …

Both lances exploded. To any unmartial watchers, it must have looked exactly like the first pass. To me, it was one of the most remarkable pieces of jousting I'd ever seen. The two men trotted past each other, reined in, and touched hands. Fiore was beaming.

There was Camus. He was in armour, and he appeared, suddenly, both broader and taller than I remembered, and he was wearing his argent instead of Achaea's colours. His visor was odd, lacking the perforations most visors had, the 'breaths'. And it was *down*.

That made no sense. On a hot day in a city square on stone, it was an impossible choice.

I turned to Marc-Antonio. Bibbo was there, and Ewan.

'Where is the count?' I asked.

'Half a mile away. There was an accident,' Bibbo said, with disgust. 'Stefanos came, and Sir John sent us.'

'Look at Camus,' I said.

Marc-Antonio nodded. 'No one could have their visor down,' he said.

Bibbo said, 'It's not Camus.'

That hadn't even occurred to me.

'Where is Geneva?' I asked.

Bibbo shook his head.

I prayed. That's all I could think of. I had clues, but not enough to form a pattern.

'Can we put someone over there to watch them?' I asked.

Stefanos, having returned sweating from his run, jumped up. He was just twelve years old, and his brother had been killed by poison. 'Let me go,' he said.

Ewan went into the crowd and bought some Milanese boy's long gown, clerical black. He bought it right off the boy, and came back. 'Ye owe me two florins,' he growled. 'Here, lad. Don't be killed, now.'

'I have a dagger,' the Greek boy said with magnificent courage, as if his tiny dagger would stop Turenne's men-at-arms.

The jousters were ready. The archers turned outward, and watched the crowd.

Fiore waggled his spear-point at Boucicault. They were friends now – united by their contest.

They flew at each other. Fiore's horse seemed to leap on its first step. Boucicault's went back on its haunches and then launched. Both men, I thought later, tried to lean into their blows. Both gathered their horses perfectly at contact.

One more time, both lances seemed to detonate like the bombs of the German handgonners, and this time, both men rocked in their saddles. Rocked back, sat up, and continued down the lists through the wall of sound of a crowd of twenty thousand or more.

My heart was pounding.

It was my turn.

While the crowd roared on and on, a dozen Visconti guardsmen appeared and began to move the barriers. They left only the little walled enclosure that marked the inner lists. The royal couple's viewing box was directly above my corner.

I walked to it. Marc-Antonio followed me, carrying my helmet and my spear and my gauntlets. A bench was brought. It was damned hot and I was almost oily with sweat under my harness. I wondered how much the other bastard was suffering.

He walked across the sand from where Turenne and the French were gathered. He was attended by two boys in Turenne's livery. One carried a heavy pole-hammer with a massive head and a spike above it, like a heavy spearhead. The other carried a sword belt with a long-sword.

Gian Galeazzo rode up behind me. 'Together now,' he said. His voice betrayed his emotion. 'Bow to my sister.'

I made a full *reverentia* to the couple. Prince Lionel saluted us, and Violante waved.

'I'd like to see who I'm fighting,' I said, loudly enough to carry. I turned to look at the man. He was half a head taller than Camus: my height, to the width of an eyelash.

Gian Galeazzo smiled, a little too broadly. 'The Bourc Camus, I understand?' he said.

I shook my head. 'That's not Camus,' I said.

Turenne had mounted one of the stools and had begun to address the crowd. I could hear him, claiming that I had killed my wife's husband, that I had betrayed the King of Cyprus, that I was a false knight.

The two boys passed behind the strange knight, and I wondered at the sheer size of the head of the pole-hammer – a massive weapon.

'Not the Bourc Camus?' Gian Galeazzo asked. He was absolutely genuine. His puzzlement was real.

'Ask him to open his visor,' I shouted.

I was growing very angry, because Turenne was standing forty feet away, repeating every slur ever spoken against my wife, not just me. Every whiff of scandal, every possible lover.

'Shut him up,' I spat at Gian Galeazzo.

'I give the orders here,' he said. He was terrified, and yet smug.

But then he turned to the strange knight. 'Show us your face and declare your style,' he said.

The man opened his visor without demur. It was de Lesparre. I was not very surprised; I knew he hated me, and I knew how big he was.

'Where is the Bourc Camus?' I asked.

'He is indisposed. He expected that you will try some coward's cheat. I was proud to take his place. I will prove on your body what a caitiff you are.'

'There now,' Gian Galeazzo said. 'All settled.' He smiled.

I walked to the lists, and was admitted. They tied a scarf with the Visconti colours to my left arm, and my helmet went on my head, and the gauntlets on my hands. I still didn't see it.

Fiore was leaning on my corner of the lists, ignoring the prince, who was trying to praise him.

'Look at his pole-hammer,' Fiore spat. I was trying to ask something, and he actually punched my shoulder. '*Look* at it.'

Marc-Antonio held a cup of water to my lips and I drank.

I closed my eyes, knelt, and tried to imagine the three wise men kneeling before the Christ child. I rose, thinking of my first blow – of how obviously my opponent intended to pin me in my corner. Everything about his body language suggested that he was going to charge.

My visor went down. Gian Galeazzo was still on horseback, outside the tiny ring. I had the royal couple at my back. Turenne was now nowhere to be seen, and there were ten thousand people pressing close around the lists, and another ten thousand beyond them.

I looked at my opponent. He was bouncing up and down on the balls of his feet, six feet and more of armour and muscle. His great pole-hammer was held across his body, the head back and the butt-spike pointing at me. I looked at it, and whatever Fiore had seen, I didn't see. But I did know some tournament tricks. I saw the white wand go up, I saw my enemy's tension. I rotated my hips, from a weight-back *garde* to a weight-forward one.

He sprang forward before the twitch of the white wand – a virtual leap of six feet, meant to pin me against the barricade.

I had already moved. And Gian Galeazzo, in an odd display of fairness, called halt, all twenty trumpeters braying out the sound. I nodded.

My opponent had moved too early. He had also revealed something of his intentions. I went back to my corner, and took up my *garde*, this time with my spearhead pointing well off to my right, off line – *porta di ferro.*

Fiore said, 'He has something in that hammer.'

That made no sense to me.

When the wand dropped, I powered forward like a man going into an enemy line of battle. So did he, but without the convulsive leap of his first attempt. He thrust with the iron butt-spike, a clear provocation, to enable the swing of that massive hammer. I tapped the iron aside.

That was not the response he'd expected. He tried to turn me, and, remember, the lists were small.

I was not interested in turning. Fiore always tells you to do the easy thing first. I thrust at one of his hands.

And I caught him, a tiny blow, between the fingers. But my borrowed spearhead was sharp, and blood flowed over the haft of the great hammer.

And I rotated my spearhead up, glided it over his hands … My spearhead vanished under his arm and we struggled.

In any public deed, that was the end of the bout, because I could see his blood. Perhaps for a heartbeat I relaxed. I expected the baton to drop …

He smashed at me with the haft.

I had nowhere to retreat, so I met him, haft to haft. Then he pushed me, and while I am big, he was bigger. Fiore, and all that dancing, saved me – our hafts remained locked. He swung the whole weight of his hammer at me as we pressed together, and for such a huge head, it moved with astounding speed. But then, so did I. I got the spear out from under his arm and cut. We crashed together like warhorses, and his blow went past my head, and the crossbar on my spear had the head of his hammer, so that he could not land a blow with it, but his shaft slammed into my shoulder even as my rising parry ended in a thrust to his shoulder.

Then a great many things happened at once.

The two of us were instantly blind, surrounded by something that stung the eyes and made me cough. I thought for perhaps a single heartbeat that it was dust. But it tasted like metal.

Stefanos screamed, '*A l'arme!*'

The pain of de Lesparre's blow went through me like a red-hot spear. My left shoulder had been abused repeatedly for two years, and in one blow, his haft alone broke something. I couldn't breathe.

De Lesparre grunted and danced back, cursing. I was blind, and all

I could do was stab with the blade of my spear, one-handed – my left arm was almost inert. I pressed forward.

De Lesparre slammed the butt of his pole-hammer into my helmet. I didn't see it coming. It should have put me down, but it only staggered me. My good helmet held the blow, and I stumbled. I still couldn't see.

He hit me again, but his back was pressed against the oak poles of the lists.

De Lesparre coughed. He was right in front of me, and people were screaming. Sweat saved me – the sheer volume of sweat pouring down my face got the powder out of my left eye, and I had a glimpse of him. The air was like the haze of a battlefield after an hour of cavalry fighting, except that the haze was pale grey or white, like flour, but it tasted like metal. De Lesparre was as blind as I. Even as I watched, he swung a blow with both hands, and I saw powder spraying from the head of his hammer. He missed me and hit the wooden barricade, and a great puff of the stuff slopped over the crowd.

And he was bleeding badly. My first cover and thrust had scored, right under his right arm, when I thrust over his bleeding hands. I thrust again, overhand, like the men in the statues I'd seen in Outremer. I put my spearhead into the rent in his maille. He coughed, and threw a sloppy cut, and stumbled and I tried to pull my spear back, one-handed, but I couldn't. Again, I got a glimpse of the action. He was bent over, and my spear was five fingers deep in his side.

I let go.

He screamed, coughed, and brought his pole-hammer up.

I stepped in, kicked my own spear haft knowing it would hurt him, and drew my dagger right-handed. His right arm was slow and my left wrapped it as I entered into this close space, and there we were in the stinking dust, faceplate to faceplate.

It was, despite my broken left shoulder and the intense pain I was in, pretty much the play I'd imagined, except that, as my shoulder was hurt and his right arm was pouring blood, we neither of us had much grip on each other. But he tried to cock the hammer back one-handed.

Behind him I saw flame.

How to put this . . .

In one beat of my heart, I understood what I had been seeing: what Stefanos saw when he shouted. I understood what the deception was for, why Geneva was not there, and why they had duped de Lesparre the blowhard.

I could see the man with the burning cord in his left hand and the clay pot in his right.

I pivoted on my right foot, and slammed my dagger into de Lesparre's visor, but I used the blade, not to kill him – as a scythe, out behind his head, clutching his neck like an iron claw. Weight change. Right foot between his legs.

The dagger rolls outward, and my hips pivot, and he is on his back.

I stepped forward onto my right foot, and threw my dagger. It struck the bomb-thrower sideways – not blade first as in a romance – but I threw hard, all the desperation of the hour, and it hit him in the head.

And Stefanos, the unlikely hero, stripped the clay pot from his hands and tossed it. It seemed to sail through the air forever. More importantly, he appeared to have thrown it *at* Prince Lionel.

But the boy's aim was true. The clay pot vanished over the edge of the well head.

There was the sound of the pot breaking, and then a flash of intense heat and light went straight up out of the well, as if it were a great cannon planted in the earth.

The bomb shocked us all to silence. I couldn't hear anything, but I do not think anyone made a noise. I had de Lesparre at my feet, and I didn't even think to fall on him. I stood, stupefied.

Then I saw Gian Galeazzo.

He was *smiling.*

I looked down at de Lesparre. He was in a bad way. I struggled to get my visor up, threw down my gauntlets, and knelt by him, even as Marc-Antonio came and took my helmet right off my head.

'Christ,' de Lesparre said. 'What is this stuff?'

I missed the next few minutes. William Boson did it all. He got Prince Lionel out of the box and surrounded him with English soldiers. Lionel was panicked for his bride, who had, it appears, been summoned away just before I was to fight. Emile was with her, safe.

They took me to my pavilion. I could walk, and de Lesparre, who seemed to me uncomprehending of the role he'd played, was carried.

I stopped twice to cough. It was terrible, that stuff, and my eyes burned. Emile appeared and began to pour water on my eyes before my armour was off. The hellish stuff from de Lesparre's hammer was all over me, but very little of it had penetrated my armour, even at the maille.

'Don't touch it,' Peter Albin shouted, coming in. I have no idea how much later that was – most of my harness was off. His wife came in with hot water and towels.

Albin tasted it and spat. '*Arsenico,*' he said, 'with hellebore and mustard powder. Something like that. Sweet Virgin Mary. What hellish stuff.'

He pinned me, with Marc-Antonio, and with a feather made me vomit. That was grim. Caterina began to wash any part of me touched by the powder.

Then I was given water. My stomach began to gripe.

Ewan and Gospel Mark were doing the same with de Lesparre – none too gently – and Albin snapped at them and went to bandage his wound. They made me vomit again.

Emile was just cleaning my face, and Albin was fussing over my collarbone, when Count Amadeus entered. Some men went on one knee, and some continued their work.

The Green Count was in an apotheosis of emerald magnificence. I was stained in sweat and vomit.

He ignored me and looked at Albin. 'Well?'

'His collarbone is broken,' Albin said. 'Otherwise, much as usual.' He smiled.

The Green Count bowed to Emile and then to Caterina.

Emile burst into tears. Having worked like a mule for half an hour, I think she'd been ready for worse news.

Count Amadeus came to me. He nodded, as if we were old friends.

'Guillaume, I know you have done us a fine service. And I know you would lie down and sleep. But if you can manage, put on your fine clothes and join us for dinner. Because,' he looked at Emile, 'because victory in these awful things is in appearances.'

Emile washed me, Marie dressed me, and I had fresh braes and a fresh shirt. Every motion of my left side hurt. But the griping in my stomach calmed, and Albin mixed me something – dates and honey and wine, he said – and I drank it off, and was better for it.

I wore the pink cote-hardie, and my lovely belt of enamel plaques, and the two orders I had earned over my hood. Emile also changed, and her pink matched mine to perfection. Really, for once in my life I was a great noble, and too damned hurt to really enjoy it.

I walked the five-minute walk to the square, and I was cheered when I left the pavilion, a wonderful thing. I bowed and waved my hand, my right hand, and a guard of my own archers closed in around me and Emile and Caterina and Sister Marie, and we reached the palace square alive and untouched.

And so I attended the wedding dinner, the most outrageous feast of my lifetime, with my arm and shoulder in a fine brocade sling. We were late, of course. And being late, we made an entrance, even though the Visconti were wearing matching cloth of gold, even though Violante looked like the goddess Venus come to Earth, or perhaps the very keeper of the garden of chivalric love that poets write about.

We had missed four courses. Chaucer will tell you more, but there were eighteen in total, each a double, one of game and one of fish, and there were thousands of guests. And at every course, the master of ceremonies, now in magnificent cloth of gold and miniver, was giving away incredible gifts to the newly married couple and other guests.

Food is the very best drug of all. I sat with Emile, and Master Chaucer was at my right hand, and Petrarca himself was across the table, and Monsieur Machaut sat not three places away – almost the only French dignitary present, as it appeared that the rest had chosen not to attend. Boucicault and his lady were there; he came and congratulated me.

He shook his head. 'Bad business,' he said. 'I told the king not to trust Turenne.'

'Or the Prince of Achaea?' I asked him, and he would not answer.

I ate and ate, and felt better – my stomach remained calm enough.

Emile asked me why they had involved de Lesparre.

Before I could answer her, the Lady Violante rose, was kissed by her new husband, and then went out into the square to her brother, who stood like a statue of a pagan youth. He didn't look at her, and she ignored him, took a cord from his hand, and pulled. A thousand doves were released into the soft evening air, and a cheer went up that terrified them, and they went in all directions. Not merely rising out of the square, but roosting, or colliding, or rushing madly between the buildings.

The next course was marvellous – cheese gnocchi in jugged hare, or so my palate told me – and I ate a dish. Gian Galeazzo called out my name. I had time to turn. People were applauding, and there, on a mannequin, was a whole harness, all white, with pretty latten edges – everything complete in the latest Milanese style with the heavy shoulder pieces that could keep a man safe, and with my arms engraved across the breastplate. The master of ceremonies beamed at me, and I rose, winced, and went to him. My legs had stiffened up just from a brief spell of sitting. I was very tired, despite having fought only once, for perhaps two hundred heartbeats.

I was eye to eye with Gian Galeazzo. I bowed, and he bowed. He waved at the armour. I rather expected it to explode, or reveal snakes.

He looked at me and said quietly, 'How little you understand.'

I bowed again, a little confused, and went back to my place, and Chaucer here gave me a cup of wine and started to tell me of the attempt on the count, and how it was foiled – but that is not my story.

Trout was served, an amazingly fat fish, in a mint sauce. I ate mine, and Emile mocked me for my eating. I happened to glance up at Sister Marie, who was serving my lady directly – still part of our security arrangements. She was staring over my shoulder, to where the master of ceremonies stood.

'No,' she breathed.

There was the boy, and he had another cord in his hand, as he had had for his sister's doves.

Carts had rolled up: more birdcages. Everyone was slower than Sister Marie in realising that they held Icelandic falcons – dozens of them. A fortune in birds.

Gian Galeazzo had the oddest look on his face. Not triumph. Not dejection.

How little you understand.

He pulled the cord, and the cages opened. Falcons leaped into the air like chargers into battle.

Above us, above a thousand noble guests in their very finest clothes – a fortune in silk and cloth of gold and pearls and lace – there circled half a thousand doves, symbols of peace and a happy marriage, and perhaps even more ancient symbols than that.

The falcons hit them, and it began to rain blood across the square.

And Gian Galeazzo stood in the centre. He stood proudly, his back straight, and then, as the blood began to fall, he turned and looked at Bernabò, and he bowed.

Bernabò looked as if rage might cause him to ignite like a giant torch.

People scrambled onto the church portico, or into the palace gates, to avoid the rain of blood. But it touched everyone, like a curse.

And there they all were, Master Froissart, all the players: representatives of England and France, the Pope, Genoa, Venice, the Holy Roman Emperor, and Florence. We were all poised on the edge of the abyss. The Union of Churches had failed, the Emperor was at war with Milan; everything we had won in the Holy Land was being abandoned so that the kings and princes of Europe could squabble. The future held nothing but war, and the birds showered us with blood.

I met Emile's eyes, and as we huddled under the palace gates, she kissed me.

'We lived,' she said.

'We should go back to Jerusalem,' I said. 'It's safer there.'

HISTORICAL NOTE

I am always delighted to return to the world of William Gold. Perhaps that's because this is what I did for my thesis, way back in my university days; perhaps it is because this is what I love to re-enact; perhaps because this world, the world of England, Italy and Outremer in the late fourteenth century, speaks to me in a way that only a few other epochs in history speak to me. All of history interests me, but I confess that William Gold's period seems especially vibrant and especially relevant.

Many of the characters in this series are historical personages, not creations of my pen, although I confess I've chosen to give them life in ways that are fictional. So William Gold himself is an historical character; he was one of Hawkwood's lieutenants, and he really was 'William the Cook'. We don't know a great deal about him, which is convenient for the historical fiction writer. We do know that he was knighted on the battlefield in front of Florence, and that he was one of the captains of Venice (possibly 'the captain') during the 'War of Chioggia', which will be the climactic event of this series and was one of the most important conflicts in Medieval history – certainly the most important war about which most people have never heard. To round out his character, I have given him a lifelong acquaintance with Geoffrey Chaucer, and I have suggested that his (fictional) self might be the basis for Chaucer's Knight in *The Canterbury Tales*.

Fiore Furlano di Liberi was also an historical personage. Fiore is known to us now as the great sword master of the fourteenth century, and author of some of the earliest treatises on fighting, both in and out of armour, with sword, spear, poleaxe and lance, on horse and foot, as well as wrestling and dagger fighting. The most accessible of his manuscripts is in the Getty Museum and is known as MS Ludwig XV 13. From his manuscripts we can understand the whole art of

Armizare, or knightly combat, in ways that had been completely lost. I practice Fiore's art every day. I owe the maestro a huge debt of gratitude.

Rainerio I Acciaioli, Duke of Athens and Corinth (Nerio) is also an historical figure. The cousin, nephew, or just possibly bastard son of the incredibly rich and powerful Florentine banker and knight (a fascinating combination) Niccolò Acciaioli, Nerio carved a magnificent dukedom out of the remnants of Frankish Greece, fought with and against the Turks, and led a life of adventure and warfare that deserves a set of novels of its own. He began from more modest origins; certainly he was always rich, but he virtually sprang from the head of Zeus onto the world stage when he took Corinth sometime between 1367 and 1371 (an event that is central to this book). It is my suspicion that rumours of Nerio created the character of Theseus in Chaucer's 'The Knight's Tale'. His presence as one of Gold's friends is a novelistic attempt to explain how Chaucer might have gotten to know so much about Acciaioli and the Duchy of Athens.

Miles Stapleton, the last of Gold's close friends (of whom there are four, as a nod to Dumas and D'Artagnan, Athos, Porthos, and Aramis) is a fictional creation, but a representative one. Outremer was full of Englishmen in the late fourteenth century: there were Englishmen at Alexandria and a company of Englishmen is still remembered on Lesvos as serving the Gatelussi princess. The real-life Miles Stapleton was a generation older and died at Auray in 1364. Our character is (fictionally) his nephew and inheritor, while also being related to Lord Grey. Grey and Scrope and a number of other named Englishmen served at Alexandria and were later acquaintances and friends of Chaucer and Gower at the court of Richard II.

The principle events of *Sword of Justice* are historical. The last months of the Green Count's crusade follow his itinerary as closely as possible; my descriptions of the Turkish occupation of Thrake is at least in part based on the research of my friend Giorgio Kefetzis, and any errors are mine. I travelled the road from Istanbul to Thessaloniki twice while writing this book, and I confess that I used the historical sites that I most enjoyed as locations: the fine fourteenth century Byzantine castle far above the plains of Thrake is located very close to modern Alexandroupolis, and my friend Chris Vermijweren shot arrows from there, four hundred feet above the plain, and showed us how effective an archer could be. And in Italy, the Green Count's route to Rome follows the 'Via Francigena', or the Pilgrim's Way, from Florence to Rome. In preparation for this book, I walked it with two friends; Jon Press, who often serves as my squire when I fight in tournaments, and Alessio Porto, who is now my Italian translator for my books. I visited almost every setting in Italy from Venice to Rome, and I owe a debt of thanks to Jon and Alessio for their cheerful support.

I could never have attempted a subject this complex without reading some great scholarship. One man stands above all others in this field, the historian Kenneth Setton, without whose books there would be no William Gold. Setton's magisterial, remarkable, superb work *The Papacy and the Levant* gives almost painless access to the translations of the Papacy concerning all of the crusades and with matters of trade and politics throughout the Latin East.

Almost as vital to my novels as Professor Setton is Professor William Caferro, whose invaluable work *John Hawkwood: An English Mercenary in Fourteenth-Century Italy* remains, to me, the single best primer on the life of Hawkwood, his world, and the finances and politics thereof.

And I cannot ignore Eugene Cox's *The Green Count of Savoy*. Although some of his information is dated (the book was written in 1967) his research was close to impeccable, and I would have had a much harder time following the Green Count with William Gold if Cox had chosen another subject.

Beyond the bare bones of history it is essential to understand, when examining this world of stark contrasts and incredible passions, that people believed very strongly in ideas – like Islam, like Christianity, like chivalry. Piety – the devotional practice of Christianity – was such an essential part of life that even most 'atheists' practised all the forms of Christianity. Yet there were many flavours of belief. Theology had just passed one of its most important milestones with the works of Thomas Aquinas, but Roman Christianity had so many varieties of practice that it would require the birth of Protestantism and then the Counter-Reformation to establish orthodoxy. I mention all this to say that to describe the fourteenth century without reference to religion would be completely ahistorical. I make no judgement on their beliefs – I merely try to represent them accurately. I confess that I assume that any professional soldier – like Sabraham or Gold – must have developed some knowledge of and respect for their opponents. I see signs of this throughout the work of the Hospitallers – but that may be my modern multiculturalism.

The same care should be paid to all judgements on the past, especially facile judgements about chivalry. It is easy for the modern amoralist to sneer – the Black Prince massacred innocents and burned towns, Henry V ordered prisoners butchered. The period is decorated with hundreds, if not thousands, of moments where the chivalric warriors fell from grace and behaved like monsters. I loveth chivalry, warts and all, and it is my take – and, I think, a considered one – that in chivalry we find the birth of the modern codes of war and of military justice, and that merely to state piously that 'war is hell' and that 'sometimes good men do bad things' is rubbish. War needs rules. Brutality needs limits. These were not amateur enthusiasts, conscripts, or draftees. They were full-time professionals who made for themselves a set of rules so that they could function – in and out of violence – as human beings. If the code of chivalry was abused – well, so are concepts like liberty and democracy abused. Cynicism is easy. Practice of the discipline of chivalry when your own life is in imminent threat is nothing less than heroic – it required then and still requires discipline and moral judgment, confidence in warrior skills and a strong desire to ameliorate the effects of war. I suspect that in addition to helping to control violence (and helping to promote it – a double-edged sword) the code and its reception in society did a great deal to soften the effects of PTSD. My reading of the current scholarship suggests that, on balance, the practice of chivalry may have done more to promote violence than to quell it – but I've always felt that this is a massively ill-considered point of view – as if to suggest that the practice of democracy has been bad for peace based on the casualty rates of the twentieth century.

May I add – as a practitioner – that we as a society have chosen to ignore the reality of violence, and the hellish effect on soldiers and cops – and we have done so with such damning effectiveness that we have left them without any code beyond a clannish self-protection. Chivalry should not be a thing of the past. Chivalry is an ethic needed by every pilot, every drone controller, every beat cop and every SWAT team officer, every clandestine operator, every SpecOps professional. I often hear people say that such and such act of terror or crime justifies this or that atrocity. 'Time to take off the gloves.'

Rubbish. If you take off the gloves, *that's who you are.* Whether you do it with your rondel dagger or your LGB (Laser Guided Bomb) or your night stick. There need to be rules, and the men and women facing fire need to have some.

A word about the martial arts of the period. The world sees knights as illiterate thugs swinging heavy weapons and wearing hundreds of pounds of armour. In fact, the professionals wore armour that fitted the individual like a tailored steel suit, with weight evenly distributed over the body. We have several manuals of arms from this period, the most famous of which is by a character in this series – Fiore di Liberi. The techniques are brutal, elegant and effective. They also pre-date any clear, unambiguous martial manual from the East, and are directly tied to combat, not remote reflections of it. I recommend their study, and the whole of Fiore's MS in the Getty collection is available for your inspection at http://wiktenauer.com/wiki/Fior_di_Battaglia_MS_Ludwig_XV_13. If you'd like to learn more, I recommend the International Armizare Society http://www.armizare.org/.

AUTHOR'S NOTE

My greatest thanks still have to go, first and foremost, to Richard W. Kaeuper of the University of Rochester. The finest professor I ever had – the most passionate, the most clear, the most brilliant – Dr Kaeuper's works on chivalry and the role of violence in society makes him, I think, the pre-eminent medievalist working today, and I have been lucky to be able to get his opinions and the wealth of his knowledge on many subjects, great and small. Where I have gone astray, the fault is all mine. To Professor Kaeuper's work I must add the works of Professor Steven Muhlberger on chivalry and the minutiae of the joust and tournament, as well as the ethics of chivalry themselves. Several hours of conversations with Steve have not only been delightful but helped me with some of the themes of this book.

Not far behind these two, I need to thank the two masters with whom I've studied and trained these last years – Sean Hayes of the Northwest Fencing Academy and Greg Mele of the Chicago Swordplay Guild. To these modern masters this book is dedicated. I'd also like to thank all the people with whom I train and spar – the *Compagnia* mentioned below. Re-enacting the Middle Ages has many faces, and immersion in that world may not ever be a perfectly authentic experience, but inasmuch as I have gotten 'right' – the clothes, the armour, the food or the weapons – it is due to all my re-enacting friends, including Tasha Kelly (of La Cotte Simple, a superb web resource) Chris Verwijmeren, master archer, and Leo Todeschini, JT Pälikkö, Jiri Klepac and Aurora Simmons, master craftspeople. I cannot imagine writing these books without all the help I have received on material culture, and I'm going to add more craftspeople – all worth looking up – Francesca Baldassari and Davide Giuriussini of Italy, and Karl Robinson of England.

Throughout the writing of this series I have used (and will continue to use), as my standard reference to names, dates and events, the works of Jonathan Sumption, whose books are, I think, the best unbiased summation of the causes, events, and consequences of the Hundred Years' War. I've never met him, but I'd like to offer him my thanks by suggesting that anyone who wants to follow the real events should buy Sumption's books!

As Dick Kaeuper once suggested in a seminar, there would have been no Middle Ages as we know them without two things – the horse and Christianity. I owe my horsemanship skills largely to two people – Ridgely and Georgine Davis of Pennsylvania, both of whom are endlessly patient with teaching and with horseflesh in getting me to understand even the basics of mounted combat. And for my understanding of the church, I'd like first to thank all the theologians I know – I'm virtually surrounded by people with degrees in theology – and second, the work of F. C. Copleston, whose work *A History of Medieval Philosophy* was essential to my writing and understanding the period – as essential, in fact, as the writings of Chaucer, Gower, Boccaccio and Dante. But I'd also like to thank Fr. David Harrison, and my friend Ms Elisabeth Beattie and the parish of St Mary Magdalene for their constant support and theological study advice.

My sister-in-law, Nancy Watt, provided early comments, criticism, and copy-editing while I worked my way through the historical problems – and she worked her way through lung cancer. I value her commitment extremely. As this is her favourite of my series, I've done my best for her. I'm pleased to say that after seven years, she is still alive and reading – and working. I write all these books imagining that she is sitting and listening to me tell the story.

And finally, I'd like to thank my friends who support my odd passions, and my wife and child, who are tolerant, mocking, justly puzzled, delighted, and gracious by turns as I drag them from battlefield to castle and as we sew like fiends for a tournament in Italy.

Six years ago, we formed the 'Compagnia della Rosa nel Sole' and we now have 190 members to recreate a company like John Hawkwood's that fought in Italy in the late fourteenth century. Our company has given me (already) an immense amount of material and I thank every member. We're always recruiting. Interested? Contact us at www.boarstooth.net.

William Gold is, I think, my favorite character. I hope you like him. He has a long way to go. This is book four of six.

Christian Cameron
Toronto, 2018

Can't wait for the next

CHRISTIAN CAMERON

novel?

Turn over for an extract from *Killer of Men*, the first novel in his Long War series.

Arimnestos is a farm boy when war breaks out between the citizens of his native Plataea and their overbearing neighbours, Thebes. Standing in the battle line for the first time, alongside his father and brother, he shares in a famous and unlikely victory. But after being knocked unconscious in the mêlée, he awakes not a hero, but a slave.

Betrayed by his jealous and cowardly cousin, the freedom he fought for has now vanished, and he becomes the property of a rich citizen. So begins an epic journey out of slavery, as the emerging civilization of the Greeks starts to flex its muscles against the established empire of the Persians.

As he tries to make his fortune and revenge himself on the man who disinherited him, Arimnestos discovers that he has a talent that pays well in this new, violent world – for like his hero, Achilles, he is 'a killer of men'.

Available now from Orion Books

1

The thing that I remember best – and maybe it's my first memory, too – is the forge. My father, the smith – aye, he farmed too, because every free man in Boeotia counted his wealth in farmland – but Pater was the bronze-smith, the best in our village, the best in Plataea, and women said that he had the touch of the god upon him, because he had a battle wound that made him lame in his left foot, and because his pots never leaked. We were simple folk in Boeotia, not fancy boys like Athenians or joyless killers like the men of Sparta – we valued a man who made a pot that didn't leak. When Pater pounded out a seam, that seam held. And he liked to add more – he was always a man to give more than he got, so that a housewife who paid him ten hard-won drachmas and a bowl of potted rabbit might find that Pater had put a carefully tooled likeness of Demeter or Hecate beneath the rim of the pot, or worked her name into the handle of the cauldron or tripod.

Pater did good work and he was fair. What's more, he had stood his ground twice in the storm of bronze, so that every man knew his measure. And for all that, he was always ready to share a cup of wine, so the front of the smithy had become a gathering place for all the men of our little village on a fair day when the ploughing was done – and sometimes even a singer or a minstrel, a *rhapsode*. The smithy itself was like a lord's hall, as men brought Pater their quarrels – all except his own bloody family, and more of that later – or came to tell him their little triumphs.

He was not much as a father. Not that he hit me more than a dozen times, and every one deserved, as I still remember. I once used my father's name to buy a knife in the *polis* – a foolish thing, but I wanted that knife. It broke in my hand later – yet another tale, lass – but I meant no harm. When Pater learned that I had pledged his name for a simple blade he'd have made me himself, he struck me with the whole weight of his fist. I cried for a day from the shame.

He had the raising of us all to himself, you see. My mother was drunk from the time I first remember her – drinking away the forge, Pater would say when the darkness was on him. She's your grandmother, lass – I shouldn't speak ill of her, and I'll try to tell her true, but it's not pretty.

She was the daughter of a lord, a real lord, a *basileus* from down the valley in Thespiae. They met at the Great Daidala in the year of the Olympics, and the rumour of my youth had it that she was the wildest and the most beautiful of all the daughters of Apollo, and that Pater swept her up in his great arms and carried her off in the old way, and that the basileus swore a curse on their marriage.

I respect the gods – I've seen them. But I'm not one to believe that Hera comes to curse a woman's womb, nor Ares to push a spear aside. The gods love them that love themselves – Mater said that, so she wasn't a total failure as a mother, I reckon. But she never did aught to love herself, and her curse was her looks and her birth.

She had three children for Pater. I was the middle one – my older brother came first by a year, and he should have had the smithy and maybe the farm besides, but I never faulted him for it. He had red hair and we called him 'Chalkidis', the copper boy. He was big and brave and all a boy could want in an older brother.

I had a sister, too – still do, unless Artemis put an arrow into her. My mother gave her the name of Penelope, and the gods must have been listening.

I know nothing of those first years, when Pater was as handsome as a god, and Mater loved him, and she sang in the forge. Men say they were like gods, but men say a great many things when an event is safely in the past – they tell a lot of lies. I'll no doubt tell you a few myself. Old man's prerogative. I gathered that they were happy, though.

But nothing ended as my mother expected. I think she wanted something greater from my father, or from herself, or perhaps from the gods. She began to go up in the hills with the maenads and ran wild with other women, and there were words in the forge. And then came the first of the Theban years – when the men of Thebes came against us.

What do you know of Thebes? It is a name in legend to you. To us, it was the curse of our lives – poor Plataea, so far from the gods, so close to Thebes. Thebes was a city that could muster fifteen thousand hoplites, while we could, in an emergency and freeing and arming our most trustworthy slaves, muster fifteen hundred good men. And this is before we made the Great Alliance with Athens. So we were a lonely little polis with no friends, like a man whose plough is broken and none of his neighbours have a plough to loan.

They came at us just after the grain harvest, and the men went off to war. Whenever I hear the *Iliad*, thugater, I weep when I hear of mighty Hector's son being afraid of his father's shining helmet. How well I remember it, and Pater standing there in his panoply, the image of Ares. He had a bronze-faced shield and a splendid helmet he had forged himself from one piece of bronze. His horsehair plume was black and red for the smith god. He wore a breastplate of solid bronze, again of his own making, and thigh guards and arm guards of a kind you scarcely see any more – aye, they were better men. He carried two spears in the old way, and long greaves on his legs, and when he stood in the courtyard with the whole panoply he gleamed like gold.

Mater was drunk when she poured the libation. I can see it in my head – she came out in a white *chiton*, like a *kore* going to sacrifice, but the chiton had purple stains. When she went to bless his shield she stumbled and poured wine down his leg, and the slaves murmured. And she wept, and ran inside.

So Pater went off to fight Thebes, and he came back carried by two men on his *chlamys* and his spears, and his shield was gone. We lost. And Pater lost most of the use of his left leg, where Mater spilled the wine, and after that there was nothing between them but silence.

I suppose I was five. Chalkidis was six, and we lay in the loft of the barn and he whispered to me about Pater's part in the battle and about our cousins – the grandsons of Pater's father's brother. Aye, thugater, we count such relations close in Boeotia. Pater had no brothers – his father must have read Hesiod one too many times – and this batch of surly cousins were the nearest relations I had on Pater's side. On Mater's side they scarcely allowed that we were kin – until later, and that's another tale, but a happier one.

My brother said that Pater was a hero, that he'd stood his ground when other men ran, and he saved many lives – and that when the

Thebans took him, they hadn't stripped him, but ransomed him like a lord. I was young and I knew nothing of ransom, only that Pater, who towered over me like a god, was unable to walk and his mood was dark.

'The other Corvaxae were the first to run,' Chalkidis whispered. 'They ran and left Pater's side open to the spears, and now they slink through the town and fear what Pater will say.'

We were the Corvaxae – the men of the Raven. Apollo's raven. Look up, lass – there's the black bird on my *aspis*, and may the gods send I never feel it on my arm again! You know what the sage says – count no man happy until he is dead. I pour a libation in his memory – may his shade taste the wine.

The black bird is also on our sails and on our house. I was five – I knew little of this, except that I knew that Pater told me it was a good omen when a raven landed on the roof of the smithy. And our women were Corvaxae, too – black-haired and pale-skinned, and clannish. No man in our valley wanted to cross my mother, or my sister, in their day. They were Ravens of Apollo.

And the truth is that my story starts in that fight. It is from that day that the other Corvaxae turned against Pater, and then against me. And from that day that the men of Plataea decided to find a new way of keeping their little town free of Thebes.

It took Pater almost a year to get to his feet. Before that year, I reckon we were rich, as peasants in Boeotia measured riches. We had a yoke of oxen and two ploughs, a house built of stone with a tower, a barn that stood all weather and the smithy. Pater wore the full panoply when the muster was called, like a lord. We ate meat on feast days and we had wine all year.

But I was old enough to understand that at the end of that year we were not rich. Mater's gold pin went, and all our metal cups. And my first bad memory – my first memory of fear – is from that year.

Simonalkes – the eldest of the other branch of the Corvaxae, a big, strong man with a dark face – came to our house. Pater had to walk with a crutch, but he rose as fast as he could, cursing the slaves who helped him. My brother was in the *andron* – the men's room – pouring wine for Simon like a proper boy. Simon put his feet up on a bench.

'You'll be needing money,' Simon said to Pater. Not even a greeting.

Pater's face grew red, but he bowed his head. 'Are you offering me aid, cousin?'

Simon shook his head. 'You need no charity. I'll offer you a loan against the farm.'

Pater shook his head. 'No,' he said. If Pater thought that he was hiding his anger, he was wrong.

'Still too proud, smith?' Simon said, and his lip curled.

'Proud enough to stand my ground,' Pater said, and Simon's face changed colour. He got up.

'Is this the famous hospitality of the Corvaxae?' Simon said. 'Or has your whore of a wife debased you, too?' He looked at me. 'Neither of these boys has your look, cousin.'

'Leave my house,' Pater said.

'I came to tender help,' Simon said, 'but I'm met by accusations and insults.'

'Leave my house,' Pater said.

Simon hooked his fingers in his belt and planted his feet. He looked around. 'Is it *your* house, cousin?' He smiled grimly. 'Our grandfather built this house. Why is it *yours*?' Simon sneered – he was always good at sneering – and snapped his fingers. 'Perhaps you'll marry again and get an heir.'

'My sons are my heirs,' Pater said carefully, as if speaking a foreign language.

'Your sons are the children of some strangers on the hillside,' our cousin said.

Pater looked as angry as I'd ever known him, and I'd never seen two grown men take this tone – the tone of hate. I'd heard it from Mater in the women's quarters, but I'd never heard it rise to conflict. I was afraid. And what was I hearing? It was as if cousin Simon was saying that I was not my father's son.

'Bion!' Pater shouted, and his biggest slave came running. Bion was a strong man, a trustworthy man with a wife and children who knew he'd be freed as soon as the money came back, and he was loyal. That's right, thugater. Melissa is Bion's granddaughter, and now she's your handmaiden. She's never been a slave, but Bion was once. As was I, lass, so don't you wrinkle your nose.

'You'll be even poorer if I have to kill your slave,' Simon said.

Pater thumped one crutch-step closer and his heavy staff shot out and caught Simon in the shin. Simon went down and then Pater hit him in the groin, so that he screamed like a woman in childbirth – I knew that sound well enough, because Bion's wife provided him with a child every year.

Pater wasn't done. He stood over Simon with his staff raised. 'You think I'm afraid of you, you coward!' he said. 'You think I don't know why I'm lame? You ran. You left me in the bronze storm. And now you come here and your mouth pours out filth.' He was panting and I was more afraid, because Simon was wheezing, down on the floor, and Pater had hurt him. It was not like two boys behind the barn. It was *real*.

Simon got himself up and he pushed against Bion. 'Let go, slave!' he croaked. 'Or I'll come back for you.' He leaned against the doorway, but Bion ignored him, linked an arm under his chin despite his size and dragged him from the room.

All the *oikia* – the household, slaves and free – followed the action into the courtyard. Simon wouldn't stop – he cursed us, and he cursed the whole oikia, and he promised that when he came into his own he'd sell all the slaves and burn their houses. Now I know it for what it was – the blusterings of an impotent but angry man. But at the time it sounded like the death curse of some fallen hero, and I feared him. I feared that everything he said would come to pass.

He said that he'd lain with our mother in the hills, and he said that Pater was a fool who had risked all their lives in the battle and who sought death rather than face his wife's infidelity. He shouted that we were all bastards, and he shouted that the basileus, the local aristocrat, would come for the farm because he was jealous of Pater.

And all the time Bion dragged him from the yard.

It was ugly.

And when he was gone, Pater wept. And that made me even more afraid.

It seemed as if the roof had fallen in on our lives, but it was not many weeks later when Pater brought the priest to the forge, all the way from Thebes. He rebuilt the fire and the priest of Hephaestus took his silver drachma and made a thorough job of it; he used good incense from the east and he poured a libation from a proper cup, although made of clay and not metal as we expected. Because Chalkidis and I were old enough to help in the forge, he made us initiates. Bion was already an initiate – Hephaestus cares nothing for slave and free, but only that a craftsman gives unstintingly to his craft – and he advanced a degree. It was very holy and it helped to make me feel that my world was going to be restored. We swept the forge from top to bottom and Pater made a joke – the only one I can remember.

'I must have the only clean forge in all Hellas,' he said to the priest.

The priest laughed. 'You took that wound fighting us last year,' he said. He pointed at Pater's leg.

'Aye,' Pater allowed. He was not a man given to long speeches.

'Front rank?' the priest asked.

Pater pulled his beard. 'You were there?'

The priest nodded. 'I close the first file for my tribe,' he said. It was a position of real honour – the priest was a man who knew his battles.

'I'm the centre man in the front rank,' Pater said. He shrugged. 'Or I was.'

'You held us a good long time,' the Theban said. 'And to be honest, I knew your device – the raven. Apollo's raven for a smith?'

My father grinned. He liked the priest – a small miracle in itself – and that smile made my life better. 'We're sons of Heracles here. I serve Hephaestus and we've had the raven on our house since my grandfather's grandfather came here.' He kept grinning, and just for a moment he was a much younger man. 'My father always said that the gods were sufficiently capricious that we needed to serve a couple at a time.'

That was Pater's longest sentence in a year.

The priest laughed. 'I should be getting back,' he said. 'It'll be dark by the time I see the gates of Thebes.'

Pater shook his head. 'Let me relight the fire,' he said. 'I'll make you a gift and that will please the god. Then you can eat in my house and sleep on a good couch, and go back to Thebes rested.'

The priest bowed. 'Who can refuse a gift?' he said.

But Pater's face darkened. 'Wait,' he said, 'and see what it is. The lame god may not return my skill to me. It has been too long.'

The fire was laid. The priest went out into the sunshine and took from his girdle a piece of crystal – a beautiful thing, as clear as a maiden's eye, and he held it in the sun. He called my brother and I followed him, as younger brothers follow older brothers, and he laughed. 'Two for the price of one, eh?' he said.

'Is it magic, lord?' my brother asked.

The priest shook his head. 'There are charlatans who would tell you so,' he said. 'But I love the new philosophy as much as I love my crafty god. This is a thing of making. Men made this. It is called a lens, and a craftsman made it from rock crystal in a town in Syria. It takes the rays of the sun and it burnishes them the way your father burnishes bronze, and makes them into fire. Watch.'

He placed a little pile of shavings of dry willow on the ground, then he held the lens just so. And before we were fidgeting, the little pile began to smoke.

'Run and get me some tow from your mother and her maidens,' the priest said to me, and I ran – I didn't want to miss a moment of this *philosophy*.

I hurried up the steps to the *exhedra* and my sister opened the door. She was five, blonde and chubby and forthright. 'What?' she asked me.

'I need a handful of tow,' I said.

'What for?' she asked.

We were never adversaries, Penelope and I. So I told her, and she got the tow and carried it to the priest herself, and he was tolerant, flicking her a smile and accepting the tow with a bow as if she were some lord's kore serving at his altar. And all the time his left hand, holding the lens, never moved.

The light fell in a tiny pinpoint too bright to watch, and the willow shavings smoked and smoked.

'I could blow on it,' I said.

The priest looked at me strangely. Then he nodded. 'Go ahead,' he said.

So I lay down in the dust and blew on the shavings very gently. At first nothing happened, and then I almost blew them all over the yard. My brother punched me in the arm. The priest laughed.

Quickly, I ran into the shop, where Pater stood by his cold forge with a distant look on his face, and I took the tube we used for controlling the heat of the forge – a bronze tube. I ran back into the yard, put the end of the tube near the pinpoint of light and gave a puff, and before my heart beat ten times, I had fire.

The priest wasn't laughing any more. He lifted the tow, put the flames in the midst and caught the tow, so that he seemed to have a handful of fire, and then he walked into the forge at a dignified pace, and we followed him. He laid the fire in the forge under the scraps and the bark and the good dry oak, and the night-black charcoal from mighty Cithaeron's flanks. The fire of the sun, brought down from the sky by his lens, lit the forge.

Pater was not a man easily moved, but he watched the fire with a look on his face like hunger in a slave. Then he busied himself managing the fire – the hearth had been cold for a long time, and he needed coals to accomplish even the slightest work. So my brother and I carried wood and charcoal, and the priest sang a long hymn to the smith god, and the fire leaped and burned through the afternoon, and before long there was a good bed of coals.

Pater took down a leather bag full of sand from his bench, and he had Bion cut him a circle of bronze as big as a man's hand. Then, with that hungry look, he took the bronze in his great hand and set the edge to the leather bag. and after a brief pause his rounded hammer fell on the bronze in a series of strokes almost too fast to see.

That's another sight I'll never forget – Pater, almost blind with his lust to do his work, and the hammer falling, the strokes precise as his left hand turned the bronze – strike, turn, strike, turn.

It was the bowl of a cup before I needed ten breaths. Not a priest's holy cup, but the kind of cup a man likes to have on a trip, to show he's no slave – the cup you use to drink wine in a strange place, that reminds you of home.

Outside, the shadows were growing long.

In the forge, the hammer made its muffled sound against the leather. Pater was weeping. The priest took the three of us and led us outside. I wanted to stay and see the cup. I could already see the shape – I could *see* that Pater had not lost his touch. And I was six or seven and all I wanted was to be a smith like Pater. To make a thing from nothing – that is the true magic, whether in a woman's womb or in a forge. But we went outside, and the priest was holding the tube of bronze. He blew through it a couple of times, and then nodded as if a puzzle had been solved. He looked at me.

'You thought to go and fetch this,' he said.

It wasn't a question, so I said nothing.

'I would have thought of it too,' my brother said.

Penelope laughed. 'Not in a year of feast days,' she said. One of Mater's expressions.

He sent a slave for fire from the main hearth in the kitchen, and he put it in the fireplace in the yard. That's where Pater kindled the forge in high summer when it was blinding hot. And he blessed it – he was a thorough man, and worth his silver drachma, unlike most priests I've known. Blessing the outdoor hearth was something Pater hadn't even considered.

Then he built up his little fire and the three of us bustled to help him, picking up scraps of wood and bark all over the yard. My brother fetched an armload of kitchen wood. And then the priest began to play with the tube, blowing through it and watching the coals grow brighter and redder and the flames leap.

'Hmm,' he said. Several times.

I have spent much of my life with the wise. I have been lucky that way – that everywhere I've gone, the gods have favoured me with men who love study and yet have time to speak to a man like me. But I think I owe all of that to the priest of Hephaestus. He treated all of us children as equals, and he cared for nothing but that tube and the effect it had on fire.

He did the oddest things. He walked all over the yard until he found a whole straw from the last haying, and he cut it neatly with a sharp iron knife and then used it to blow on the flames. It gave the same effect.

'Hmm,' he said.

He poured water on the fire and it made steam and scalded his hand, and he cursed and hopped on one foot. Penelope fetched one of the slave girls and she made him a poultice, and while she nursed his hand, he blew through the tube on the dead fire – and nothing happened except that a trail of ash was blown on my chiton.

'Hmm,' he said. He relit the fire.

Inside the forge, the sound had changed. I could hear my father's lightest hammer – when you are a smith's child, you know all the music of the forge – going *tap-tap*, *tap-tap*. He was doing fine work – chasing with a small chisel, perhaps. I wanted to go and watch, but I knew I was not welcome. He was with the god.

So I watched the priest, instead. He sent Bion for a hide of leather, and he rolled it in a great tube, and breathed through it on the fire, and nothing much happened. He and Bion made a really long tube, as long as a grown man's arm, from calf's hide, and the priest set Bion to blow on the fire. Bion did this in the forge and he was expert at it, and the priest watched the long tube work on the fire.

'Hmm,' he said.

My brother was bored. He made a spear from the firewood and began to chase me around the yard, but I wanted to watch the priest. I had learned how to be a younger brother. I let him thump me in the ribs and I neither complained nor fought back – I just stood watching the priest until my brother was bored. It didn't take long.

My brother didn't like being deprived of his mastery. 'Who *cares*?' he asked. 'So the tube makes the fire burn? I mean, who cares?' He looked to me for support. He had a point. Every child of a smith learned to use the tube – as did every slave.

The priest turned on him like a boar on a hunter. 'As you say, boy. Who would care? So answer this riddle and the Sphinx won't eat you. *Why* does the tube air make the fire brighter? Eh? Hmm?'

Pater's hammer was now going *taptaptaptaptaptap*.

'Who cares?' Chalkidis asked. He shrugged. 'Can I go and play?' he asked.

'Be off with you, Achilles,' the priest said.

My brother ran off. My sister might have stayed – she had some thoughts in her head, even as a little thing – but Mater called her to fetch wine, and she hurried off.

'May I touch the lens?' I asked.

The priest reached up and put it in my hand. He was down by the fire again.

It was a beautiful thing, and even if he said it had no magic, I was thrilled to touch it. It brought fire down from the sun. And it was clear, and deep. I looked at things through it, and it was curious. An ant was misshapen – some parts larger and some smaller. Dust developed texture.

'Does it warm up in your hand when you bring down the sun?' I asked.

The priest sat back on his heels. He looked at me the way a farmer looks at a slave he is thinking of purchasing. 'No,' he said. 'But that is an excellent question.' He held up the bronze tube. 'Neither does this. But both make the fire brighter.'

'What does it mean?' I asked.

The priest grinned. 'No idea,' he said. 'Do you know how to write?'

I shook my head.

The priest pulled his beard and began to ask questions. He asked me hundreds of questions – hard things about farm animals. He was searching my head, of course – looking to see if I had any intelligence. I tried to answer, but I felt as if I was failing. His questions were hard, and he went on and on.

The shadows grew longer and longer, and then my father started singing. I hadn't heard his song in the forge in a year – indeed, at the age I was at, I'd forgotten that my father *ever* sang when he worked.

His song came out of the forge like the smell of a good dinner, soft first and then stronger. It was the part of the *Iliad* where Hephaestus makes the armour of Achilles.

My mother's voice came down from the exhedra and met Pater's voice in the yard. These days, no one teaches women to sing the *Iliad*, but back then, every farm girl in Boeotia knew it. And they sang together. I don't think I'd ever heard them sing together. Perhaps he was happy. Perhaps she was sober.

Pater came out into the yard with a cup in his hand. He must have burnished it himself, instead of having the slave boys do it, because it glowed like gold in the last light of the sun.

He limped across the yard, and he was smiling. 'My gift to you and the god,' he said. He handed the cup to the priest.

It had a flat base – a hard thing to keep when you round a cup, let me tell you – with sloping sides and a neatly rolled rim. He'd riveted a handle on, simple work, but done cleanly and precisely. He'd made the rivets out of silver and the handle itself of copper. And he'd raised a scene into the cup itself, so that you could see Hephaestus being led to Olympus by Dionysus and Heracles, when his father Zeus takes him back. Dionysus was tall and strong in a linen chiton, and every fold was hammered in the bronze. Heracles had a lion skin that Pater had engraved so that it looked like fur, and the smith god was a little drunk on the happiness of his father's taking him back.

The priest turned it this way and that, and then he shook his head. 'This is king's work,' he said. 'Thieves would kill me in the road for a cup like this.'

'Yours,' Pater said.

The priest nodded. 'Your gifts are unimpaired, it seems,' he said. The cup was its own testimony. I remember the awe I felt, looking at it.

'Untouched by the rage of Ares,' Pater said, 'I owe more than that cup, priest. But that's what I can tithe now.'

The priest was visibly awed. I was a boy, and I could see his awe, just as surely as I had seen Simon's fear and rage. It made me wonder, in a whole new way, who my father was.

Pater summoned Bion, and Bion poured wine – cheap wine, for that's all we had – into the new cup. First the priest prayed to the smith god and poured a libation, and then he drank, and then Pater drank, and then Bion drank. Then they gave me the cup, and I drank.

'Your boy here has a gift too,' the priest said, while the wine warmed our bellies.

'He's quick,' Pater said, and ruffled my hair.

First I'd heard of it.

'More than quick,' the priest said. He drank, looked at the cup and held it out to Bion, who filled it. He started to pass it back and Pater waved at him.

'All servants of the smith here, Bion,' he said.

So Bion drank again. And let me tell you, when the hard times came and Bion stayed loyal, it was for that reason – Pater was fair. Fair and straight, and slaves know. Something for you to remember when you're tempted to a little temper tantrum, eh, little lady? Hair in your food and piss in your wine when you mistreat them. Right?

Anyway, we drank a while longer. It went to my head. The priest asked Pater to think about moving to Thebes – said Pater would make a fortune doing work like this in a real city. Pater just shrugged. The joy of making was washing away in the wine.

'If I wanted to be a Theban,' he said, 'I'd have gone there when I was young.' He made the word *Theban* sound dirty, but the priest took no offence.

And then the priest turned back to me.

'That boy needs to learn his letters,' he said.

Pater nodded. 'Good thing for a smith to know,' he agreed.

My heart soared. I wanted nothing – *nothing* – more than to be a smith.

'I could take him to school,' the priest said.

Pater shook his head. 'You're a good priest,' Pater said, 'but my boy won't be a *pais* in Thebes.'

Again the priest took no offence. 'You won't teach the boy yourself,' he said. No question to it.

Pater looked at me, nodded, agreeing. 'No,' he said. 'It's my curse – I've no time for them. Teaching takes too long and I grow angry.' He shrugged.

The priest nodded. 'There's a hero's tomb with a priest up the mountain,' he said.

'Leitos,' Pater said. 'He went to Troy. Calchas is the priest. A drunk, but a good man.'

'He can write?' the priest asked.

Pater nodded.

The next morning, I rose with the sun to see the priest go. I held his hand in the courtyard while he thanked the god and Pater for his cup, and Pater was happy. He reminded Pater that I was to learn to write, and Pater swore an oath unasked, and the thing was done. I wasn't sure what I thought about it, but that was Pater's way – a thing worth doing was done.

The priest went to the gate and blessed Bion. Pater took his hand and was blessed in turn. 'May I have your name, priest?' he asked. Back then, men didn't always share their names.

The priest smiled. 'I'm Empedocles,' he said.

He and Pater shook hands the initiates' way. And then the priest came to me. 'You will be a philosopher,' he said.

He was dead wrong, but it was a nice thing to hear at the age of six or seven, or whatever I was.

'What's your name?' he asked.

'Arimnestos,' I answered.